Praise for the novels of Joyce Lamb

TRUE VISION

"Lamb knocks it out of the Chicago ballpark with this fast-paced romantic mystery. Combining paranormal elements, a carefully crafted mystery and a powerful romance, *True Vision* has something for everyone. Readers will be looking for the next book in the trilogy as soon as they finish reading this one."

—*Romantic Times*

COLD MIDNIGHT

"Impossible to put down! A spine-tingling whodunit constantly keeps you on the edge of your seat with scenes that will make your toes curl . . . Joyce Lamb is a highly talented writer who knows how to write a captivating suspense novel."   —*Manic Readers*

"Tension runs high throughout the entire story and the drama is terrific . . . Well crafted and intriguing."

—*Huntress Book Reviews*

"The interaction and emotion between the characters [are] very entertaining . . . This is a page-turner."

—*Night Owl Reviews* (Top Pick)

"An enjoyable romantic police procedural."

—*Midwest Book Review*

continued . . .

Berkley Sensation Titles by Joyce Lamb

COLD MIDNIGHT
TRUE VISION
TRUE COLORS

TRUE COLORS

Joyce Lamb

BERKLEY SENSATION, NEW YORK

THE BERKLEY PUBLISHING GROUP
Published by the Penguin Group
Penguin Group (USA) Inc.
375 Hudson Street, New York, New York 10014, USA
Penguin Group (Canada), 90 Eglinton Avenue East, Suite 700, Toronto, Ontario M4P 2Y3, Canada
(a division of Pearson Penguin Canada Inc.)
Penguin Books Ltd., 80 Strand, London WC2R 0RL, England
Penguin Group Ireland, 25 St. Stephen's Green, Dublin 2, Ireland (a division of Penguin Books Ltd.)
Penguin Group (Australia), 250 Camberwell Road, Camberwell, Victoria 3124, Australia
(a division of Pearson Australia Group Pty. Ltd.)
Penguin Books India Pvt. Ltd., 11 Community Centre, Panchsheel Park, New Delhi—110 017, India
Penguin Group (NZ), 67 Apollo Drive, Rosedale, North Shore 0632, New Zealand
(a division of Pearson New Zealand Ltd.)
Penguin Books (South Africa) (Pty.) Ltd., 24 Sturdee Avenue, Rosebank, Johannesburg 2196,
South Africa

Penguin Books Ltd., Registered Offices: 80 Strand, London WC2R 0RL, England

This is a work of fiction. Names, characters, places, and incidents either are the product of the author's imagination or are used fictitiously, and any resemblance to actual persons, living or dead, business establishments, events, or locales is entirely coincidental. The publisher does not have any control over and does not assume any responsibility for author or third-party websites or their content.

TRUE COLORS

A Berkley Sensation Book / published by arrangement with the author

PRINTING HISTORY
Berkley Sensation mass-market edition / January 2011

Copyright © 2011 by Joyce Lamb.
Excerpt from *True Calling* by Joyce Lamb copyright © by Joyce Lamb.
Cover art © by Kablonk!/Masterfile.
Cover design by Annette Fiore DeFex.

ISBN: 978-0-425-24035-9

BERKLEY® SENSATION
Berkley Sensation Books are published by The Berkley Publishing Group,
a division of Penguin Group (USA) Inc.,
375 Hudson Street, New York, New York 10014.
BERKLEY® SENSATION and the "B" design are trademarks of Penguin Group (USA) Inc.

PRINTED IN THE UNITED STATES OF AMERICA

10 9 8 7 6 5 4 3 2 1

For Lisa Kiplinger, who works behind the scenes to make me a better writer, a better person and a better friend.

ACKNOWLEDGMENTS

Thanks to:

- My awesome critique partners: Joan Goodman, Diane Amos, Linda Cutillo, Maggie Hoye, Susan Vaughan and Lina Gardiner. You guys are the BEST! You're pretty awesome writers, too.

- Ruth Chamberlain, Lisa Hitt, Charlene Gunnells, Chantelle Mansfield and Karen Feldman McCracken, for reading and re-reading and still being so enthusiastic.

- Danielle, Michael, Nikole and Zach, for keeping me young and sorta, kinda hip. I think.

- Glenn and Di, for providing me with a bed-and-breakfast away from home.

- Julie Snider, for creating the best bookmarks ever, and always in record time.

- Rebecca Chastain, for saving my butt so many times, as great copy editors do.

- Grace Morgan, for your absolute wonderfulness as a literary agent.

- Wendy McCurdy and Katherine Pelz, for all your hard work on my behalf.

- And Mom, as always, for everything.

CHAPTER **ONE**

Alex Trudeau spotted the flashing lights of a police cruiser and pulled onto the shoulder of the beach road. She'd heard the call for emergency vehicles over the scanner when she'd been only a mile away. Hopping out of her dark red Jeep Liberty SUV, she dragged her camera equipment out and then took off at a jog toward the scene of the accident.

The heat of the Florida sun baked the asphalt under her feet, but she barely noticed as she ran, dodging the drivers and passengers who'd pulled over and gotten out of their cars to gawk. As she neared the mangled wreckage of a silver minivan upside down in the ditch, she started snapping shots even as her stomach clenched. Could anyone have survived an accident so violent that it shattered the windshield and caved in the roof?

Her heart skipped, and she lowered the camera, watching in awe as Lake Avalon police detective John Logan delivered a hysterical woman from the wreckage to bystanders who ran up to help. With blood pouring from a gash at her temple, the woman screamed, "Get my baby! Get my baby!"

Alex's journalistic instincts snapped back into gear when Logan, tan and muscular in his khaki police uniform, turned back toward the van that had started to smoke. Big, black clouds, the kind that looked like a precursor to a fiery explosion, billowed upward. She could tell by his determined stance that he was going back for the driver's baby.

Where the hell were the fire trucks? At least firefighters were experts at this kind of thing. Yet, she'd known John Logan for two years, considered him a good friend, and he wasn't the kind of man to stand around and wait for someone else to show up and do what he could do right now.

"Her back tire blew," a bystander said. "I saw it explode just before the van flipped."

Alex listened only vaguely, her heart pounding as Logan plunged into the billowing smoke.

The driver continued to scream, "My baby girl! My baby girl!"

Alex counted the seconds as she waited for Logan to reappear. Sirens sounded in the distance, but they seemed so far away, her focus having narrowed down to the spot where she'd last seen Logan. She should have been taking more pictures of the chaotic rescue scene, but fear for him had constricted her chest muscles so much she could barely breathe.

Come on, Logan, where are you?

This can't end in tragedy, she thought. Logan was too good, too kind. She accepted that bad things happened to good people. Not this time, she prayed. Please.

And then he stumbled out of the smoke, a small child of maybe two or three years old cradled in his arms.

Alex released the breath she'd held and brought the camera up to take the picture, already knowing it would make headlines. There was nothing newspaper readers loved more than a ragged hero streaked with blood, carrying a crying, soot-smudged child away from wreckage that looked like no one should have survived. Especially a hero as good-looking as John Logan, his eyes even more blue in a face blackened by smoke. The child looked tiny and helpless in his large, muscled arms.

Logan delivered the bawling little girl to her mother, his eyes streaming from the smoke. Sweat made his short, dark brown hair spike. He was filthy, yet he'd never looked more gut-wrenchingly handsome. Then, surprising Alex, he walked over to her, his teeth flashing white in his streaked face.

"You got here fast," he said.

A thrill raced through her that he'd noticed her among all the bystanders. Maybe that meant something. "I heard the call on the scanner."

"Does this mean you're back at work at the paper?"

She managed to prevent her smile from faltering at the reminder that she'd technically died three months ago. A man gunning for her sister had shot Alex by mistake. Three zaps from defibrillator paddles in the ER had revived her.

"Been back for a while," she said. "Guess we just haven't run into each other."

His grin widened. "I find that unacceptable."

She felt the heat in his starburst blue eyes. He made her nervous. In a good way. A *very* good way. Before the shooting, she'd thought they were gearing up for their first kiss. After the shooting, he'd visited her in the hospital and had dropped by her house a couple of times after her release, armed with the makings for hot fudge sundaes and DVDs of old, quirky dog-themed movies like *Best in Show* and *Beethoven*. That he'd known her well enough to cater to her love of sugary treats and animals had thrilled her. She'd thought, This is the man of my dreams. But then he'd pulled back, and she'd thought maybe he'd lost interest. She had to admit she was pretty pathetic after taking a bullet to the chest. No doubt, her inability to carry on a conversation, or watch an entire movie, without drifting to sleep had been a huge turnoff.

But she was better now, and here John Logan stood, grinning at her after saving a helpless child from certain death. Things were looking up.

"What're you doing for dinner tomorrow?" he asked.

Now we're talking. "I've been craving some of that tasty grilled shrimp they serve at Antonio's Beach Grill. You?"

"What a coincidence. I've been craving that, too. Shall we make it a date?"

A big, dumb smile spread through her entire body, more intense than anything she'd felt in a long time. In fact, ever since the shooting, she'd felt different. She figured death did that to people, made them more aware of the people around them. Made them feel emotions—compassion, pleasure, pain, anticipation—on a deeper level. Or maybe her senses just *seemed* sharper, like a head that felt lighter, and better than before, once a blinding headache faded. Whatever the cause, she thought she might have a serious crush on this man.

She nodded. "It's a date."

He thrust out a hand. "Shake on it?"

She laughed, low and breathless. Could the man *get* any more appealing?

The instant their fingers touched, everything around her made a dizzying shift . . .

I'm choking on smoke, eyes tearing as I fumble a door open and lurch inside the van, drawn by the cries of a small child. I'm not losing this one. Not this time.

Where is she? Can't see a damn thing.

"It's okay, it's okay. I'm coming. Talk to me, kid, talk to me."

The inside of the van is hot, too hot. Just give me time . . . and then something warm and soft brushes my fingertips.

I close my fingers around a soft, pudgy leg, trying to be

*gentle even as the need to hurry, hurry clenches in my gut.
I use the leg to guide me to a car seat. Strapped in, the seat
and the kid. Glimpse of pink flowers on a white T-shirt. A
little girl. Small and helpless and counting on me.*

This *child's not dying, damn it.*

"Just hang on. I won't let you down."

*I can't see, can't find the mechanism that releases the
straps. And I smell hot metal, burning plastic and rubber,
hear a weird, ominous crackle. Flames? Oh, Jesus, oh, Jesus.*

*Still no straps, hands frantic as they move over the
screaming, squirming kid, searching, searching. Finally,
there it is. The latch. Jesus, the metal's hot.*

*Everything is so hot, making the sweat pour into my
eyes, stinging along with the smoke. Two more seconds
and the latch is free, the girl all but sliding out of the seat
into my arms.*

*I crawl backward, out of the death trap, into humid,
smoke-choked air. My lungs ache, burn, my throat raw.*

*But I've got the girl, this sweet, warm, wriggly child,
in my arms, and nothing else matters.* This *time, I saved
the—*

An explosion shook the world.

Logan scrambled to Alex's side and leaned over her, not
caring that the van had burst into a ball of fire. The con-
cussion had knocked them both to the ground and sent
bystanders screaming and running. He had no idea why
Alex had gone catatonic when he'd taken her hand, and no
amount of calling her name had snapped her out of it.

This time when he said her name, though, she blinked
open brown eyes that reminded him of dark chocolate.

"What happened?" she asked, clearly disoriented.

"You tell me."

She shook her head, then squinted as though the movement made her dizzy. "It's too weird."

"What?"

"For a minute there, it was like I knew exactly what you went through trying to get that baby out of the van. Like I was there . . . or like I was . . ." She trailed off, her expression puzzled.

"Like you were what?"

"Like I was you."

Before he could respond, she sat up. He helped her, not sure she should even be sitting up, and brushed at ashes that floated down onto the shoulder of her emerald green polo. Her shoulder-length, reddish brown hair had curled further in the Florida humidity, sticking to the perspiration dampening her skin. He smoothed it back from the side of her face as he searched her eyes for lucidity. Damn it, they'd just had a breakthrough. He'd *finally* asked her out on an actual date. Defying death could boost a man's confidence. But his heart had lodged in his throat all over again, just like it had after she'd gotten shot.

"Tell me what happened," he said.

"I don't know." She coughed and looked around, dark eyes widening at the chaos. "What the hell?"

"Van exploded." He slipped a hand under her elbow to steady her when she took it upon herself to get to her feet. "Maybe you should—"

She was already up, swaying toward him at the same time that she grabbed at the camera dangling from her neck. She looked it over as carefully as a mother checking a child for injury. Then, apparently satisfied, she stepped to the side, trying to peer around him for a look at the burning wreckage. "I need to get—"

"Alex—"

She lifted the camera, heading straight for the inferno.

Logan sighed and let her go. That was Alex, after all. Give her a camera and breaking news, and she became utterly focused on her job. Part of being a photojournalist, he supposed. And he guessed that focus meant she was okay.

He kept an eye on her, though, watched as she snapped photo after photo from every angle possible as firefighters sprayed down the van and paramedics tended to the little girl and her mother.

Alex Trudeau at work was something to behold. She wasn't a glamour puss in the least and had to keep shoving her hair out of her face as the wind picked up. After a while, she hastily secured it with a band she dug out of a pocket. The ponytail-securing pose knocked him right in the gut. With her toned arms up, quick fingers at work in the thick, unruly curls, her shirt clung to palm-sized breasts, emphasizing her flat stomach and the subtle flare of hips in khaki slacks.

Freckles dotted her nose and cheeks, and her chin sported the most adorable, subtle cleft. She was captivating as hell, he thought for the thousandth time since he'd met her two years ago. As he watched, she threw her head back and laughed at something one of the firefighters called out to her, and she was so stunningly beautiful that Logan's world shifted under his feet.

He wanted her. Yearned for her. But he'd taken a step back after the shooting for fear of rushing her. Or taking advantage. Or myriad other ways he would have been a jerk if he'd made a move on her at such a vulnerable time.

She wasn't vulnerable anymore, though, and his pulse ratcheted up a notch at the possibilities.

As long as she never had to know what gave him nightmares.

CHAPTER **TWO**

Butch McGee wiped the bloody knife against the thigh of his new Levi's as he flipped open his cell phone. Who was calling him at five in the fucking morning? He didn't like the interruption in the adrenaline rush of watching the light die out of the eyes of his latest conquest, so when he spoke, his voice had an edge. "Yeah."

"I've found him."

He grinned as he heard the familiar voice. They didn't get to talk nearly enough. "Found who?"

"John Logan. His picture's in fucking *USA Today.*"

Butch dropped his Bowie hunting knife next to the bound body on the bed as the thought of finally, *finally* getting revenge chased all annoyance from his brain. "Where is he?"

"He's a cop in Florida."

"No shit? Where in Florida?"

"Lake Avalon. Podunk town between Naples and Fort Myers."

A mere hour-and-a-half airplane ride from Atlanta. Butch could be in Lake Avalon in a matter of hours. "You got any information on him? Like where he lives?"

"Nope. I'll have to leave the detective work up to you."

Butch studied his fingernails, noting that blood outlined them like tiny black red picture frames. He'd gotten carried away this time, let the passion of the kill drive him to new heights. A small grin touched the corners of his mouth. He had new heights yet to explore. "Any special requests, my brother?"

"Yeah. Make him suffer."

CHAPTER **THREE**

Shortly after eight thirty A.M., Alex ambled into the kitchen to let six sleepy mutts into the backyard for their morning ritual and retrieve the pile of newspapers on the front porch. She'd spent a frustrating night tossing and turning. Every time she closed her eyes, she relived those disturbing, disjointed moments inside the minivan. Her father had often told her she had a vivid imagination, but nothing about yesterday's experience seemed imagined.

She had no hope of coming up with an explanation, other than maybe she'd become so focused on lusting after Logan that she somehow projected herself into his shoes, which was ridiculous, because if she were going to do that, she would project herself into his *pants* . . .

She pushed the thoughts aside, deciding to add the mystery to the list of other disturbing things that had dogged her imagination since she'd gotten shot and almost died. It shouldn't have surprised her, after all, that such an intense brush with death had changed, and sharpened, her perception of the world around her.

After pouring herself a cup of coffee and grabbing a protein bar from the cupboard, she ambled over to the table. Idly sipping, she shifted the newspapers around to take in the day's front-page news according to *The Miami Herald* and *The Tampa Tribune*.

War. Death. Destruction. Economic trouble.

Same old, same old.

As she sat, she pulled *USA Today* out from under the *Orlando Sentinel* and scanned the front before flipping to the next page. When she reached page five, she almost bobbled her coffee. There, in full-color newsprint, John Logan materialized out of a swirl of black smoke, a tiny little girl clutched in his able arms. The sight struck her breathless, not because the national media had picked up her photo, but because the country's biggest newspaper declared Logan a hero.

Grinning so hard her cheeks ached, she picked up the phone and called the managing editor at the *Lake Avalon Gazette*.

"Mac Hunter."

"It's Alex. Have you seen *USA Today*?"

"Hell, yeah," he said with a booming laugh. "I was just getting ready to call you. I told you that picture was a headliner."

The pleased tone of his voice made her grin even more. They'd been good friends since her father had hired him at the newspaper a few years ago. Mac had had a rough time lately, just as she had. "So how's it going?"

His sigh gusted over the line. "You don't have to check up on me, you know."

"I'm not. I called to gloat."

"Yeah, right. Don't worry, okay? I'm doing great."

She didn't believe him. He hadn't been "great" since before they'd ended up in the hospital at the same time, victims of the same psycho who'd targeted her sister. Mac's skull fracture had healed, but he was still dealing with a lot of stress—work and personal—that had Alex worried. "You know you can talk to me any time, right?"

"Yep. You've told me several times already."

"Just making sure."

"You don't have to rescue me, Alex. Besides, you already have your hands full with all those furballs you've saved from uncertain fates. Are you coming into the office later?"

"Nope. I'm off the next two days. Going over to help Charlie in the garden."

"Enjoy the time off. And try not to gloat too much."

She hung up with a smile, then headed for the bedroom to don her jogging clothes. Five minutes later, she hit the pavement, her trusty, blind German shepherd at her side in his harness and short leash. She'd started running a couple of weeks ago to rebuild her strength and stamina since the shooting. The time outdoors and quality time with Dieter, the latest addition to her growing menagerie, never failed to put her in a good mood. Today, it gave her time to think about her upcoming date with John Logan, Lake Avalon's man of mystery.

She didn't know a lot about him, other than the sight of him in his police uniform put a hitch in her heart rate. She didn't normally have a thing about men in uniform— just *this* man in uniform. And that thing had started the moment they'd begun flirting at the scenes of crimes, accidents, fires and other newsworthy events that she'd photographed for the next day's newspaper while he kept order. From day one, the day he'd started as Lake Avalon's newest police detective two years ago, she'd thought he was beyond hot. And he just kept getting hotter the more she got to know him.

Now, finally, they were going to go on a date. Soon, she would know whether this intense attraction extended beyond flirty conversation.

Dragging her attention outward, she made kiss-kiss noises at Dieter, who kept an even pace at her side, trusting her implicitly to guide him. Kind of funny, considering he had been a guide dog before he developed cataracts. His tail kept up a constant wag, his ears perked and nose twitching.

As they paused at an intersection to let a car pass, she rubbed his ears. "You're a good friend, Dieter."

She could swear he grinned up at her in response.

As they neared home at a leisurely pace, she perused the neighborhood she loved. Nothing fancy. Just older, simple, one-story homes in various pastel shades of stucco lining narrow streets with gravel shoulders and no sidewalks. Large trees—royal palms, jacarandas, holly and banyan— crowded the yards, arching over driveways, roofs and streets. The delighted screams of playing kids at a nearby school filled the air, complemented by the occasional barking dog or lawn mower.

On her block, she turned Dieter loose for his routine mad dash to the house. He knew what came next: breakfast. He *loved* breakfast. Alex laughed as she jogged toward the driveway that led up to her peach stucco house nestled among the trees. The two-bedroom home was small, but it had a large screened-in back porch and an even larger fenced-in backyard, perfect for the pooches.

A sharp bark startled her, and her steps faltered. Dieter barked only when he thought it necessary: an unusual noise outside or a stranger in their midst.

She broke into a run. "Dieter?"

She was halfway up the driveway when she saw the source of the shepherd's excitement: John Logan was laughing his ass off as Dieter pinned him to the stucco with both paws on his shoulders and licked at his face with a sloppy tongue. Logan balanced a flat box of Krispy Kreme doughnuts on one palm as he scrubbed at the dog's ears with his free hand.

"Dieter, down!" Alex exclaimed, horrified.

The dog obediently dropped back to all fours and loped over to her, pink tongue dangling as he happily panted.

Alex flashed Logan an embarrassed smile. "Sorry about that. I think he likes you."

"It's good to be liked." Logan grinned at her, looking good enough to devour. Freshly shaved. Hair still damp from a shower. Tall and broad-shouldered, tan and handsome in an untucked white T-shirt, khaki cargo shorts and well-worn Nike running shoes. He held out the iconic white and green box. "Hot doughnuts now."

Accepting the box pleased Alex more than two dozen roses ever could have. She loved doughnuts as much, if not more so, than Dieter loved breakfast. "A whole dozen? You're the best."

Logan's lips twitched. "I was hoping you'd share."

She pretended to ponder that idea. "What's the occasion?"

"You made me a star."

"*You* made you a star. I was just lucky enough to be there with a camera." She gestured him inside. "Do you mind putting on fresh coffee while I feed the mutts? They get cranky if they have to wait. Everything you need is above the coffeemaker."

Inside, she headed for the screened-in porch that branched off from the kitchen. While she prepared doggy breakfasts, Logan rinsed out the coffee carafe and filled it with fresh water.

As he scooped coffee into a clean filter, he listened to her talking to the half-dozen strays she'd rescued over the years.

"How's your morning going, Raquel? Are you getting anything done? Must be tough to accomplish anything with Gus sniffing your butt all the time."

Logan shook his head and chuckled. He could listen to her talk to her best friends all day, her smoky, contralto voice smoother than the best jazz. And, to be honest, he was relieved to find her cheerful and brimming with energy this morning. He easily could have waited until tonight to acknowledge the fantastic photo she'd taken of him doing his job—or he could have called. But he'd wanted to see her in person, to reassure himself that no ill effects lingered from that odd moment when they'd touched at the scene of the accident and she'd gone catatonic.

Alex's conversation in the other room resumed. "Where's Artemis? Oscar, have you seen Artemis? Did you chase her into the closet again?"

Logan pictured the shy cocker spaniel cowering in the back of the closet to escape the aggressiveness of a high-energy wiener dog with a back so bad his hind legs had been paralyzed for years. The dachshund used his front legs to pull himself around on a tiny cart, but that didn't stop him from stalking the other pooches in his version of playtime.

During Logan's first visit after she'd been released from the hospital, Alex had availed him of the cruel history of each of the pack. He admired the way she'd taken them in when no one else wanted them and loved them with all she had, gradually healing their wounds and their hearts. A part of him wondered whether he was drawn to her because he sensed she could do the same for him.

Her triumphant voice interrupted his thoughts. "There you go, Artemis. You're so brave. Look out, Dieter, you just tripped Gus. Geez."

Logan couldn't help but smile as he pictured the playful German shepherd who'd just accosted him in the driveway getting in the way of Gus, a beagle-bloodhound mix with a shiny red coat and one eye. Squirrel-chasing incident, Alex had told him with a tender smile as she'd stroked Gus's ears.

Raquel, a brown and white corgi, had lost her floppy ears and half her tail while alerting her family to the fire fast-consuming their mobile home. Her family survived thanks to her, but the fire rendered the family homeless, including Raquel. Alex took her in the instant she heard the story and nursed the dog back to health.

Phoebe, a brindle greyhound who was small for her breed at only fifty-five pounds, had lost her front right leg to amputation after a bad break at the dog track. That didn't stop her from running like a jack rabbit, especially when a squirrel was involved.

Alex returned to the kitchen then, curls caught in a bouncy ponytail and cheeks flushed from her morning jog. Her joy of life seemed to emanate from every pore, and damn, if he didn't find that even more sexy than the toned curves of her compact body.

"Mm, that coffee smells divine." She gestured at the table. "Have a seat."

As he settled onto a chair, he took in the massive spread of newspapers. "Not much of a newshound, are you?" he teased.

She grinned as she turned with coffee cups in hand. "More like a news whore."

While she grabbed napkins from a drawer, he flipped open the doughnut box. "You're good enough to work for *National Geographic*, you know."

She beamed as she sat across from him. "Really?"

"Hell, yeah. Have you ever sent them your portfolio?"

She shook her head as she reached for a doughnut and sank her teeth into it all in one fluid motion. "I like it here," she said as she chewed.

The way she enjoyed the warm, gooey doughnut, her pink tongue chasing the sugary glaze clinging to her top lip, fanned a hunger inside him that had nothing to do with food. Jesus, this woman would drive him crazy if he didn't get to kiss her soon.

She stopped chewing suddenly and cocked her head. "What?"

He realized he'd been staring. But how could he not? A flushed, sexy woman in shorts and a tank top . . . okay, focusing now. Or trying to. "Uh—"

"Do you think it's weird that I like it here?" she asked.

"Why would I think that?"

"I'm a small-town girl with small-town dreams and no desire to flee my family. Very uncool."

"Your devotion to your family and Lake Avalon is one of the things I like best about you."

"Really?"

"Yes. Besides, I like it here, too."

She reached for a second doughnut. "What made you want to be a cop?"

The change of subject threw him at first, but then he shrugged. "I wanted to help people. Make a difference."

"That's not very specific."

He took a sip of coffee. No one had ever expressed a desire for more information than that, which had always suited him just fine. "I don't know. It just happened. Why did you want to be a photojournalist?"

"Dad gave me his old Nikon one day when I was bugging the crap out of him and let me loose. I don't think Mom was too happy when I started coming home covered with grass stains and dirt from crawling around on the ground trying to get the perfect shot of a squirrel. Or from falling out of a tree while snapping a pic of the neighbor's cat stalking a bird it had no hope in hell of catching."

"Fun."

"I thought so. When Dad realized how into it I was getting, he took me to work with him and showed me how to develop my own photos." Her fond smile washed over him. "Those are some of my best memories with my dad, hanging out with him in the darkroom at the *Lake Avalon Gazette.*"

Logan sipped more coffee, amazed at how much information she managed to share in one breath and even more amazed at the enthusiasm with which she shared it. She made him laugh. She made him smile. She made him think the world wasn't such a cold, dark place after all. Which just affirmed all over again what he'd suspected three months ago when this lovely, lively woman almost died: He could fall for her. Hard and fast.

Alex set her elbows on the table and gestured at him with her third doughnut. "I answered your questions. Now you answer mine."

Time to go. He pushed back from the table and rose. "Much as I'd love to stay and chat, I have to report for duty. Is a rain check okay?"

Her dark eyes narrowed as they perused him. "Are you dodging?"

He barely managed to resist the urge to lean down and kiss the tip of her adorable nose. "Yep."

"I'll just nail you tonight during our date—I mean . . ." Her cheeks flushed a brighter red. "Crap."

His grin broadened. "I'm counting on it."

CHAPTER **FOUR**

After a good couple of hours on her knees helping Charlie yank weeds out of her garden, Alex sat back on her heels. She pulled off a gardening glove and ran a hand through hair curling further in the humidity. She imagined Logan's fingers in it, imagined him gripping her head while he kissed her, hot and hungry. A warm flush climbed up from the pit of her stomach that had nothing to do with the sun beaming down on her. For the hundredth time, she chided herself to stop thinking about him. But she couldn't help it. He consumed her thoughts. She couldn't wait to get her hands on him, couldn't wait for that first searing kiss.

Deciding she needed something cool to drink, she pushed to her feet. "I'm going inside for some water. Want any?"

Charlie stripped off her gloves and then used the back of one hand to push back wisps of dark hair that had escaped from her ponytail. She looked healthy and tan and well rested in a pink tank top and navy shorts. "I'll come in, too. I'm ready for a break."

Alex extended a hand to help her sister to her feet, but Charlie ignored the offer and rose on her own. The brush-off stung, and Alex debated whether to say anything. If Charlie's distance hadn't become so obvious lately, she wouldn't have. But now she was irked. The snub had pissed all over her good mood, and that just wasn't right.

She huffed out a breath. "I don't have cooties, you know."

Charlie stilled in the act of brushing the dirt off her knees. When she looked at Alex, her golden brown eyes brimmed with regret. "Damn, Alex, I'm sorry."

"Sorry for what? Not hugging me anymore? Because, you don't."

"I was hoping you hadn't noticed."

"How could I not notice? You used to hug me every time you saw me, and then you just stopped. I thought at first that you were afraid you'd hurt me, because of the . . . you know. But I'm fine now, and you still make an effort not to touch me."

"I . . . I don't . . ."

"You flinch, too. When I get too close. You flinch away."

"Alex—"

"I hope you know that I don't blame you for the shooting. It was an accident. He was a psycho, and I was in the wrong place at the wrong time."

Charlie held up a shaking hand. "Alex, please."

Alex fell silent, worried now. Her sister wasn't one to tremble. She reached out to grab her hand, to stop it from shaking, and Charlie jerked back so violently she ended up on her butt in the grass.

Alex stared at her in shock. "What the hell is going on with you?"

Charlie pulled in an uneven breath as she pushed to her feet and swiped at the loose grass clinging to her shorts. "It's not me."

"Well, it's not *me*," Alex countered. "Look, I know how you are, how you're all about protecting me from stuff you think might hurt me, but this is getting ridiculous. We used to be so close."

"We're still close—"

"You won't *touch* me." Alex took a step toward Charlie, only to watch her back away. Like she had the plague. Hurt burned in her throat, and she put her hands up and did her own backing away. "Fine, whatever. Keep your secrets, as usual. I'll catch you later."

She turned away, ignoring it when she heard Charlie come after her. "Alex, wait."

"Forget it, Charlie. I can take a hint."

"Alex, damn it!"

She paused and faced her reluctantly. "What?"

"Let's just . . . can we go inside and have a drink and talk?"

Alex kept her face impassive. "Don't do it to humor me."

"I'm not."

"Good. I could use a margarita."

In the kitchen, surrounded by sunlight, the lemon-fresh scent of dishwashing liquid and a tense silence, Charlie got out margarita glasses and the necessary ingredients.

"I was just kidding," Alex said with a small smile. "It's kind of early for booze, don't you think?"

"We're both going to need it," Charlie replied, far too serious as she filled the glasses with ice and then splashed in tequila and margarita mix. After setting one glass in front of Alex, she took a seat across from her sister.

Alex picked up the glass and drank with a clink of ice cubes. "Mm, good one."

Charlie didn't smile as she toyed with her own glass instead of drinking. "I'm not sure how to do this."

Alex sat back. "If you're breaking up with me, just say it." Her attempt at humor didn't even register on her sister's tense face. "Okay, how about this? Let's talk about something else for a bit, ease into it."

Charlie nodded, looking way too relieved.

"I talked to Mac this morning," Alex said. "He sounded . . . good."

"Wasn't it my turn to check on him?"

Alex shrugged. "We had business to discuss."

Charlie's lips twitched into a smile. "You used the photo of Logan as an excuse to call him."

"Busted. But the good news is Mac didn't sound as stressed. At least, he sounded *less* stressed. And a bit like he might be tired of us hovering."

"I wish he'd just get out of town for a while," Charlie said. "He went back to work too early, in my opinion."

"We could let him use the cabin. It'd get him out of town for a week or two."

Charlie thought that over. "That's not a bad idea."

"He probably just needs more time. Head injuries take time to heal."

"Working twenty-four hours a day doesn't help."

"He's better, though. I can tell," Alex said.

"Or maybe he's just getting better at hiding it." Charlie sighed and shook her head. "And maybe I'm channeling your thing about rescuing the wounded."

"You say that like it's a bad thing."

Charlie laughed. "Awesome shot of Logan, by the way. Really amazing."

Alex smiled despite her anxiety. She never tired of compliments from her big sister. "Helps that I had such a gorgeous subject."

"Helps that you know how to take a great photo. What's up with you and that gorgeous subject anyway? Rumors are flying all over work that you two are an item."

A warm wave of anticipation for their date tonight flooded Alex's stomach. "We're working on it."

As Charlie nodded her approval, her forehead creased. Apparently, she'd started stressing again about the conversation they weren't having.

"Come on, Charlie. What's going on?"

Charlie drew in a breath. "Have you felt different? Since you were shot."

Alex gazed at her for a long moment. So it was going to be one of *those* conversations. Where Charlie fished for information on what Alex was feeling or had felt or might feel tomorrow. A maddening habit her sister had picked up since the shooting, as though she expected Alex to be different in some way. And she was . . . different in some way. But putting it into words . . . hell, Charlie was the writer. Alex expressed herself in pictures.

"Yeah, I do feel different," she said finally. "How could I not? I died in the ER."

Charlie flinched at that but moved on. "I don't mean physically. I mean, it is physical, but it's mostly . . . emotional. Well, hell, maybe it's mostly physical. I don't know."

"You're not making any sense. You know that, right? It's kind of funny, really, coming from you. You're the one who always knows what to say and precisely how to say it."

"You're giving me way too much credit on that."

"Just say it, Charlie. Lay it out for me, and we'll go from there."

Charlie closed her eyes as though to gird herself. Alex felt so bad for her that she reached across the table and grasped her hand.

The world turned inside out . . .

I yank on my hands, but they're tied, and there's pain, oh, God, pain in my temples, behind my eyes, rippling in waves. I try to talk, forcing the words out through lips that don't want to move.

"You need help." Nausea cracks my voice. "You're hurt. You're probably bleeding internally. I can help you. Get you to the ER."

The man wavering before me, pale and sweaty, takes a step back only to double over with a harsh groan. "This is your fault," he says. "You broke something inside me."

I jerk at my wrists. What if he passes out and I'm stuck here like this? "I can't help you if you don't untie me."

But he drops to the gritty concrete floor and starts to retch.

Desperation races through my blood like fire. I'm going to die here, like this, tied and helpless and alone.

"Untie me."

I'm begging now, knowing this is it, this is the end. And then lightning blasts behind my eyes—

Alex's head snapped back, and for a moment, she felt it loll, weightless yet incredibly heavy.

"Alex!"

Charlie's frantic voice broke through the confusion, and Alex managed to lift her head and open her eyes. The Herculean motion made everything around her swim, and the next thing she knew, she was on her knees on the floor, her stomach heaving.

Charlie jumped back with a shout but quickly recovered and helped Alex to her feet and down the hall to the bathroom. Tears squeezed out of her eyes as she vomited until nothing more came up.

She leaned back against the side of the bathtub and tried to get her breathing under control, conscious of the sweat running down the sides of her face and her spine.

Charlie handed her a washcloth, and Alex pressed its cool wetness to her face. She winced at the flare of pain in her cheek, as though someone had struck her.

Breathing easier, Alex looked up at her deathly pale sister. "Did you hit me?"

Charlie knelt before her and grasped Alex's ankle as though to ground herself. "You weren't answering me. I didn't know how else to snap you out of it."

Stomach-clenching horror slid through her. "Snap me out of *what*?" She'd blacked out? Had an epileptic seizure? What?!

"Alex, you had an empathic flash."

CHAPTER **FIVE**

Butch McGee settled into the rental Mustang in the parking garage at Tampa International Airport and unfolded the road map the nice girlie at the Hertz counter had given him. She'd batted her eyes at him more than once, but as much as he'd been tempted to flirt back and score a little afternoon delight, he'd stayed on track. He had a destination: Lake Avalon.

He couldn't deny his anticipation of the moment when he had John Logan on his knees and begging for his rotten life. The thing he loved most about his art—and there were plenty of benefits to choose from—was the begging.

He found Lake Avalon with the tip of his finger. An easy drive, he decided. Straight shot down Highway 41. He'd be there in a few hours, maybe even have John Logan squinting against the glare of his favorite Bowie blade by morning, if he was lucky.

And Butch McGee was always lucky.

CHAPTER **SIX**

Whistling softly, Logan ambled down the alley that separated a restaurant and a bar. It smelled of Mexican food and cigarettes. He found what he was looking for squatting with his back against a lime green stucco wall, cigarette smoke creating a cloud around his shaved head. The teenager—Logan assumed he was about sixteen—went by the name Justin Parker. Not his real name, though, as Logan had discovered when he'd tried to track the boy's parents.

"You again," the teenager said. His voice rasped as though he'd smoked since coming out of the womb.

"Yep, me again," Logan said with a nod. "Brought you something." He held up a McDonald's bag that held four double cheeseburgers and the three Krispy Kreme doughnuts that he and Alex hadn't devoured.

The boy snorted and blew twin streams of smoke out his nostrils. "You do know that crap will kill me, right?"

Logan shrugged as he balanced the bag on the kid's knee. "So will starving."

Justin pressed his lips together as he eyed the bag.

Promises of tasty goodness floated out of the bag, somehow overpowering the offensive alley odors. He looked ravenous, his dark-rimmed blue eyes intense with hunger, his cheeks pale. Already thin to begin with, he'd lost weight since Logan had met him the first time a few weeks ago, his cheeks beginning to get that hollowed-out look. Logan hoped that sickly pale appearance didn't have anything to do with drug use.

Logan waited him out, hands in his pockets as he nonchalantly studied the ugly green stucco that belonged to a Mexican restaurant. The Green Iguana. Good, inexpensive margaritas. Salsa exactly the way he liked it: strip-the-skin-off-the-roof-of-your-mouth hot.

The rattle of the paper bag drew his attention down, and he watched Justin plunge a hand inside and pull out the first paper-wrapped cheeseburger. "Is it a double?" he asked as he unwrapped it like a precious birthday gift.

"You bet."

Justin sank his teeth in and rolled his eyes with ecstasy.

As Justin ate, Logan leaned against the stucco across from him, this one a mustard yellow. It belonged to a bar that Logan suspected turned into a strip club after hours. One of these nights, he planned to stop in and flash his badge. That should be enough to scatter the ne'er-do-wells into the night, at least for a while.

"So," he said, hands still pocketed. "What're you up to today?"

Justin grunted as he swallowed a huge mouthful, already ripping into a second sandwich. "What do you think?"

"I'm guessing a bunch of feeling sorry for yourself."

Justin nodded and chewed. "Sounds good to me."

"I don't suppose you took my advice and went to see Dr. Paige?"

"Waste of time." Burger muffled his words. Some color had returned to his cheeks, so the food was already doing some good.

"She works with kids like you all the time," Logan said. "She might have some insight."

"I don't need insight from a bleeding-heart social worker to know I'm screwed up."

"You're not the only one, you know."

"Yeah? What would you know? You look pretty well fed to me. What're you hanging out with me for anyway? You think you're going to get some?"

"I'll pass, but thanks for the offer."

Justin scowled as he plunged his hand into the bag for the third time. His eyes widened, though, when he pulled out a doughnut. "What the hell?" he breathed.

"It's a doughnut."

"I can see that, dumbass. I just haven't had one of these in a long time."

"A doughnut?"

"No, a Krispy Kreme. Jesus."

Logan smiled. "Yeah, I praise the Lord when I eat them, too."

Justin closed his eyes as he took the first bite and chewed. His expression said he'd tasted something beyond decadent. "It's fresh," he said softly, eyes still closed.

Logan felt a tug at his heart at how much this kid missed the finer things in life. He cleared his throat. "I've been there."

"To Krispy Kreme?" Justin asked. "It smells like heaven. Mom used to take me there after school sometimes. When I was a kid and got good grades."

Logan didn't point out that he was still a kid. "I meant I've been where you are now. Living on the streets."

Justin peered into the bag and grinned when he spotted two more doughnuts. "Hot damn." As he tore into the second one, he said, "It could be worse. This could be freaking Chicago or New York. I don't get cold at night. Much. And there's this cop who brings me food on his lunch hour."

"I can get you some help. Get you a place to sleep."

"You're talking about a foster home, right? I'm not going into the system. The system is screwed."

Logan couldn't argue with that. A front-row seat could provide a hint of the problems, but a starring role during a long-term run made the flaws glaring. "I can help with that. Make sure you get a decent place."

Justin studied him as he chewed. "What's in it for you? I already told you I don't do guys."

"Not yet you don't. And that might not be around the next corner, but it probably will be around the one after that."

"No freaking way. I don't do that shit. It's *disgusting*." He spat out the last word a bit too vehemently.

Logan squatted, bracing his forearms on his knees, so that he was eye to eye with the teenager. "I've been here, Justin. I know what I'm talking about. There comes a point where you don't feel you have a choice."

Justin's eyes rounded. "You—"

"And then there's gangs. They make it sound like family, but it's not. Your family doesn't kill you if you decide to leave the fold."

Justin finished off the last doughnut with a thoughtful look on his face. "You're trying to scare me straight?"

Logan chuckled and shook his head. "You're too smart for the streets, Justin. You're too smart to flush your life down the toilet because your parents don't know shit about how to deal with you. Instead of being bitter and pissed off, you can do something about it. You can prove that you're better than this."

"Hey, my mother obviously doesn't give a crap about me, 'cause here I am. So what am I supposed to do? Where am I supposed to go? I have *nothing*."

"Yeah, it sucks. But you know what? You're in charge now. You're the one who decides what happens next. I'm just trying to give you some decent advice. This is the first step, sleeping in an alley and depending on the kindness of a stranger to keep you fed. You can spend the rest of your life wallowing and making bad decisions until you finally die young. Or you can get off your ass, brush yourself off and do something about it. Don't do what I did, kid. Don't roll over and play dead."

Justin looked him up and down with narrowed eyes. "You look like you turned out okay, cop."

"Took me a while. I'm offering you a shortcut."

Justin glanced away, working his jaw as though either biting back angry words or suppressing tears.

Logan rose and his knees popped. Withdrawing a pre-paid cell phone from his pocket, he tossed it to the boy. "I programmed my number into speed dial number two," he said. "When you decide you're going to do something constructive, give me a call."

He turned and walked away without looking back, hoping like hell that he'd made an impression. Maybe it'd take a few, or even a dozen, more visits. He just hoped he could turn the kid around before he had no choice but to do his duty and haul him into the system.

CHAPTER **SEVEN**

Alex shifted in the passenger seat of Charlie's new Escape hybrid, wondering if she should tell her sister to slow the hell down. But Charlie seemed hell-bent on going wherever they were going. "Where are you taking me again?"

"To see someone who can help."

"You seem to know what's going on. Why don't you just explain it to me?"

"This is different. *Yours* is different."

Alex rubbed at the center of her forehead. That made no sense, but her brain felt too foggy to sort it out.

"Headache?" Charlie asked.

"A little."

"Are you seeing flashes of light?"

Alex squinted sideways. "No. Why?"

Charlie kept her eyes on the road, but the coiled tension in her shoulders unfurled a little. "Good. That's good."

Alex decided to try another tack. "What makes you think I had . . . what did you call it? An empathic flash?"

Charlie braked for a stoplight. "You said something in

the hospital after you were shot. You were out of it, but it was something you couldn't possibly have known unless you'd gotten an empathic hit off me."

"I don't remember this."

Charlie went on as if Alex hadn't spoken. "I was sitting with you, holding your hand, and when you woke up, you were agitated. You said something about a body under the stairs."

"I *really* don't remember this." And didn't want to. A body under the stairs? Holy crap.

"You couldn't have known what I saw, Alex. Unless you saw it through my eyes."

"This is nuts. It's . . . it's . . ." She trailed off, at a loss.

"What happened when you touched my hand earlier?" Charlie asked.

"You know what? Let's just go back to your house so I can get my car. I don't want—"

"Think about it. What did you see?"

Alex shook her head and stared out the passenger-side window. She didn't want to relive those moments. The pain and fear had felt all too real, all too powerful. She shied away from the memory as surely as she shied away from the idea of a root canal without a painkiller.

"Whatever it was," Charlie said softly, "it happened to me."

Alex turned her head to look at her sister. "What?"

"You had an empathic flash on something that happened to me."

Alex's nausea returned in full force. "You should pull over."

Charlie didn't hesitate to swing the car onto the shoulder of the beach-access road.

Alex stumbled out the door and made it a couple of yards away from the car before doubling over. Nothing came up this time, her heaving stomach hollow and raw, almost painfully empty. Oh, God, this can't be real. Don't let it be real.

Her knees buckled, and she braced her hands in soft green grass and tried to catch her breath. A dream, a nightmare. That's all this is. Time to wake up now.

Please.

Charlie appeared at her side and placed her hand on Alex's back, soothing in gentle circles. She handed Alex a fresh bottle of cool water, the cap already removed, and waited while she took a shaky drink. Several minutes passed before Alex thought she could speak coherently.

"He did that to you," she whispered. "That man who tried to kill you. He kidnapped you and . . . tied you up."

Nodding, Charlie stroked her palm over Alex's hair in a calming gesture. "But I'm okay now."

"I didn't know it was so . . ." She couldn't find an adequate word. "Horrible" wasn't horrible enough.

"You'd been shot, Alex. You needed to focus on your own recovery."

Alex closed her eyes and took several deep breaths to fight the churning of her stomach. Perspiration beaded on her upper lip, and she swiped the back of her hand over it. The world hadn't made much sense to her before, but now . . .

"We should get back into the car," Charlie said. "It's cool there. You'll feel better."

Alex didn't say anything as Charlie guided her back to the SUV, but she was thinking she'd never feel better again. How had Charlie survived such terror? And how the hell had Alex tapped into it?

Once they were back in the car, Charlie flipped the air-conditioning on high and pulled back into traffic, calm as you please.

"How?" Alex asked. She figured she didn't have to elaborate at this point.

"I don't know. It probably has something to do with when you were shot. You weren't empathic before that."

"How do you know?"

"Because I was, and I could tell you weren't like me."

"Have you always been . . ." She couldn't bring herself to say the word. Didn't want to acknowledge that it even existed. As if that would make a difference in how screwed up everything was.

"Some," Charlie said. "But it didn't become what it is now until after . . ."

"After?"

"Remember the woman I saw get killed when she was hit by that car? She was our cousin. And also empathic."

Alex put a palm to her forehead and pressed against the growing throb there. "I thought we didn't have any cousins."

"Surprise."

Alex didn't respond to her sister's attempt to lighten the mood. "So if that woman was our cousin, why are you just now telling me?"

Charlie sighed softly. "I didn't tell you when I found out because she was murdered and someone was coming after me. I didn't want to make you a target. And we haven't had much alone time since then to discuss . . . things."

Alex narrowed her eyes against afternoon sunlight that had turned blinding and wished she had sunglasses. "Things about Mom, you mean. Mom and her slew of secrets."

Charlie nodded. "Yeah."

"Which appears to include a cousin we didn't know about."

"Yeah."

Alex chewed at her lower lip. "Is it okay if I file that information away for later and we just hit the highlights?"

"I think that's a good idea, considering."

"So this cousin was empathic?"

"Yes, and when she died," Charlie said, "I was holding her hand. AnnaCoreen thinks I—"

"AnnaCoreen?"

"She's a friend who has some experience in this sort of

thing. She thinks that when Laurette—that's our cousin—died, I absorbed her empathic ability, and that it super-charged mine."

Alex couldn't stop the laugh that slipped past her lips. "This sounds . . . I don't know . . . just weird." And completely freaking unbelievable.

"I had a hard time at first, too. You'll get used to it." Charlie paused, wet her lips. "I mean, you'll get used to the *idea*. I haven't gotten used to the ability. I don't think I ever will."

Alex stared through the windshield as the scrubby landscape gave way to beachside restaurants, hotels and gift shops. The Gulf of Mexico was a glittery backdrop in the sun. Everything about this moment felt surreal.

"So what happens?" she asked.

"I'd rather hear how it's happening for you."

Alex's brain went blank. She had no idea. All she remembered was spinning disorientation and the incredibly intense sense of being not herself anymore. The first time—or at least the first time she'd become totally aware of what happened—had been right after Logan pulled that little girl out of the burning van. But then the van had exploded, and the chaos had distracted her until later that night. By then, she just hadn't known what to think.

"Alex?"

She blinked. "You first."

Charlie didn't try to dodge, which was unusual for her. "It happens when I make skin-on-skin contact with another person. I relive something traumatic that happened to them recently. It's just a flash, and then it's over." She paused as she pulled over to the side of the road in front of a fuchsia shack sporting a neon sign advertising psychic readings for ten dollars.

"So that's why you wouldn't touch me?" Alex asked. "Because you didn't want to . . . what? Feel what it was like when I got shot?"

Charlie's lips curved slightly, but it was a sad smile. "I already felt that. I was there, remember?"

And then it hit her. Charlie hadn't been protecting *herself*. Alex sank back against the seat. "You didn't want me to feel what you went through when you were kidnapped."

"And you ended up being blindsided by it anyway. I'm sorry I let my guard down."

Alex squinted at the pink shack, wondering idly why Lake Avalon Beach even let such an eyesore take up precious beach property. Thinking that was easier than thinking about what she'd just learned.

She rubbed at her burning eyes, then winced as her fingers brushed a tender place high on her cheekbone, almost like she had a bruise. No way had Charlie struck her hard enough to leave a bruise, and it had much more likely been a slap rather than a punch anyway—

"Your empathy is different from mine," Charlie said softly. "When you touched me, you were gone. For a long time."

Alex turned her head to look at her sister, noted how pale she still looked despite the tan from working in her garden.

Charlie took in a shaky breath before she went on. "I had to slap you to bring you back." She tried to smile at Alex but managed only a grimace. "I don't know how, but your ability is different."

Alex glanced down at her tangled hands in her lap. Different, great.

Suddenly, Charlie grasped Alex's chin and angled her head up, her eyes becoming scrutinizing slits. "What the hell? I didn't hit you *that* hard."

Alex pulled back with a wince at the painful pressure on her jaw. "Ow."

Charlie's gaze dropped to Alex's hands, as though searching for something she was afraid to find. Gentle this time, she curled her fingers around Alex's right forearm and lifted her hand to inspect the raw, red skin and bruises encircling her wrist. Her other forearm sported similar injuries.

Charlie let out a shocked breath. "Oh, God."

Alex stared at her wrists, her own disbelieving "Oh, God" echoing in her head. She remembered being inside Charlie's head, remembered struggling to get free of the tight bonds around her wrists.

Somehow, what had happened to her sister then had carried over into her own reality.

CHAPTER **EIGHT**

You still thinking you'll turn that kid Justin around?"

Logan glanced up at his lunch companion. Noah Lassiter had a bacon cheeseburger in one hand and a can of Coke in the other. In a navy polo, white shorts and sun-streaked hair, he looked like a tourist, minus the sunburn. Fleeing his life as a police detective in Chicago in favor of private investigation in Lake Avalon, along with living with Charlie, seemed to agree with the man.

"Yeah, I do," Logan said.

"Why don't you just take the kid into custody and get it over with? He'll get the help he needs that way."

"He needs to make the choice."

Logan took a drink of Coke and squinted out at the pedestrian traffic that flowed past the sidewalk cafe. People in shorts, tank tops and sunglasses mixed with men and women in business suits or khaki pants. Tourists and residents alike out for lunch or a stroll. Since it was May, residents outnumbered the tourists, most of whom had returned to their northern homes after Easter. But the weather was still comfortable ahead of the dense humidity of summer.

After finishing off his burger, Noah flipped open a notebook he'd pulled out of his back pocket. "I did the checking you requested and came up with zilch on the kid's background. None of the Parkers in Lake Avalon have heard of him."

"Damn. I knew the name he gave me was bogus, but I was hoping it had a family connection."

"He's probably a *Spider-Man* fan."

Logan arched an inquisitive brow. "How do you figure?"

"Peter *Parker*. Teenage boy dealing with the rejection and feelings of inadequacy that go with growing up. Odds are Justin's first name is for real, though it's unlikely he's a closeted superhero."

Logan smirked. "Or maybe he just likes the sound of Parker."

Noah sat back and began tilting his half-empty soda can from one side to the other. "You got a vested interest in this kid?"

"You could say."

"Care to share?"

"Not really."

"Mind if I make an observation?" Noah asked.

"There's nothing to worry about here."

"I don't know about that. You get tense when you talk about him."

"Kids living on the street make me tense."

"It's more than that. Charlie's friend AnnaCoreen would say there's something dark inside you."

Logan snorted as he tossed his crumpled napkin onto the wrought-iron table. "Please."

"You haven't met AnnaCoreen. She knows things."

"What the hell are you talking about?

"She *knows* things."

Logan cocked his head, ready to laugh, until he realized Noah was serious. "You mean, like a psychic? That's such bullshit."

"You'd be surprised."

"No, I don't think I would. Don't tell me you buy into that crap."

Noah said nothing as he drained his Coke, but it was clear that he disagreed.

"Why are we even talking about this?" Logan asked. "I'm just looking out for a homeless teenager I caught Dumpster diving behind the Iguana a couple of weeks ago."

Noah slipped his notebook back into his pocket. "You didn't have anyone to take you in, did you?"

Logan stiffened. He shouldn't have gotten defensive, damn it. He should have let the "there's something dark inside you" roll off his back. Like a damn duck. But, no, he'd had to let his feathers ruffle, and now he looked like a pitiful jerk. "Just forget it."

"Does Alex know?"

"There's nothing to know."

"She should know. Guy like you has issues to work out. Intimacy issues."

Logan opened his mouth to tell the man to fuck off when he caught the glint in Noah's eyes. The bastard was trying his damnedest not to laugh.

Logan let his shoulders relax. "You've been rifling through Charlie's *Cosmo*s, huh?"

Noah leaned forward and dropped his voice. "I read it for the pictures. Did you know that there's a position called the Amazing Butterfly?"

CHAPTER **NINE**

Are you kidding me?"

Charlie flashed Alex an amused, albeit grim, smile at her reaction to the hot pink shack with its rusted tin roof. "If you're nice to her, she'll read your palm for free."

"Charlie, come on. A beachfront psychic is going to explain this?" Alex glanced down at the bruises and red skin on her wrists. Were the injuries already fading? A fingertip dragged over a particularly purple mark returned an answering twinge that did indeed feel less intense than it had only minutes ago. What the hell?

She started to shake again. She must be dreaming, in a sleep so deep that her subconscious had visited an insanely lucid world, where everything was turned upside down and crazy. Or maybe she was dead. Maybe she'd never recovered from the gunshot and this was hell.

"It's not."

Alex jolted. She'd completely lost the thread of conversation. "What?"

"It's not a dream," Charlie said.

"What, are you psychic, too?"

"No. I've just been there."

"God, Charlie. *God.*"

Charlie craned her neck to look at the rundown shack through the window on Alex's side of the car. "Anna-Coreen is waiting for us."

Alex turned her head to see a petite older woman in blue jeans, a blousy white top and flat sandals waving from the sidewalk leading to the shack. She had short springy strawberry blond hair and, even from the car, Alex could see she wore simple, if any, makeup. That woman was a beach psychic? Not the garish character she'd expected.

"Come on," Charlie said and pushed open the driver's door.

Alex followed Charlie reluctantly. She knew the polite smile she offered the psychic as they approached couldn't get any stiffer. This was going to be such a massive waste of time, and all she really wanted to do was lie down and jam a pillow over her head.

Then, as if things couldn't get any weirder, Charlie shared a warm hug with the faux psychic and brushed a light kiss over one of the older woman's awesome cheekbones.

"Alex, this is AnnaCoreen Tesch," Charlie said.

Alex nodded in greeting but kept her hand to herself. No way did she plan to touch anyone else until she knew what the hell was going on.

AnnaCoreen's lips took on an amused quirk as she looked Alex up and down. "My goodness, but you are gorgeous."

Alex felt her eyes widen. Okay, not what she was expecting. And *so* beside the point. Somehow, she'd fallen down her very own rabbit hole. Perhaps this was the Queen of Hearts. No, had to be the Mad Hatter. Or maybe Charlie was the Mad Hatter . . . Man, that would suck. The most sane, logical woman on the planet suddenly a crackpot? An *empathic* crackpot.

AnnaCoreen glanced from Alex to Charlie and back again. "So very obviously sisters, too. Look at the both of you, all that thick dark hair and lovely shades of brown and gold in your eyes. Your Nana must have just wanted to eat you both up when you were youngsters."

Laughing, Charlie launched into a story. "Nana pretended to capture and eat Alex's nose once, saying it was the best white chocolate she'd ever had, and Alex screamed bloody murder until she gave it back."

AnnaCoreen smiled, showing perfect white teeth. "Oh, that's precious. Truly precious."

Alex smiled tolerantly. "I hate to be a party pooper, but—"

Charlie cast an apologetic look at the older woman. "She's not on board yet."

AnnaCoreen's grin didn't falter. "How can she be? She's been blindsided."

Alex almost rolled her eyes. Please. This was such bullshit. Whatever was going on with her . . . well, it'd go away. She'd get a good night's sleep, eat better, do some exercise, and she'd be fine. "Look—"

"I'm afraid there are no miracle cures for empathy, my dear child," AnnaCoreen said. "Why don't we go inside, have some tea and talk? You'll feel better afterward."

As AnnaCoreen turned, Alex gave Charlie a questioning look.

Charlie shrugged. "She does that sometimes."

"Does what?" Alex wasn't willing to concede what she'd been thinking.

"Reads your mind."

"Can she? For real?"

"I don't know."

"If that woman is psychic, I'll eat my camera," Alex whispered as she followed Charlie and AnnaCoreen around the side of the ugly shack.

"Probably be more pleasant for you in the long run if you said you'd eat a box of doughnuts," Charlie whispered back. "Krispy Kremes."

Alex didn't respond, too taken aback as they followed

a brick path through an explosion of flowers in vibrant oranges and pinks and reds to the back door of a small bright yellow house trimmed in white. She could hear the gentle roll and retreat of the Gulf waves on the other side of the house, scent the salt and flowers in the air. Under her shoes, the grit of sand rasped. So very normal on such an abnormal day.

"Relax," Charlie said softly. "If you're not convinced in ten minutes, we'll leave."

Alex shot her a rueful glance. "You think it'll take only ten minutes?"

"I'm sure of it."

Alex forced her shoulders back and tried to roll the tension out of her neck. "Okay. Ten minutes. And I'm not drinking anything in that ten minutes. She probably doses you with some kind of potion. Or, wait, I bet she hypnotizes you."

"You'd buy hypnotism over empathy," Charlie said in a dry tone.

Alex shook her head. Charlie wasn't the only one who'd lost her grip. "You know what I mean."

AnnaCoreen opened the back door to the house and gestured them inside. "Have a seat in the front room while I make some tea."

Alex bit back the urge to grumble "I hate tea" under her breath. And, honestly, she couldn't bring herself to be such a grump in a kitchen so open and bright. Everything was white and accented by bright reds, blues and yellows. It smelled like lemon, like Nana's kitchen always had, and Alex felt a tug at her heart.

Charlie led Alex into a sunroom surrounded by floor-to-ceiling windows. French doors opened onto a wrap-around porch, beyond which stretched a white-sand beach that ended where waves glittering in the sun began. Three white rocking chairs sat in a row, wooden seats covered with yellow-and-white-striped cushions.

Charlie plopped into one, settled back and started to rock. For a moment, Alex saw her as she'd been twenty years ago. Big sister showing her the wonders of Nana's overgrown backyard. "These orange ones are Nana's favorite flowers." "Don't touch that. It's got prickles." "Nana says a hedgehog lives under the porch. I've never seen him. She calls him Brutus and feeds him Vienna sausages. Gross."

Alex checked her wrists. Still bruised and red, but maybe less so.

"Sit," Charlie softly ordered.

Alex did as she was told. "You *are* the one who told me the Tooth Fairy was Dad, right? And Santa doesn't exist."

"I was a bitchy little kid. I never should have done that."

"That's not the point."

"We're going to figure it all out, Alex. Trust me."

Alex took a breath and decided she could spare ten minutes if it made her sister happy.

When AnnaCoreen returned, Charlie rose to her feet to accept the tray of lemonade, glasses and what looked like homemade lemon bars. "Changed your mind on the tea?" Charlie asked, sounding faintly disappointed.

AnnaCoreen waved a dismissive hand. "I thought we'd try something different since we have a new guest."

Alex did her best to smile politely, even as she eyed the pitcher of ice-laden lemonade with a thirst she hadn't acknowledged before. Lemonade was *way* better than tea. And as she accepted the first chilled glass from Anna-Coreen, she told herself she hadn't really meant it when she told Charlie she wouldn't drink anything. The first sip carried a tart zing of flavor across her tongue so strong her ears tingled.

Charlie mm'd in delight as she sank her teeth into a lemon bar. "These are fantastic."

The older woman settled onto the remaining rocking chair, to the right of Alex, and sipped lemonade. "A friend made them."

"Your friend's a goddess," Charlie said around a powdered-sugared mouthful.

"A god, actually," AnnaCoreen replied, a smile curving her lips.

Charlie arched one brow, apparently thinking the same thing Alex was: That smile looked a little naughty.

"So, a good friend then," Charlie prodded.

Alex had to admire her sister's curiosity. A reporter to the bone.

"Oh, yes. A good friend." AnnaCoreen sipped more lemonade. Her bright blue eyes twinkled.

Alex couldn't help checking her watch. Had it been ten minutes yet?

"Let's talk about what brings us together today," Anna-Coreen said.

Charlie shifted from inquisitive to purposeful in a heartbeat. "Alex is empathic, too."

Way to ease into it, Alex thought as she buried her nose in her glass for a long drink. When her hand started to shake, she lowered the glass and cupped it in both hands in her lap.

"But it's different for her," Charlie continued. "She has—"

"Bruises." AnnaCoreen's gaze flicked down to Alex's wrists.

The trembling in Alex's hands intensified. She *really* didn't want to do this.

"They look better now than they did before," Charlie said. "Like they're fading. Are they fading, Alex?"

Alex felt AnnaCoreen's steady gaze on her, as though she could check Alex's blood pressure by sight—one-twenty over freaked the hell out.

Unnerved as much by the scrutiny as the question, Alex prodded her wrist with one finger while ice chattered in her lemonade glass. She couldn't stop shaking. Couldn't stop wishing she were anywhere but here. Anything but empathic. She still didn't know what that really meant. Except stark, raving terror when she touched her sister.

The memory of Charlie's fear in that boiler room twisted her stomach, and she swallowed the bile at the back of her throat. Don't think about that, she told herself. That didn't even happen to you.

But it felt like it did. God, it felt like it did, and she didn't know how she would ever live with her sister's memories. Was that what she faced now? A lifetime of coping with other people's pain and terror?

"Oh, dear." AnnaCoreen rolled from the chair to her feet in one smooth motion an instant before Alex's glass exploded in her hand.

"Crap!" Charlie jumped up.

· Alex sat there, stunned as pink-tinged lemonade dripped onto the wooden floor of the porch. Luckily, she'd no longer been holding the glass over her lap or she'd be drenched.

"It's okay, dear," AnnaCoreen said to Alex. "I'll get some towels."

As she disappeared into the house, Charlie knelt beside Alex's chair. "Are you okay?"

Alex flinched back before Charlie could put a hand on her knee, the jerky movement tilting the chair back on its rockers. "Don't."

Charlie drew back, and the surprised color in her cheeks faded. "God, Alex, I'm sorry. I know this is a lot to take in. I didn't realize you were so . . ."

As her sister trailed off, Alex tried to crack a smile. "Strong?"

"Yeah," Charlie said, her lips tight. She began gathering the bigger chunks of glass and stacking them gingerly in one hand, careful to avoid contact with Alex in any way.

Alex glanced down at the palm of her hand, where blood welled from a cut that she didn't yet feel, despite the lemonade that should sting. "She knew that was going to happen," she said, her voice dull to her own ears. "AnnaCoreen. She was already on her feet."

"She's kind of spooky that way."

"Is she really psychic?"

Charlie shrugged. "She may just be an ace at reading people. She probably saw your hand tighten on the glass."

"She's helped you a lot?"

Charlie raised her head and met Alex's eyes, a conviction there that made Alex shiver. "I don't know if I could have handled any of it without her."

"How does it work? Why us?"

"AnnaCoreen can explain. It helps when you know the . . . I don't know what you'd call them . . . the logistics, I guess."

"There are logistics?"

Charlie smiled. "In the sense that there's logic? No."

AnnaCoreen returned with a roll of paper towels and a bright yellow hand towel. "This is for your hand," she said, holding out the towel. "I'll get some antiseptic and bandages in a moment."

Alex hesitated to use the towel. It was thick and luxurious, like new. The blood pooling in her hand would surely ruin it.

"Don't worry, dear. I have others just like it." AnnaCoreen knelt to sop up lemonade. "Luckily, the cut's not that deep."

Alex pressed the clean, obviously expensive cotton to her palm and winced at the answering twinge. "How do you know it's not that deep?"

"If it were, you'd be dripping blood all over my porch," AnnaCoreen said simply, then rose to her feet, a wad of used paper towels clutched in one hand. "That's the worst of it. I'll ask Richie to hose off the porch later. Otherwise, the ants will throw a party."

Charlie perked up. "Richie?"

AnnaCoreen either didn't hear or chose not to answer, because she strode back into the house without a word.

Charlie grinned at Alex. "I think she has a boyfriend."

Alex had to laugh at Charlie's enthusiasm. She obviously cared deeply for the older woman.

AnnaCoreen returned with a first aid kit and a fresh glass, which she handed to Charlie. "Get your mind out of the gutter and pour your sister a refill."

"You still trust her with a glass?" Charlie asked as she dutifully poured lemonade.

AnnaCoreen, kneeling at Alex's feet, set the first aid kit on Alex's knee and held out a small, fine-boned hand. "Let me see."

Alex didn't move, her gaze riveted on AnnaCoreen's waiting hand. What if . . .

"It's okay, dear," AnnaCoreen soothed. "Let me help you."

Tension coiled in Alex's belly, muscles tensed so hard they began to ache. She couldn't do it. Couldn't just reach out and—

AnnaCoreen took the choice away from her and clasped Alex's injured hand with cool fingers. And the world tilted . . .

I'm falling, uncontrolled and wild, grabbing for the railing, trying to stop my tumble, to slow it. Every stair step slams into my ribs, shoulders, head, knees. I hit bottom, and stars explode in my eyes, darkness encroaching at the edges and threatening to blot out the light.

It's dark, the concrete cold and damp. Everything hurts. Oh, Lord, everything hurts so much. My head, my back.

He's thumping around upstairs, stomping from one room to the next, dresser drawers thudding as he yanks them clear out of the furniture. He's looking for evidence, but there's nothing to find, nothing to prove his fears.

Except Richard is coming. Richard will be here any

minute, coming to help me pack, and that's all the evidence he'll need. He'll kill us both for what he thinks we've done.

I need to move, to get up. I need to find something to defend myself.

He'll come down here and make me pay, make me hurt for doing nothing more than trying to find a way out.

The door at the top of the stairs jerks open, and the sudden piercing light hurts my eyes. Oh, no, oh, no, oh, no.

He thunders down the stairs. He's so angry and, oh, Lord, he's unbuckling his belt. When he looms over me, terror pins me to the cold concrete floor. If I could move, I'd try to scoot away.

"Don't do this. Please don't do this."

He snarls and falls on me. He rips my blouse open, and a moan of despair escapes my throat. I know not to fight back, but it's hard not to.

"Please, Frank, I won't leave you. I made a mistake. I won't go, I promise."

He's not listening. He's breathing hard, his face red with fury. "You're mine," he grunts. "You'll always be mine."

He goes to work on his fly and zipper with one hand, the other holding me to the floor. My hands claw at his arm as he shreds my pantyhose and shoves my skirt up around my hips.

I can't help it. I start screaming, a strangled, pathetic sound that carries no volume because his fingers are tightening on my windpipe—

Little.

Black.

Stars.

"Alex!"

Her head felt weightless and weird. Empty. Nobody home.

"Answer me! Alex!" Charlie sounded frantic.

"Calm down, child, she's okay now." Another voice, this one soothing and calm. "Look, she's focusing."

Alex realized her eyes were open, and she blinked

them several times, until her sister and AnnaCoreen Tesch appeared before her, both on their knees at her feet and peering up at her as if she'd just spontaneously combusted.

An odd throbbing burned through her left cheek, and Alex raised a hand to touch it.

Charlie raked both hands through her hair before stumbling to her feet and over to the railing for support. "Jesus."

"Are you back with us?" AnnaCoreen searched Alex's eyes, her countenance as soothing as a trauma nurse trained in calming hysterical patients.

Alex nodded, which was a mistake, because dizziness welled through her head as quickly as the bile rose in her throat.

"Easy," AnnaCoreen murmured. "Breathe through it."

Alex closed her eyes, swallowed hard. "I'm going to be sick."

"No, you're not," the older woman said firmly. "You're going to breathe."

Alex tried to nudge the woman aside so she could get up, but AnnaCoreen refused to budge. "Listen to me, Alexandra Lee, and do what I tell you to do."

Alex looked at the woman in surprise. How could she possibly know her middle name? And what did it matter? She was going to hurl all over her if she didn't get the hell out of her way.

AnnaCoreen grasped Alex's left elbow with a strong hand to still her, then dug the blunt end of her thumb against the inside of her elbow. With her other hand, she did the same thing in the middle of Alex's right forearm. "Breathe in," AnnaCoreen ordered. "Do it."

Alex complied, if only to get the woman to let her go more quickly. Ribs that felt bruised protested the deep inhalation.

"Breathe out."

Alex exhaled, wincing at the answering pain. She hurt like she'd been beaten. Or had fallen down the stairs.

"Again."

After several more inhalations and exhalations, the nausea began to subside. Whatever AnnaCoreen was doing—acupressure, Alex assumed—worked.

Behind AnnaCoreen, Charlie began to pace. "I can't believe how much this sucks. Nobody ever has to punch me to snap me out of this shit."

AnnaCoreen turned her head slightly to address Charlie. "Charlie, dear, would you mind giving your sister and me a few moments alone?"

Charlie left the porch mumbling something about a stiff drink.

AnnaCoreen turned back to search Alex's face with eyes that no longer twinkled, a grayness to her complexion that hadn't been there before. "Better?"

Alex nodded.

After releasing her wrist and elbow, AnnaCoreen bent her head over Alex's palm and quickly cleaned the shallow cut with a round of antiseptic-soaked cotton. As she tore open a palm-sized piece of gauze, she said, "Your sister had to strike you to bring you around."

"She did last time, too. It's like I get stuck."

AnnaCoreen pressed the gauze to Alex's palm, then wrapped more gauze around it to hold it in place. "Please accept my deepest apologies."

Alex had no idea what she meant.

The woman secured the gauze with white tape, and Alex noticed that AnnaCoreen's fingers trembled. "I assumed your empathy was like your sister's," she said, her voice so soft Alex had to strain to hear her. "I had no idea."

"So you know what's happening to me?"

AnnaCoreen got stiffly to her feet and sat in the rocking chair next to Alex's, a tension in her body that hadn't been there when she'd welcomed her into her home. "Understand that I'm not a scientist or doctor. All I know is what I've learned from studying your sister's ability."

"Maybe just start with Empathy 101."

AnnaCoreen actually seemed relieved at that, as if simple empathy was something she could deal with. "Empaths, in the most basic terms, are very in tune with the feelings of those around them. They absorb others' emotions into themselves and feel them as if the emotions are their own. The stronger the feelings, the stronger the absorption. Your sister has told me that she experienced that before the accident that claimed your cousin's life. Do you think perhaps you did as well?"

Alex shook her head. "I'm probably the most self-centered person you've ever met."

"I don't believe that for a moment. You open your home to damaged animals that no one else wants, do you not?"

Alex narrowed her eyes. Another psychic guess? "Charlie told you that."

"Of course," AnnaCoreen said with a small, knowing smile. "I have a theory, if you'd like to hear it."

"Okay."

"You surround yourself with animals because it's too painful for you to be around people."

"Because I'm empathic," Alex said, unable to quell the doubt in her tone.

"Animals give you the companionship you crave without burdening you with troubling emotions."

"Other people's problems raise my blood pressure, and the unconditional love of my pets brings it back down. Aren't there studies that say that's normal?"

"Even now, you're rationalizing your ability."

"Rational," Alex said with a snort. "That's not a word I expected to come up in this conversation."

AnnaCoreen didn't let Alex's sarcasm derail her explanation. "Charlie's ability appears to be based on energy. Contact with another person's energy, through a simple skin-on-skin transfer, sparks her ability, a kind of empathy with some retrocognition thrown in that we've been calling super empathy."

Alex blinked at the older woman. Retro what? She was so lost.

Before Alex could say "huh?" or start fidgeting with impatience, AnnaCoreen continued. "The body is made up of electrical impulses. Everything you do, feel and think originates as an electrical impulse inside your brain. We're all surrounded by an energy field made up of these electrical currents. Most of them bleed off as we go about our day, but some are stronger than others and remain with us as a kind of . . . residue. Say you stub your toe. That's much more painful, or traumatic, than, say, nicking yourself while shaving your legs. Your toe may hurt for a few days after the injury, whereas the minor nick is forgotten by the time it stops bleeding. Charlie's ability allows her to tap into that residual energy. She absorbs it into herself and experiences the event as if it happened to her. The more traumatic the event, the more powerful the residual energy and the more powerful the retrocognitive, or postcognitive, empathic experience."

"But Charlie said she absorbed our cousin's ability when she died and that triggered hers. Nothing like that has happened to me."

"That's not entirely true. After you were shot, you had to be revived at the hospital."

"This has something to do with *that*?"

"My theory is that when they used the defibrillator paddles to restart your heart, the jolt of electrical energy somehow supercharged your ability. How many times did they shock your heart before it responded?"

Alex swallowed hard, the nausea back. "Three times."

AnnaCoreen nodded. Alex had confirmed her theory, but instead of looking pleased, AnnaCoreen appeared even more concerned. Perhaps three times the shock meant three times the supercharging.

Alex didn't give AnnaCoreen a chance to voice that concern as she plunged ahead. "If it's residual energy, wouldn't it wear off after a few days? Like the pain of the stubbed toe goes away?"

"That was my assumption, based on Charlie's experience."

Alex didn't like the fact that AnnaCoreen spoke in past tense. "But she was kidnapped three months ago. Shouldn't that energy have faded by now?"

"It should have, according to what we know about Charlie's empathy."

"So what the hell's going on?" Alex couldn't help that her voice rose. She wanted answers, but every answer brought up more questions.

"Half an hour ago," AnnaCoreen said, "I would have assumed that because Charlie's experience was so intense, it has taken longer for the residual energy to evaporate."

Half an hour ago, Alex had been at the bottom of some basement stairs, unable to move and terrified of a man stomping around overhead. Something about that experience had changed AnnaCoreen's assumptions about Alex's ability.

Alex could no longer sit still. She had to move, get up and pace, maybe run as far and as fast as possible. As she shifted to rise, pain tightened around her torso, and an involuntary moan escaped her lips.

AnnaCoreen got quickly to her feet and, before Alex could stop her, hiked up the hem of Alex's T-shirt to just below her breasts. Alex opened her mouth to protest, but the blood draining from the older woman's already pale face stopped her.

"Good Lord," AnnaCoreen breathed. She straightened, and with one cool finger, she tilted Alex's head back until her narrowed eyes could focus on her throat. Her brow furrowed with what looked like pain.

"What is it?" Alex asked. Not that she really wanted to know at this point.

"You have bruises on your throat, too. As though someone tried to strangle you."

Strangle?.Holy crap. A strong, thick hand on her throat that pinned her to cold concrete flashed through her brain. "Is it similar to the injuries you sustained in the past?"

AnnaCoreen nodded, lips so tight they'd gone white.

"What the hell is happening to me?" Alex asked.

"It's like an empathic stigmata," AnnaCoreen murmured, then grasped Alex's forearm and studied her wrist. "The marks you arrived with are gone. How long ago did you flash on your sister's captivity?"

Alex stared first at her right wrist and then her left, trying to assimilate the fact that not long ago, she'd had large purple bruises and raw skin, and now all signs of the injuries had vanished. How was that even possible? Of course, how she *got* the bruises wasn't even possible, so why should it shock her that they'd healed in an unbelievable amount of time?

"How long, Alex?" AnnaCoreen prodded.

"An hour and a half maybe?"

"So the marks fade fairly quickly," AnnaCoreen said.

Drawing away, Alex fought back a shudder. Could this get any worse?

"Clearly, your empathic ability goes well beyond residual energy from a recent traumatic event," AnnaCoreen said. "I believe it's more of a postcognition hybrid with strong empathic overtones. Whereas Charlie's ability is more empathically focused with only slight postcognition, yours appears to be both empathic and acutely postcognitive. You relived Charlie's deepest, darkest memory, one that will never leave her."

A horrible thought struck Alex. "Will this happen every time I touch her?"

"You've touched her since, have you not?"

"Yes. I think so. Nothing happened."

"Perhaps once you've made the connection to the energy, it's somehow discharged. Like static electricity. That's how Charlie's ability works, too."

"So it's like the energy recognizes me," Alex said. "Like syncing an iPod."

AnnaCoreen's lips quirked with the hint of a smile. "I'm afraid I don't know how that works."

"Once you plug your iPod into your PC the first time and set it up, your PC recognizes the iPod the next time you plug it in. It's, like, 'Hi, how ya doing?' instead of 'Who are you and what do you want?' "

"Yes, that's possible. Sort of like a cookie that gets placed on your hard drive the first time you visit a Web site. The next time you visit, the Web site recognizes you because of that cookie."

Alex laughed softly, not at all amused. "I'm a technological wonder."

"These are all semi-educated guesses, of course."

"So, really, what's happening is that my postcognitive empathy hybrid whatchamacallit can tap into something further back in someone's past than Charlie's can, right? I mean, her thing happened three months ago, so . . ." She trailed off, and despite her effort to keep it at bay, she thought of another woman, this one writhing in agony after being ruthlessly shoved down a flight of stairs.

Focusing on AnnaCoreen, she tried to frame her question tactfully. "That man. He was your husband?"

AnnaCoreen nodded, and her hand gripped the arm of the rocking chair. Her tension was back. "He was a good man when I married him, but our life together didn't develop as planned."

"Did he . . ."

AnnaCoreen knew exactly what she meant and gave her a sad smile that didn't touch her eyes. "No. My friend—"

"Richard." The name from the . . . flash, that's what Charlie called them, the name from the flash came to her as easily as the fear and pain.

"Yes, Richard. He arrived before Frank could hurt me further."

Alex struggled to focus on AnnaCoreen and not the memory. God, it was going to haunt her forever. As it apparently haunted AnnaCoreen.

When the older woman added nothing more, Alex got that she no longer wanted to talk about it. But Alex had one more important question, and a cold band of dread began to tighten around her chest. "How long ago did it happen?"

"Thirty-two years."

CHAPTER **TEN**

Butch McGee pulled the Mustang to the curb and killed the engine in front of 3481 Colonial One Place. John Logan lived here, and Butch planned to wait, ensconced in his comfy leather seat, for him to come home.

He imagined what it would be like to kill the man who'd killed his brother. He hoped he had the control to keep from slitting Logan's throat right away. Torturing him first, that would be the most satisfying. Over several days would be even better. But he'd need to prepare for that first. Get a storage unit. Those were the best for what he did. Secluded after closing time and usually in the middle of nowhere because no one wanted an ugly storage place in their backyard.

Easy to clean up afterward, too. If the floor got stained, all you had to do was say you spilled some red paint. Oops. The setup and even the aftermath were easy: No one questioned what you brought in or what you hauled out. As long as you hauled it out before the smell set in, everything was copacetic, peripatetic and chic. That's why he preferred the climate-controlled kind. Took things longer to rot.

So it was settled. He'd hold off on outright killing the son of a bitch in favor of torture. His brother would prefer that anyway. He couldn't participate in the act, so Butch would draw it out to make it extra special when he shared the grisly details with him on the phone.

Maybe it'd even be a nice change of pace. He'd never tortured a man. He normally practiced his art on women. Something about the way they screamed and begged made the act all the more sweet. They bargained, too. He imagined a man like John Logan would threaten to kill and maim. Give a man a gun, and he thought he was fucking God, charged with deciding who lives and who dies.

But a woman, ah, yes, a woman had something to trade. He loved that look they got when he let them think they had a choice in offering themselves to him. Power zinged through him every time with that first heavenward thrust, because he knew that when he was done, after he geysered into them like a high-pressure fire hose, the edge would be taken off and the real fun could begin.

Swallowing hard, Butch carefully steered his brain away from such distracting thoughts. Now was not the time to get off track. He had vengeance to wield.

As soon as John Logan arrived home, he'd get started.

And if he got *really* lucky, John Logan would have a girlfriend.

CHAPTER **ELEVEN**

A re you okay?"

Alex glanced sideways as Charlie steered the small SUV into the beach traffic and couldn't think of a thing to say. Fatigue burned in her bones, in her brain.

"It gets better," Charlie said. "I know that seems impossible now."

Alex had to laugh. Either that or weep, and once she started to laugh, she couldn't stop. Soon, she was laughing so hard she couldn't breathe. It really was hysterical when you thought about it. Empathic postcognition. Touch a friend and get thrust into their worst nightmare in high-definition, 3-D, surround sound. But wait, there's more! Afterward, their aches and pains, their bruises, are yours. Maybe even their gaping wounds. And the psychological torment that followed? All yours, too. Scars on the inside. Scars on the outside. The deal of the century.

She buried her face in her hands, and as the laughter subsided, the weeping started, because, oh, God, she couldn't bear all the pain that other people carried with them, couldn't imagine closing her eyes to sleep tonight only to relive having her wrists bound and a psychopath stalking her or a hard hand squeezing her throat while a monster ripped away her clothes.

She'd know now. She'd know what tortured the people she cared about. Know their pain, their torment, their fears. She'd know what they hid behind sunny smiles and warm laughter. The worst thing that had ever happened to them would happen to her. She'd *live* every detail.

She couldn't live like this. She . . . just . . . couldn't.

Slowly, she became aware of the hand on her back. Stroking and soothing.

The car wasn't moving anymore. Alex wiped her eyes and raised her head, saw that they were parked behind her Jeep in Charlie's driveway.

Charlie handed her a handful of Kleenex and said nothing as Alex blew her nose. She'd cried for a long time, and Charlie hadn't said a word, driving in silence while Alex's world crumbled.

"I'm sorry," Alex whispered, her voice thick and ragged.

Charlie blew her own nose, and Alex realized she hadn't been crying alone.

"How do you do it?" Alex asked.

"I try to avoid contact as much as I can. You'll become more aware of your personal space and learn how to anticipate what other people are going to do so you can protect yourself from unexpected contact. You'll get used to it."

"You're so casual about it. How is that possible?"

"I've had some time to adjust," Charlie said. "You'll adjust, too. AnnaCoreen sent me to a friend of hers, a doctor. She prescribed some drugs that help blunt some of the more . . . intense stuff."

"I don't want to take a bunch of drugs."

"I know. Neither do I." Charlie paused and took a breath. "Alex, you need to pay close attention to how you feel after an . . . episode."

"Episode," Alex repeated with a disbelieving snort.

"That's a nice way to put it. Like it's a TV show to look forward to. Next on *My Empathic Life*: Our distraught heroine jumps off the nearest bridge only to be rescued by a firefighter who's recently recovered from being nearly burned to death in a fire where he failed to save a family of four."

"That's a disturbingly detailed scenario," Charlie said dryly.

Alex gave a hollow laugh that choked off at the end. "I can't do this, Charlie. I really can't. Even with drugs. I'm . . . I'm . . ." She couldn't think of a word strong enough.

"What?" Charlie prodded. "You're what?"

"Tired." That wasn't even close to describing the leaden weight of exhaustion that bore down on her, but it was all she could come up with. "I'm just really, really tired."

"That's probably your version of flash fatigue. You need to sleep and recharge."

"Recharge, huh? So I can be drained all over again like a battery?"

"You'll get through this," Charlie said. "I get through it, and you're a lot stronger than I am. Trust me."

That surprised Alex. "Why would you think I'm stronger?"

"You just let yourself fall apart while I sat right next to you. That took more strength than holding it in would have."

"Your ability to spin my blubbering breakdown into something positive is astounding."

Charlie shrugged. "Your ability to form a coherent sentence after what you've been through today is astounding."

Alex clenched her fist around the balled-up Kleenex, and the small cut in her palm twinged. "AnnaCoreen. Something . . . terrible happened to her."

Charlie gave a grim nod, her lips drawn tight. "I kind of figured."

"You were right about her, though. I'm sorry I was so skeptical."

"The first time I went to see her, I was just as dubious."

"Does Noah know?" Alex couldn't imagine how Logan would react. Like Noah, he was an analytical cop. Everything had a reasonable explanation. Maybe she was getting ahead of herself anyway. Maybe she and Logan would go out once, and that'd be it. He'd never have to find out.

"Yeah, Noah knows," Charlie said.

"And he's okay with it?"

"He doesn't have much choice, really. It's part of me. Are you worried about Logan?"

Alex nodded.

"Have you gotten empathic hits off him?"

"Only once that I was aware of. Right after he saved the girl in that wreck."

"So it was an immediate trauma that you flashed on. That's similar to what happens with mine. Maybe your empathy reacts differently to different people. I mean, that makes sense, right? No one's body chemistry is exactly the same. With Logan, maybe you'll flash only on recent stuff that happens to him. There's going to be a learning curve for you both, but if he loves you, he'll adjust."

If he loves you. Wouldn't *that* be something? Just thinking about the possibility made her heart skip. "Did it take Noah long?"

"No. He had the advantage of knowing about our cousin's ability."

"Our cousin. That's still unbelievable."

"I know. We've spent our whole lives thinking we had no family beyond each other and Mom and Dad." A tiny pause. "And Sam, of course."

Alex's eyebrows shot up as it hit her that their oldest sister might also be . . . "Do you think—"

"I have no idea. She hasn't returned my calls since after we knew you were going to pull through the shooting."

"Oh." Alex studied Charlie's clenched jaw. "You're ticked at her."

"We can talk about Sam later. Our focus right now is you." Charlie captured Alex's hand and gave it a squeeze, a small grin playing at the corners of her mouth. "There are perks to the curse."

Alex arched an eyebrow. "Yeah? Like what?"

Charlie's grin turned sly. "I can't ruin the surprise. Just trust me."

Twenty minutes later, Alex parked her Jeep in the garage, then waved good-bye to Charlie, who'd insisted on following her to make sure she arrived home safely. Alex let herself into her house and received the exuberant welcome of half a dozen mutts who acted like they hadn't seen her in days rather than a few hours.

As she scratched ears and murmured endearments, she realized she wanted nothing more than a long nap. First, though, she needed some food. She hadn't eaten since the doughnuts with Logan this morning.

The surprisingly subdued dogs followed on her heels, not making a sound while she looked in the fridge for something to eat. She cocked her head at them, smiling slightly when they cocked their heads back, their eyes intent on her, as though they knew she'd changed in some fundamental way.

"Right," she muttered, then raised her voice and said, "I'm empathic."

Doggy ears pricked, and adoring eyes blinked.

"Not just regular empathic, either. If there is such a thing. But mega I-can-relive-your-horrible-past empathic."

Not one pooch raced howling from the room. A good sign?

And then it hit her that she'd rubbed the ears and patted the bellies of living beings who'd endured terrible, painful tragedies. A broken then amputated leg. A bad back. A damaged eye. A missing tail and ears because of burns sustained in a fire.

Thank God her so-called empathy didn't kick in when she loved up her kids.

She decided she didn't have the energy to eat.

Within another minute, she hit the sofa and instantly dropped into a deep sleep.

CHAPTER **TWELVE**

Logan rang Alex's doorbell for the second time, wincing at the cacophony of barking that responded. No Alex, though, which was obvious after the first time he'd rang, but he'd wanted to be sure.

He balanced the bouquet of fresh daisies on his fore-arms while he checked his cell phone again. Maybe she'd left a message that he'd missed. No messages. No missed calls. Had she stood him up for their first date? He couldn't imagine that she had. She simply wasn't wired that way. Must be a miscommunication. Or something unexpected had come up.

Still, he had an uneasy feeling, so he walked around the side of her house and to the detached garage. Cupping his hands around his eyes, he peered through one of the dinner-plate-sized square windows in the garage door. Her Jeep Liberty SUV sat inside.

Okay, now he was worried. She could be out for a run, he thought, as she had been when he'd dropped by unan-nounced this morning. But tonight he wasn't unannounced. And it was almost dark. Would she go running in the dark?

Deciding he'd rather look like an idiot now than find out later that something was wrong and he'd done nothing, he opened the gate that led to her back door. He discovered the door was unlocked and eased it open, calling her name at the same time. "Alex?"

Several mutts on a tear barreled into the kitchen, and he quickly stepped inside and blocked them before they could bowl him over and escape outside.

"Whoa, whoa, whoa. Sorry, but I'm not your dinner, guys."

As they calmed down, he bestowed some head pats and ear rubs. "Do you know where your mom is? We have dinner plans."

And how stupid was it that he was asking half a dozen animals as though they would actually answer?

"Okay, well, if it's all right with you, I'm going to take a look around. I promise not to do anything uncool, okay? I just want to see if your mom is here." He'd set the flowers on the kitchen table when a thought struck him. "Does anyone need to go out?"

Phoebe and Artemis ran to the door and took turns woofing, which struck Logan as the doggy equivalent of the pee dance. He opened the door, checked to make sure he'd latched the gate, then waited while four of the six dogs shuffled out into the backyard.

With the remaining two dogs—Gus, the beagle-blood-hound, and Dieter, the German shepherd—trailing in his wake, he walked into Alex's dim living room and felt along the wall for the light switch and flicked it up. His heart stopped dead when he saw her, out cold on the sofa.

"Alex?"

She didn't stir, even as Gus and Dieter each nudged her arm with their noses and whined.

Logan fought panic as he crossed to her. She'd slept through frantic barks, two ringing doorbells and at least two phone calls. No one who wasn't seriously ill snoozed *that* soundly.

"Alex? Hey, Alex."

He had his palm on her forehead and two fingers pressed to the pulse point in her throat when she snapped her eyes open on a gasp. He twitched back as she sat up so fast their heads almost knocked together. At first, she didn't seem to recognize him, her dark eyes huge and startled in her pale face.

Logan raised his hands, palms out. "It's just me."

She focused on him after a moment and blinked slowly, as though having trouble getting oriented. "Hey."

"Hey. You okay?"

She started to respond, but then Dieter reared up and landed his front paws in her lap while Gus plopped his butt on the tile floor and let out a high-pitched yip. Alex gave Dieter a quick, distracted hug before gently pushing him off.

Logan spotted the bandage. "What happened to your hand?"

"I broke a glass." She sounded terrible. Like she had the flu. The shadows under her puffy eyes added to his alarm. Had she been crying?

"Are you sick?" he asked.

She ran both hands back through rampant curls. "No. I'm . . ." She trailed off, as if she had no clue what to say.

He reached for her chin, intending to angle her head so he could check her pupils, but she flinched back from the contact.

His concern went into overdrive when she brushed his hand away and got up from the sofa. Everything about her was off. She was tense and drawn, so pale her eyes looked sunken. She hadn't looked this strung out and sick since the first week after she died in the ER and was shocked back to life. His stomach clenched at the memory.

As he followed her into the kitchen, noting that she didn't quite walk in a straight line, he wondered if she was drunk. Before the shooting, she and Charlie would sometimes meet for margaritas after work. Maybe they'd resumed the tradition . . . except he hadn't noticed any alcohol on her breath.

"Um, did you maybe forget about our dinner plans?" he asked. On top of alarming, this was awkward. He didn't know whether to go or stay. He sure as hell didn't want to go until he knew she was indeed okay.

"You were coming at eight," she said. "Are you early?"

"It's eight fifteen."

She stopped and stared at her watch as though she didn't believe what it told her. "Oh."

"Alex, are you okay?"

She raised her head, a spaciness in her eyes that made them appear out of focus. "Yes, of course. I must have napped more deeply than usual." She headed for the door. "I need to feed the brood. It's way past dinnertime for them."

She faltered by the kitchen table, her eye caught by the daisies. "You brought me flowers?" she asked softly.

"They reminded me of you."

"That's so sweet. Thank you."

"Anytime."

She continued onto the porch area, and Logan paused in the doorway between the kitchen and the porch to watch her scoop dog food from a large Rubbermaid container into multiple doggy dishes. Dieter and Gus dug in as if they hadn't been fed in days.

"Want me to let in the others?" Logan asked. "I let them out when I got here. They seemed desperate."

"Sure, thanks."

As soon as he opened the door for them, four hungry dogs tore past him, through the kitchen and onto the porch, where they started to noisily chow down.

When Alex just stood there and watched the dogs eat, Logan said, "So . . . dinner?"

She ran another hand through her hair, obviously distracted. "I'm sorry I'm so out of it. I don't know what my problem is."

"If you don't feel like going out, we can go another time."

She seemed to think about that suggestion for a moment.

"Or," Logan said quickly, because he didn't want to leave her alone yet, "we could stay in, and I could cook for you."

She smiled faintly. "That sounds good. There's pasta and spaghetti sauce in the pantry, if you want. And a bottle of red wine, I think."

"Perfect."

"Do you mind if I hop in the shower? I was helping Charlie in her garden."

"No problem."

She flashed another smile at him, this one bright and devastating. He would have fallen straight into it and drowned if he hadn't noted that it was fake. More than anything so far tonight, that faux smile, coming from the most genuine woman he'd ever met, bothered the hell out of him.

Twenty minutes later, Logan had doctored a jar of spaghetti sauce with chopped onions, bell peppers and fresh garlic. With sauce simmering, pasta boiling, and the pups lounging in the backyard, he opened the bottle of pinot noir he'd found in the pantry and poured two glasses.

He'd just finished lighting two tapered candles on the table when he turned to find Alex leaning against the kitchen doorjamb, her arms loosely crossed, a smile tugging at the corners of her mouth. "You've been busy."

Seeing her standing there, hair damp and a rosy hue in her cheeks, looking refreshed and relaxed, chased away the bulk of his concern. He'd startled her out of a deep sleep earlier. No reason to worry. Still, he couldn't completely shake the notion that something about her was off.

Then she wiped all thought from his brain as she walked over to him and took one of his hands into both of hers. She stared up at him with an expectant expression, and he wondered what she was looking for. Whatever it was, he'd give it to her, no questions asked.

Her brow creased and she stiffened briefly, a breath catching in her throat. And then, just as quickly, she relaxed and looked down at their joined hands. Smiling, she eased her thumb over the back of his hand in a soft caress that had his body reacting in an entirely too eager way. She seemed fascinated by the texture of his skin, or perhaps the movement of her thumb mesmerized her. Either way, he had to clench his jaw to keep from leaning into her and diving in. But, Jesus, he wanted to. He'd wanted to for so long.

As if she'd read his mind, she raised her head and stared into his eyes, invitation blatant in her dark gaze. He didn't need to be asked twice. He lowered his head and claimed her mouth with his. The first touch of their lips shocked him, revving his heart and spinning his head. He'd known all along that kissing her, tasting her, would be good, but he hadn't expected it to turn so quickly into heat and lust and desperation. Before he realized what he'd done, he had her backed against the counter, his hands buried in her hair and his mouth fused to hers.

She smelled like Christmas cookies and tasted just as sweet. He couldn't get enough, didn't want to ever let her go, yet he still sensed something was wrong. She seemed a little too desperate, a little too eager. And while his ego—and body—wanted to rejoice, his brain told him to slow things down or they would both regret it. Easing back from her, he put his hands on her arms when she tried to recapture his retreating lips.

"Dinner's getting cold," he said, a rasp in his voice that betrayed his outward show of control.

Faint disappointment clouded her features, as though she wanted *him* for dinner. And as she backed away, cheeks flushing pink, he could have kicked himself. What the hell was *wrong* with him? He wanted her, wanted to taste and touch and love, and she'd just offered herself on a silky platter. What kind of idiot said, "Wait."

She turned before he could get a read on her expression.

He'd given her the wrong impression and didn't know how to fix it. At the same time, he didn't want to rush. They had something good here, something promising. They'd gotten to know each other over the past several months, built a friendship before a romance. And he knew her well enough to recognize that she wasn't herself right now. He wanted—needed—to know that her head was in the game, their game, before they raced to the next level.

On top of all that, he knew a damn good thing when he had it, and Alex Trudeau was not the kind of woman a man took to bed on impulse, then dealt with the consequences later. She was the real thing, and he planned to make all the right moves at all the right times.

Retrieving the wineglasses, he set them on the table, then pulled a chair out for her.

She watched him with inquisitive eyes, as though trying to figure out where they stood.

He searched for something to say to break the tension. "Please don't tell me you're not hungry. I slaved over a hot stove all day."

She cracked a smile at his exaggeration, and her shoulders relaxed. As she sat, she inspected the bowl of pasta sauce. "Looks like you added stuff."

"Yep."

"Better watch it. You're going to spoil me."

"I plan to."

"I love the sound of that." She loaded up her plate with spaghetti and sauce.

Once he had his own plate filled, he asked, "What'd you do today?" Probably not the most covert way to seek clues to her . . . off-ness, but he had to start somewhere.

"Helped Charlie in her garden."

Too much time in the sun could explain her sluggishness. And maybe she'd overdone the activity. She was still healing, after all.

She twirled pasta onto her fork. "Can I cash in my rain check from this morning or is it too soon?"

He took a drink of wine and wished he'd had a follow-up question about her day ready sooner. But he supposed he couldn't dodge talking about his childhood forever. He was surprised she'd let him dodge it as long as she had. He set down his glass and took a breath. "My parents died when I was four."

"Oh, God, I'm sorry." Her compassion was a wave of warmth that enveloped him. "What happened?"

"Truck driver on the road for fourteen hours dozed off at the wheel, crossed the center line and smashed head-on into their Niagara Falls tour bus."

"That's awful."

"I went to live with my only remaining grandfather, but by the time I hit six, Papa was destined for a nursing home. He fought hard for me, but social services had other ideas." He paused, trying to suppress the bitter twist to his lips. "Foster care sucked. Nine different homes in seven years, and by then I wasn't cute anymore. Nobody wanted a thirteen-year-old with a chip on his shoulder."

"God, Logan." Alex pushed back her plate.

"I survived." He angled a chin at the pasta she'd abandoned. "You're not eating."

"How?" she asked, ignoring his observation.

"Joined a gang." The ease with which he said it should have shocked him. But, then, this was Alex. She could get anyone to open up when she peered at them with her empathetic gaze.

"A gang? For real?"

"I got busted early on. By an old cop determined to save me from myself. Officer Mike was probably the only person, besides my grandfather, I can remember caring about what happened to me. He died a few years ago. Old age."

"I bet he was proud of you."

He wondered what Officer Mike would have said about his colossal mistake in Detroit. "Your turn," he said, before she could drill him some more.

"My turn for what?"

"You told me how you're close to your dad because of his Nikon and the newspaper biz, but what about your mother?"

She shrugged. "That story is boring."

"Not to me. And, hey, I showed you mine."

She flashed him an amused smile. "If you yawn, I might smack you."

"As long as you smack me on the ass, everything's cool."

She laughed before taking another drink of wine. "My mother is most interested in high society. It drove her nuts that all three of her daughters turned into tomboys rather than girlie girls."

"Why do you think that happened?"

"I guess we all gravitated toward Dad. He talked to us, listened to us, challenged us. Mom just tried to tell us what to do and got wenchy when we disappointed her. My sisters and I can be a bit . . . contrary."

"So you and Charlie both ended up working at the family newspaper. What about your other sister? What's her name?"

"Sam. She's the oldest. Can you tell Dad wanted boys? Mom calls us by our full names. Charlotte. Samantha. Alexandra. Dad's a bit contrary himself."

"And where's Sam?"

Her expression had relaxed as they talked, but now it tensed again. "I don't know. She took off as soon as she turned eighteen. She checks in every now and then, but no one really knows where she is or what she's doing. It's kind of weird, like she's a spy or something."

"I could try to track her down, if you want. I have friends in the FBI."

"That's nice of you to offer, but Charlie and I decided a long time ago that if Sam needs us, she knows how to reach us."

"That must be tough to accept."

"I admit that I really miss her."

Logan searched for something to say to lighten her mood. "So . . . why six dogs and no cats?"

She gave him a crooked smile. "Charlie has a cat, so that angle's covered." But then the smile faltered. "Apparently, I surround myself with dogs because people cause too much pain."

He couldn't stop his brows from arching. Not the answer he was expecting.

She shook her head and picked up her wine. "Forget I said that. It's just something someone said earlier that I want to believe is a load of baloney."

"You *want* to believe it, but you don't." Come on, Alex. Talk to me.

She toyed with her glass, swirling the last half inch of wine in the bottom. He thought she might actually start spilling what was on her mind, but instead, she set down the stemware and scooted back from the table. "Want to take the mutts for a walk with me? They've been cooped up most of the day."

She was avoiding him, but at least she didn't ask him to leave, or even hint that she wanted him to. For now, he'd let her get away with it. "Sure, a walk sounds great."

CHAPTER **THIRTEEN**

The walk with the menagerie and Logan helped relax Alex some. Now, they sat on the sofa, hands loosely linked, and watched a *Seinfeld* rerun. Leaning against the warmth of Logan's body, feeling his strength seep into her, comforted her, though the aimless wanderings of Jerry and friends through a parking garage did little to distract her from her circling thoughts.

She knew Logan was worried about her, could sense the tension in his muscles, but she didn't know how to tell him what was on her mind. Blurting, "Hey, guess what? I'm psychic," didn't strike her as a good approach. He'd think she'd lost her mind. And maybe she had. Maybe she *would* if she touched the wrong person.

Besides, she didn't know where she and Logan stood now. He'd pushed her away when they'd kissed in the kitchen. Well, all right, he hadn't *pushed* her away. But he'd made it clear that he was more interested in dinner than walking her backward down the hall to her bedroom.

And, damn it, kissing had been the wrong thing to do just then anyway. They hadn't even graduated to hand-holding at that point, though they did round that base on their walk. The moment he'd caught her fingers with his had made her heart give a happy jump. So maybe he'd insisted on dinner instead of what she'd wanted—the physical release that would wipe her whirling mind clear—because he'd sensed her turmoil.

God, she was *still* so freaking confused. Was she empathic or not? Earlier, she'd touched Logan deliberately, had taken his hand in hers and waited for the impact of something that had happened to him in his past. A test of sorts. If she couldn't handle what haunted him, then how could she handle a relationship with him? Mostly, she'd succumbed to curiosity about her ability. She still wasn't sure how this empathy thing worked—or whether she even believed something so unbelievable could exist. Instead of a trauma from Logan's early life hitting her, though, she'd experienced the intensity of his fear and concern for her when he'd found her dead asleep on the sofa. A recent trauma, rather than a blast from the past. So maybe Charlie was right. Maybe with Logan, she wouldn't get thrust into his past like she had with AnnaCoreen and Charlie. Different body chemistries and all that. Maybe she'd flash only on his most recent terrifying moment, and that was it. She thought she could live with that.

With that mystery possibly solved, she'd looked into his eyes and wanted nothing more than to kiss him and forget everything that had ruined her day . . . and possibly her life.

Then he'd stepped back.

Wham. More confusion.

She *hated* confusion. *Hated* angst. She'd decided a long time ago that she would live her life as a happy person, wasting no time on the dark stuff that got other people down. Getting shot, and almost dying, had further cemented that goal in her mind. Life was too short to get caught up in unnecessary drama and worries about what *could* happen.

•

Logan shifted to loop his arm around her shoulders and draw her closer against him, keeping his fingers tangled with hers in his lap. Then he pressed a kiss to her temple. "When you're ready to talk, I'm here," he murmured.

Tears instantly burned her eyes. How did she get so lucky? Here she was, cuddled up with one of the greatest guys ever, watching sitcoms on the sofa, surrounded by six dozing dogs . . . it was exactly what she'd always wanted. No way in hell would she let some *stupid* psychic ability wreck that.

She vowed then to never tell Logan about her empathy. It had no place in her life, in their relationship. She'd find a way to suppress it, take drugs if she had to, avoid going out in public . . . whatever it took to keep other people's past traumas from ruling her life.

She relaxed fully against Logan and closed her eyes, smiling as he gently rested his chin on the top of her head. She was still so tired. Dropping into sleep in this man's arms felt like the most natural thing in the world . . .

The child looks up with wide, blue eyes, so young, so innocent, his bottom lip quivering as one tear tracks a dirt-smudged cheek. My hand trembles, finger poised on the trigger, my heart thudding in my ears. Sweat trickles into my eyes, and I furiously blink the stinging away. Focus. You have to focus.

Someone's shouting. Someone else—another child?—screams. It's all distant, surreal. All that matters is the boy staring up at me, pleading with large, terrified eyes. He can't be more than six. Too thin, scraggly blond hair, dirty face and dirtier clothes. He has a scrape across the bridge of his nose, and he's trying desperately not to blubber.

Despite the effort, the little boy's face screws up, and he begins to cry in earnest. "Daddy! Where's Daddy?"

My finger jerks on the trigger.

The gunshot is deafening.

Alex bolted up with a scream of denial. Strong hands fumbled to hold her down, and a fresh burst of stunned horror shot through her, her own hoarse scream echoing in her ears.

"Hey! Whoa, whoa, it's okay, it's okay."

She struggled, in a panic because she didn't know where she was or who had hold of her. The hands that gripped her arms gave her a firm shake. "Alex, it's okay. You were dreaming."

The words finally penetrated the lingering shock. She sagged back into the sofa cushions, blinking against the lamplight and only now becoming aware of the dogs' frantic barking. Logan was braced over her, his tanned face pale. He looked as though her screams had jerked him out of his own deep sleep.

She relaxed in slow degrees, heartbeat still frantic, lungs fighting for air. Everything was fine. Logan was here.

She sat up. "Nightmare. The dogs—"

"I'll take care of them."

He got up and strode into the kitchen, beckoning the mutts to follow. Dieter lingered behind and rested his chin on her knee. She scratched his ears with both hands, then cupped his head to look into his earnest, though sightless, puppy-dog eyes. "I'm okay, sweetie."

The treat cabinet in the kitchen opened, and Dieter's ears pricked, but he stayed put. She gave him a nudge. "You'd better go before the others eat yours."

The German shepherd trotted out of the living room.

Alex heard Logan open the back door. His voice, low and soothing, grew fainter as he went outside with the pack and assured the animals that Mommy was fine.

She sank back against the sofa cushions and dragged a hand through her sweat-damp hair. Her whole body felt warm and sticky, her brain muzzy with sleep. A nauseating horror clutched at her. She'd shot a child in her dream.

A small, helpless little boy. Where the hell had *that* come from?

Logan returned from tending to the mutts and sat down next to her. "You okay?"

She nodded.

"Sure?"

She closed her eyes and swallowed against the urge to be sick. She'd never had such a horrific dream before, though she'd definitely had some doozies after she'd gotten shot. Charlie had suggested cutting back on pain medication, which had done the trick. Until now.

Logan scooted closer and put both hands on her shoulders, rolling the tight muscles with his large, gentle fingers. Through the cotton of her shirt, she detected a tremor in those strong fingers and turned her head to glance at him. He looked tense, his jaw set, a you-freaked-me-the-hell-out muscle flexing at his temple. She couldn't blame him. The first time they'd fallen asleep cuddling, and she'd awakened screaming. Poor guy.

"Want to tell me about it?" he asked.

She rolled her shoulders, distracted by the heat of his hands through her shirt, distracted further by the heat gathering low in her belly. Was it twisted that she shifted so quickly from the revulsion of the dream to how much she wanted to turn into this man's arms and ask him to kiss away the lingering distress?

"Is it about when you were shot?" he prodded.

She shook her head. "No."

"Then what?"

"I . . . don't think I . . . It's too . . . disturbing." Her head started to throb like it had after her empathic trek through Charlie's encounter with her kidnapper. The terror of that memory returned, and her stomach knotted further. A chill moved up her spine, a trail of goose bumps in its wake.

"Maybe talking about it would help," Logan said.

Somehow, she didn't think so. Nothing would help

dispel the memory of her hand holding the gun that shot a little boy. It was just too . . . revolting.

She pushed up from the sofa and shoved wayward curls behind her ears. She needed some time to herself, time to get her head clear. "I'm really sorry, but I think I need to go to bed."

"Are you sure you're okay? You're awfully pale."

She tried a reassuring smile. "I'll be fine. Thank you for dinner. I'm sorry I've been such lousy company."

"Are you kidding me? Other than that nightmare, this has been the perfect evening."

Her attempt at a smile turned genuine. "You're sweet to say that."

"I mean it. How about you go lie down right now, and I'll take care of letting the dogs in from outside?"

She kissed him on the cheek, lingering for a moment to inhale his fresh, soapy scent. She yearned to ask him to stay but feared he'd balk at such an offer after the somewhat disastrous kitchen kiss. And, really, she had no energy for anything but sleep anyway. Exhaustion pulled at her like anchors sinking through Gulf waters.

She gave him one last smile. "You're the best."

CHAPTER **FOURTEEN**

Butch McGee ambled into the Lake Avalon Public Safety Building and tapped the ring-for-service bell. An attractive young woman with a wavy blond ponytail and chic square eyeglasses hurried over to help him. She wore a simple white blouse tucked into a straight skirt and had sparkly blue eyes, peach-sized breasts, a small waist and slim hips. Librarian by day and stripper by night. His grumpy mood—caused by John Logan failing to show up at home last night or this morning—lifted.

She returned his smile, showing lovely white teeth with a slight gap in the middle. A sucker for a handsome man. "May I help you?"

He leaned on the Formica customer-service counter, turning on the I'm-a-hunky-but-clueless-guy charm. "I sure hope you can. I'm . . ." He trailed off and cocked his head with an embarrassed smile. "Well, I hope you won't hold it against me when you hear why I'm here."

"Oh, I doubt I'll do that," she replied with a soft, lilting laugh.

He breathed in the fresh breath of her laugh and wished

he had time to spend with her. Quality time that they both would enjoy. He would love making her scream.

"Long story short: My family and my brother had a parting of ways a few years back. My fault, I'm afraid. He moved away and never looked back, and well, my mother's heart has been broken ever since. Yesterday, I spotted his picture in the newspaper and drove straight here from Detroit to see him." He let his smile tremble just slightly, reeling her in. "It's been my goal in life to bring home Mom's little Johnny."

Sheila, according to her shiny gold name tag, made an I'm-so-sorry face and reached out to grasp his hand. Her skin was warm and soft against his, and he had to swallow against the surge of want. He had such a hard spot for beautiful women.

He tried to focus himself. "Anyway, I saw in the newspaper that my baby brother is not only a hero, but he's a police officer here in Lake Avalon."

"Are you talking about John Logan?"

He nodded. "Yes. Johnny Logan. Do you know how I can reach him?"

She shook her blond ponytail. "I'm not allowed to share his contact information."

He did his best to look crestfallen. "Not even to mend an old woman's broken heart?" Cheesy bullshit, but who knew? Maybe once he mixed it with wounded-dog eyes and a beseeching can-you-help-me-out-here expression, it'd work.

Sheila glanced around, as if checking to make sure no one nearby could overhear. "I'd get into a lot of trouble if I gave out his info, but someone at the newspaper might be able to help you."

He leaned in closer, taking a moment to breathe in her flowery perfume. Holy Christ, this woman smelled like heaven. The need churning to life inside him began to overwhelm the bone-shaking satisfaction he'd found during his last kill. He needed to find John Logan soon, or he'd have to find a way to take the edge off.

"Who at the newspaper?" he asked, keeping his voice low, like hers.

"A good friend of Logan's, Alex Trudeau, took the photo you saw."

"And you think he'll point me in Johnny boy's direction?"

Sheila's eyes glinted at that. "Alex Trudeau is a she, and rumor has it she knows your brother quite well." She winked at him, clearly happy to help without breaking any rules. "If you know what I mean."

Butch's heart swelled, and his cheeks heated with excitement. It sounded as though John Logan *did* have a girlfriend. "Do you know how I might contact Alex Trudeau?"

"I can't give you that information, either, but I believe she's listed in the phone book."

CHAPTER **FIFTEEN**

Alex woke slowly, aware first that she felt . . . better. *Much* better. Sitting up, she ran her hands through her out-of-control curls to try to tame them. The action reminded her of Logan's fingers clutched in her hair as he kissed her breathless and aching. Right before he'd stepped back. Damn. It figured she'd think of that first thing.

She pushed back the pang of disappointment that knotted in her belly and got out of bed. Right now, she was hungry, which she considered a good sign. When she'd fallen into bed last night, slightly nauseated and fighting a headache, she'd thought she'd never want food again.

First, she stopped in the bathroom to take care of business and wash her face. The mirror told her that empathy wreaked havoc on a girl's face. Dark circles rimmed her eyes, and her skin looked ashen, her cheeks hollow. If she stretched out on her back and rested crossed hands over her chest, she'd look ready for a coffin. Lovely.

Breakfast would help, she decided. A heaping plate of protein and carbs to chase away the pallor, to restore energy. Then she'd figure out her next step. No way in hell did she plan to just sit back and let her new psychic ability drive a stake into what she had with Logan. If she was going to learn how to cope without him knowing she could drop into his head right after something bad happened to him, she had to get busy.

As she walked down the hall toward the kitchen, she wondered why the brood of pooches hadn't spent the night sprawled in various positions around her bedroom as usual. In the arched doorway that led to the living room, she stopped to see each member of the menagerie occupying a different area of carpet, some still dozing, others lifting their furry heads to ask with their eyes how she was today. She saw why in the next instant and stopped to stare, eyes welling within a heartbeat.

Logan was sprawled on his back on her sofa, in cargo shorts and nothing else, one tantalizingly veined forearm thrown over his eyes, his other hand resting flat on his muscular abdomen. A light snore told her he hadn't heard her stir, and that was fine with her, because it gave her a chance to admire that tan, ripped body.

Her mouth watered, and she swallowed, getting familiar now with the tightening low in her belly when she was around him. A woman would have to be dead not to appreciate the planes and valleys and ridges of this man's physique. The fact that he'd camped out on her sofa after she'd so unartfully fled to bed last night just made him all the more appealing.

Determined to do something nice for him, to make up for the night before, she went into the kitchen, a trail of furry critters in her wake. She fed them, taking care to lavish lots of affection on each, shooed them out the back door into the warm sunshine, then got started on breakfast for humans.

She'd transferred the last of the sizzling bacon to a paper-towel-covered plate when Logan's hands settled on her shoulders from behind, his palms warm against skin bared by the straps of her tank top. Instant tension stiffened her spine, but when nothing nasty happened in her head, she relaxed again. The empathy was behaving as she expected.

She turned toward him with a smile, faintly disappointed to see that he'd donned his white T-shirt. "Good morning."

He studied her face for a moment, eyes narrowed and critical. Any second now he would probably try to take her temperature. She figured she must look better than she had in the mirror earlier. Caffeine and a couple of bacon strips—not to mention the sight of the tantalizing beefcake snoozing on her sofa—had done wonders to perk her up.

"I'm fine," she said when he continued to scrutinize. "I had a bad day yesterday, but it's over."

"You sure?" he asked, Scope-fresh breath wafting over her face.

"Positive." She took a chance and sealed the assurance with a kiss, one hand holding the plate of bacon, the other resting against his stubbled cheek.

He didn't respond at first, and she thought, Crap, here we go again. Somebody fetch me a dunce cap.

But then he started kissing her back, and she nearly dropped the bacon as he stepped into her, forcing her back against the counter. He angled his head to take the kiss deeper, one hand settling at the curve of her waist, the other coming up to cup the back of her neck.

He tasted like cool water and mint, and she sank into his scents and textures, losing herself in the stroke of his tongue, the contact of his warm hand against her nape, the growing nudge of his erection against her hip.

He lifted his mouth from hers just an inch. "You have no idea how much I've been wanting you," he breathed against her cheek.

Her knees weakened, and the bacon plate almost slid off her hand. Luckily, she held on to her composure and the dinnerware. "I have a pretty good idea," she replied, canting one hip against the bulge in his cargo shorts.

He groaned, low and hot. "There's nothing sexier than a beautiful woman holding a plate of fresh-fried bacon."

She thought he'd kiss her again, perhaps venture a palm up to her breast to cop a quick feel, but instead he eased back and rescued the plate. "Shall we eat?"

She stood frozen in shock as he placed the bacon on the table, then moved to the coffeemaker to pour himself a cup. *Again* with the food over sex? What the—

"Does your coffee need freshening?" he asked over his shoulder.

"Uh, sure." Okay, she thought. She could deal. He had a hard-on the size of Florida, but he wanted food more. Interesting. *Mystifying.*

She shook herself out of her bewilderment and—okay, she'd admit it—disappointment, and used a spatula to scrape scrambled eggs from the skillet into a bowl.

"There's toast," she said.

"Yum." He reached around her to snag the slices out of the toaster, taking a second to brush his lips over the side of her neck.

She froze again, her heart stuttering at the light, random embrace. Good God, was this his idea of foreplay? Because it was working. With a capital F.

"Coming?" he asked as he pulled out a chair and settled.

Suppressing a snicker at his deliberate word choice, she joined him at the table.

"What?" he asked as he sank his teeth into a crisp slice of bacon. "Are you blushing?"

"No." Yes.

Flashing a knowing grin, he helped himself to a heap of scrambled eggs. "So, what was going on yesterday?" he asked. "You weren't yourself."

She hesitated, not sure what to say. "I had a headache"

seemed so cliché. And while that wouldn't be a total lie, it still struck her as dishonest. She really didn't want to lie to this man. Yet, she couldn't imagine telling him the truth. So, what, was she going to spend their entire relationship lying to him?

"Alex?"

She met his inquisitive gaze and forced a smile as she dug into her breakfast. "Like I said, I had a weird day. It's over now." She forked up some eggs, followed them with bacon, willing the off-kilter sensation inside her to click back into place. Everything would be fine.

"You were sweet to stay the night," she said.

"Sweet had nothing to do with it. I was worried about you."

A rush of warmth started in her stomach and spread outward. She couldn't believe her absolute blind luck that this incredible man had landed in her life. "So . . . we're a thing, right? A boyfriend-girlfriend thing."

A broad grin took over his face. "I've been thinking so, yes."

"Excellent. Because there's something I want to do."

"Yeah? What's that?"

"Have sex."

She grasped the hem of her shirt and whipped it over her head.

"Hey, I wanted to do that," Logan protested, catching her shirt against his chest as she tossed it at him.

And then his breath stopped at the sight of all that exposed creamy skin. My God, he thought. She was so . . . so beautiful. And her breasts, tantalizingly cupped by a very Alex-like, no-nonsense white cotton bra, were perfect. Not small, not big. She had the Goldilocks of breasts: just right. And he couldn't wait to touch and taste.

When she turned and walked out of the kitchen, he scooted his chair back and followed without thought, his eyes on the sway of her hips and then the deft work of her fingers as she reached behind her to unhook her bra and let it drop to the hallway floor. He stepped over it without hesitation. In the bedroom, she turned to face him, naked from the waist up, and he stopped in midstride, gulping as all the blood in his body surged downward so quickly he felt dizzy.

But then he spotted the scar, halfway between her collar bone and her right breast, and his lust cooled. Dark pink and slightly raised, it stood out as a testament to both the psychosis of a madman and her indomitable will to live.

As if she knew the direction of his thoughts, she caught his chin in her strong, warm fingers and urged his gaze away from the mark.

"Don't look at that," she said. "Look at me."

He gladly gazed into her rich brown eyes and lost track of himself for a moment. So alive, he thought. So vibrant. And here with *him*. He didn't think he deserved her, deserved this, but that didn't stop him from cupping one of her soft breasts with a suddenly shaking hand.

She let her head fall back, making a low humming sound deep in her throat as he grazed his thumb over her hardening nipple. While he stroked and swallowed and stared reverently down at the smooth skin of her arched throat, his mouth dry, she hooked her thumbs in the waistband of her shorts and wiggled out of them.

In a matter of seconds, she stood naked in front of him. Grinning and rosy, eyes glittering with intent. "You're still dressed."

He returned her grin and stripped faster than he'd ever stripped in his life.

She watched with one eyebrow lifted, not the least bit shy as her gaze fixed on the erection he freed from his shorts. He heard her soft intake of breath and grew harder still. This is all for you, baby.

She stepped forward and grasped his face in her palms, kissed him, openmouthed and wet and deep, and he was lost all over again. So easily. She sucked him in, and he went willingly, drowning in her sweet almond scent, lost, so lost.

When her fingers curved around his cock, her grip firm and hot, his knees went so weak they almost buckled. Jesus, he wouldn't last, not if she kept touching him like that. His synapses started to wildly misfire, sending come impulses to every cell in his body. The incredible glide of her palm on him robbed him of the ability to speak, hell, breathe. He needed to tell her to slow down. Oh, Jesus, slow the fuck down . . .

As if sensing he was too close, she released him and gave his shoulders a light shove, sending him bouncing onto the bed. He didn't care if she didn't want to take it slow. They'd do slow later. Much slower, much later.

She straddled him, trapping his cock between their bodies, rubbing her heat over him so lightly he couldn't stop himself from rearing up and catching his hands in her hair. While he kissed her, tasting bacon and coffee and Alex, she shifted position, lifted her hips and . . . sank . . . down . . . onto . . . him.

He went still, his mouth still on hers, his breath locked in his lungs, every muscle in his body tensed to the point of pain. Holy Christ. Tight. Wet. Heat. If she moved, he'd explode.

She rested her cheek against his and let out a shaky breath.

Neither moved for a long moment, savoring this first joining, breathing steadily and evenly, focusing. Once he thought he had himself under control, he cradled her against him and changed position, levering her back so that her head was at the foot of the bed and he was braced over her, his weight on his rigid arms.

She arched on his first thrust, her breath hitching. "Oh . . . God." It came out choked and hoarse.

He grinned and did it again, closing his eyes at the exquisite slide of hot, grasping satin.

Her breath caught again, her body going so taut he thought she might already be climaxing. But then she said something under her breath that he didn't catch.

"What was that?" he asked with a chuckle, following the question with another long thrust that had her grabbing at his hips as if to hang on. He'd never been with a woman so responsive to every move.

She swallowed hard, her head bowed back against the mattress. "I can . . . I can feel you."

He couldn't stop the low laugh. "I would hope so."

"It's . . . it's . . . I . . ." She trailed off on a long moan as he filled her to the hilt and paused to grind against the spot he knew needed the most attention. He felt her internal muscles jerk as she sucked in a harsh breath, and then he was fighting for control all over again. He laid his cheek against hers and breathed slow and easy.

Baseball. Gun cleaning. Shaving. Changing the oil in the pickup. Untangling the garden hose. Changing that annoying plastic cord in the weed whacker.

The chanted list of unsexy guy stuff didn't work. He . . . was . . . too . . . close . . .

From the catches in her breath and the way her fingers dug into his hips, he surmised he wasn't alone. Impossible, considering how little he'd done to get her there. Regret washed through him. He'd meant to make this first time last, draw it out until sweat drenched them both and she was gasping and begging.

But he had to thrust. He'd make it up to her later. Later, he vowed, would rock just as much as this did. More.

Opening his eyes, he gazed down at her, surprised to find her dark eyes open and fixed on his, bright with awareness. She was in the game, no doubt about it, so maybe cutting it short wouldn't be so bad.

He began to thrust, keeping his strokes long and slow when his body would have preferred short and fast. If anything, she was going to go up and over before he did, he decided. It was the least he could do.

As he moved, he trapped her hands on either side of her head and held them there, slid his knee up to nudge her thigh higher on his to grant him deeper access. He focused on her breathing, tried to gauge where she was based on its choppiness.

With him, he realized. Right with him, her wrists straining against his grip, her hips rising in perfect cadence to meet his thrusts. She murmured something, and he leaned his head down so he could hear her.

"I . . . can . . . feel you. I can . . . oh, God . . . I can . . . I feel . . . everything . . . it's . . . it's . . ."

He didn't think she realized what she was saying, and then it didn't matter, because he felt the familiar tightening in the boys, knew the point of no return had arrived. He tried to slow down, to stop, but she whispered a fierce "No!" and pistoned her hips faster, blinding him to his intentions. He had no choice but to let his focus narrow down to the wet heat clamping around his world, and on the next thrust, everything inside him imploded, pleasure rippling out from the center of his body to every nerve ending, every cell.

Amazingly, she was coming, too, her body as rigid as his as he held her tight against him, mindlessly grinding into her heat, not breathing, every muscle taut and straining, his head back and his mouth open, a long, low groan rasping out of his throat.

When his senses finally returned, it took him a few seconds to comprehend that while all the tension had drained out of his body, Alex's legs still clutched tight around his hips. She clung to him almost desperately, her breath uneven, her mouth open against his shoulder.

Holy crap, he thought. Multiples the first time?

He lifted his hips, thanking all the gods in the universe that he was still semierect, and drove slowly into her. His breath hissed through his teeth at the intensity of the dragging sensation against his supersensitized flesh, but when Alex's head arched sharply back against the bed, he didn't care. Jesus, she was so responsive. So incredibly *there* with him. Never had it been like this, never so intense and easy and . . . shared.

And then her hips bucked once, twice, and for a long moment, while her internal muscles clamped down hard on his cock, her body convulsed in his arms, her arms tight around him, her mouth pressed to his shoulder as involuntary whimpering sounds escaped her throat.

He held her for at least a minute, waiting for the shuddering aftershocks to fade and her muscles to relax. When her arms finally loosened, he eased back and looked down at her with what he was sure was the stupidest, loopiest smile he'd ever given a woman in bed. But he couldn't help it.

"Hey," he said, his brain too fried to come up with anything clever. He was pretty sure they'd just destroyed some brain cells.

She smiled, her eyes so unfocused he had to laugh. "Hey."

He trailed a light finger over the scar above her breast. "You okay? Did I hurt you?"

Her smile grew, but her eyes remained dreamy. "Nope."

"Nope what? Nope, you're not okay? Or nope, I didn't hurt you?"

She sighed. "Yeah, that one."

He chuckled, figuring she must be fine or she wouldn't look so sated and relaxed. He watched her a few moments, expecting any second to hear her breathing drop into the even in-out that meant she'd fallen asleep.

Instead, she opened her eyes and gazed up at him, looking for all the world as if she'd smoked an entire joint by herself and flown dangerously close to the sun. "Logan?"

"Yeah?"

"I've never had good sex."

He cocked his head. "Never?" Not even *now*? he wanted to ask as his ego deflated. He'd thought he'd done pretty damn well considering the minimal foreplay.

"Not until just now."

He relaxed and laughed—whew—and slid to the side, drawing her against him so he could hold her as close as possible. He was never letting her go.

"If I were a generous woman, I'd make you go out and do that to as many women as possible, so they'd all know what it's supposed to be like."

"But you're not generous?"

"Nope. You're mine." She snuggled her head under his chin and kissed his chest just over his heart. "All mine."

Within a minute, her breathing was slow and even.

Logan held her, unable to stop grinning.

All mine.

He loved the sound of that.

CHAPTER **SIXTEEN**

*T**he young boy stares at the gun in my hand with round blue eyes, bottom lip trembling. A tear tracks through the dark shadows of dirt on his cheek. My finger flexes on the trigger, and a voice screams in my head: Don't do it! For the love of God, don't!*

He can't be older than six, though he looks small for his age. Malnourished probably. And dirty, as though he hasn't seen the inside of a bathtub in weeks. He needs to be saved, and yet the gun I point at him can't possibly accomplish that.

Sweat drips into my eyes, and I blink it away, my heart thudding against my ribs. Focus, God, focus.

Shouts ring out all around me. Angry, frantic shouts. Someone screams in a high, thin voice. Another kid? My God, how many are there? How many have these bastards . . .

Rage rips control from my mind just as the boy begins to cry out for his daddy. "Where's Daddy? I want Daddy!"

My finger squeezes even as my brain shrieks, "NOOOOO!"

Alex shot awake with a strangled scream. A male voice

issuing the same shout echoed in her ears just as Logan jolted up beside her. He grasped her arm with one hand, as though to steady himself, and shock and fear that she didn't recognize as her own surged through her. She twisted violently away from the intensity of the emotions, further surprised when the mattress beneath her disappeared. She hit the floor on all fours, the pain of impact singing through her knees and aching head. On the other side of the bedroom door, the dogs raised holy hell.

"Jesus, Alex, are you okay?"

She sat back on her heels and met Logan's startled gaze. He looked as disheveled as she felt, his hair flat on one side and standing up on the other. His bare, muscled chest rose and fell as though he'd just finished a labor-intensive workout.

She had a vague recollection of him snuggling up to her back after they'd made love and looping his arm around her waist to draw her back against him. She'd fallen to sleep in his arms, his breathing slow and steady against the side of her neck. Everything would be okay, she'd thought. Turbo postcognitive empathy could kiss her ass.

"Alex?"

She blinked him into focus and felt sick. Everything was *not* going to be okay. Oh, God, maybe it never would be again. "I had a dream," she said, voice husky.

He lay back and ran his hand over his face and back through his hair. "Was it the same one as last night?"

She nodded. The memory of his outburst of denial mirroring hers reverberated in her ears, and realization hit her like a vicious blow to the chest. The nightmare wasn't *her* nightmare at all. "I shot a little boy."

He went so still she couldn't tell if he was breathing. Then he sat up, his complexion suddenly a sickly pale that made dark shadows appear under his eyes.

"That's what you were dreaming just now, isn't it?" she

said. "A little blond boy, dirty and thin. He was screaming for his daddy."

Logan swung his legs over the side of the bed and got up. "What the hell is going on here?"

She gazed up at him, feeling small and vulnerable. She was between him and the bedroom door, blocking his escape. She couldn't pretend that she wasn't psychic. Empathy was a part of her, and she knew now that hiding it from the people closest to her, from Logan, was not going to work.

"I'm empathic, Logan. I tapped into your nightmare while you were having it."

He stared down at her in disbelief. "Are you . . . are you kidding me? You're what?"

"Empathic. It happened when my heart stopped. The . . . the defibrillator—"

His sharp laugh cut her off. "Alex, come on, is this some kind of joke? Did you Google me or something and find the news stories? Because this isn't funny."

"I'm not joking, Logan. You had a nightmare, and I . . . I had it, too."

"This is crazy. It's . . . it's just crazy. Does it have something to do with what happened to you yesterday? Because you're being weird again, like you were last night. It's freaking me out."

"*You're* freaked out. Try being in my head."

He knelt in front of her and reached for her hands to help her up, but she drew them back, hating the way his eyes narrowed and darkened as she did it.

He braced his hands on his thighs. "Look, this is . . . this is . . . Hell, we just need to take some breaths and get oriented."

"I *am* oriented. I'm empathic. Some kind of postcognitive or retro something or other. AnnaCoreen explained it in a way that I can't wrap my brain around enough to repeat at the moment—"

"Wait a minute. Did you say AnnaCoreen?"

"Yes."

"That's your sister's psychic friend?"

She nodded, hope taking root. "Yes. That's her. She's—"

"Did Noah put you up to this?"

"Noah? What? No, I—"

Logan laughed, but it wasn't amused, as he straightened. "That son of a bitch. He ribbed me yesterday about AnnaCoreen's crap, and then, what, he called you up and got you to be in on the joke?"

"This isn't a *joke*."

He swung away from her to pace. "Oh, man, he got me. You both got me. I had no idea what a good actress you are—"

"Logan!"

He stopped and turned to face her. Anxiety etched deep lines in his forehead, and his eyes seemed to plead with her: Please tell me it's a joke.

"I'm not acting."

He shook his head, his expression anguished. "Alex . . ."

"I'm sorry," she said softly, not sure why she was apologizing but feeling compelled. He just looked so . . . disappointed. And doubtful. He didn't believe her, and she was the one apologizing. Did that even make sense?

"We've got a good thing here," he replied, his voice low. "A really good thing. The *best*."

"I'm not trying to . . . mess it up. But you have a right to know that I can . . . that I've been inside your head."

"You know that what you're saying is impossible. Right?"

"I know it *sounds* impossible."

"No, it *is*. This is the stuff of TV shows and books and faux psychics who rip off tourists at the beach."

"That's what I thought, too."

"Alex, please. What are you doing?"

"I'm being honest. That's what you do when you love someone. You tell the truth."

He squeezed his eyes shut and pressed his lips together before turning away. "Jesus," he murmured as he braced both hands on the dresser.

Alex swallowed, feeling shaken. He hadn't even noticed what she'd said. *That's what you do when you love someone.*

He needed time. That was all. Once he had some time to think, he'd remember that she wasn't a flake or a nutcase. Maybe they could go see AnnaCoreen together. For now, though, she thought she should back off, give him some space. God knew she hadn't been ready and willing to accept the truth the first time she'd heard it.

She braced herself to speak normally even as emotions whirled through her. Don't leave me. God, please, please, don't leave me. "I'm . . ." Her voice cut out, and she took a breath and tried again. "I'm going to take a shower."

She didn't hear if he responded, because a roar had begun in her ears. He didn't try to stop her, didn't say, "No, wait, let's talk about it. Help me to understand."

He let her go.

Logan got into his truck and slammed the door shut. The sun glinted off the hood, and he squinted, remembering he'd left his sunglasses sitting on Alex's kitchen table. Fuck.

Instead of going back in to get them, he cranked the engine and backed out of her driveway. He knew exactly where to go for answers.

It took ten minutes to get to Charlie's. If anyone had an explanation for this madness, it was Alex's trusted sister.

When he rapped on the screen door, though, it was Noah's voice that called out permission to enter. Logan found the other man sprawled on the kitchen floor, his head disappearing into the cupboard under the sink.

"Gotta leak?" Logan asked.

Noah grunted. "Garbage disposal gave up the ghost this morning. I don't know what the fuck I'm doing, either." He scooted out and sat up, swiping a grimy hand through his sweaty hair. "You know anything about replacing garbage disposals?"

"That's what plumbers are for."

Noah scowled. "That's what Charlie said."

Logan glanced around, trying not to appear too impatient. "Is she here?"

"Nope. Got called into work on her day off again. Her boss is a slave driver."

"Mac Hunter? He was great about Alex's time off after the shooting."

"I just get the impression the guy depends too much on Charlie. He had a thing for her, you know. Back before . . . well, me."

Logan nodded, not at all interested in assuaging Noah's insecurities. It's not like they were best buds. "So when do you expect her back?"

Noah angled his head to peer up at him as he wiped his grubby hands on a white dishcloth. "Why? What's up?"

"Nothing. I just need to talk to her."

"Is everything okay with Alex?"

Logan stiffened in spite of his effort not to. "Of course. Why wouldn't it be?"

"I'm just asking. No need to get your shorts in a knot." Noah pushed to his feet and dropped the filthy dish towel on the counter as he went to the fridge and pulled it open. "Want a beer?"

"Can't. I'm on duty in an hour."

Noah handed him a Sam Adams with a smirk. "I won't tell anyone."

Logan stared down at the beer in his hand while Noah jerked a chair out from the table and sat down with a groan. "You know any plumbers around here?"

Logan twisted the cap off the bottle and took a long

swig. It felt cold and refreshing going down. Maybe the alcohol would clear his head. God knew he needed *something* to help him think.

"Hello?"

Logan focused on an annoyed-looking Noah. "What?"

"Plumbers? Lake Avalon? Know of any? Maybe one I could call to come get this damn thing fixed before Charlie gets home?"

"Oh. Sorry. My landlord takes care of all that stuff for me."

"Lucky bastard," Noah muttered.

Then, with a sigh, Noah pushed himself up, set aside his beer and crawled back under the sink. "Want to hand me that red doohickey with the teeth?"

Logan scanned the tools. Even he knew that red doohickey with the teeth was called a pipe wrench. "You're in way over your head."

"Just hand it over and shut the fuck up, would you?"

Logan slapped the wrench into Noah's waiting palm. He'd finish his beer and be on his way.

"So what's the problem?" Noah asked, his voice almost drowned out by the metallic clanking of the wrench as he tried to adjust its grip.

Logan hesitated to respond. Noah would laugh his ass off. "There's no problem."

"Yeah? Then why stop by unannounced to talk to Charlie? You and Alex have a fight?"

"Hell, no." But the words sounded choked. Yeah, they'd had a fight. Their first. And who knew it'd be so soon after the first time they'd made such incredible love? And about something so . . . unbelievable?

"So you want to talk about it?" Noah asked, obviously out of his element in more ways than one.

Logan snorted. "What is this? *Dr. Phil*?"

"Charlie's not here, butthead. If you want to talk to someone, I'm all you've got. Take it or leave it. I don't give a shit. Hey, you see a Phillips-head screwdriver out there somewhere?"

Logan spotted the tool and handed it over.

"So is it the psychic thing?" Noah asked.

Logan stilled, waiting for the other man to snicker. Jesus, he'd never hear the end of this. But Noah said nothing, pipes rattling as he worked, as though they were discussing the chances of the Miami Heat making it to the NBA finals.

"Because, you know," Noah said, "I was pretty freaked out when I found out about Charlie."

Logan plopped back down onto the chair, all the air leaving his lungs. "Charlie's psychic, too?"

"The technical term is empathic. But, yeah."

Logan rubbed at his eyes. The whole world had gone screaming insane. "Cue *The Twilight Zone* theme."

Noah scooted out from under the sink and sat up. "You don't buy it?"

"Hell no. Do you?"

"Yeah, I do."

"It doesn't make sense. I mean, she said she tapped into my dream. Don't you think that's . . . *odd*?"

"Only if it wasn't your dream."

Logan didn't know what to say to that as an image flashed through his head of a dirty six-year-old boy sprawled on a filthy, scarred hardwood floor with a bullet wound in his chest.

"It's not possible," he said, more to himself than to Noah. "She found out somehow and instead of just confronting me, she cooked up this . . . this twisted scenario to . . . to . . ." To what? He didn't even know.

"You think Alex is that manipulative?"

"No, of course not." Damn it, Logan didn't know what to think. Nothing made sense anymore.

"What did she find out?" Noah asked, as casually as he'd offered Logan a beer earlier.

Dropping his head back, Logan dragged his hands through his hair. "Fuck." No way did he plan to share that info with *anyone*.

Noah clearly got the message, because he moved on. "You trust Alex, don't you?"

"Yes, damn it. Of *course* I trust her."

"Then why don't you believe her?"

"Because it's not possible. That shit doesn't exist."

Noah pushed to his feet. "There's someone we need to go see."

CHAPTER **SEVENTEEN**

In the shower, Alex tried to shove Logan from her mind. She'd have to figure out a way to deal later, depending on what he did next. He'd either come back to her or not. Instead of obsessing about which it would be, she'd decided to pay a visit to her mother to ask some key questions about their psychic history. Charlie might not have any luck having a conversation with the woman, but Alex could usually cajole something out of her. Probably because she knew how to avoid the button on her forehead that said "push here to irritate the hell out of me." Charlie seemed to live to poke that button, something Alex never understood. Yes, their mother could be cold and unemotional, but she was their mother. A little respect went a long way.

At her parents' front door, Alex paused to check her sneakers for mud. Wouldn't help with her goal if she tracked something in on the clean floor. As she perused the bottoms of her shoes, her eye caught on the word scrawled prettily across the mat in front of the door: WELCOME.

When they were teenagers, Charlie had explained irony to her by using their mother's welcome mat as an example.

"It says 'welcome,'" Charlie had said, "but have you ever seen Mom throw open the door with a cheery hello and a great big smile? Nope. That's ironic. A black fly in your chardonnay? That's just bad luck. And unsanitary."

Tears welled in Alex's eyes, and she shook her head. Why was she even crying about a stupid welcome mat anyway? But it wasn't the damn welcome mat. A butterfly could have landed on the tip of her nose, and she'd probably burst into tears. She honestly couldn't imagine a day when her life wouldn't suck now that she had super-turbo bullshit empathy.

Maybe, though, just maybe, her mother could help. Charlie had said their cousin, the one they'd had no idea they had, was empathic. That meant there was an aunt or an uncle, and perhaps more cousins. If empathy were indeed genetic, and it appeared to be, maybe someone somewhere on some branch of their family tree knew how to get it under control. Singing a song in her head—Charlie said that worked for her—wasn't going to do it. Alex feared that if she was going to survive her new ability . . . gift . . . *curse*, then she needed answers. She needed coping mechanisms.

With a deep breath and a swipe at her wet lashes, Alex opened the front door and walked into her parents' house. It smelled like warm chocolate chip cookies or perhaps chocolate cake. Someone was baking, which surprised her, because her mother had never been one to bake when Alex was a kid. She had been too busy lunching with her high-society friends and arranging charity events.

Alex paused in the foyer to peruse the family photographs artfully arranged on the wall. Just like in real life, no extended family existed there.

"Mom? Dad?"

The door to her father's office whipped open within seconds, and her father ambled out with a huge grin on his face that eased the tight band encircling Alex's chest. She walked right into his arms and received his engulfing hug and peppermint scent without a second thought.

After he set her back from him, his hands on her arms, she realized her mistake. Luckily, she wore a long-sleeved T-shirt (on purpose), and he'd pressed his kiss to the top of her head. No skin-on-skin contact, thank God. She *really* didn't want to know her father's darkest nightmare, and it shocked her to realize that she had no idea what that would even be. Perhaps the moment six months ago when it hit him that he'd gambled the family newspaper's future, and that of everyone who worked there, and lost.

He hadn't stopped grinning. "How's my littlest angel?" he asked.

She couldn't help but smile. Losing the paper, in her opinion, had been the best thing that ever happened to Reed Trudeau. He looked healthy for the first time in her memory. And smiling! It helped that his loss had been a bored billionaire's gain, and the *Lake Avalon Gazette* lived on. No harm, no foul.

He cocked his head and would have cupped her chin in that way he did when he was concerned about her if she hadn't stepped back. "I'm fine," she said, and felt her lips quirk on the lie. A Trudeau tradition. No matter what happened, the answer was always the same. She and Charlie got that from their mother. The queen of "fine."

"You don't look fine," her father said as she walked to the large windows that looked out on a rolling green hill that sloped down to the bank of the peaceful Caloosa-hatchee River. "You've been crying. Come into my office and talk to me."

Her father, the king of the pensive silence, wanted to *talk*. Alex tried to rub the chill out of her arms. She didn't think she'd ever be warm again. "Is Mom here?"

"Last time I saw her, she was in the kitchen supervising her latest protégé in the art of the perfect chocolate chip cookie. The DAR is having a bake sale."

A laugh bubbled into Alex's throat. As if Elise Trudeau had any idea how to make the perfect chocolate chip cookie. Any fresh-baked cookies she and her sisters had had as children had come from their Nana's oven. It amused her, too, that her mother appeared to still be angling for the perfect daughter, one who baked and wore frilly dresses and belonged to the Daughters of the American Revolution. The exact opposite of her own girls.

Elise walked into the living room from the kitchen, a pristine white apron tied around her narrow waist and a sunny yellow dish towel in her hands. She saw Alex and paused, clearly not planning to bestow a bear hug similar to her husband's. "Hello, Alexandra. I thought I heard voices."

Alex had learned long ago not to wince at the stilted use of her full name. "Hi, Mom."

While the past few months had been freeing for her father, her mother seemed even more distant than usual. She looked tired, too. Worn and haggard. As though her secrets had begun to wear her down.

Reed started to move away. "Well, I'll just get back to reading the paper and let you girls chat." He stopped suddenly. "Oh, and Alex, fantastic photo yesterday of Officer Logan. I'm not surprised national media snatched it up. It's Pulitzer-quality work."

Alex managed a small smile. She'd take Logan over a Pulitzer any day. "Thanks, Dad."

Once they were alone, her mother watched her with a question in her eyes. "You wanted to chat?"

"I want to know about my relatives."

Elise blinked at the uncharacteristic bluntness. Or perhaps it was the actual statement that shot her eyebrows up toward her hairline. "We don't—"

"Yes, we do. I want the truth, Mother." Alex hadn't intended to be so undiplomatic, but her nerves were frayed. And her life among people hung in the balance. Without some way to control her empathy, she faced a life in seclusion. She was *so* not the recluse type.

Her mother's complexion heated, and her lips thinned. If she'd been a cartoon, steam would have billowed out of her ears. Instead of answering, she pivoted on her heel and started to stalk back to the kitchen.

Alex lashed out with one hand and grabbed her mother's bare arm.

And felt the world shift into a different reality.

The grungy hallway smells like urine and garbage, and I can't believe Mr. Nelson lives in such a rank apartment when he can afford to live somewhere with hardwood floors and arched ceilings. Kind of a dumbo, if you ask me. If you've got it, flaunt it. There isn't anything that makes it more obvious he's a moron than what he let me do to him.

Mr. Nelson isn't the only moron here. I let him get to me. Dad warned me. So many times. "Think with your head, not with your heart."

Well, I thought with my heart. And now it's good-bye, carefree existence living off the laurels of others. Hello, shame.

I used to think Dad knew everything. I used to think he could save the world. I was a stupid little girl then. Eager to please. Eager to make Dad proud of me. Look what I can do, Daddy! I can trick unsuspecting good Samaritans out of their cash as easily as the next girl. See how well I've listened and learned? From the best, Daddy. You're the best.

And now the guilt . . . it's eating me alive. I can't sleep, can't eat. And instead of walking away like the good little grifter I was raised to be, I'm walking down this stinking hallway, hoping I can make everything that's wrong right again.

I hesitate before Mr. Nelson's door. I can do this. Come on, I can do this.

I don't want to.

I have to.

It's my own stupid fault. I reveled in the success of my first solo con, high on my power to manipulate. I wanted to see the aftermath. I wanted to point and laugh when Mr. Nelson realized that all his savings was gone forever, that he fell for a pretty teenager's sob story, and had no idea that while I twisted his heart around my little finger, I was sifting through his thoughts and emotions, searching for the one vulnerability I needed to get my job done.

I found it fast: a missing daughter about my age. Money sitting in the bank, earmarked for a high-priced private detective to find her and bring her home. Bingo. Almost too easy for a first time.

Afterward, Agnes and Rena begged me to walk away without looking back. That's how we do things. Con and run. There's a good reason for that, it turns out.

I didn't listen to my older sisters, and it changed everything. Now, the absolute devastation on Mr. Nelson's face when he realized what happened is burned into my brain.

I stole a desperate man's hope.

But I'm going to fix it. Dad's going to hate me. Maybe Mom and Agnes and Rena will hate me, too. But I can't do this. I'm not like them.

I'm not like them.

I can make it on my own. I'm smart and resourceful. Dad says so every day. All his girls are the smartest and most resourceful.

And I have Ben now. Wild and wonderful Ben. As soon as I'm done here, I'm going to ask him to run away with me.

What we did last night . . . oh my God. He felt so good inside me, and I must have felt amazing to him, considering how quickly he finished. I can't wait to make love with him again, can't wait for it to feel so good I lose control like he did. I'm the one, he said. None of the others matter to him anymore. Agnes and Rena are so wrong about him. They'll see soon enough.

Taking a breath, I raise my hand to knock on Mr. Nelson's

door. There's no response. Maybe he's not here. But his car is downstairs, so I try again.

Another knock goes unanswered, and I start to get antsy, standing in the dark, possibly unsafe, hallway, a plastic Winn-Dixie bag filled with twenty-dollar bills bound together by rubber bands. I try the knob, and it turns. I can leave the cash on his table. I won't even have to face him again.

I push open the door and step inside. There's a lamp on in the living room, but it's not very bright. I glimpse the back of Mr. Nelson's head where he sits in the recliner in front of the turned-off TV. Oh, so he's here after all.

"Mr. Nelson? It's me. Eli—" I break off. No, not Eliza. "It's Jenny," I amend. "I brought your money back." I stop behind the chair, uncertain now, because he hasn't acknowledged me.

"I . . . I'm sorry," I say. "I made a mistake. I . . . um . . . I hope you're able to find your daughter."

He doesn't move.

I take a step closer. "Mr. Nelson?"

Nothing. Not even a grunt.

"Should I just leave the money right here? On the floor by the door?"

Silence.

"Look, Mr. Nelson, I understand that you're upset, but I'm trying to fix this. You don't have to say anything, okay? I'll just leave the money and go. Um, good luck, okay?"

I can't stand not seeing his face, not seeing the relief in his eyes as I return to him the key to finding his lost child. Even if he's still mad, I still want to see that I've given him back his hope. Everyone should have hope.

I set down the bag of money and walk over to the chair, noticing for the first time the odd metallic scent in the stale air. I don't recognize it until I'm staring at Mr. Nelson and what's left of the lower half of his face. The gun is still in his limp, pale hand.

Oh, God, oh, God, oh, God, he's dead, he's dead, he's dead.

I try to scream but instead end up on all fours, gagging and choking. Sobbing.

I killed him. I killed Mr. Nelson. I killed—

Alex opened her eyes and blinked blearily up at the woman hovering over her. Her mother had fear in her dark brown eyes. And knowledge. As if she knew where Alex had been and it scared the absolute living crap out of her.

Alex raised a hand to the throbbing in her cheek.

"You weren't responding," her mother said, voice low and strained.

Alex pushed herself to a sitting position, surprised that she'd been flat on her back in her parents' foyer and hadn't even known it. Her mother made no move to help her as she shakily shifted to her knees, her head light and dizzy, then to her feet.

"How long?" Alex asked. Her throat felt raw, as though she'd been screaming. But if she had, her father would have come running, and his office door remained firmly closed.

"About a minute."

Alex met her mother's gaze and wondered why the woman didn't try to get help from her husband. Her child had been in distress. Catatonic for a full minute, an eternity during an emergency, and she'd done nothing. Except slap her out of it. As if she'd known exactly what to do.

Alex walked slowly, carefully, into the living room and sat on the white sofa. She swallowed several times, fighting back the urge to be sick. Wouldn't be good to puke all over Mom's white carpet.

Starting to shiver, she looked up to see her mother staring at her with lips pressed together so tightly they'd turned white. Her mother said nothing, asked no questions, not even: Are you all right?

"Don't you want to know?" Alex asked.

Her mother gripped the towel in her hands, the towel

she'd hung on to despite her daughter's catatonic state. She'd twisted it into a tight, narrow column of cloth. "You should leave now." Steady, unblinking.

Alex closed her eyes, so tired she couldn't shake the vague nausea that clung to her system. She didn't have the energy to argue, barely had the energy to stand on wobbly legs and walk to the door.

Her mother shut it softly behind her, and Alex paused on the front porch, one hand braced on a freshly painted column, and breathed in the humid air.

She couldn't think straight enough to sort through what had just happened. But she knew she'd learned far more about her mother's past than any "chat" would ever reveal.

For now, she needed to get herself home before she fell flat on her face.

And then she'd find Charlie.

CHAPTER **EIGHTEEN**

Paint the mother pink," Logan drawled as Noah parked the SUV in front of prime beachfront property occupied by a wreck of a tiny little windowless house.

Noah cast him a tolerant glance. "Whatever you might think as you walk in there, try to remember that Anna-Coreen deserves some respect."

Logan rolled his eyes. As if he would disrespect an old lady just because she knew how to shake down gullible tourists. This was crazy. His lieutenant was already irked that he'd requested some personal time at the last minute. But Noah had insisted, and Logan wanted answers. *Logical* answers, though, which he most likely would not get from a beachside psychic who, if Noah's end of the fawning cell phone conversation Logan'd just heard was any indication, knew how to snow the best.

"Try to keep an open mind," Noah said. "I know that'll be tough for a dipshit like you, but try."

Logan's first instinct was to defend himself. But instead he rubbed the back of his neck, remembering how sick Alex had looked last night and still this morning. Wrung out and pale and exhausted. And he'd walked out on her. But, damn it, what was he supposed to do? First, she wouldn't talk to him, and then when she did, she offered him an unbelievable story.

They got out of the car, and Logan followed Noah around the side of the pink shack to the back where a small sunshine yellow house with white trim sat on the beach. They walked through a garden filled with flowers and green grasses that smelled fresh and crisp. The waves of the Gulf rolled ashore a short distance away.

Now *this* was a nice place.

The woman who answered Noah's knock surprised Logan. He'd expected a wicked bloodred manicure, too much eye makeup and flyaway, Farrah Fawcett hair. This woman had soft strawberry blond curls and tastefully made-up eyes and lips. Her pretty blue eyes sparked with affection when they landed on Noah. She received his kiss on the cheek with a sunny smile.

"I was so pleased to hear from you, Noah," she said, then smiled at Logan. "Hello. You must be Alex's significant other."

He forced himself to smile back at her as he took her hand. "Nice to meet you, too, ma'am." *Ma'am.* Jesus. He felt like a third-grader caught in the little boys' room with a porn magazine.

Her eyes crinkled at the corners with genuine amusement. "So you say."

Logan reclaimed his hand, irked at the knowing look the other two shared.

AnnaCoreen stepped back and swept her hand toward the interior of the house with a flourish. "Please come in, boys."

The doorbell rang, startling Alex awake and bringing a horde of noisy pooches barreling into the living room.

Blinking several times, she was surprised at the gloom of the house. Her head felt fuzzy and full, and it took her a moment to realize she'd apparently slept for several hours. And she'd slept so deeply that even the usual antics of the rambunctious pack hadn't disturbed her.

Pushing herself up, she pulled a hand through her hair and stumbled—sheesh, it was like she was hung over—to the front door.

She checked the peep hole and saw a clean-cut late-thirtysomething guy wearing a friendly smile on the other side. She pulled open the door. The man, with short wavy brown hair and a slim physique, started grinning like he'd just bluffed his way to a huge poker pot.

"Alex Trudeau?" he asked.

He looked downright ecstatic, and Alex had the muzzy thought that maybe he worked for Ed McMahon and she'd just won the Publishers Clearing House sweepstakes. That'd fit right into this bizarre week. She'd use her winnings to build a time machine so she could go back and change . . . something. Hey, if super-duper Doppler empathy 3000 existed, why not time travel?

"Yes, I'm Alex," she croaked. She needed coffee. Strong and black. "Can I help you?"

He nodded, his grin widening to the point that it resembled the Joker's freakish leer. "It's my lucky day."

CHAPTER **NINETEEN**

Logan sat with his elbows braced on his knees and his head spinning. None of this is happening, he thought. It can't be happening. How could these apparently reasonable people believe the implausible words coming out of their mouths? Especially Noah. A fellow cop. A fellow devotee to truth and logic. Or so Logan had thought.

"You'll adjust," AnnaCoreen said softly. "Give it time."

Logan tried to wrap his brain around the facts, such as they were. "But how . . . why now? I mean, Alex wasn't always . . ." Jesus, he couldn't say it. That would acknowledge that he believed it. And he didn't. He *couldn't*. Not without letting go of logic and reason and . . . and *reality*. "Wouldn't I have known? I mean, it's not like we just started seeing each other. We've been friends for a long time."

"Alex and Charlie both had latent tendencies," Anna-Coreen said. "It took their respective traumas to awaken them." She glided to her feet with an almost supernatural grace. "I'm going to refill the tea pitcher and give you some time to absorb everything."

He watched her go, wanting to dismiss her as a crackpot. Wanting to get up and walk away. It was just so . . . far-fetched. Yet, he stayed put. If they'd been talking about anyone besides Alex, he would have harrumphed his way out the door long ago. But this was *Alex*.

Logan glanced at Noah to find him sitting quietly, elbows resting on the arms of his rocking chair as he gazed at the sparkling tips of gentle Gulf waves. The man's pores oozed serenity.

Logan didn't get it. "You accept all this?"

"I do," Noah said with a confident nod.

"How can you? You were a cop."

"I've seen Charlie in action."

Logan sat back, his chair rocking back on its rails. "Jesus." He kept saying that. But . . . *Jesus*. "They can see inside our heads," he said. "No one should have that power."

Noah shifted as though Logan hadn't just ruffled his feathers but plucked several. "It's only a big deal if there's something inside your head you don't want Alex to see."

"Aren't there things inside your head you don't want Charlie to see?"

"Not anymore."

"Then you're a perfect man, and I'm not."

"It's not that black-and-white."

"Isn't it? She gets to know what I'm thinking, and I don't get to know what she's thinking. How can it possibly be a balanced relationship?"

"Sounds to me like you've got a lot to hide," Noah said.

"She should have told me. I wouldn't have . . ." He trailed off and tried to swallow the bitterness. "I wouldn't have touched her." He closed his eyes tight. Fuck.

"There's more that AnnaCoreen hasn't told you yet," Noah said.

"What more can there be?"

"It's important. For Alex's safety."

Logan pushed up out of the rocking chair and stalked to the side of the porch. Bracing his hands on the white railing, he glared at the glittering water. He wanted to go back to two days ago when everything with Alex had been perfect and promising. Not a conflict in sight. No unexpected visits to the dark recesses of his past. No worries about how much it would take before the woman he was falling for started to hate him.

Behind him, Noah said, "These flashes Alex gets . . . they can be debilitating. You're going to have to keep an eye on her, make sure she limits her contact."

Logan faced the other man, a new kind of dread slithering inside his gut. "What are you talking about? Debilitating how?"

"Charlie calls it flash fatigue. Too many trips into people's heads, and . . . well, she gets migraines. A couple of times, she's had seizures."

"Seizures?!" Logan had to stop himself from hauling Noah out of his chair by the front of his shirt. "Are you kidding me? Seizures? Like, put a piece of rubber between her teeth so she doesn't bite off her tongue seizures?"

Noah raised his hands in a placating gesture. "Everything is controllable."

"Really? Because it all sounds very out of control." And he couldn't handle out of control. Not when it involved Alex and seizures and the threat of losing her because of what he kept buried deep inside him. "You know what? This is too much. I'm out of here."

He turned toward the door into the house but stopped when he saw AnnaCoreen standing there, a full pitcher of tea and ice in hand.

Her softly wrinkled face wore an expression of sympathy. "You're confused," she said. "Overwhelmed."

"It doesn't take a psychic to figure that out."

One perfectly shaped eyebrow ticked up. "Angry, too. Interesting."

Logan resisted the urge to brush by her, rudeness be damned. Yeah, he was pissed off. Why was that a news flash? "What's interesting about it?" he asked through clenched teeth.

"The reason for your anger."

He crossed his arms and cocked his head. "And what's that?"

"You're afraid she'll find out."

"Find out what? Just spit it out. I'm not a twenty questions kind of guy."

"Logan," Noah warned.

"No, hang on," Logan said. "I want to hear what the psychic has to say. Looks like she's going to psychic-analyze me."

AnnaCoreen's lips curved. "Amusing."

Logan returned her smile but felt more like he'd bared his teeth. She had no idea what made him angry. No, infuriated. He wanted to rip something apart with his bare hands.

"You care deeply about her."

Logan's shock set him back a step. That wasn't what pissed him off at all. No way. He acknowledged that he cared deeply for Alex. She was his lover and his best friend.

But now his best friend was psychic. Now he had no defenses. Any time she wanted to tiptoe through the tulips in his head, she could, and he couldn't do a damn thing to stop her.

"But you don't deserve affection, do you?" AnnaCoreen said. "You don't deserve Alex."

He opened his mouth to respond. He should have snorted his disbelief. Should have flipped the woman the bird and stomped the hell out of there. But he couldn't move, nailed to the spot by AnnaCoreen's shrewd gaze.

"You did something dreadful that haunts you," she went on. "You fear that Alex will see firsthand what you did, experience it as if she did it herself, and then she'll know the man you really are. You're powerless to prevent her from seeing it, and you've convinced yourself that once she finds out the truth, you'll lose her." Her eyes softened. "But you're forgetting something."

"What?" It came out a croak. He didn't bother to tell her she was wrong. She wasn't. God help him, she wasn't.

"You and Alex have been friends for months now, and it appears that she's flashed only on your dream. Is that correct?"

"As far as I know." He'd shared as many details of said dream with AnnaCoreen as he had with Noah, which was zip. She'd still figured out, or perhaps *knew*, that the nightmare was associated with a terrible memory.

But then another memory struck him. Alex *had* flashed on something else: when he'd stumbled away from the burning wreckage of a minivan, a little girl clasped in his arms.

For a minute there, it was like I knew exactly what you went through trying to get that baby out of the van. Like I was there . . . or like I was . . .

Like you were what?

Like I was you.

But why would she flash on only that and his dream and not—

AnnaCoreen's voice interrupted his whirling thoughts. "Perhaps her ability manifests itself differently with you, because of your closeness."

"How so?"

"Charlie's flashes with Noah are more powerful because of the intensity of their relationship. She shares certain . . . feelings with Noah that she doesn't with anyone else. Alex's empathy could be damped for the same reason but with the opposite effect. Because you're both so in sync, so to speak, her ability doesn't acknowledge that your electrical pulses are separate from her own."

Logan frowned even as hope flared. Being that in sync . . . that'd be a good thing, wouldn't it?

AnnaCoreen went on. "It's also possible that you're in such deep denial that when you're conscious, your body suppresses the electrical impulses associated with your bad memories. Alex tapped into the dream you had only because you were relaxed enough in sleep to allow it the opportunity to surface from your subconscious. If that's the case, I would assume she could also tap into your energy during circumstances in which your defenses have been breached." She paused to smile softly. "It's actually quite promising that you can let your guard down with Alex. That shows how much you care for her."

Logan said nothing as he processed this new possibility. That he cared for Alex wasn't news to him. That sleeping with her, or letting his guard drop during other intense situations, such as saving a child from certain death, could expose things to her he didn't want exposed . . . well, that was just . . . disturbing. He didn't know if he could handle such vulnerability. And would Alex continue to care about him once she knew—

"A word of caution here, if I may."

At AnnaCoreen's softly spoken words, he refocused on her face—and the censure in her otherwise kind expression. "You appear very concerned about how Alex's ability affects *you*. If you truly care about her as much as you seem to, then perhaps you should spare some thought for how it affects *her*."

He sat down heavily, a sick knot forming in his gut. He saw Alex in his mind's eye, pale and exhausted, trying hard to hide her anxiety, trying hard to explain something she herself didn't quite understand.

She'd been thrust into her own worst nightmare, and all he could think about was what it meant for *him*. He'd walked out on her, left her to deal on her own. He'd all but called her a *liar*. He was *such* a prick.

"You're human," AnnaCoreen said, soothing now. "I'm sure you'll make it up to her."

He looked up, thinking at first that he'd spoken aloud. But he hadn't.

AnnaCoreen gave him a knowing smile and lifted the tea pitcher. "More tea?"

CHAPTER **TWENTY**

Butch's heart raced with anticipation as he knelt on the cool concrete floor and tied the final knot securing his captive's bare left ankle to the leg of the wooden Queen Anne chair. He'd scored the piece on the way to his newly rented, garage-sized storage unit. A kitschy little antique store on the side of the road with the catchiest name—Mimi's Old Stuff—had leapt right out at him. Thinking of how much fun he and Alex Trudeau were going to have very soon, he'd charmed the matronly woman running the store into cutting the already attractive price of the chair in half. He'd oohed and aahed over everything from her yippy toy poodle—the Mimi in the shop's name—to the gaudy faux-diamond ring on the owner's right hand. She'd had overbleached hair and an overgrown ass, and he'd flirted like she was Meg Ryan in her When Harry Nailed Sally days.

Christ, he loved women. Spring chickens. Old hens. Willowy housewives. Plump executives. If they had breasts, he wanted nothing more than to get into their pants, or skirts. He loved making them scream. Loved how they shook and shuddered and keened. Loved that instant when they went still and breathless, right before the hot, wet—safe—place inside them accepted the heart of him.

Resting his damp palms on the thighs of his jeans, he raised his head and gazed at his captive. While she was relaxed like this, he could appreciate the things about her, about women in general, that made him ache with anticipation. She wore navy cotton shorts that left her long, pale legs vulnerable, and he had to resist the urge to stroke his fingers over her skin. Swallowing hard, he lifted his gaze from her legs to the white tank top that conformed to the perfect shape of her breasts—no bra, lucky, lucky, lucky. He wished that her eyes were open and looking at him, and wondered about their color. He'd had only a glimpse of them—deep and dark and curious—before he'd zapped her with the stun gun.

She'd gone down like a hooked largemouth bass landing in the bottom of a fishing boat on Lake Michigan. She hadn't twitched nearly as much as he'd expected . . . anticipated. Rather, the zap had knocked her cold. He'd worried at first. Had he set the voltage too high? But, no, he'd used the same setting on other women, and they'd merely dropped and twitched, then stared at him with dawning horror widening their lovely eyes.

Alex Trudeau, though, hadn't regained consciousness as he'd carried her out of the house to the Mustang parked at the curb. Not a peep had escaped her as he'd charmed his way around her concerned neighbor. She hadn't stirred when he'd pulled behind an abandoned gas station outside her neighborhood and transferred her to the trunk, where he tied her hands and feet, just in case. She'd remained just as insensate while he'd fireman-carried her through a side door into the closed storage facility. Stupid teenager running the place hadn't even noticed him messing with the door when he'd given him the tour of the place.

Unit 4410 resided on the fourth floor, accessible by

elevator. The empty storage compartment was big enough for a car and smelled of new plastic, courtesy of the fresh sealant lining the edges along the floor. Florida bugs, the stupid teen had told him, could be persistent critters. That sealant would stop pooling blood, too, Butch had noted. So convenient.

Butch trailed his fingertips, light as a feather, over Alex Trudeau's delicate ankle and around and up the gentle curve of her calf, marveling at such unblemished skin. No scars, not even on her knees. She apparently hadn't been a clumsy child. He almost regretted the marks he would soon make. Maybe he would have given it a second thought if the anticipation hadn't sent blood rushing down between his legs.

Pulling in a calming breath, he closed his eyes and focused on breathing and counting. Don't rush. Take your time. The payoff will be worth it. Fifteen. Fourteen. Thirteen . . .

The tension bled away in slow degrees. Ahhhhh.

Before he got started, he had a phone call to make. He pulled Alex's cell out of his pocket and flipped it open.

Logan didn't understand at first why his teeth hurt so much, but when a pang shot through his jaw, he realized he'd been clenching his teeth hard enough to crack fillings. It didn't take a rocket scientist—or psychic—to know the source of his apprehension. He was an asshole. When Alex had stood there in the bedroom, telling him something that had to terrify the crap out of her, he'd stalked around like a bully, accusing her of messing with him and refusing to believe her. Then he'd walked out on her.

Christ, AnnaCoreen was right. He *didn't* deserve Alex.

But as much as he admired her, as much as he *adored* her, he just couldn't completely accept what Noah and AnnaCoreen had told him. He had to keep at least one foot planted in reality, even if they didn't.

The way he saw it: Alex was a photographer by profession. She saw the world in ways that people who weren't photographers didn't. She intimately understood light and shadows, black and white and all colors of the spectrum. It was her job, her talent. She was damn good at it. And perhaps, somehow, her intense awareness, her profound understanding of how things fit together to create a stunning photo, sometimes transcended the normal perception of the average person.

She was special, no doubt about it. So special that he was already falling for her. But empathic to an extreme . . . or at all? Come on.

How she knew about his nightmare he couldn't—and didn't want to—figure out just yet. Clearly, she knew more about his past than he'd ever shared.

He couldn't blame her if she'd researched him. He wasn't one to talk about his past, or even spend much time dwelling. It was over. Done. Buried. He preferred living in the present. He only wished that she had asked him about it instead of doing her own digging. They were a couple now, so that meant they needed to trust each other.

"I can hear your teeth grinding," Noah said from the driver's seat.

Logan glanced sideways at him. "And that surprises you? Considering."

"I'm guessing it bothers you that Alex can see inside your head. If it's any consolation, it's not that easy. Like Charlie, she can't control what she sees. And it has to be a trauma of some kind, something that ramps up the body's electrical impulses."

"And you're okay with Charlie poking around in your head?"

Noah sighed, shrugged. "It sucked at first."

"Just at first?"

"I did some bad shit back in Chicago, but I told Charlie about it, and we're good."

"You told her because she saw it?"

"No, because she needed to know what I'd done," Noah said.

"But you feared she'd find out, so you had no choice but to tell her."

"That's one way to look at it, yeah. Jesus, Logan, what the hell? You act like you skinned puppies and ate them alive."

Logan laughed harshly under his breath. "Nice. I just—" His ringing cell phone interrupted him, and he fumbled to get it out of its place clipped to his belt. He recognized the number flashing on the caller ID display as the one belonging to the cell phone he'd given to Justin. "John Logan."

For a long moment, nothing but the hiss of static responded. Then a tentative, "It's Justin. Parker. I . . . I was wondering if, you know, if you could . . . if you could help me."

Logan wanted to get back to Alex as soon as possible, but it was also monumental that the teenager was already reaching out. "Of course, I can. Where are you?"

"I'm outside the Green Iguana."

"I'll be there in ten minutes. You'll wait for me?"

Justin didn't say anything, and Logan was sure he heard the boy's breath catch. Right about then, the call waiting signaled another call coming in. Logan ignored it. He'd get back to whoever it was. At the moment, he couldn't afford to lose the troubled teen.

"Justin, it's going to be okay," he said into the silence. "Asking for help is one of the most difficult things to do, and you've done it. We're going to try real hard to make everything be okay now."

"Okay. I'll be here."

"Great. And good job, okay? It took a lot of guts to make this call. I'm proud of you."

Logan disconnected, then checked his list of missed calls. The other call had come from Alex, but she hadn't left a message. He tried her number back, but the call went straight to voice mail. She must have turned off her phone already.

He waited for the tone, holding his breath. "Hey, it's me. Sorry I missed you just now. I'll explain later. I have a thing to take care of, and then I'll come by, okay? I . . ." His voice cut out for a second, and he swallowed. "I miss you. I'll see you soon." After hanging up, he stashed the phone back in its holster. "Jesus, I'm a lame bastard."

"It sounds like the Justin project is finally paying off," Noah said.

"Yeah. Hopefully, he'll tell me his real name so I can track down his parents. Better yet, he'll tell me what he's running from. Thanks again, by the way, for checking up on him for me every now and then."

"No problem," Noah said. "The Iguana happens to have kick-ass guacamole, so it was a treat to stop by a couple of times a week." He paused. "Look, it speaks volumes that you're trying to find a way to deal with this kid without letting him get screwed over by the system. A lame bastard wouldn't bother. You're a good guy, no matter what's inside your head."

Logan could only hope Alex agreed.

CHAPTER **TWENTY-ONE**

Butch closed the cell phone and smiled at his sleeping charge. She'd stirred while he'd used her phone to call her beloved. That tiny movement, indicating she was close to waking up, had caused such a surge of excitement that he'd decided to have a little fun before getting her boyfriend all riled up. Besides, he didn't want to leave a message. He wanted to hear John Logan's voice when Butch began the process of ripping out his heart.

"Are you with me, Alex?" He spoke in a soft yet conversational voice. He didn't want to startle her awake. She'd be frightened enough once she realized he'd virtually immobilized her. It wouldn't take her long to register she was not in a good predicament.

When she didn't stir in response, he stepped closer. "Aleeeex," he sing-songed. "Wakey-wakey."

He stroked the back of his hand down her soft cheek, tender as a new lover.

Her head jerked back, and she looked up at him with wide, dark eyes.

He smiled at her, his heart, and other parts, swelling with excitement. "Well, hello."

But something was wrong. She didn't appear to see him. Her eyes . . . her eyes had a weird cast to them. Glazed over, unseeing.

She looked blind.

It's dark. And the space is small and . . . and smells gross. Like stinky socks. I miss the smell of sheets after Mommy washes them. Clean and fresh. And safe.

The floorboards outside the door creak, and I hold my breath.

I'm not in here. I'm not in here. Go away.

He jerks open the closet door, and the empty hangers above my head clatter together. I try to make myself smaller.

"There you are," he says, kind of nice. "I've been looking all over for you. You can't hide, you know."

A whimper squeezes out of my throat.

No, please. I'll be good. I'll be so good.

"Come on out here." He opens the door wider.

I shake my head, tighten my arms around my curled legs.

"Come on out here. Now."

I squeeze my eyes shut. No, no, no.

"Tyler Ambrose. You need to come out. Right now."

I rest my forehead on my knees. Wish myself away. Far, far away.

He squats right in front of me. His breath stinks. Like cigarettes.

"Get out here."

He reaches in and jerks me forward, and rough hands lift me up by the arms. He throws me across the room, and I hit the wall, hard, and slide down to the floor. It hurts. Everything hurts. Tears burn my eyes, but I try not to let them fall.

"You can't hide from me, young man. You'll never be able to hide."

I want to hide anyway.

He digs in the pocket of his red flannel shirt and takes out cigarettes. He uses a square silver lighter to light one, then plays with the lighter for a while, flicking the metal lid back and forth.

"They gave you to me, you know," he says. "They didn't want you anymore."

I don't believe him. No way would Mommy have let this ugly, smelly man take me away. Mommy's trying to find me right this second. Please find me, Mommy. Please find me soon.

"You were a pain in the ass to them, with your budding psycho issues," the icky man says. "Setting a trap for a harmless squirrel, then taking it apart is a bad sign to them, Tyler. Very bad." He sucks on the cigarette, making the tip glow red. "That means they're relieved to be rid of you. So I've got you all to myself. Forever."

His grin is creepy. "First thing we're going to do is give you a new name. Tyler's such a pussy name. How about Butch McGee? You want to be Butch McGee?"

I don't even know what "a pussy name" means.

"Butch it is," he says, and nods. "I like it."

He grasps my wrist and drags me closer. "What do you say we have us some fun, Butchie?"

I start to cry. I'm afraid, so very afraid—

And then he twists and touches the tip of his cigarette to my belly.

Butch stumbled back, stunned as much by her sudden ragged shriek as the way her body convulsed violently against her bonds.

"Holy shit," he ground out and had to brace himself with one hand against the concrete wall of the storage unit.

His heart rat-a-tat-tatted against his ribs. What the hell was *that*? One moment catatonic and unresponsive, the next letting loose a blood-curdling scream.

Whatever the hell just happened, Alex Trudeau no longer looked blind. She stared at him through wide, watering eyes, her sweat-damp cheeks as pale as white cotton sheets.

He straightened, smiling at her with all of his teeth. Whatever just happened, it didn't have to ruin his fun. "Welcome back, Alex."

She blinked at him, eyes dazed and distant. Disoriented.

Butch angled his head to the side and watched her. Already, he could tell she was like no woman he had ever enjoyed. No pleading. No questions. No demands to let her go. It was almost as if she had no idea who she was.

"Alex." He said her name softly, invitingly, to remind her, just in case. "My name is Butch. We're going to have some fun."

She flinched at that, and her eyes focused on his face and widened with what looked like recognition.

His heart rate tripped. She *knew* him. How was that possible?

Then she bent forward, as much as her hands bound behind her would allow, and vomited.

"Fuck!" Butch jumped back, out of the splash zone.

She heaved until nothing came up, then remained pitched forward, arms and tied wrists bearing her weight, as though she didn't have the strength, or presence of mind, to sit back and take the pressure off her shoulders.

Butch wanted to hit her for making a mess. Had to fight against the urge to take out his knife and take a few swipes at her then and there. Not enough to kill her. Just enough to make her sorry. He knew all about punishment and pain. Knew exactly how far to go to make her regret what she'd done yet not far enough to render her unconscious and thwart his pleasure.

He had to remind himself that he had to keep her alive

long enough to ensnare John Logan. And have some fun, of course. Eye on the objectives.

First things first: Clean up the mess. He couldn't work with the stench. And it'd hamper his enjoyment even more to step in that shit in the middle of his work.

Without saying a word, he rolled the pleated metal door upward and stepped out. "Don't go anywhere," he told her, and chuckled at his joke. As if she could do more than breathe the way he had her trussed up.

After rolling down the door, he secured it with a padlock and headed to Wal-Mart for a bucket and a mop.

CHAPTER **TWENTY-TWO**

Alex concentrated on breathing through her mouth. The smell and the aftertaste of vomit were the least of her worries, as was the hideously stinging burn on her belly. She tried to think around the buzz in her brain, which sounded like the hum of a fluorescent lamp. Where was she? How did she get here? She couldn't remember anything that came before the moment the closet door opened and she saw the man who tortured her . . . no, tortured a little boy. That didn't happen to *her*. Not directly.

Still, her heart beat erratically with remembered terror, and she twisted her wrists against her bonds, wincing as they tightened. Her legs were similarly immobilized, each strapped to a front chair leg. Even the chair was unmovable, secured to the floor by bolts and hinges driven through the concrete.

Her mind flashed back to another time when she'd been bound and helpless, raging pain in her head and lightning sparking in her eyes. No, wait, that wasn't her memory. It was Charlie's. Yet it felt like hers, and the remembered terror tasted acrid.

Shoving away the choking memories, she looked around, blinking in the dim light cast by lanterns placed in each corner of the small space. They must have been battery-operated, perhaps the source of the buzz in her ears. A shiny red toolbox occupied one corner, but she shied away from that for now, focusing instead on where she was.

Concrete blocks formed three walls, the fourth a wide, pleated metal door about the length of a single-car garage. Sealant coated the cement floor, a chemical odor underlying the stink of vomit in the unmoving air. God, a storage unit?

If so, it had to be one in a facility of many, and there was nothing to indicate sound-proofing. She started screaming.

"Help! Help me!"

She shouted for a long time. Over and over, so loud her ears rang with the echoes, adding to the persistent hum inside her aching skull.

"Can anyone hear me? Please help me! Hello? Is anyone there? Hello?"

When her voice gave out, she had hot tears dripping off her chin. She had no idea what time it was. Had to be well after closing time.

The toolbox, its lid thrown back to expose the contents, drew her eye. She couldn't help it. Call it morbid curiosity. Or a need to know what horrors lay in store.

The box looked new and cast a long shadow in the lantern light. Her head started to spin as she registered the assortment of tools. Power drill. Needle-nose pliers. Ball-peen hammer. Hunting knife.

A cigarette lighter. The silver square kind that people engraved for gifts. Just like the one in the flashback. Perhaps the same one?

And was that a syringe sticking out of the lower drawer?

Oh, God, oh, God, oh, God.

She jerked at her bonds again, groaned at the answering cinch. The man knew how to tie a knot.

She closed her eyes, tried desperately not to see the face of the man who'd tortured a child. Butch McGee, to be exact. No, wait. Tyler Ambrose. The psycho had changed the child's name, stolen his identity. He couldn't have been older than eight or nine at the time.

As she remembered her fear . . . no, *his* fear, a *child's* fear, her heart skipped, uneven and hitching.

The burn on her stomach, just above her belly button, screamed as every breath she took shifted the fabric of her tank against the wound. She could still hear the sizzle of burning flesh, could still smell it. Still taste the absolute terror of a child. No matter your age, fear tasted the same. Like metal. Like blood.

What did Butch McGee want with her?

Maybe nothing, not from her specifically. Maybe, like his tormenter, he'd brought her here for his own fun.

"Logan," she whispered.

CHAPTER **TWENTY-THREE**

As Logan pulled into Alex's driveway, he noticed the uncharacteristic darkness of her house. He checked his watch, thinking maybe it was later than he'd thought. But, no, it was just after ten P.M. She should have been home for at least an hour, even if she'd had to work late.

He would have come by long ago, but Justin had stood him up. Logan had hung around the Green Iguana for three hours, waiting and hoping the kid would show. Several calls to the cell phone he'd given the kid had gone unanswered. Cold feet, Logan figured. Hopefully, the boy would try again.

As he got out of his truck and slammed the door, he could already hear the dogs going nuts . . . but they weren't inside. They were in the backyard. Now that was *really* unusual. Alex never left them outside when she wasn't home.

He let himself through the gate in the fence, barely managing to hold his own against the onslaught of barking and whining.

"Hey, hey, hey," he admonished as he forged ahead through a sea of fur to the back door and inside. He immediately went to the doggy cabinet. "Pipe down. No one's going to let you starve. Jesus."

He filled their dishes as he'd watched Alex do the night before, surrounded by a chorus of huffing and whining.

"Where's your mom?" he asked. "Did she take off and forget to let you in?" Highly unlikely, but he couldn't imagine what else could have happened.

Instead of burying their noses in kibble, Gus and Raquel sat down and stared up at him with cocked heads and inquisitive eyes. Phoebe hobbled between him and the door that led into the living room in a doggy version of pacing. Dieter and Oscar took turns nipping at his ankles, and Artemis sat in the living room doorway and whined.

Normally, the whole pack would have attacked dinner with an energy that would make an exhausted man envious. Something was seriously wrong.

Logan walked into the living room, the source of all the furry consternation. Maybe Alex was sleeping on the sofa again. Except his arrival had made enough of a racket, thanks to the chorus of fervent hellos, to wake the dead. Fearing a repeat of the night before—Alex all but comatose on the couch—he flipped on the light in the living room. The sofa sat empty.

He had started to turn back toward the kitchen, when he noticed that four of the dogs had started to mill around the front door, sniffing and whining. Both Phoebe and Artemis sat smack dab in front of the door and gazed forlornly up at him, as if to say, "You know this is wrong, right?"

That was when he noticed the front door hung open a bare inch.

Heart skipping, he stopped himself before he could take the two steps over and open it fully. Alex could have left it open when she left. She wasn't the most conscientious person about unlocked doors and windows. She trusted her environment—and her half-dozen woofy security alarms. Except she used the front door only for guests. She came and went by the back door, the most expedient route to her Jeep in the garage.

Still . . .

He took a moment to study the area around the door, his detective brain telling him not to jump to conclusions, while his boyfriend brain screamed at him to get on the phone to his fellow cops at work. Drawing in a calming breath, he shut down his boyfriend brain for a moment. So Alex had done a few things out of character. Their argument this morning could explain everything.

Pivoting, he headed back toward the kitchen and the back door, a crew of panting dogs on his heels, Dieter's nose bumping against his ass every few steps.

Logan was traversing the short cobblestone walk between the house and the garage when his cell phone rang. He pulled it off his belt absently, more interested in whether Alex's Jeep was in the garage.

Before he answered it, he glanced at the display and saw Alex's name and cell number. Shoulders sagging with relief, he stopped walking and answered. "Perfect timing. I was getting totally paranoid. Where the heck are you?"

"Hello, John Logan."

Logan's head snapped up, and he turned back toward the garage. He could see through the window in the door that Alex's SUV was indeed parked inside. Dread clamped hard in his chest.

"Who is this?" Logan demanded.

"The better question would be: What do I want?"

The voice, deep and over-the-top casual, didn't sound the least bit familiar. "Is Alex there?" Logan asked.

"Yes, but she's tied up at the moment." A soft, dark chuckle.

Logan's heart started to thud like a hammer against his chest wall. "Who is this?"

"This is your worst nightmare, John Logan. I've got your girlfriend, and she's going to provide a little down payment on what you owe me."

"Look, I don't know who you are or what you think you're doing—"

"I'll make it simple for you. I'm avenging my brother. I'm doing it by sharing some of my own personal magic with your girl. When I'm done, I'll give you a call back, and we can talk about what happens next. Sound good?"

"Let me talk to Alex. I want proof that this isn't some kind of sick joke."

"You're not in control here. I am. I'll decide when you can talk to your precious Alex. I'll be in touch."

"Wait! Don't hang up! If you want me, then tell me where you are, and I'll be there. Alex has nothing to do with—"

"Oh, but she does. You care about her. I cared about my brother. You took him from me. See where I'm going with this? It's the biblical eye for an eye."

"Who is your brother? I have no idea who you're referring to."

"You will."

"But your beef is with me. I'm the one who took away your brother. Not Alex. You and I, we can work something out."

"Of course we can. But you need to suffer first. You need to be frantic, wondering what I'm doing to your girlfriend." He paused to snicker. "I'll give you a hint. Alex—I can call her Alex, can't I? She's special. I noticed that right away. I'm not sure in what way, but I intend to find out. And are you listening carefully, John Logan? Alex and I are surrounded by some very sharp objects that are capable of cutting very deeply. But don't worry. I'll make sure you can still recognize her when I'm done."

"Listen, you twisted son of a—" A click sounded in his ear. "Fuck!"

CHAPTER **TWENTY-FOUR**

A rattle of metal against metal brought Alex's head up, and every muscle went rigid as the door of the storage unit rolled up, revealing Butch McGee holding a mop, a jug of water and an overstuffed Wal-Mart bag. A rush of fresh air washed over her.

"Miss me?" he asked as he strode into the unit and dropped his purchases on the floor. "Christ, it reeks in here."

He didn't spare her a glance as he unscrewed the top of the jug and splashed the contents into the bucket. He followed that with a couple of squirts of dishwashing liquid, then dunked the mop in a few times until suds formed and the scent of lemons floated into the air.

"I should make you do the cleanup," he muttered as he started mopping.

He looked so . . . normal. He wore new blue jeans, a dark gray T-shirt with some kind of writing on it under a long-sleeved denim shirt and bright white Nike tennis shoes that had to be new. His hair, a dark brown with lighter highlights, was cut short, the curl in it suggesting that left to grow, it would get wild and wooly. His eyes when he glanced her way were a lighter color—gray perhaps, or blue. She couldn't tell in the shadows. She wouldn't say he appeared harmless, but he certainly didn't have "kidnapper" written all over him.

"What do you want?" Her voice rasped like the roughest grade of sandpaper.

He shrugged as he worked. "I just want to have a little fun. If you relax and keep an open mind, maybe you'll have some fun, too."

Picturing his kind of fun, she started jerking at bonds that only tightened around her already abraded wrists. Pointless, she knew. But she couldn't help it. She had to do *something*.

He paused in his mopping. "Still trying to yank your way out, are you? I would have thought you were smarter than that."

"Why?" she asked, breathless.

"Why what?"

"Why my house? Why did you . . ." She trailed off. Was it completely self-centered to ask? If not her, some other woman would most likely be tied to this chair. But, God forgive her, she'd take that trade in a heartbeat. As long as she didn't know the other woman.

"Why did I pick you?" Butch asked. "Is that what you want to know?"

She nodded, fully embracing her lack of heroism.

"Would it ease your mind if I told you it wasn't *you* that made me pick you?"

She narrowed her eyes. Either the man talked in riddles or he'd fried some of her brain cells with the stun gun.

He laughed, deep and low and creepy, as he returned his attention to the cleanup. "I picked you because of your boyfriend." A sly grin curved his lips. "John Logan."

Alex hitched in a surprised breath. "What?"

"John Logan was a bad, bad boy." He braced both hands

on the end of the mop handle and rested his chin on them, like Mr. Cellophane in a Broadway production of *Chicago*. "Bet he's never told you how bad he's been."

"You must have him mistaken for someone else. John Logan is a cop."

Butch's grin grew. "You think being a cop makes a person perfect?"

"He's a *good* cop."

"He's the worst kind of cop." A scowl of disgust chased away his playful grin. "The kind that kills without remorse. Or impunity."

"You're wrong."

Butch slammed the mop into the bucket, sloshing sudsy water over the sides. "I'm not wrong!"

Alex clamped her lips shut. Okay, stupid thing to say, considering. She tried another desperate tack. Lying. "You won't be able to use me as bait."

"That's where *you're* wrong, Alex Trudeau. I know about you two, you and John Logan. Rumor has it you're a couple of lovebirds."

"Wherever you got your information, it's wrong. Logan . . ." She trailed off, her voice giving out as her brain took a moment to whisper that maybe it wasn't a lie after all. Maybe Logan *didn't* want her now that he knew the truth.

She tried again. "Logan doesn't love me. He won't negotiate with you to save me."

"Oh, yes, he will. I've already talked to him, and he made all kinds of tantalizing threats."

Alex closed her eyes and tried to breathe, to remain calm. She had to figure out a way to escape, before this madman dragged Logan into this hell.

Butch said nothing more as he finished up the mopping and set the bucket, water and mop outside the door of the storage unit. Then he rolled the door down and faced her. "Now, where were we?"

Alex pressed back in the chair, terror spiking into her

heart. She thought of the bright red toolbox in the corner. The hammer and drill and syringe . . .

He approached with a soft, almost affectionate, smile. "We're going to enjoy ourselves, Alex Trudeau. And then I'm going to invite Lover Boy to come watch."

He reached out and, with gentle fingers, stroked from her temple down to her cheekbone.

The world dropped out from under her.

"Butchie! Where are you, Butchie?"

His shadow shifts the light under the crack of the closet door. Any second he's going to whip open the door and yell at me for hiding again. But I can't help it. He hurts me no matter what I do. I want to die.

But dying scares me. I've been so bad, and bad people go to hell. Why else would he punish me all the time?

He jerks the door open and stares down at me. "Why do you think you can hide from me? I always find you."

He drags me out of the closet and kneels in front of me. His breath smells of booze, and anger makes his eyes black. I don't wonder anymore what makes him angry. Obviously, I do.

Then why did he take me?

But I know why. Because Mom and Dad didn't want me anymore. I made them angry, disgusted them. I believe him now. It must be true. Otherwise, they would have rescued me long before now.

He sits back on his heels. "You don't cry anymore, Butchie. Why?"

I'm not Butchie! But instead of screaming it, I stare up at him, paralyzed. It's a trap. It's always a trap.

"You used to cry for your mommy. Cry for your daddy. Why don't you cry anymore, Butchie?"

I watch him with dry eyes. Any second now, he's going to lash out. He's going to hurt me, make me pay for . . . something, I don't know what.

My stomach aches. It's been so . . . very . . . long since

Mom . . . Mommy . . . tucked me in and whispered, "I love you, my sweet little blond-haired boy."

I'm not that sweet little blond-haired boy anymore. Sometimes I'm so angry. I just want to . . . scream and scream and never stop.

"Answer me, Butchie. Why don't you cry for your parents anymore?"

"Because I hate them." I want to hurt them, like I've been hurt. With cigarettes and fists and boots. I want to take them apart the way I did that squirrel, the one that turned them against me.

He smiles down at me, and hope surges through me. Maybe he won't hurt me today.

"Does that mean you're happy here with me, Butchie?"

I nod, thinking I've found the key to this prison. If I say what he wants to hear, maybe he'll let me go.

He draws me to my feet, and I stand before him, the top of my head reaching the middle of his chest. At first, my head barely topped his belt buckle. Maybe someday I'll be big enough to fight him, and I can try again to escape.

"I've been waiting to hear that," he says. Something different is happening here, something that gives me hope. Maybe I'm going to get to see Mommy again.

If only I had known!

He moves only one hand as he slips it into his pants pocket and withdraws something shiny. I hold my breath as I watch, terrified it's the cigarette lighter. Seeing that silvery square object, so small and harmless before the flame flicks to life, can make me pee my pants.

"I got you a present. Close your eyes."

I shut my eyes. I can't help the hope that's welling inside me. It's over. All the punishment is over.

"Look, Butchie."

I open my eyes to see my present. I think at first that the small, slim item in his palm is a stubby pen. Looking up at him, I ask, "What is it?"

He's grinning, and dread clamps down on my throat. His eyes have that crazy light like when he burns me, when I cry out from the pain.

He pries at the thing with his dirty fingernails and unfolds a short blade.

A knife.

"It's time to move on to something more interesting," he says.

I jerk my head up, unable to keep the betrayal from scrunching up my face. No, no, no. I can't take any more. I've had enough pain, enough, enough, enough, and something snaps inside my head and I start screaming. "No! I won't let you!"

He grabs my arm as I turn to run. "It's not for you," he says as he holds me in place. "Come, I'll show you."

I force myself to stop struggling, confused and somehow hopeful again. Not for me?

He leads me out of my room, and I notice it smells like new plastic and wood and . . . tires? And there's a wall where there used to be an open basement. He's been hammering and sawing for days. What he's been building fills me with a dread so intense it twists my stomach.

"No." I fight his grip. I want to go back to my room. It's safe there.

"It's okay, Butchie. We're going to have fun. You'll see."

It's a brand-new room. The floor is rubber. The walls are shielded in clear sheets of hard plastic. One of the walls holds a window, like an interrogation room on a police show on TV. There's a drain in the middle of the floor.

And then I see her.

Bound and gagged and curled in the corner, red-rimmed eyes streaming with tears as she watches us approach.

"You've been such a good boy, Butchie, so much better than any of the other boys before you, that I've decided you can be my apprentice."

He hands me the pocket knife, blade extended.

I stare at it for a long, blank moment.

"Go ahead," he tells me, giving me a little nudge toward the terrified girl. "That's your present."

Someone else's pain. Someone else's screams. My heart races at the thought. Maybe he'll leave me alone now.

"I'll teach you everything I know," he says, his hands on my shoulders. "It'll be fun."

I turn and plunge the blade into his thigh.

He releases an inhuman scream and slams me with the back of his hand.

CHAPTER **TWENTY-FIVE**

Logan, heart pounding and sweat beading on his upper lip, paced the tile in Alex's kitchen as he replayed the kidnapper's words in his head.

I'm avenging my brother.

I cared about my brother. You took him from me.

It's the biblical eye for an eye.

That's the only clue he had to go on. A vengeful brother.

How many men had he arrested over the years? In Detroit and in Lake Avalon? How many had brothers? Hundreds. Maybe a thousand.

Christ, he had nothing else. *Nothing.*

Meanwhile, that psycho was cutting into Alex. His stomach heaved, and he stopped his frantic pacing to bend forward and brace his hands on his knees. He had to think. *Think.*

The front doorbell rang, and he froze. He'd called work but specifically told the crime scene people to come to the back door so as not to disturb any evidence—evidence that the gaggle of dogs had already sniffed, trampled and drooled all over. But still . . .

Logan ran out the back door, hopped the fence and strode around the side of the house.

Charlie, on the front porch with her palm flat on the door as though about to push it open, started when she spotted him. "Logan, God! You scared the crap out of me. Why's the door open?"

Then, as she focused fully on him, the arched lines of surprise in her forehead flattened into worry lines. "What's the matter?"

He didn't know what to say. *Alex has been kidnapped. I have no fucking clue who took her. And it's about me. Oh, Jesus, it's about me.*

Before he could form a response, Charlie stepped off the porch and approached him. "Is Alex here? I've been trying to reach her, and she's not answering her cell. I got worried."

"She—"

He broke off when Charlie stood before him. Shadows of suspicion, and anger, darkened her usually open expression. Noah must have told her what had happened between him and Alex. Or maybe Alex told her. Not that it mattered. Jesus, Alex was *gone*. He had to *think*.

"What?" Charlie asked, impatience adding to the angry red in her cheeks. "Where's my sister?"

"She—" His voice deserted him, and he heard the guy's voice in his head: *Alex and I are surrounded by some very sharp objects that are capable of cutting very deeply. But don't worry, okay? I'll make sure you can still recognize her when I'm done.*

Logan flinched as Charlie reached out and firmly grasped his forearm with a cool hand, and then her whole body stiffened on a swift intake of breath.

"Alex has been kidnapped," he blurted. "I don't know who took her. I have no fucking idea."

Horror filled Charlie's eyes as she drew her hand back, the color washing out of her face.

"He's going to hurt her," Logan said, and turned away, jamming both hands through his hair. "I don't know who he is. I don't know. I don't even know where to start."

"We need to call Noah."

"And you think he'll know? I'm the one this guy wants to hurt, and I've got nothing."

Charlie headed for her car in the driveway and retrieved her cell phone from the cubby between the seats. She thumbed a button with a shaking hand. "We have to start somewhere."

CHAPTER **TWENTY-SIX**

A lex opened burning eyes and blinked several times.
Even the dim light of the battery-powered lanterns
stabbed at her temples. God, her head hurt, pressure and
pain vying for dominance inside her skull.

"Welcome back."

She forced her thousand-pound head up to see her captor sitting on the floor to the right of her chair. He had his
knees up and his forearms braced on top of them, his back
against the concrete wall of the storage unit. A normal guy
with a ready, albeit too wide, smile and a teasing glint in
grayish blue eyes.

"Where did you go?" he asked.

She blinked again, starting to shake her head to clear it,
then thinking better of the motion as the pain gripping the
top of her skull throbbed. Nausea churned in her stomach,
and she swallowed convulsively.

"Water?"

At the polite offer, she focused on him, then on the clear
Evian bottle he held out toward her. That was when she
realized her hands were no longer tied. She straightened in

the chair, gripping its arms as her fight-or-flight response kicked into high gear.

"Don't." He spoke softly, as though he'd just given her an affectionate "hello."

"There's nowhere to go," he said. "It's well after closing time. So there's no one out there to help you even if you managed to overpower me, find the key, get the door open and get out."

He nodded toward the padlock looped and locked through a gap in the door's track. The door would open only a few inches with the lock blocking its path, not enough for her to get through.

"Water?" He jiggled the bottle, making the water slosh inside.

Alex reached for it and uncapped it. She hesitated before drinking, wondering about drugs. Her gaze darted to the syringe sticking out of the toolbox, and she figured he had other means to deliver drugs, means that a guy like him would probably enjoy more than simply slipping her a Mickey.

The cool water slid down her raw throat and hit her empty stomach. For a moment, she thought it was going to come right back up. Mr. Creepy Kidnapper wouldn't like that one bit. Thankfully, it stayed put, so she took another swallow.

Her captor watched silently, a small, pleased smile curving his mouth. "Better?"

She nodded. "Where are we?" she asked, not expecting an answer but hoping.

He leaned forward to fish around in his back pocket, then scowled. "Paperwork's in the car. Sorry. It's a new place, though. Nice and fresh and clean. Secluded. Near the river. Caloosahatchee, is it? I like the name of that. It's Indian." His eyes crinkled as he grinned. "But, of course, you know that. You live here."

He cocked his head as if expecting an answer, but she

had no idea what to say. Something like: "Yeah, I've lived here my entire life. I'm going to die here, too, right? Right? Sliced into tiny little pieces small enough to feed the fish in the river."

Finally, he sighed. "I gave you a straight answer. Now, it's your turn."

She shifted, every move sending a dizzying swirl through her senses. The pain, a squeezing, stabbing throb in both temples, clenched its way down both sides of her neck. Intermittent light flashed at the edges of her vision, like sparks thrown off a dying sparkler. Was this the flash fatigue Charlie had mentioned?

He pushed to his feet, shrugging out of his long-sleeved shirt. She could read the rock-band writing on his shirt now. Nine Inch Nails. Not what she expected. This unassuming, soft-spoken guy seemed more like the Barry Manilow type.

He moved toward her, and she tensed, pressing back against the chair, terrified he would touch her again. She didn't know what frightened her more: staying right here with this madman or going back into his past and experiencing firsthand what turned him into a madman.

He didn't touch her this time as he walked behind her chair and circled around it in a thoughtful, pacing loop. "Where do you go?"

She squinted her eyes to try to think better. It didn't help. "Go?"

He paused in front of her, one hand absently stroking his chin. "Are you meditating? Going to a happy place? What?"

She groped for something to say, anything to keep from angering him. "I . . . I'm scared. You're scaring me."

"But you go somewhere. In your head. I can see it in your eyes. You're not here with me." He studied her face for a moment before resuming the circle around her chair in slow, measured steps. "And when you come back . . . it's very strange, Alex. Like nothing I've ever seen. Last time, you passed out. It took a good five minutes for you to come around. So I'll ask you again. Where did you go?"

She swallowed hard against nausea. The sparks in her vision were getting more rapid, more like lightning, more like the explosions of light in her trek into Charlie's experience at the hands of a psychopath. A distant roar in her ears sounded like a tornado on the horizon, spinning ever closer.

"My happy place," she said, trying to sound strong. "I go to my happy place."

"I don't think I believe you. Why would you scream coming out of your happy place?"

"Because I'm scared. I want to stay there." She closed her eyes. She couldn't focus, couldn't think. "Could you please stop circling me? You're making me dizzy."

He stopped before her and leaned forward, bracing one hand on an arm of the chair. "Tell me about your happy place. What is it like there?"

She breathed through her nose. Any second now, she was going to be sick again, and considering how angry he got last time, she couldn't imagine his reaction if she spewed in his face.

"Alex," he said, soothingly. "I'm just trying to understand."

He reached out to brush hair off her forehead, and she grabbed his wrist to stop him, to stop contact. But she'd miscalculated. His wrist was bare. So, skin-against-skin and thinking, oh, shit, she spiraled away.

The dickhead's going to be ticked when he gets here and I haven't figured out this goddamn algebra. Why do I have to do this anyway? It's not going to help me with real life. I don't even have a real life. I'm like Holden Caulfield and his stupid I-don't-know-what-the-hell-I'm-doing-here shtick.

"Life is a game, boy," Mr. Spencer had told Holden. "Life is a game that one plays according to the rules."

And who makes the rules? I have no goddamn clue who does in the real world, but for me, it's him. Psycho Von Bulow and his "One day you're going to need to know what other young men know. Else, how are you going to function out there?"

Like he's going to let me go at some point. Yeah, when he's dead.

I don't even know what "out there" is like anymore. Not in reality. I read the books he throws at me. Didn't at first, but then I failed his tests and paid for it in spades. So now I watch the movies and TV shows and documentaries. But "out there" doesn't exist. It's all a dim memory. I remember being a clueless kid who thought an offer of candy at the mall from the guy who lived down the street couldn't possibly be a bad thing. I mean, come on. That guy helped Mom shovel the driveway the day it snowed a shitload and Dad got stranded at work. It's not like he was a stranger.

Groaning, I push back from the desk and get up.

Dropping to the floor, I work on some pushups. The dick-head's getting afraid of me, getting afraid of my strength. He's wary when he comes in now, careful to immobilize me before he gets out his toys. Our toys, he calls them. Like a hunting knife is a toy. Goddamn fucking fuck.

One day soon I'm going to get that fucking stun gun away from him and shove it down his fucking throat and zap him into fucking hell.

I hear him beyond my door, and my heart just about chokes me. He said he'd have a surprise for me if I solved the math problems correctly. A surprise could be good, could be bad. Best not to defy him, either way.

Swiping a hand through the sweat in my hair, I get back to my desk and read the algebra problem. Two trains are traveling toward each other along the same track but one *hundred fifty miles apart. One train goes sixty miles per hour, and the other goes ninety. How long before they collide?*

Fuck, that's easy! Any bonehead could figure that one out.

At the rattle of keys at the door, I jump to my feet. The dickhead steps into my room with a wide smile. His hair is gray, and he's so fat that his gut hangs over the waistband of his black pants. I hope he has heart disease. High cholesterol. Cancer growing in his gut. No, better: Cancer growing in his nads.

"How's Butchie today?"

Butchie wants to rip out your intestines, you disgusting old fart. "Fine, thank you."

"Did you finish your homework?"

"Yes."

"Did you get the train question?"

"Yes."

"And?"

"They'll collide in an hour. Together, the trains are going one hundred fifty miles per hour. It'd take an hour to go one hundred fifty miles, and they're one hundred fifty miles apart."

"Excellent. You've earned your surprise."

My heart leaps a little, though I'm unsure. His idea of a surprise could be cutting off my balls and feeding them to me with some McDonald's special sauce. The Hannibal Lecter of kidnapped boys.

"Turn around."

I quickly obey. Hesitating could invite a zap from the stun gun, depending on his mood. He loves that fucking thing. Probably strokes it while he's jerking himself off.

The familiar cool metal snaps around my wrists. Before I stun gun him to death, I'm going to cuff him. I'm going to light a few cigarettes and play up and down his back for a couple of hours, and then I'm going to take his knife and—

He gives my arm a pat. "Come with me."

I follow him out of my pathetic, dank room and glance toward the stairs that lead up, up, up to escape. Heaven. Home.

I want to make a run for it, but the memory of last time stops me. He let me get to the top before he zapped me, and then I rolled down the steps, feeling each goddamn bounce. Broken ribs suck.

"Wait here," he says.

He leaves me in the Play Room. His name, not mine. It has a couple of chairs that have restraints, a rolling stool that swivels and a wall of toys. No. Tools. He calls them toys. The room is soundproofed. It must be. Because no one comes running at the screams. Mine or the others'.

He returns, and my breath stops when I see what he's got with him.

Not a bound-up present ripe for playtime, but another boy, the same age as the others. Eight or nine, the same as when I got here. I don't even know how old I am now. He calls me a teenager, so I'm at least thirteen. Feel more like thirty.

"Look, Butchie, I brought you a new friend. This is Brian. Brian, meet Butchie."

The kid has terror in his eyes. Absolute, pants-shitting terror. I'm familiar with that look. I've seen it on other kids just like him, other boys who have come and gone. Other little boys who didn't please the dickhead, who failed some kind of perverted test. I've passed the test, apparently, because he keeps me. He keeps me, and he makes the others disappear.

Something snaps inside my head. I think I even hear the crack. I am not, no way, no how, not in this fucking lifetime going to let him try to break another little boy who looks just like me.

I fling myself at him, at the goddamn fucker that's kept me here. No, not that. Who. The fucker who's kept me here. His form of English class has paid off.

This is the fucker who's stolen my life, who's turned me into a freak . . . and I'm screaming and screaming and screaming . . .

Stars explode in my head, and I fall back against my bound wrists, not realizing at first that he punched me. Something warm and wet is on my face, pouring from my nose, and I taste blood, and that makes me smile. I want to taste his blood. I want to bathe in his blood. See? Twisted. The dickhead's fault.

Baring my teeth, I snarl and struggle and launch myself at him all over again, like fucking Cujo, man, and when his fist crashes into the side of my face, it doesn't stop me. I want his blood, I want his blood, I want his blood . . . I'm Dracula. I'm Lestat. I'm the American werewolf in London. I'm fucking Freddy Krueger, Jason and Michael Myers all rolled into one.

Someone is crying and whimpering, and I know it's Brian, poor little lost boy Brian, crying for his Mommy and asking for more like Oliver goddamn Twist. You're going to thank me for this, Brian. I'm going to be your ever-loving Artful Dodger here.

Just give me a minute.

My teeth are close to the dickhead's throat, and I snarl and snap but catch nothing but air.

He's yelling my name—not my name, but the name he gave me—over and over again, fumbling behind him for something, for . . . what? And I see it. I see it!

The stun gun.

I roll, because my hands are cuffed behind me. On my back, I grope frantically for the weapon I can no longer see.

He finds it first.

And he shoves it against my belly.

While I'm writhing from the first shock, my lungs in spasm, while I'm fighting the darkness clawing at my vision and screaming—"Run, Brian! Run! Run!"—he reloads and zaps me again.

Reloads.

Zaps.

Again.

CHAPTER **TWENTY-SEVEN**

Standing in the kitchen door, watching two crime scene guys go over every inch of the living room for evidence, Logan glanced down at his cell phone for the hundredth time to make sure it received a signal. All the bars were present and accounted for. And yet no one called. Likewise, no one answered Alex's cell each time he tried her number.

Behind him, Charlie said, "You're not doing her any good by staring holes into the CSU guys' backs."

He couldn't bring himself to look at her. He already knew that terrified looked pale on her, pale and hollow-eyed. Like Alex had looked last night and this morning. God, he was an ass. He should have listened, should never have walked away. If he'd stayed to talk things through . . .

Useless to think like that. Useless to regret. But what he was doing now—watching other people do their jobs while he did nothing—there wasn't much more useless than that.

He wanted to look for evidence. He wanted to canvass the neighborhood with the rest of his fellow cops, looking for someone who might have seen something. He wanted to *do* something other than stand around like a jerk and wait for someone else to find the woman he loved. And, God help him, he *did* love her. No way could he feel this helpless and sick, this certain that life would end if anything bad happened to Alex, about a woman he only liked.

He heard Noah walk up behind him but was glad the other man didn't do anything supportive, like pat him on the shoulder. It wouldn't take much to send him right over the edge, and he wasn't even sure what going over would look like. Howling, screaming rage probably.

"You said the guy mentioned a brother," Noah said.

Logan swallowed the lump in his throat and nodded. "He said I took his brother. I must have arrested him at some point, maybe sent him to prison."

"Anyone stand out in the past few months or so? Maybe someone who made a threat?"

"No. No one."

"What about arrest records?" Charlie asked. "We can start with the most recent and work backward."

Noah shook his head before Logan had a chance.

"What?" Charlie asked, looking from one to the other. "We're just going to sit around and wait for something to drop into our laps?"

Noah crossed to her and cupped her face in his big hands. "We know what we're doing."

She grasped his wrists, as if to hang on. "Can you please do it faster? Alex . . ." She trailed off, unable to finish.

"We'll find her," Noah said, then rested his forehead against hers. "We'll find her."

Logan looked away and swallowed hard. He sided with Charlie. They weren't going to find Alex by waiting around for the phone to ring or a magic DNA sample or fingerprint to turn up that told them exactly where to look.

But he didn't know where to begin. Even if he arrested on average one man a week who ended up in prison, there'd be more than a hundred after two years. And that assumed he was one lazy-assed cop, which he was not. The most unhelpful part, though: Family connections weren't listed in arrest records. There was no way to know which men he arrested had brothers.

The back door opened, and fellow Lake Avalon police detective Don Walker stepped inside. He was tall and thin, with angular features and a full head of floppy dark hair. He looked more like a thirty-year-old Paul McCartney than a man in his fifties thinking about retiring into a less-demanding job with regular hours.

A young woman with short blond hair and a sun-reddened nose followed Don into the kitchen. Logan recognized her as the owner of a pug who lived several houses down. Alex didn't always remember the names of neighbors who shared her street, but she knew their animals without fail. She referred to this woman as Clarence's Mom.

"Hi," the woman said with a small, nervous smile.

Don gave Logan a significant look that said, "We'll find her, man," before consulting a small spiral-bound notebook. "This is Rose Brown. She saw Alex with a man this afternoon."

A surge of questions rushed to Logan's tongue, and he must have taken a sudden, eager move toward her, because Rose stepped back and bumped against Don's arm.

"Oh, sorry," she said.

Logan forced himself to back off. He trusted Don. The man was his friend and a damn-good detective. He wouldn't fuck this up. But, God, it was *Alex*.

To Rose, Don said, "Tell us what you saw. Every detail you can remember is important."

She nodded, her cornflower blue eyes wide. "I'm so sorry I didn't call 911 when it happened—"

"Start from the beginning," Logan cut in, then seeing Don's arched eyebrow, he added more softly, "Please."

"I was walking Clarence. It was about two thirty. I come home every day at that time to walk him. I wasn't even paying attention, actually. Too busy thinking about what to fix for dinner later, when Clarence started barking." She paused with a tremulous smile. "He loves Alex. She always has dog biscuits in her pockets and knows the proper way to do a belly rub."

Logan's throat felt too thick to swallow. Alex, God, Alex.

"So Clarence started barking and going a little bonkers," Rose went on. "And that's when I saw the man carrying Alex to his car."

Logan's vision washed white for an instant. "He was carrying her?"

"He said she fainted, and he was taking her to the emergency room."

"And you let him take her?" He could do nothing to temper the edge of hysteria in his tone.

"Logan," Charlie warned.

Logan glanced at her, and he wondered how the hell she was managing to hold it together. But then he saw: Her hands were clasped so tightly with Noah's that their fingers were white. They had each other, and he was losing Alex.

Rose said, "He told me he was her cousin from out of town. He said she'd had the flu and was probably dehydrated and got dizzy. He was certain she was okay, but he wanted to be sure. He even invited me to go with them. He seemed . . . sincere."

"What kind of car?" Don asked.

"A new Mustang convertible. White. A rental."

"How do you know it was a rental?" Logan asked.

"It had one of those bar code stickers on the windshield."

"Rental indicates he's not from around here," Logan said.

"What about the tag number?" Don asked, nodding and taking notes.

"I caught a glimpse as I walked away. Florida plate. JR something. I remember only because I noticed it was the abbreviation for junior. My ex is a junior. Maximilian Endicott Jr. I should have known he would be a dud just by that name."

"Can you provide a description?" Don asked, steering her back on track.

Rose winced, her freckled forehead creasing. "I know this is no help, but he just looked normal."

"Tall? Short? Thin? Heavy?" Logan had to fight to keep his tone patient.

"Medium height, I guess. Not short, but not six feet tall, either. Regular build. You know, not skinny but not muscular. Short brown hair. A little curly, but it was short, so not a lot curly."

"Wearing?" Don asked.

"Jeans. A gray T-shirt. It had a band insignia on it. Something from the nineties, like Nirvana. Something with an N. I think." She sighed, blowing at her wispy bangs. "I know this isn't helping."

"You're doing fine," Don said. "What about glasses? Tattoos? Scars?"

"He wore sunglasses. I didn't notice scars or tattoos. It's not like I talked to him for ten minutes. He put Alex in the car and took off. He even said he'd call Logan"—she glanced at him—"on the way to the ER. Everything he said sounded right. I'm so sorry I didn't—"

"Did he have an accent?" Don asked.

Logan had to concentrate to keep from groaning. He'd talked to the guy himself, and he hadn't detected an accent.

The question drew Rose's eyebrows together, and she squinted. "Like Southern?"

"If he wasn't from around here," Don said, "he might have had a regional inflection in his voice."

Rose's eyes widened as she glanced at Logan. "Actually, he sounded a lot like you."

Logan turned away and took a few jerky steps. "Shit."

"What?" Charlie and Noah asked at the same time.

"He's got a Midwest accent like me. The son of a bitch is from Detroit."

Butch checked his watch for the twentieth time and suppressed a loud groan. He'd moved his numb butt from the cold concrete to the cushioned seat of the chair an hour ago. At his feet, Alex Trudeau lay unconscious, her shallow breaths hitching every few moments.

She must be epileptic. What else would explain the sudden violent convulsions that had flung her from the chair, bouncing her head against the hard floor of the storage unit? She'd had a seizure, plain and simple. Her nose bled like she'd been punched, but luckily she hadn't bitten off her tongue. That would have severely limited his entertainment. More than it was already limited.

What disturbed him more than anything, though, was what she'd screamed as her body repeatedly seized.

Run, Brian! Run! Run!

He wondered if her Brian had obeyed—and how weird was it that they both had a Brian that they'd urged to run? His Brian hadn't obeyed. Butch had opened his eyes to find himself back on his bed in his room (ccll), muscles still quivering from stun gun aftershocks. And there at the foot of the bed sat his newest best friend.

Brian Lear.

At least that's what the dickhead said Brian's name was. But it could very well have been that he liked Lear jets. Or Norman Lear sitcoms. Maybe *All in the Family* set him off.

Butch had gotten his name because the dickhead liked the Janis Joplin song "Me and Bobby McGee."

Which Butch found a bit ironic these days, considering. If freedom really was just another word for nothing left to lose, then he was about as free as you could get. John

Logan took away everything that was important to him, and now he had nothing to lose by making the son of a bitch pay.

A soft moan drew his gaze to the floor, where his captive shifted, eyelids fluttering.

He sat forward in the chair, elbows on his knees. "Alex, my sweet. You're testing my patience. We've spent several hours together now, and we haven't played at all. You do know that's not fair, right?"

When she made no response, her chest barely rising and falling, he nudged her in the ribs with the toe of his new Nikes.

Nothing. Not even a twitch this time.

What a buzz kill.

CHAPTER **TWENTY-EIGHT**

In Alex's backyard, surrounded by oddly subdued pooches, Logan made a cell phone call to Detroit. The single light by the back door pushed back the midnight darkness, and the air hummed with the sounds of busy insects and the occasional call of a bird. The night smelled earthy and a bit musty, humidity thick and swirling like a cloud. Lightning flashed among the dark clouds in the distance as a storm rolled east across the state from the Gulf. A muted roll of thunder followed.

"Lieutenant Packard." The memorably gruff greeting tweaked Logan's guilt.

"Phil, it's John Logan. I hope I didn't wake you."

A long pause competed with the crackle on the line, followed by a muttered, "Hell, no. I'm sitting here channel flipping. How long's it been, asshole?"

Logan laughed in response. Asshole. Fucker. Dickweed. Shithead. His friend's casual use of expletives hadn't faded in two years. "Too long. I'm sorry about that."

"You should be. I thought we were buddies."

"We were. We *are*. I just . . . I needed some time."

"Time to forget you have goddamn friends here, apparently."

"I never forgot that, Phil. And, hey, congrats on the promo. Lieutenant now, huh?"

"Right after you split, actually. They needed someone to fill Tucker's position after he got the boot."

Damn. Logan hadn't thought of Ed Tucker, his former lieutenant, as a possibility for Alex's kidnapper. Yet when Logan busted up the sex ring he'd stumbled into, he'd also busted two of Tucker's subordinates who'd taken bribes to protect the brothel, acts that had cost Tucker his job as well. Yet, if Tucker was behind the kidnapping, Logan would have recognized his voice.

"So what the fuck is up?" Phil asked. "I figure there's a reason for this call."

Logan felt like a jerk for contacting his good friend after so long only because he wanted something from him, but he didn't bother easing into it. Phil would understand. "Yeah, I need some help."

"There's a surprise. And here I thought you called me up to meet for pancakes."

"A man has kidnapped my girlfriend. Says he wants revenge because I took his brother away from him."

"Shit."

"Can you tell me off the top of your head, do either Kendricks or Hudson have brothers?"

"Well, hell, Logan. Kendricks alone has three. Two of them are on the force. Far as I know, they're not on the take like their big bro was, though. Third's a firefighter in Chicago."

Logan pulled out his notebook and started taking notes in the dim light. So much for hoping for one brother each. Or, better yet, one brother between the two. "Do you know their names?"

"Christ, let's see. All started with M's. Our guy was Matt, so his brothers are . . . Mark and Mick, the two who are cops. Mitchell, the youngest, is the one down in Chicago."

"What about Hudson?"

"He has a twin. Name's Tim." Phil snorted. "Jimmy and Timmy. You wouldn't think a kid with a twin named Timmy would grow up to be a cop on the take. Fucking idiot."

"Did either Kendricks or Hudson ever say anything to you about getting back at me?"

"Are you shitting me? They had long, involved conversations about how they were going to take you apart, piece by piece. You fucked up their lifelong plans. They were looking at retirement at forty."

Logan's control slipped a notch. "Women and little kids were being forced into sexual slavery. I was supposed to walk away after stumbling into that?"

"You're preaching to the choir, buddy."

Logan dragged in a calming breath. "Sorry. I'm on edge."

"Understandably. And maybe you shouldn't consider just the brothers of Kendricks and Hudson. A lot of people paid for what those fuckholes did on the job. Tucker drank himself into liver disease. His kids haven't talked to him in two years, and he technically didn't do anything wrong."

"Except overlook the fact that two of his cops were buying cars and boats and vacation homes."

"Yep, there's that."

"Does Tucker have brothers?" Logan asked.

"Nope. A couple of sisters."

"Finally, a break."

"He's got some pretty fucking loyal brothers-in-law, though."

Logan's call waiting beeped. "Hold on." He switched over, his hand starting to shake. This was going nowhere fast, and he had no idea what to do next. "Yeah?"

"It's Reese. I was driving by that new storage place

over on Via Del Mar. There's a white Mustang convertible parked in the lot after closing time. It's got a bar code in the window."

"What's the tag?"

"JR 3418."

Logan started running toward the driveway and his car. "I'm on my way. Call for backup."

Butch stood by the open door and gazed down at his very disappointing captive. She had yet to regain consciousness, and he was tired of waiting. This was getting him nowhere. And it certainly wasn't getting him *off*. His number one requirement for satisfying vengeance: It had to give him a happy. Alex Trudeau was not giving him a happy. In fact, all she'd done was flip him out and make him clean up vomit. *Not* fun.

So screw it.

He'd take a step back and regroup. He'd go find some pleasure elsewhere in this intriguing little town, which would help him regain some patience and perspective. Maybe that tasty morsel at the Lake Avalon Public Safety Building or the one at the rental car place at the airport didn't have plans tonight. He could easily be persuaded to partake in some tantalizing shrimp and some tantalizing woman.

He stopped to gaze down at the massive waste of his time shuddering on the floor, blood trickling from her nose. Maybe by morning, she'd snap out of her stupor and gift him with what he wanted. What he needed. Until then, he was out of this cold, sterile, concrete-and-tin-can hole.

Before leaving, he lifted her into the immobilized chair, resecured her wrists and ankles and gagged her, though he doubted she'd be able to make much noise in her current state. The tremors in the muscles of her arms and legs, and the way her head lolled forward, concerned him, but not enough to do anything about it. He planned to kill her, so whatever was wrong hardly mattered. He just wanted to have some fun first.

And he wanted her to survive long enough for him to take her apart in front of John Logan.

After locking up, he took the elevator down to the lobby. He saw the cop right away, illuminated by the obscenely bright parking lot lights, shining his massive flashlight through the windshield of the Mustang.

Crap.

Butch scooted down the hallway to the door he'd used to get in and slipped outside. The moldy scent of wet earth made his nose itch, and he swiped at it as he tread lightly toward the front of the building.

The cop was talking into a cell phone, but Butch couldn't make out what he said. He was a big guy, tall and muscular, just the kind of guy that Butch would have to take by surprise to overpower. Not that that made him nervous. He'd taken down a few muscle-bound he-mans in his lifetime. He and his brothers had trained well, from the moment they'd all agreed to execute their own version of a coup.

Butch lingered at the corner of the building, waiting to see what happened next. Maybe the cop would mosey along without mishap. He might have stopped to run the tag on the solo car in the lot of a closed business. Butch should have parked somewhere else and walked to the storage place, but he'd been irked at the extra trip to Wal-Mart for the bucket and mop, and had gotten impatient. More proof that he really should work on his patience.

Keeping that in mind, he watched the cop. Most likely, he would get back into his squad car and drive off. Or maybe call a tow truck to haul away the illegally parked car.

A disturbing thought occurred to Butch. What if the woman who'd caught him carrying his unconscious captive to the car had called the cops? But, no, she had bought every word he'd fed her, he was sure of it. She'd been the type who wanted to believe everyone had good intentions, especially in *her* neighborhood.

Of course, John Logan was probably the type who went door-to-door asking questions and demanding answers, no matter what time of day it was. The woman might have described the Mustang, which wouldn't normally have been a giveaway, considering how many of them roamed the roads of tourist paradises. But one going solo in an empty parking lot . . . Well, damn. He'd done this to himself. And now he'd have to take care of it before anyone else showed up.

He really didn't want to start killing people, especially cops, before he'd had a chance to do what he'd come to do. He also firmly believed in doing what had to be done to support the greater good. And his greater good was far from supported with a cop snooping around.

Of course, he could just walk away. If the police were on to his rental, he couldn't very well get into it and drive away. They'd find him in a nanosecond. And if he killed a cop, well, that would just be stupid. He'd have the whole of the Lake Avalon Police Department breathing hellfire down his neck. Not conducive to achieving his goals.

Better to walk away. It'd be a hike back to the hotel, but it'd give him time to think, to clear his head. To work on his patience.

CHAPTER **TWENTY-NINE**

Logan, with Noah's car just about plastered to his bumper, yanked the steering wheel to the left and fishtailed into the parking lot of the new Palm Storage facility.

Lake Avalon police sergeant Darrell Reese met him at the door of his pickup as he jumped out. The sergeant, a man Logan had shared many a beer with after hours, didn't waste time with greetings. "The place is deserted. I took a walk around back, and there's trampled grass outside a side door that's unlocked."

"Which way?" Logan asked, unsnapping the holster under his arm.

Reese pointed toward the right side of the four-story, red-and-blue-stucco building. "Around that way. Backup's on its way."

Logan had no intention of waiting that long. He shot a glance at Noah. "You want to help Reese check out the car?"

Noah gave a quick nod. As Logan drew his Glock and headed for the grassy strip between the building and a tall chain-link fence, he glanced back once to see Reese open the driver's door of the Mustang. Unlocked. That'd help.

Just inside the door of the storage facility, Logan paused and listened, Glock gripped in both hands but angled toward the floor. A breezy night made the metal rafters overhead shift and pop, and a chorus of crickets chirped from all directions.

If not for the Mustang in the lot, he would have assumed he was alone here. Maybe this was a waste of time. Maybe the Mustang's battery died or the driver met some friends for dinner and had yet to return to pick it up. Maybe it was a coincidence that the tag started with JR.

His cell phone trilled on his belt, sounding as loud as a bomb in the stillness of metal and concrete, and he snatched it up. "Yeah?"

"Try unit 4410," Noah said. "Fourth floor. I'm on my way."

Logan looked around for a stairwell and, seeing none, started running down the hallway toward what he assumed would be the lobby, his shoes slapping at the floor.

Spotting a door marked STAIRS, he plowed through and took two steps at a time to level four. His breathing harsh and his heart thundering, he traversed clean walkways with concrete floors that had a shiny new coating. Fluorescent lights tripped by motion sensors winked on overhead as he ran, his eyes scanning for the numbered sign that would mark row forty-four.

When he stood before unit 4410, staring at the padlock securing it and wishing for bolt cutters, he heard the clomp of running feet. Noah.

Logan didn't wait for his friend. If he broke the law, violated someone's right to privacy or the search-and-seizure laws, he didn't care. Alex might be on the other side of this door, and nothing was standing in his way. Screw the lack of a search warrant.

He raised the Glock and took aim. It took two deafening shots to destroy the lock, and by then, Noah had arrived. While Logan poked at the remnants of the lock to get them out of the way, Noah checked the other aisles to make sure no one tried to sneak up on them.

Logan's hands shook as he hauled the door up.

And there she was. Chin resting on her chest, wrists and ankles secured to a fancy antique chair. She looked dead. His knees almost buckled. "Oh, God."

Behind him, Noah ground out, "Son of a bitch."

Logan lunged forward, blind with fear and deaf to the rest of the universe. His world consisted at that moment only of Alex tied to a chair and not moving, Alex not smiling up at him and saying, "Thank God, you found me in time."

He *hadn't* found her in time.

He leaned over her, his whole body trembling as he reached out to check for her pulse.

Noah was there in an instant, knocking his hand away before he could make contact with her skin. "Don't!" Noah snapped. "Don't you remember anything AnnaCoreen told you?"

Logan gripped the arms of the chair to brace himself and took in the cords tied around Alex's bare wrists and ankles. "How are we supposed to get her out of this chair if we can't touch her?"

"Use these." Noah whipped out two pairs of latex surgical gloves that had been stuffed in his back pocket and tossed one set at Logan.

Logan stared at the gloves in disbelief. "Are you serious?"

"As a heart attack." Noah snapped on his pair as if he did it every day of his life.

"You carry these around with you?"

"Since I met Charlie. You never know when there's going to be a situation like this. They come in handy at crime scenes, too."

As Logan struggled with his own pair—damn it, his hands shook so much he could barely maneuver his fingers into the latex—Noah gently cupped Alex's head and angled it back, exposing her features to the dim light.

"Fuck," Noah breathed.

Logan couldn't speak, his breath stolen by the dried blood at her nose and the stark purple of the bruises marring the absolute whiteness of her features. She'd been struck more than once, fist-sized evidence on the left side of her jaw and temple. Murderous rage spewed through his veins. He would *kill* the man who'd done this to her.

"Her pulse is erratic," Noah said.

Logan got the gloves in place and slid his hand over the back of hers, still tied to the chair, and squeezed to let her know he was there, that she was no longer alone in this hellhole. Guilt joined the rage boiling in his gut. It was because of him that she was tied to this chair, bleeding and unconscious.

"Logan."

He blinked and focused on Noah, who was working on the knot at Alex's left ankle. "Call for an ambulance," Noah said. "I'll get her untied."

"No," Logan said, and it came out guttural and choked. "I'll untie her. You call the ambulance."

He nudged his friend aside and knelt at Alex's feet. She was so still, so pale, and his covered fingers fumbled with the knots in the thin cord. He could see the raw skin underneath, and he had to swallow back the surge of nausea that accompanied the rage. Son of a bitch, son of a bitch, *son of a bitch*.

Noah returned—Logan hadn't realized he'd stepped out of the unit—and swore under his breath as he knelt off to the side, near the toolbox.

"What is it?" Logan asked, not taking his eyes off his work.

"The bastard had plans," Noah said softly.

The last cord dropped free, and Logan braced Alex's body as she slumped forward. Her head lolled onto his shoulder, and he buried his face in her hair and breathed in the almond scent. The skin of her arms against his was cool and clammy. Oh, God, he thought. Shock.

"Hang on, sweetie. I've got you."

"Damn it, be careful," Noah snapped. "You're getting all over her."

Logan shifted her quickly away from contact with his bare arms, moving his hands to her shoulders. He still didn't buy what Noah and AnnaCoreen had told him about empathy—no doubt, they'd exaggerated—but he wasn't going to carelessly put Alex at risk, either.

He looked around for a way to shield her so he could carry her out. Seeing nothing he could use, he stripped off his T-shirt and draped it around her shoulders like a shawl that covered her bare arms. Noah stripped his off, too, and wrapped it around her legs, holding it in place while Logan lifted her into his arms.

"Make sure the EMTs are wearing gloves," Noah said. "The more we can limit contact, the better. We don't know what's going on right now with her system."

Logan nodded, and cradling her still, limp body against his chest, he carried her out of her concrete prison.

CHAPTER **THIRTY**

Awareness returned as a floating sensation and the illusion of Logan, smelling of soap and spearmint gum, wrapped all around her. A sigh of absolute contentment coursed through her. This was nice.

"Alex?"

She didn't open her eyes, didn't want to acknowledge she was dreaming and that Logan wasn't there, that her subconscious conjured the safest thing in her head and took her there to escape her captor and his sadistic past. She concentrated instead on the strong heartbeat under her ear, the scent of Dial filling her head.

"Baby?"

Vertigo whirled for a moment, and she clutched at his strong, warm arm, tensing as a cool breeze sailed across her skin, as if a door had opened, letting in fresh air. Unfamiliar sounds invaded her senses. A man shouted something she didn't catch, and she heard running feet and the spin of small rubberized wheels on pavement. A different voice, this one female, issued a command, but it also made no sense to her.

The floatiness ended abruptly, and she panicked as Logan's arms let her go. "No!" She screamed it in her head, but nothing came out.

"She's coming around," Logan said from somewhere above her. He sounded too far away, and she opened her eyes to seek him out, to beg him to come back.

"What's her name?" The woman again, and this time she was right in Alex's face, blocking her from finding Logan, and shining a bright light into her eyes.

Alex moaned at the stabbing pain from the light and tried to push it away. It hurt too much, made the pain in her head expand and pulse.

"Alex," Logan said, from even farther away. "Her name is Alex."

"Alex," the woman said, "can you hear me?"

She pushed again at the hand connected to that damn piercing light. "Stop."

"Do you know where you are, Alex?" the woman asked.

"Logan?" She couldn't see him, couldn't hear him, and panic started to set in. Was this another flash into her kidnapper's head? But, no, that didn't track. She wasn't Alex during those trips. She lifted her head and strained to see around the irritating woman asking her irritating questions. "Logan?"

Movement at her side distracted her, and a man, not Logan, wrapped something around her upper arm and started pumping it tight. She focused on him because she had no choice, because she already sensed the woman would be no help. He had kind eyes and a flop of curly blond hair on his forehead. "Where's Logan?" she asked him.

"Alex," the woman repeated, "I need to ask you a few questions. Just bear with me, okay?"

Alex gave one last, energetic push at the maddening penlight, managing to knock the woman back a step. And then, thank God, Logan was there. Without his shirt. Wow, what an impressive sight. All those defined muscles and that smooth, smooth skin.

She reached out and grabbed his arm so she wouldn't lose him again and felt him tense, felt him pull away, and thought, That was weird. But then he was leaning over her and smiling, his eyes shiny and bright, and his hand resting on her hair. She could have drowned in those eyes.

"Hey," he said, stroking her hair. "I missed you."

"I missed you, too." She expected him to kiss her then, to plant one on her that would wipe her brain clean and hit the "reset" button. When he didn't, fear began to creep in on her. Something was wrong. With her? With him?

"BP's one-seventeen over seventy-two. Pulse is sixty-five."

Alex turned her head, remembering the guy with the blood pressure cuff. That's when she realized she lay on a gurney and that the two harried people getting between her and Logan were paramedics. Alarm brought her to a sitting position. Thankfully, no one tried to force her to lie back down, though the woman did put a hand on her shoulder as if to brace her.

Alex shoved aside her first inclination—to ask, "What's going on?"—and went with her second. "I'm fine. I must have passed out for a little bit, but I'm fine now." She gave the woman, a redhead with a splash of freckles across her nose, what she hoped was a reassuring smile. "Thank you for checking me out, though."

"Alex—" Logan began, only to be cut off when Charlie arrived at the side of the gurney, frantic and white-faced. When she saw Alex sitting up and talking, her shoulders dropped and she heaved a sigh of relief.

"Jesus, Alex, what the hell? I thought we were going to find you in little pieces."

Alex managed an answering smile, even as it ran through her head that Charlie's quip landed disturbingly close to where Alex had expected to be about now. She had no idea why her captor took off, but it hardly mattered now. Logan had found her. She was safe.

Except . . . she had a vague recollection of things not seeming so good not too long ago. And, God, she was tired. Fatigue clung to her brain like damp cotton candy, insidiously sticky and melting onto already foggy brain cells.

Determined to fight off the exhaustion, at least until she got free of the clinging do-good EMTs, she swung her legs over the side of the stretcher.

While the two paramedics and Logan protested, Alex pushed them back and hopped down. Her knees threatened to buckle, thanks to the surprising weakness in her legs, but she managed to stay upright by bracing a hand on the gurney's black vinyl pad.

"I'm fine," she said, and forced a smile even as a dizzying kaleidoscope of flashing red and yellow diamonds danced in front of her eyes.

"You need to get checked out at the ER," the female paramedic said.

"Really, I'm fine," Alex said. "Don't I look fine?" She regretted the question as soon as she said it, because four pairs of eyes said, "You look like fifteen-day-old leftovers not fit for a starving dog."

"I'm fine," she repeated, just to make it clear.

Logan started to protest again, but Noah chose that moment to join them, and when he saw Alex, his brows shot up. "Oh, hey, how you doing?" He couldn't hide his shock.

"I'm—"

"Fine," Logan cut in. "She wants to go home instead of the ER." Noah, his confident expression said, would be his reinforcements.

"You should definitely get checked," Noah agreed. "You were unconscious ten minutes ago. And those bruises—" He broke off then, his brows arching even higher as he peered closely at her face. "Oh." He cast a glance at Logan. "Must have been a trick of the light."

Logan didn't respond, the worried creases of his forehead seemingly permanent.

Relieved that whatever bruises she'd sustained from Butch's past had already faded, Alex shot Charlie a help-me-out-here look. She *really* didn't want to go to the ER and endure a bunch of questions she had no idea how to answer. Not to mention all those people touching her, intending to help. All those potential nightmares . . .

But Charlie wasn't going to help. "You really do need to get checked out," she said with an apologetic shrug. "Maybe Logan can pull some cop strings with his friends at the ER. You know, get you in and out fast."

"The police are going to want to talk to you, too," Logan said.

"But—"

"Alex," Logan cut in, "You've been bleeding."

She cast Charlie a questioning look, and her sister gestured sympathetically at her own nose.

Alex tested the skin above her top lip, felt the caked blood. "Oh."

An expression of such intense concern crossed Charlie's features that Alex laid a hand on her sister's arm to reassure her. When Charlie stiffened, Alex realized what she'd done and snatched her hand back. A panicked "oh, shit" rang in her head.

But nothing happened. The world didn't fall away, the earth didn't tilt, and she didn't spiral headfirst into Charlie's latest trauma—finding out her sister had been kidnapped by a psychopath. She stayed firmly inside her own aching head.

Anxiety tightened Charlie's jaw. "First stop: ER. Then we're going to see AnnaCoreen."

CHAPTER **THIRTY-ONE**

It's gone," Alex said the instant AnnaCoreen opened her door.

Alex couldn't help the relieved laugh that sputtered out of her. Thank the Lord and all his angels, her super-duper Doppler 3000 empathy was gone! So was her headache, for that matter, vanished as if it had never existed. Her head felt light and airy, amazing. And not because she'd gotten drugs at the ER. There, all she'd gotten was a clean bill of health after a nurse checked her vitals and poked her for blood and a doctor shined another of those damn penlights in her eyes. They confirmed what she already knew: She was fine. Better than fine.

The worst part at the ER had been telling Detective Don Walker—a man she knew well from years of shooting news photos at the scenes of crimes and accidents—what had happened with Butch McGee. But she'd managed to numb up every raw nerve inside her and tell Don everything she could without sounding like a total whackjob. Luckily, she'd had an incredible adrenaline high to see her through it all.

And now, here they all were on AnnaCoreen's doorstep because worrywart Charlie insisted.

The poor psychic, wearing a pink satin and lace bathrobe and a sleepy expression, let her gaze travel first over Alex, then Charlie, then Noah, then Logan, then back to Alex.

"See? We woke her up," Alex said, shooting Charlie an I-told-you-so glance that probably appeared crazed, considering how she hadn't been able to stop smiling her ass off since they'd left the ER. She was free. Free!

"It is three in the morning," AnnaCoreen said in a sleep-roughened voice and blinked a couple of times against the brightness of the porch light.

"We're so sorry," Charlie said. "But I didn't know what else to do. Something odd is happening with Alex's empathy."

Alex laughed again and said, "It's gone. Check it out." She placed her palm flat against AnnaCoreen's forearm, just below the lacy short sleeve of her bathrobe. She glanced from one woman to the other and back again and started to grin even more. "Nothing. Not one little thing. I had a nurse all over me at the ER, and a doctor, and nothing, nada, zip."

Charlie exchanged a concerned look with AnnaCoreen. "Is that even possible?" Charlie asked.

The disorientation from a doorbell dragging her from a sound sleep began to clear from AnnaCoreen's eyes, and she stepped back. "You'd better come in. I'll get dressed."

"Are you sure?" Alex asked, hesitating after Charlie had already stepped into the kitchen. "We could come back tomorrow or the next day. There's no emergency here. I mean, look at me."

As she smiled to prove it, she wondered if she'd showed too many teeth, because neither AnnaCoreen nor Charlie appeared amused or happy.

Noah gave her a nudge at the small of her back, giving

her no choice but to join Charlie in AnnaCoreen's dimly lit kitchen.

As AnnaCoreen padded barefoot through the kitchen to the door that led to the living room and the bedrooms, she said, "Make yourselves at home. I'll be right back."

Alex shrugged and glanced at Logan. "Personally, I think we shouldn't have bugged her."

Charlie hit a light switch, and Noah got busy with the coffeepot. As Charlie opened a cabinet to retrieve coffee cups and Noah started scooping copious amounts of ground coffee into a filter, Alex turned to Logan, who lingered in the doorway, and smiled. "Hey."

His answering smile didn't erase the concern from his eyes. "Hey."

She went to him, snaked her arms around his waist and leaned into him, tipping her head back so she could nip at his chin. She ran her hands up under his shirt in the back, reveling in the feel of his smooth, clean skin against her fingers and palms. She'd never take this ability to touch, to caress, for granted again. "Kiss me?"

His eyes darkened with awareness of her, and relief helped chase some of the mounting fatigue from her muscles.

He granted her request, and as his warm, moist lips touched hers, she sighed and let her eyes slip closed. Like this, with him, nothing mattered but the moment. And as the heat shot through her, she pressed against him, her fingers in his hair and her heart pounding against his. If they had been alone, she would have wrapped her legs tight around his waist and ground herself against the part of him she desperately wanted inside her. She hadn't thought she'd ever get to do this again, touch him, kiss him, love him. She wanted to revel in it.

But Logan murmured something against her lips, and his hands grasped her arms as he urged her back from him.

She stared up into his face in surprise. "What?" she asked.

"You're scaring me a little right now," he said softly, as though he didn't want Charlie and Noah to overhear.

"What? How? Why?"

"You're a little . . . manic."

"Manic? No. Are you kidding? That's crazy. I'm fine. Don't I seem fine?"

When his eyes widened at the rapid-fire response, she started to laugh, only vaguely aware of how Noah and Charlie had turned to watch them.

"Okay, yeah," Alex said, nodding, "I am a little wired at the moment. A lot wired, actually. But you know what? I'm just psyched, you know? A lot happened tonight and I survived, and the best freaking part of all is that whatever that psycho did to me *cured* me. Isn't that wild? All those god-awful forays into his ghastly past, and now I'm all better. He's the most screwed-up nutjob on the planet, but do I care? No freaking way. He freed me." She whirled toward her sister. "Hey, Charlie, we should set you up with this guy. A couple of hours of his kind of shock therapy, and you'll be giddy, too."

Charlie stared at her without saying anything, her complexion a pasty white.

"What?" Alex asked, spreading her hands in front of her and looking from Charlie to Noah to Logan. "You guys, come on. Stop looking at me like that. I'm fine. Great. Fantastic. Really."

About then, a wave of dizziness smacked her in the forehead like she'd run head first into a steel girder. She staggered back against Logan, plastering her palm against her forehead to keep her brain from finding a way out of her skull. "Whoa," she said in a soft, dazed voice.

Logan caught her against him. "Alex?"

A serious case of vertigo turned the world sideways, and she saw Charlie take a lurching step toward her before the lights winked out.

Logan caught Alex as she sagged and swept her up in

his arms. For the second time tonight, he cradled her, limp and still, against his chest. He cast a helpless, questioning look at Charlie, but she shook her head and covered her mouth with a trembling hand.

AnnaCoreen stopped in the kitchen doorway. "Oh, dear," she said when she saw Alex's unconscious form.

"She passed out," Logan said unnecessarily.

"Yes, let's get her into bed then."

The older woman gestured for him to follow her down a short hallway to a guest bedroom that smelled of lavender and vanilla. She pulled the covers back on the double bed and fluffed the pillows before stepping back so Logan could deposit his cargo.

"Get her shoes," AnnaCoreen said as she rested her hip on the side of the bed and set her palm against Alex's forehead as though checking for a fever.

Logan pulled Alex's shoes off and dropped them on the floor, his attention on everything AnnaCoreen did, his heart beating in an uneven staccato. The doctor had said he found no evidence of a head injury, or *any* injuries. Still, Logan didn't like the uncertainty, didn't like seeing Alex, normally so alive and sparking with energy, lying so incredibly still.

The older woman lifted Alex's right wrist and held it lightly to check her pulse. After about a minute, AnnaCoreen sighed. "She's sleeping." She sent him a soft smile. "The adrenaline ran its course."

"Is that why she was so manic just now? Adrenaline?"

AnnaCoreen nodded as she rose, gesturing toward the door to indicate they should take their conversation out into the hall so as not to disturb Alex.

Once she'd closed the guest-room door, AnnaCoreen said, "Alex has experienced something truly horrific, Logan. She doesn't know how to cope with it."

"Is it because of the . . . you know, empathy?"

Her blue eyes narrowed before regaining their serenity. "You still don't believe."

He sidestepped that issue. How could he *not* believe? Yet . . . damn it, he didn't *want* to. It would change everything between him and Alex. "She said it was gone, that she was cured. And she was touching all of us, and nothing happened."

"It's more likely that her ability somehow ran its course after many hours of intensity. Her body's own safety mechanisms kicked in to protect her from further harm."

"But Charlie needs drugs to . . . what? To"—he floundered for the right words—"to snap her out of the . . . flash stuff."

"Perhaps if Charlie's flash fatigue were allowed to run its course unaided, her own safety mechanisms would also kick in. Or it's possible that the differences in Alex's empathy extend to flash fatigue, as well."

"So you're saying you don't know what the hell is happening and it's all a big fat guessing game for you."

AnnaCoreen's lips tightened. "I can appreciate your skepticism, young man, but I don't imagine it's going to be useful for Alex. I fear your negative energy is going to have a very adverse effect."

Logan stared at her in disbelief. Young man? Negative energy? What the hell dimension was he in?

Apparently done with him, AnnaCoreen started to walk by him, but he grasped her arm to stop her, forcing gentleness into his grip, and started to ask the question foremost in his brain.

Before he could form it, AnnaCoreen's features softened, and she gave his arm a maternal pat. "Alex is going to be fine once she's had a good night's sleep."

CHAPTER **THIRTY-TWO**

Butch lingered in the frozen-food aisle at Lake Avalon's twenty-four-hour Publix grocery store. He'd picked up a new rental car, a Ford Fusion—sangria red and quite peppy, though certainly no Mustang—then driven to the store to get dinner to take back to his new hotel room. He roamed the aisles for an hour, restless and hungry and not interested in any of the offerings, not even the fresh shrimp and king crab legs.

All he could think about was Alex Trudeau. He'd so anticipated some quality time with her. And felt massively cheated.

"Excuse me."

He jolted and stepped aside as a woman in a pink linen dress and pearls reached past him to open the freezer door. The scent of gardenias washed over him. Oh, how he adored women who smelled like flowers.

She dropped her newly scored pint of Ben & Jerry's Chunky Monkey into her cart, then consulted a list jotted on a crumpled yellow Post-it Note.

So very pretty. She had exaggerated curves that some

might call buxom or hippy. Butch called them perfect, just like the rest of her. Straight light brown hair that brushed her shoulders. Milk white skin pinkened by the sun. Delicate hands with chewed-short fingernails.

No rings.

She glanced at him over the black rims of her trendy rectangular eyeglasses, and his heart gave an excited bump. Brown eyes. He *loved* brown eyes. Especially ones as deep and dark as hers. Alex Trudeau had brown eyes like that. But, no, this wasn't about her. This was about this Chunky Monkey–loving woman who shopped for groceries alone late at night.

He grinned at her, cranking up the goofy-guy charm. "Maybe you can help me decide," he said. "Chubby Hubby or Chocolate Fudge Brownie?"

CHAPTER **THIRTY-THREE**

When Logan returned to the kitchen, he found Charlie and Noah hunched over cups drained of coffee, talking in low voices, their hands clasped between them. He paused in the doorway before they noticed him and admired their deep connection. Their intimacy made him ache for what he and Alex had had so briefly before all hell broke loose. So much more than lovers, they were friends on a level that some people never knew.

We'll get it back, he thought. There's no other option.

In the meantime, he needed to think like a cop, not like a worried, pissed-off lover.

Charlie and Noah looked up as he entered, and he answered the questions on their faces. "She's okay."

His voice broke on the last word. Well, shit. Alex was okay, or "fine" in her words, but he wasn't the least bit fine. He felt wrung out and raw, yet so relieved that tremors shook his knees.

Charlie rose and pointed at the chair she'd left. "Sit. I'll pour you some coffee."

Logan obeyed, resting his elbows on the table and

scrubbing his hands over his face. Alex had been missing for hours, yet it seemed like days.

He told himself to focus on the fact that they had found her, that she slept, peaceful and relaxed, in the next room. He itched to go back to her, to stay close in case she needed anything, but he also knew he needed to do something more productive than sigh with relief. Her kidnapper was still out there. And Logan had a score to settle with that fucker.

"AnnaCoreen went back to bed," Charlie said as she set a cup in front of him. "She said we should wake her if there's a change or we need anything."

Logan nodded as he stared down at the steaming coffee.

"Who is this guy?" Noah asked.

Logan rubbed at his eyes. He'd already answered these questions for Don Walker. "I don't know. Alex gave his name as Butch McGee. I don't recognize that name at all, but he said I took his brother away from him."

"Assuming he's from Detroit," Noah said, "I don't suppose anyone stands out from your days there. Someone who made a threat?"

Logan grunted under his breath. "Get a pen and a note pad, the legal length. I'm a damn cop. How many people did you tick off before you left the Chicago PD?"

"Good point," Noah said.

Logan drummed his fingers on the table, an anxiety-driven gesture he couldn't quell. Better than punching walls. "Alex gave Don a fairly generic description, but nothing she said rang a bell. I got the sense she was on autopilot at the time, so I'll ask her again when she's feeling better, see if I can get more specifics out of her."

"We don't have to wait for her," Charlie said. "I could—"

"No," Noah cut in, his hand clamping hard enough around hers that she winced. "Absolutely no way in hell are you going to try to flash on what happened to her so you can see what the guy looks like."

Her eyes narrowed, and she and Noah had a long conversation that involved only the intensity of their gazes. Finally, Noah sighed. "At least not until we know more about what happened to her," he added.

"We have other ways to get a picture of this guy," Logan said, annoyed that these two acted as though turbocharged empathy wouldn't blow a normal person's mind. Or that it was a newfangled, legit way to solve a crime. "How about some good old-fashioned detective work?"

Noah shrugged one shoulder and cocked his head at the same time, as though acknowledging that he'd gotten carried away on the superpowers. "The Mustang was rented at Hertz. I suggested to Don that he have his team check their security cameras. They were already checking the cameras at the storage facility."

"Good," Logan said. "Don's a good cop. He'll do what needs to be done."

"So you're not working the case?" Charlie asked.

Logan blew out a breath. "My lieutenant already yanked me off. Conflict of interest, he said, and ordered me to take a few days off."

"Not that that will keep you out of it," Noah said.

"Nope. And the boss knows that. But the illusion of being off-duty will free me up to do whatever needs to be done to find Butch McGee fast."

"Meanwhile," Charlie said, "what are we going to do to ensure the evil bastard doesn't get at my sister again?"

Logan clamped his teeth tightly together until he could trust his voice not to fail him. "I'll take care of that."

CHAPTER **THIRTY-FOUR**

Goofy-guy charm, Butch thought, was so underestimated. Seducing Sally Blake, middle-school math teacher by day and sad, lonely woman with no social life by night, had been almost pathetically easy. She'd abandoned her grocery cart, and they'd gone to the faux Starbucks next to the grocery store. Over caramel macchiatos and chocolate-chip scones, they'd traded jokes about Florida's seniors, whom they affectionately called "cotton tops." He'd told her how he referred to short elderly female drivers as "knuckles," because all you could see of them when driving behind them was their hands clamped around the steering wheel. She'd laughed so hard that tears had streamed down her pink cheeks, and Butch had flushed with anticipation.

When only crumbs, crumpled napkins and paper cups holding the dregs of their coffee remained between them, she'd shyly invited him to her place "for a nightcap." She'd even offered to drive, leaving his rental in the parking lot of the open-all-night store only six blocks from her modest ranch house in a quiet Lake Avalon neighborhood. Perfect.

And now he sat on the edge of her bed, gently stroking

her supple, bare thigh, waiting for her to wake from the light sedative he'd administered right after he'd shocked her. A tingle arced through him at the memory of how her head had snapped back against his shoulder when he'd walked up behind her and zapped her in the small of the back. As she'd writhed at his feet, he'd picked up one of the wineglasses she'd poured and taken a sip of an oaky chardonnay from Napa Valley.

Life was good again.

He knew the routine once she awoke. She'd hate the restraints, beseech him with terror-drenched eyes to release her, to ungag her and let her beg for her life. He would, too. He liked begging. He liked giving them hope, then snatching it away. At times like these, *he* was in charge of hope and who got to have it and who didn't. *Him*. That felt good. Powerful. Someday, soon, he'd make Alex Trudeau beg. He'd make her beg harder than the others, because she'd denied him once already. Until then, he had Sally.

He finished the glass of wine and poured another from the bottle he'd carried into the bedroom after getting her ready. The sweat he'd worked up stripping and tying her cooled under the spin of the ceiling fan. His heart thumped fast and light in his chest. Anticipation of the moment when her pretty brown, Alex-like eyes opened and saw him for who he really was. Not a goofy, harmless guy after all. That moment of stunned recognition would be all it took to get him hard.

He had to wait thirty, fairly pleasant, minutes, thanks to the buzz from the wine. It didn't hurt that she had such pretty curves. Plump breasts that flattened and spread because of her reclining position; the nipples, surrounded by dusty rose areolas, pointed upward in the cool draft from the fan. Her hips flared out from her waist, and she had a sweet little pooch of a belly, the skin soft and silky.

Her breathing changed, and her eyes opened. She blinked a couple of times, disoriented. The muscles in her arms flexed as she tried to shift position, and when they met resistance, she popped her eyes open wide and hitched in a startled breath.

"Hello, Sally," Butch said softly.

Her head jerked toward him, and she made a sound deep in her throat, muted by the clean white-linen dish towel he'd found in the kitchen and used as a gag.

He smiled at her, hoping his affection showed in his expression. She was so perfect, so vulnerable, so . . . female.

His breathing deepened along with hers, and smiling still, his heart rate picking up, because this was it, this was his moment, he rose and began to undress. He took his time, folding his clothes and setting them on the seat of the arm chair by the bed.   ·

"You're so beautiful," he murmured to her. "So very pretty. That's why I picked you. Because you're perfect."

Her head thrashed from side to side, and she yanked violently at her restraints, her eyes wild with terror. The power he had over her surged through him, and by the time he finished undressing, he had to stop to take a few deep, calm breaths to slow the throb of blood between his legs. Don't rush it, take your time, enjoy the moment.

He paused to wish he'd stuck to his routine with Alex. The thought of standing beside her like this, while she struggled, fear of him evident in every breath, only made him harder, and he stroked himself to ease some of the urgency. He had other plans for her, he reminded himself, plans that involved John Logan. Those plans would yield double the satisfaction.

This, with Sally, would merely take the edge off.

Sighing, smiling, he reached for the sheathed Bowie hunting knife he'd set on the bedside table. The knife had a seven-inch blade and hardwood handle worn from years of use. The well-used implement of an artist.

He sat on the edge of the bed next to Sally and, swallowing hard, removed the gag from her mouth. "You can beg now, Sally."

As the pleas began to pour from her mouth, he straddled her—reveling in the heaving of her breasts, the long white column of her throat, the dark fear in her brown eyes—and positioned the knife in just the right spot, that soft, sweet spot above her belly button.

"No," she sobbed, tears rolling back into her hair. "No, please, no."

She convulsed wildly at the first shallow cut, her head arching back and a raw scream washing over his skin, like a woman in the midst of an intense orgasm. As he watched the blood well around the tip of the blade, a shuddering moan parted his lips.

Yes.

CHAPTER **THIRTY-FIVE**

Alex woke to darkness and panic. She was back in the storage unit, and Butch McGee hovered over her, taunting her by wriggling his fingers an inch above her exposed skin. What horror do you want to experience this time, my little pretty?

"It's okay, Alex." Logan's voice came from her right as he moved from the chair in the corner to sit on the side of the bed. "You're safe."

His hand slid down her arm until his fingers met and threaded with hers. She didn't think to tense until it was too late, and then . . . nothing. No foray into Logan's harrowing moments when he'd found her, tied and unconscious, in that storage unit.

Maybe it really was gone. Oh, God, please, please, please.

"How do you feel?" he asked, his voice soft in the dark.

"Fine."

"Alex."

"No, really. I mean, I'm tired, but that's it. No, wait. I'm hungry." She pushed up with her elbows. "Starving, actually."

He reached over and turned on the bedside lamp. Alex blinked and shielded her eyes until they adjusted to the brightness. The light hit his face from below, casting his eyes in deep, hollowed shadows, his expression beyond grim.

"I'm sorry," he whispered, leaning forward to rest his forehead against hers. "I'm so sorry."

She wasn't sure what he was apologizing for. Their fight yesterday morning about her empathy? More likely he was sorry that the man who'd kidnapped her had a vendetta against him, as though it was his fault he'd done his job and bad people didn't like it.

She stroked her palm over the stubble on his cheek, struck that he was shaking, and kissed him. His tongue tangled with hers, and the soft, reassuring embrace quickly turned desperate and seeking. She moaned, gasping when his warm, urgent fingers slid under her tank top and grazed the sensitive skin of her waist.

But then he backed off, his breath brushing her mouth. "You need more sleep," he murmured.

"I need you." She grasped his cheeks and kissed him again, openmouthed and wet, desperate to erase the horrors of the storage unit, desperate to get lost in the touch of this man.

She shifted to her knees, reaching for the hem of his T-shirt and eager to get him out of it, eager to remind herself of the good things, good *people*, in the world. She had one of the best right here with her, *the* best.

But, damn it, if he wasn't going to go all noble on her and set her back from him, albeit with a shaky breath that hinted at his own rampant need.

"If not sleep, then food," he said.

"I need this, Logan. With you."

But he stopped her before she could get his shirt off, his hands on her arms holding her still. "Later," he said. "I promise. First, you need to eat."

Disappointed but appreciating his concern, she nipped his nose and then his chin. "Fine, go ahead and feed me. But I won't let you forget your promise. And it's going to require a little extra on your part to make up for making me wait."

He grinned, finally, and it set everything right in the world. "Count on it. So how about you get some more rest while I go raid AnnaCoreen's kitchen?"

She nodded, smiling against his lips as he kissed her fast and hard before getting up from the bed. He left her alone with one last smile.

Instead of settling back down and doing as he'd asked— she doubted he'd be surprised—she went into the guest bathroom and took a long, hot shower. She shampooed her hair three times and lathered up with shower gel twice. Her captor hadn't done anything more than make contact a few times, but her forays into his head had left her feeling dirty and abused. She couldn't prevent the twinge of sympathy for the tormented child her kidnapper had been.

Pushing aside the memories . . . *his* memories . . . she finished the shower and, wrapped in a towel, walked back into the bedroom. The dread of putting her filthy clothes back on faded when she spotted her camera bag and red duffle resting by the door.

"Thank you, Charlie," she murmured, realizing her sister had made a special trip to Alex's house and back to bring her clean clothes and her lifeline: her camera.

The sun was coming up as she made her way to the kitchen, where she could hear the low voices of two men and the occasional scrape of a plastic spatula against a skillet. She expected to find Logan and Noah in conversation, but when she walked in, she saw a man she didn't know seated at the table with a cup of coffee in front of him. He had the salt-and-pepper hair and lined face of a man in his early sixties. Handsome, too, in a sun-worn, weather-beaten, hard-living way.

"Oh, hi," she said, casting a curious glance at Logan. He deposited an omelet onto a plate, then indicated the guy at the table with the spatula.

"This is Richie Woods," Logan said. "A friend of AnnaCoreen's."

A *friend* with sleep-flattened hair and wearing pj's. Smiling, Alex reached for the hand he offered.

"Nice to meet you," he said in a deep, gravelly drawl.

His warm, callused fingers had just closed over hers when AnnaCoreen walked in.

"No!" the older woman shouted. The teacup in her hand dropped to the floor and exploded into pieces.

Alex jerked back from Richie, shocked at the fierce expression on AnnaCoreen's usually tranquil face. The woman stared at her, white-faced and panicked, and Alex stared back. What the hell?

Richie broke the stunned silence and rose. "You okay, AnnaCo?"

Alex glanced away from AnnaCoreen when Richie rose, just awkwardly enough to suggest arthritis in his hips or knees. She saw the real reason when he stepped from behind the table and walked over to rub a soothing palm over AnnaCoreen's back.

Beneath his Bermuda shorts he wore a prosthetic leg from just below the knee down.

Alex closed her fingers over the back of the closest chair and held on as the muscles in her legs became the consistency of a stick of butter left on the counter on a warm day. A person wouldn't have to touch Richie Woods to know his worst nightmare.

She swallowed hard against the nausea as she wondered what it might have been like to touch this man before her empathy had vanished. Experiencing what caused such a severe injury . . . She couldn't even think about it. But, worse: What would her empathic stigmata have done about that missing limb?

She looked at AnnaCoreen and got why the woman had fumbled her tea and gone so deathly pale. The truth sucker punched her in the gut, and she gripped the chair harder. "You don't think it's really gone, do you?"

AnnaCoreen's brow wrinkled with sympathetic pain, and it took visible effort for her to straighten her shoulders and raise her chin. "Don't mind me, dear. I obviously over-reacted. You're perfectly fine, are you not?"

Alex watched the other woman's face. Funny that a beach psychic had such a tough time telling a convincing lie.

Logan set an omelet-covered plate on the table along with a glass of orange juice. "Sit and eat," he said gently.

As Richie knelt to start picking up the pieces of broken ceramic, AnnaCoreen stepped carefully over the mess and took Alex's elbow. "Logan is right, dear. You need to refuel. We'll take care of my silly accident."

Alex did as she was told, her movements robotic. She took a bite of eggs and chewed and watched AnnaCoreen help Richie clean up the mess on the floor. She didn't look at Logan, afraid that seeing his concern would turn her into a blubbering mess. After the broken cup had been discarded and the patch of floor mopped up, AnnaCoreen and Richie left them alone.

Logan nodded at her plate, silently urging her to eat.

"It's good," she told him, though she couldn't taste a thing. Her heart beat in her ears. She wanted to talk to AnnaCoreen. Yet she didn't want to know what the woman thought about her empathic future . . . ignorance and all that.

She reached out and grasped Logan's hand, closing her eyes when nothing happened except the familiar jolt of pleasure that came with touching him. She felt an almost desperate need to caress and stroke as much of him as she could in case her empathy-free time had a deadline, before fear of what might happen to her made it impossible to reach out.

Logan's free hand covered hers. "Your hands are like ice."

She reveled in his warmth. This was all she'd ever wanted, and if—when—her empathy came back, could Logan live with it? Could *she*?

It didn't take a genius to notice that he hadn't asked her about the empathy. He seemed perfectly fine with pretending it didn't exist. After everything that had happened, what did that say about their relationship that he couldn't even acknowledge something that was so much a part of her?

When she felt herself start to tremble, she drew away from him, aching from the thought of ever losing him, yet not wanting him to know how scared she was. She had to focus on forcing herself to eat.

"Did Charlie and Noah go home?" she asked, trying to make normal conversation.

"They went over to your place to feed and walk the dogs. Charlie brought back some stuff for you while you were in the shower."

Alex nodded, grateful all over again. "Yep, I got it."

"She's been running interference with the media. Guess they were camped out in your driveway, looking for interviews. She also said she would let Mac know you're not coming into work for a few days."

Alex started to protest, but Logan gave her a look that said, "You won't win this one, so don't bother."

She didn't have the energy to argue anyway, which meant she *really* didn't have the energy to haul around her camera equipment and deal with all the activity that accompanied photo shoots, so perhaps it was best.

Logan smiled, as though pleased she let that one go. "Charlie wants you to call her as soon as possible." Then he paused, and she sensed he was preparing to move on to a difficult topic.

He looked straight at her. "We need to talk about . . .

what happened. I know you talked to Don at the ER, but you weren't completely . . . with it at the time."

"Can we do that later? I . . . just want to . . ." She trailed off as she stirred her fork through a pool of melted cheddar that oozed out of the omelet. She didn't know what she wanted to do. Pretend that everything would be okay and life would return to normal.

"Butch McGee is still out there, Alex. We need to do everything we can to find him quickly."

Sighing, she put down her fork and pushed back the plate of half-eaten eggs. He wasn't going to let it go, so why put it off? "What do you want to know?"

"We've got his name and description, which matches the one your neighbor Rose Brown gave."

Alex angled her head, wondering if she'd somehow lost memories. "Who?"

"Clarence's mom. She saw Butch with you. He told her he was taking you to the ER because you'd fainted."

"Oh. Sure. I don't think I ever knew that was her name. She looks more like a Cathy."

"Is there anything more about McGee that you might have thought of after talking to Don?"

She pictured her captor while she stared at the corner of the napkin she folded and refolded, unable to hold back the shudder that coursed through her. The details she'd shared last night had been the usual. Height. Build. Hair color and length. Eye color. No visible scars or tattoos. She'd told the detective nothing of what she'd experienced in her flashes into Butch's frightening past, too fragile yet to go there. And leery of the inevitable skepticism. Maybe no one ever had to know about any of that.

But she knew she needed to provide Logan with as many clues to McGee's identity as possible. "His real name is Tyler Ambrose."

Logan's brows arched in disbelief. "He told you that?"

She moved on without answering that question. She didn't think he was ready to hear the truth—and maybe he wouldn't believe it anyway. "I think his brother's name is Brian."

Logan scooted his chair back almost violently and stood. "That's it," he said, the first hint of emotion in his tone. "I've killed only one man in my life. In Detroit, in the line of duty. Brian Lear. He and Butch don't have the same last name, which is odd, but they could have the same mother and different fathers."

He pulled his cell phone out and started punching numbers. "I have a friend in the Detroit PD. Phil Packard. I'm going to ask him to check Butch out for us."

As he pressed the phone to his ear, he turned and smiled at her. "This is good, Alex. You did really good."

She sat back, her shoulders drooping as exhaustion invaded every cell all over again. But, thank God, Logan now knew who Butch was. It didn't matter how she knew the details she'd just shared. They helped.

Logan covered the mouthpiece, apparently not having gotten an answer yet. "Why don't you go lie down again? I'll take care of this while you get some more sleep. Later, we can move to Charlie's house. She suggested we stay there until this blows over."

"What about the dogs?"

"We'll figure something—" He broke off and turned away. While he talked into the phone in a low voice, Alex rose. She wanted to go to him and touch him again, wanted to lean against his back, her ear pressed to the beat of his heart. She wanted him to take her to bed and make love to her one more time . . . in case everything fell apart on her again.

Watching him for a few moments, she wished he'd glance over his shoulder at her and smile, maybe even blow a kiss. Something that told her he was the same Logan she'd fallen for . . . and he believed she was the same Alex. That's all she really needed right now, some assurance that her psychic ability wouldn't cost her the one thing in her life she feared she couldn't live without.

But he kept talking, seemingly no longer aware of her presence.

CHAPTER **THIRTY-SIX**

A full thirty hours after flirting over Ben & Jerry's, Butch McGee let himself out through the back door of Sally Blake's house on the southern edge of Lake Avalon. Morning humidity thickened the air, and pine needles crunched underfoot as he strolled through her backyard and the lightly forested area behind her house. It would take him about five minutes to walk back to the Ford Fusion parked at Publix.

He should have felt rejuvenated, should have had a damn skip in his step after so long with Sally. But melancholy hooked its claws in him and wouldn't let go. While Sally had been fun, beautiful in that pitiful, begging kind of way he loved, she was no Alex Trudeau.

He thought again about Alex's desperate plea for Brian to run. The way she'd said it, screamed it, had sounded so familiar, and the echoes of her shout dovetailed with his own memories of that moment when he'd frantically yelled those same words. Alex's body had convulsed almost immediately, as a seizure had claimed her, and yet the jolting movements had reminded him of his own violent loss of control after contact with the business end of the dick-head's stun gun.

What happened to her Brian? What happened in her head that caused that seizure, so like the result of an electric shock? What about it made him feel so connected to her, as if they'd somehow climaxed together in the most intimate way?

He thought of her eyes, open but blind, such a deep, dark brown, and his curiosity spiked anew about where she went in those moments when she tensed with terror at his touch and her life force more or less faded away. Unlike any woman he'd ever known. Yet, he hadn't gotten the chance to explore this fascinating new aspect of his work. A woman who didn't plead. Who somehow left her body before he could transform its canvas into a work of art.

Their business was unfinished. He felt unfulfilled. Cheated.

Sally was supposed to have taken care of that, taken the edge off, with her warm, safe place inside; her thick, welling blood; and her desperate pleas that devolved into hopeless whimpers. Her kind of fear used to make him stronger. Used to make him smile. Used to make him come.

But Alex Trudeau hadn't pleaded. She hadn't wept. She'd gone still and silent. Eerily so. He realized now that their moments together had been so much more incredibly intimate—satisfying—than his moments with Sally . . . and even all the others. He hadn't appreciated that at the time, too annoyed that Alex hadn't played her role the way she was supposed to, the way every woman before her had, as though they knew the script and followed it to the letter.

Shriek here.

Writhe here.

Bleed here.

Die here.

Alex Trudeau was different.

How would she respond once he actually settled down to

create? He imagined the challenge of working her, manipulating her, until he received the response he desired. How much would she take? How long could she stay out of her body until his skill with a blade brought her screaming back?

The anticipation of exploring her limits had him hardening already, as though Sally Blake had served no purpose at all.

A waste of time, of talent. He'd had the perfect canvas with Alex Trudeau, and he'd walked away. It was a good thing he had, of course, because he might have gotten caught if he hadn't lost patience, but next time he would know better. Next time he would appreciate the challenge before him. Next time he would stick around until he had what he wanted, what he needed.

And then, once he understood how to control her, how to make her scream to be forever his, he'd invite John Logan to watch him create a masterpiece.

CHAPTER **THIRTY-SEVEN**

Alex rolled over and opened her eyes. She froze with fear for a second before remembering where she was. Charlie's guest room, safe. And she wasn't alone. Logan had tucked her in, then said he'd be only a shout away if she needed him. She'd asked him to stay with her, but he'd insisted she needed sleep more than she needed him. She hadn't agreed, desperate to connect with him, to somehow excise the part of herself that her kidnapper's tortured past had tainted. But she'd let him go. He had calls to make, people to talk to about Butch McGee.

Alex got out of bed and stopped in the adjoining guest bathroom to wash her face. The clock on the vanity read ten thirteen A.M. She'd slept away an entire day, and while the leftover bleariness of such a deep sleep made her fuzzy, she felt better on a physical level. Now, if only she could rid herself of the overwhelming dread that sat like a rock in the pit of her stomach.

The house was quiet, and she figured Charlie and Noah both had already left for work. She found Logan snoring on the sofa, his cell phone on the coffee table and a notepad resting on his flat belly, the pen still gripped in his fingers. She eased both away from him and put them on the coffee table, then sat on the edge of the sofa and listened to him breathe, deep and slow and even. God, he was beautiful, all chiseled edges and honed muscles.

Her fingers trembled some as she reached out to trail their tips over the razor stubble of his chin, barely making contact with his warm skin. She couldn't stand the thought of losing the luxury of touching him, caressing him.

With eyes closed, she concentrated on the man-rough texture of his unshaven cheeks, the smooth glide over his temple, the fine sandpaper of his jaw. He swallowed, and she paused with her thumb resting lightly against the rise and fall of his Adam's apple.

The entire time, she stayed in her own head. Either the empathy hadn't returned or the statute of limitations had lapsed on the energy generated by his horror at finding her in the storage facility.

His fingers clasped hers, and she opened her eyes to see him watching her, his dark gaze sleepy and warm as he kissed her fingertips, her palm. A slow smile stole across his lips as he slid his palm up the sensitive skin on the inside of her forearm, a light, feathery massage that stopped her breath.

They said nothing as he curled his hand around the back of her neck and urged her down. Their lips met, tentative at first, sweet and soft, gently exploring, then growing in intensity and need, until their tongues danced and hands began to roam.

She loved how his breath caught as she ran her hands up under his shirt and thumbed his nipples, loved the feel of his naked chest under her hands, loved the hot silky skin that sheathed hard muscle and bone, loved the thud of his heart against her palms.

Sitting up, he cupped her face in his big hands and kissed her, hot and deep and wet, until her breath grew choppy and short. He moved one hand into her hair and drew her head back so he could spread kisses down her chin and over her neck to the hollow of her throat. His other hand cupped her breast through her T-shirt, his thumb moving back and forth over its tip until her nipple pebbled and he could work it more intensely. At her first moan, low and rough with need, he stopped and pulled back from her.

She chased his mouth with hers. "Don't stop," she whispered.

But he did stop and started getting up. What was he doing? Didn't he know she needed this? Needed the connection. In desperate, haunting ways she never had needed before.

He stood, and she prevented him from moving away by hooking her fingers in the waistband of his shorts. He stilled, holding his breath as she worked the button free, her hands brushing against the hard bulge molded against fabric. He was as excited as she was, and he was going to walk away? She didn't think so.

Smoothing a firm hand over the front of his shorts, she found and shaped him with her fingers, pressing and releasing, pressing and releasing in time to the growing throb between her own legs. When he dropped his head back and groaned her name, she worked his zipper down and wriggled her fingers inside. His velvety skin was searing against her cool hand, and she listened to his breathing go shallow and fast as she gripped him and stroked. A shudder shook him, and he leaned forward a little, bracing against her, as though his knees had weakened.

Smiling, loving the effect she had on him, she withdrew her fingers just as his hands slid into her hair on either side of her head. He bent down and kissed her, his tongue meeting hers in a dance that grew more and more frenzied. As they kissed, teeth clicking together, lips crushed, she tugged his shorts down. She pulled back, laughing softly at the way he chased her mouth, but she wanted to watch as she freed the part of him that curved upward in his desire for her.

Her heart thumped with lust and hunger and love at the stunning perfection of his erection, long and thick and veined, a drop of moisture gathering on the tip. She couldn't wait to get him inside her, but she wanted to make him crazy for her first.

He tried again to tug her up, to kiss her, but she held him back with one hand on his chest and focused on what she wanted. She slid from the edge of the sofa to her knees in front of him, trailing her palm down over the front of his shirt and across his rock-hard abs. He jerked in her hand as she stroked him, then peering up at him through her lashes, she slid him into her mouth and swirled her tongue around only his tip.

Her body clutched at its core, tightening in anticipation, pulsing with pleasure so acute it felt as if he touched her as intimately as she touched him.

His body tensed, and he locked his knees, his hands clutching in her hair, his dark gaze intent on hers the entire time she sucked and licked and took him, and herself, to the edge only to back off and soothe them both with soft, sweet kisses and little puffs of breath. When his knees started to tremble, he pulled out of her mouth with a wet pop and dragged her to her feet.

"I wasn't finished," she said with a pout, her own knees weak with need. She was sure that if he'd let her finish, she would have come just as hard as he was about to.

He answered with a growl and a soul-stealing kiss. And then he kicked away the shorts around his ankles and swept her up into his arms to carry her toward the bedroom.

"This is where I intended to take you before you decided to make plans of your own," he said gruffly.

She smiled, relieved to realize she'd misread him earlier.

He hadn't been putting a stop to their lovemaking. He'd merely wanted to move it to the bedroom. She looped her arms around his neck and kissed him as he walked, her fingers sifting through his soft hair and then massaging the spot behind his right ear that made him almost lose his footing.

In the bedroom, he bumped the door closed with his hip, then deposited her on the bed, coming to rest on top of her. She moved her legs apart to cradle him, arching off the mattress as his hardness nudged her through her clothing. She was wet and aching, a frustrated throb that demanded attention soon.

"You have way too many clothes on," he complained, and set about stripping them away.

They both froze when they heard his cell phone start to ring in the other room. "Ignore it," he said after the second ring, and they started to laugh as they got tangled up in the process of removing both their shirts at the same time. Being with him felt so right. Easy and fun and so, so good.

Then he was kissing her again, going deeper and wetter, his tongue stroking and exploring, his hand . . . oh, God, his hand tickling up her ribs and capturing an already erect nipple between two fingers. She gasped as he tweaked, let out a strangled cry as he did it again and again, chuckling against her mouth at her growing restlessness.

She groped for his erection, desperate to take him into her, feeling swollen inside with the intensity of her need.

"Slow down," he whispered against her throat. "If I can wait after what you just did to me, so can you."

She moaned her frustration, but then his fingers started a more intimate exploration, and she arched against his hand, her body tensing and gathering momentum. She was already there, already ready to come, and she held tight to him, her teeth against his shoulder as the wave rolled toward her, gathering strength and speed and height.

Then his fingers left her, and she dropped her head back

with a soft shriek of frustration. He laughed again, dark and low and promising. "Hang on, sweetie. I've got you."

Instead of taking the plunge and putting them both out of their misery, he kissed his way down her torso, stopping to softly kiss her scar before moving on to suck swollen nipples, then explore every inch of her quivering belly. If he didn't touch her where she wanted to be touched soon, she was going to implode. In fact, he spent so much time on her navel, nipping and kissing and fucking it with his tongue, that she slipped a hand between them and down to relieve the ache with her own hand.

But he caught her wrist before she could slide her fingers over herself and muttered something that sounded like "No, you don't," against her lower belly, and finally, finally, he slid his tongue over the right spot. Not firmly enough, though, and he only prolonged the moment, pushing her to the point that her muscles strained and trembled on the cusp of something truly seismic.

Payback was a bitch, and he paid her back for every time she'd brought him to the edge only to back off and gentle her with soft kisses and promises of next time.

The last time, she gained enough control of herself to shift position so she could palm his erection, finding him hotter and harder than before. How he could keep denying himself, and her, she had no idea. But he wasn't going to do it for much longer, that was for damn sure. She pumped her hand on him, using the moisture at his tip to create a nice, firm friction.

His breath hissed between his teeth, and his body stiffened. Grabbing her wrists, he trapped them above her head with one hand, then used his free hand to guide himself to her. She lifted her hips to get him there faster, nearly sobbing her relief when he eased inside her that first inch. He paused, sucking in a harsh breath.

"Don't move."

Her eyes just about rolled back in her head. Don't move? Don't *move*? She moved, shoving her hips up against him, groaning at the rocking pleasure as he finally filled her.

"Oh, God," she breathed against his ear, a tremor rolling through her at the intensity of the connection, the absolute rightness of it.

He shuddered as he lifted away from her, withdrawing almost completely, then sinking back into her at a maddeningly slow pace.

Her heart shuddered right along with him, and she tugged at her wrists until he released them. She grasped his firm butt and pulled him closer, deeper, locking her ankles at the small of his back and angling her hips up so he could sink in another inch.

"Jesus, Alex," he groaned into her ear. "You're so tight and hot."

A ripple of pleasure undulated through her, and he froze in the act of withdrawal, braced on his elbows. "Oh, Jesus," he said through his teeth. "Not yet, not yet. This is too good."

But she couldn't help it, his words, his warm, moist breath on her ear, his impossibly hard heat inside her, touching her more deeply than she'd ever been touched, and she was gone. The slow build, the ebb and flow, fast and slow, of the prolonged pleasure, exploded inside her with a power that shocked her.

He held her as she convulsed, not thrusting or otherwise moving, just holding her tight against him through the storm, and somehow, the lack of movement, the pressure of him still hard inside her only served to draw out the pleasure until she couldn't breathe, couldn't move, frozen in an explosion of orgasm that eclipsed the sun.

It took her a long time to come down, her heart thudding in her ears, her breath fast and shallow. When she finally arrived back inside her body, it was to the sensation of Logan kissing the moisture from her temples, his tongue pausing to play in the shell of her ear and then tug at her ear lobe. He kissed her, his lips soft and reverent and warm, his tongue gentle and caressing. As he trailed kisses over her cheek toward her ear, he asked, "Are you with me?"

She smiled. Oh, yeah, she was with him. She was *so* with him. Forever and always.

But then she realized that his words had a more immediate and tactile meaning as he shifted back from her ever so slightly. He'd ridden out her earth-shattering orgasm without letting himself go with her. He still filled her, more than before, judging from the pressure, so either he'd gotten harder while she'd gotten off, or she'd gotten tighter around him.

He breathed through his nose, slow and measured. "We're going to have to take this slow," he murmured.

She buried her face against his neck and hugged him, her heart overflowing with an emotion so overwhelming it tightened her throat. "I love you," she whispered.

His body stilled, and he drew his head back to look down at her. He looked stunned at first, then a slow smile spread over his lips, and his beautiful, beautiful starburst eyes gleamed. "I love you, too."

She smiled, then couldn't stop a shaky, ecstatic, *relieved* laugh. Everything would be fine. Logan loved her.

They began to move together slowly and reverently, their breathing and heartbeats synchronized, and Alex felt the impossible pleasure build all over again. Inside and out, like nothing she'd ever felt before, as though they were one body, feeling the same joy in the same way. When his thrusts grew short and less rhythmic, she held on to him, hitting another high note just moments before he stiffened and began jerking against her with a long, harsh groan.

Amazingly, everything inside her tensed yet again, and as he calmed down, already softening inside her, she shot up and over on a wave higher and more intense than any before. She felt as if she'd just turned inside out and the most sensitive, most vulnerable part of her was clamped in rippling, wet, silken heat. Pleasure gushed in a hot, volcanic rush that went on and on. She had no control over her body, no control over her mind as the world narrowed down to intense, rocketing, mind-wiping pleasure.

When she came back to herself, Logan had collapsed beside her. He drew her against him and snuggled his nose into her hair, his hand sliding up and down in the perspiration on her back, while she fought for breath.

What the hell had just happened?

She'd had orgasms before. With Logan, in fact. Incredible, awe-inducing multiple orgasms. No one had ever played her body like Logan could. But she'd never felt anything like she just had. No, wait. She had, a little anyway, the first time they'd made love. She'd thought it amazing that it could be so intensely good, even when he wasn't touching her in just the right places. She'd thought it was because she cared so much for him. That emotional connection heightened the experience, made it better, made it incredible.

But now it slowly dawned on her that the force of that moment just now . . . it hadn't been because they'd professed their love. Yes, that helped. A lot. But love alone couldn't do that. Not even a man with a skilled hand and even more skilled . . . moves could do *that*.

She remembered Charlie's secret, sly expression in the car after they'd gone to see AnnaCoreen the first time. Her sister had been trying to cheer her up.

There are perks to the curse.

Yeah? Like what?

I can't ruin the surprise. Just trust me.

Perks to the curse. What could be more perk-ish, or mind-blowing, than literally experiencing a lover's orgasm?

The turbo empathy was back.

CHAPTER **THIRTY-EIGHT**

Logan held Alex close against him, unable to get enough of touching her, his heart feeling bigger somehow, fuller. No more Grinch here. Alex *loved* him. Loved *him*.

He'd hoped and prayed, but he hadn't been sure, hadn't even thought he deserved it. He'd known she liked him, a lot. But he hadn't known for sure that this wasn't . . . perhaps a transition for her. She'd almost died, and as a cop, he knew that near-death experiences often led to fast, furious relationships that celebrated the pleasures in life. Eventually, such relationships ran their course.

But this wasn't that. *This* was real. He'd insisted on taking it slow . . . well, as slow as Alex would accept. And now he couldn't believe his luck that after the hell of Detroit, he'd miraculously landed here, in Lake Avalon, in Alex Trudeau's bed, in her heart, exactly where he wanted to spend the rest of his days.

In his arms, Alex shifted, drawing him out of his sex-stirred thoughts of love and romance. The taut tension in her body surprised him. He'd probably been holding her too tightly. He couldn't deny that he didn't want to ever let her go. He wanted to stay like this, naked and together, for as long as possible.

"You okay?" he asked, pressing a light kiss to her damp temple.

She didn't answer for a moment, and a tap of concern grew into a nudge as a slight tremor passed through her body.

"Alex?"

She drew in a shaky breath. "I'm fine."

He didn't like the sound of *that*. Rolling from his side to his back, he urged her to turn toward him, but instead of snuggling into him as he hoped, she sat up and scooted to the edge of the bed.

"Alex, what's the matter? Talk to me."

"I'm going to take a shower," she said.

She didn't look at him as she walked, naked and, Jesus, gorgeous, into the bathroom and shut the door. Braced on his elbows, he stared at the closed door.

What the hell? They'd just said they loved each other. Shouldn't they have cuddled—reveled—at least a little longer? Did the fact that had even occurred to him make him the woman in this relationship?

And, well, shit, she was "fine" again. He hated it when she was "fine"—except when she really *was* fine, of course. Thank God that psycho hadn't done anything more, physically, than tie her up. The bonds alone made him want to strangle the bastard, but things could have been so much worse, and the thought of those things made Logan shudder. And the fact that he, a *cop*, was shuddering . . . Damn it, he should have pressed her more for details. She'd given him a name, albeit not the man's actual name obviously, since he was, or at least Logan *hoped* he was, Brian Lear's brother, and Logan had run with it, thanking his lucky stars that it had been that fucking easy.

His cell phone started to ring again in the other room,

and he got out of bed and strode into the living room to retrieve it from the coffee table. The caller ID flashed the name Phil Packard. Excellent. The mystery of Butch McGee was about to be solved.

"Yeah, Phil."

"Butch McGee isn't an alias."

Logan's hand tightened on the phone. "What?"

"He's for real. Social Security number. Michigan driver's license. Credit cards. Bank accounts. An apartment address in Detroit. I found his fucking birth certificate in public records."

"But Brian Lear—"

"Didn't have a brother. Neither does McGee. Or sisters, for that matter."

"But Lear is the only man I've ever killed. There has to be a connection there."

"I'll go by his apartment on my way to work," Phil said. "I'll make it look like a break-in. I'm assuming you've got fingerprints at your end."

"Fingerprints, DNA, security photos. He wasn't careful about the evidence he left behind."

"He's got balls."

"Or confidence that we don't have him in the system. I should hear from the crime scene techs here before noon. I have a feeling the perp swiped McGee's identity."

"You're probably right. You want me to e-mail the info I got on him?"

"Yes. JohnLogan@lakeavalonpd.com. I'll forward it to the detective in charge of the investigation. Do you have a copy of McGee's driver's license with the photo?"

"Yeah. I'll scan it in and send it along."

"Thanks, Phil. Oh, wait, hey, did you check that other name I gave you? Tyler Ambrose."

"Oh, yeah. Interesting hit on that one. Seven-year-old boy kidnapped thirty years ago at a mall in suburban Chicago. He was never found. How does he fit into all of this?"

Logan shook his head, confused on that one. "I have no idea. I don't suppose there was a picture."

"I couldn't find anything other than his name in a database of missing kids. He disappeared before the age of high-tech record keeping. FBI might be able to help out on that."

"Right. Good idea."

They signed off, and as Logan headed back to the bedroom, he checked his missed-calls list to discover the call he'd blown off earlier had been from Justin Parker. Luckily, the teenager had left a voice mail.

Logan's stomach seized when he heard the trembling voice. "It's me. Justin. I, uh . . . Do you think . . . Well, could you maybe meet me at the usual place, behind the Iguana? Like, in an hour or two? I, uh, I'm sorry I wasn't there last time. I swear I'll be there this time. I swear."

The call ended, and Logan checked his watch. He needed to consult with the crime scene techs as well as Don Walker and Noah to see what they'd turned up at the storage unit and with the Mustang, as well as what they found on the security cameras at the rental car counter and the storage facility. Nothing had turned up that was an emergency, apparently, or he would have heard from Noah or Don by now. But he really didn't have time for anything else.

Yet . . . Justin was counting on him, and Logan didn't like the tremor he'd heard in the boy's voice. The kid had clearly reached the end of his rope.

He tried to calculate how much time it might take to stop to see Justin then head to Noah's office. But what would he do about Alex? He didn't want her staying here, or anywhere, alone. Until they found the guy who'd kidnapped and terrorized her, he didn't plan to leave her unguarded. Hell, he didn't want to be away from her, *period*.

As if his thoughts summoned her, she exited the bathroom wrapped in a short white robe, her hair damp and curling around her flushed face. Her eyes looked glassy and red, and the realization that she'd been crying jolted him. He almost asked if she was okay, but knowing he'd get her usual pat answer stopped him.

Instead, he watched her go to the duffle Charlie had packed for her that was on the floor next to the dresser. As she pulled on underwear, a pink, form-fitting T-shirt and white knit shorts, he appreciated the view of smooth pale legs toned from daily workouts. He loved her legs, especially when they clamped around his waist, strong and insistent. He loved her arms, too. Loved trailing his tongue along the inside of her elbow until she squirmed. Loved her breasts, the way her nipples reacted to his slightest caress. And her mouth. God, her mouth. Whether stretching into a wide smile or sucking him blind . . .

Damn, he was getting hard. When would this incessant need for her back off?

Never, he hoped.

He slid off the bed and walked up behind where she stood at the mirror combing out the tangles in her hair. When he smoothed his hands down her arms, she tensed and stilled. He caught her gaze for only an instant in the reflection before it skittered away. Something was definitely off. And he had no clue what to do to set it right. Or even if he could do *anything*.

So, for now, he stuck to business. "I don't want you going anywhere alone until we track down McGee and put him away."

She didn't protest, not that he'd expected her to. That was one of the many things he loved about her: She wasn't stupid.

"I need to see Charlie," she said.

The rasp in her voice—more evidence of a crying jag in the shower—twisted the muscles in his chest. He hoped this sudden shift in her emotions didn't have anything to do with her so-called psychic ability. She hadn't mentioned empathy since she'd proclaimed herself cured at Anna-Coreen's. He hoped that meant she'd let that implausible idea go. Of course, AnnaCoreen would accuse him of being in denial about the whole thing. And, hell, maybe he was. Denial had been his middle name for years.

"How about you call Charlie to see if she can meet you at Noah's office?" he said. "I need to consult with him on a few things."

"You don't have to go to work?"

"I've been ordered to take a few days off to keep me away from the investigation."

Alex's lips quirked. "How's that going so far?"

He grinned, heartened by her teasing. "As expected."

"I also need to figure out how to deal with the dogs if I'm going to be away from home much longer."

"Charlie and Noah went over several times yesterday, and I went early this morning to take them for a long walk."

"Someone should have gotten me up for at least some of those trips. I could have—"

"We all agreed that you needed to sleep and regroup." He tucked a strand of damp hair behind her ear. "Let us take care of you for a change."

She gave an acquiescent nod, though her smile was wan. "Thank you."

"Come on, Alex, what's going on?"

"Nothing. I'm just tired."

"I've seen you 'just tired.' There's something more, but I can't help you if you don't talk to me." If she brought up empathy, they'd deal. He loved her, and no way in hell would he let some fucking psychic ability tear them apart.

"I'm not ready, Logan. I'm sorry."

"You can't dodge me forever, you know."

"I don't plan to."

He sighed. She'd given him no choice but to let it go, so he would. For now. "On the way to Noah's, there's some-one I need to see real quick. Is that okay?"

"Works for me." She started to slip past him, but he put a hand lightly on her arm to stop her. Her questioning gaze swept up to meet his, and he kissed her, slow and thorough, trying to tell her with his lips and tongue that they'd work through all the crap.

No matter what.

CHAPTER **THIRTY-NINE**

Who are we going to see?" Alex asked.

Logan glanced sideways at her. Cruising toward downtown Lake Avalon with her next to him in his truck had all the marks of normalcy. Sure, she was a bit subdued, and tense. Jesus, she was tense, had been even as they'd grabbed quick bowls of Frosted Mini-Wheats in Charlie's kitchen before hitting the road. But she'd initiated conversation when he assumed she'd prefer to stick with her own thoughts.

"His name's Justin Parker," he said. "Or at least that's who he says he is. I'm guessing sixteen or seventeen."

"And he's a runaway?"

"For a couple of weeks now. Noah and I have been taking turns keeping an eye on him. Justin asked me for help a couple of days ago, then vanished. I was hoping he'd gone home, but then he called and asked to see me."

"What's up with his parents?"

"From the little he's said, it sounds like his mother doesn't know how to help him and his father won't tolerate his screwups. Justin's I-don't-give-a-fuck attitude doesn't help."

"You seem to really understand him."

He shrugged. He preferred to think that, more than anything, he was doing his job. "I've made the effort."

"Do you see yourself in him?"

Logan kept his gaze on the road even though he'd braked for a stoplight. "I was a foster kid, and he's not, but, yeah, I do." His own honesty surprised him. But, then, he was talking to Alex. He'd always found it easy to talk to her. "Would have been nice if someone had tried to save me from myself sooner."

"How much sooner?"

He glanced at her in question. "What do you mean?"

"What did you have to go through before Officer Mike came along?"

Logan took the opportunity presented by the green light to focus on the road. "Enough."

"Interesting."

Her flat tone had him looking at her again to see her lips compressed in an unhappy line. "What?"

"I find it interesting," she said, "that when you skirt a subject you don't want to talk about, it's okay, but when I do, I'm dodging."

"That's because you are."

"But you do it, too. You don't see me getting bent out of shape about it."

"When did I get bent out of shape?"

"Just because you don't say anything doesn't mean I don't know you're irked."

He didn't speak for a long moment as he turned the truck onto the Green Iguana's street. He wasn't sure how to deal with a defensive and challenging Alex.

When the silence stretched on, she sighed. "Now you're trying to figure out how to handle me."

"Well, yeah. I'm not sure where we're going here."

"All I'm saying is that sometimes I don't want to talk about what I'm feeling or thinking."

Since when did Alex not want to talk? She *loved* to talk. "Okay," he said anyway.

"Just like you don't like to talk about your past. There's no difference."

"Actually, there's a big difference. My past is over. This is the present. And no matter how often you say you're fine, I know damn well that you're not. You *can't* be after what just happened to you. And I'm not *irked* that you won't talk to me, Alex. I'm *worried*. If you're really so psychic, how come you don't know that?"

She sucked in a sharp breath, and he jammed on the brakes to pull into a parking spot in front of the Iguana and swore under his breath. "Shit, I shouldn't have said that. I'm sorry. I'm just . . . It's okay to worry about you, isn't it? I love you. It's killing me that that bastard terrorized you to get to me."

She closed her eyes and turned her head away, and he saw her swallow hard. Was she going to cry again? He didn't know how to deal with *that*, either. The Alex he knew never cried. She laughed and smiled and poked him in the ribs. She didn't look miserable. She didn't look *haunted*.

"I'm sorry," she whispered.

Logan's heart sank into the pit of his stomach. He was *so* messing this up. "I'm not trying to make you sorry. And you don't have to apologize to me. Ever."

She looked at him, and her eyes swam with tears. "I just . . . don't know how to . . ." She trailed off, swallowing again.

He stroked the back of his hand over her cheek, his stomach doing a jittery dance when she leaned into the caress. "It's okay. You don't have to deal with anything right now. Just promise you will, okay? If not with me, then with Charlie. Or a counselor. I've seen too many people get eaten up by their demons."

She nodded, dropping her gaze, and he couldn't help but worry that she'd agreed simply to end the conversation. That's what he would have done.

He'd have to worry about that later. Right now, he needed to help a troubled boy. "Will you come with me while I talk to Justin? I don't want you sitting in the truck alone."

"Won't my presence make him uncomfortable?"

"It might, but . . . I just don't want to leave you alone. Not until McGee's been caught."

"Okay."

Logan unbuckled his seat belt and got out. The humid morning air already carried the sweat-soaked scent of spicy Mexican food. The Green Iguana was known for its huevos rancheros, and his stomach growled even though they'd just eaten.

"There he is," Alex murmured beside him. "Oh, God."

Logan spotted Justin in the next instant, and a surge of shock went through him. The boy looked as though he'd gotten into one hell of a fight. Dark bruises purpled his jaw and the left side of his face, his left eye all but swollen shut.

"Jesus, Justin, what the hell happened to you?" Logan asked.

"I ran into a door." He jerked his chin toward Alex. "Who's that?"

"This is Alex Trudeau," Logan said. "My girlfriend."

Justin's lips quirked. "You're kinda old to have a girl-friend, aren't you?"

Logan noticed Alex didn't reach out to try to shake Justin's hand, but he couldn't blame her. The kid was filthy. "So what happened?"

"I told you. I ran into a door."

"Come on, Justin. How am I supposed to help if I don't know what's going on?"

"You should probably go to the ER," Alex said, her voice soft.

One side of Justin's mouth lifted in a sneer. "Why? So they can call social services? No freaking way. Besides, I'm fine."

"Justin—"

"Look, I called you because I—" Suddenly, he tossed his hands in the air and backed off a step. "Forget it. Just forget it."

Alex touched Logan's arm to draw his attention. "Maybe I should go wait in the truck after all."

"No, I—"

"Then how about I go stand at the end of the alley? I'll stay where we can see each other, and you guys can have some privacy."

He didn't like it, but he also needed to get Justin to spill. "Okay." He gave her a quick kiss and murmured, "Thanks."

As she walked away, Justin gave a low whistle. "She's hot. Where'd you score her?"

Logan shot the teen an annoyed look. The kid's appreciation was too exaggerated to be sincere. "Knock it off."

"She have a sister?"

"Justin."

The teen rolled his eyes and shoved his hands into his pockets. "I'm sorry I interrupted your date with your *girlfriend*, but you said I could call you if I needed help."

"And you can. Any time. But you're going to have to tell me the truth, or I'll have no choice but to get social services involved. So tell me. Who hit you and why?"

Justin's eyes widened. "You think I deserved to get my lights punched out?"

"No. Why would you—"

"You're asking me why I got the crap beat out of me. Maybe I got punched because the person who punched me is an asshole. Ever think of that?"

"I didn't mean it like that." Logan dragged a hand

through his hair. Jesus, this kid liked to parse words more than anyone he knew. "Let's start over."

Justin hunched his shoulders. "Fine."

"Do you need to see a doctor?"

"No."

"Are you sure?"

"Positive."

"Are there other injuries besides what I can see?"

"Like what?"

Logan bit back a frustrated groan. "Did you maybe get hit in the ribs or kidneys? Does it hurt when you breathe? Is there blood when you pee?"

Justin frowned, lifting one shoulder. "No."

"Headache? Double vision?"

"Yeah, my head hurts. Look at my face. Wouldn't your head hurt?"

"But you don't feel like you're going to pass out or anything?"

"No. It's just bruises. And I've been punched before."

Logan had already figured as much, and his conscience poked him. He should have gotten this kid into the system right away instead of trying to wait for him to make the choice. "So who hit you?"

"Doesn't matter."

"Whoever did it can be arrested."

"No! I don't want that. Just drop it." He paced away. "Can you just . . . can you just . . ." He pulled his hands out of his pockets and shook them out as though they tingled. "Shit."

"What, Justin? What do you want?"

"I need some cash. A couple hundred dollars. I'll hit the road, go up north. I can stay with my grandma."

"Where does your grandma live?"

"She's in . . . Tampa."

So obviously a lie. "How about this? I'll drive you up there. I'd like to meet her."

Justin started shaking his head. "Screw you, man. I don't need an escort. Just forget it, okay? Go away. I'll figure something out."

"You know I can't do that. You're visibly hurt. I have a duty to—"

"You brought me a couple of cheeseburgers, okay? That doesn't make you my freaking guardian."

"You ate them, so yeah, it does. You shoulda read the fine print."

"You've got a twisted sense of logic, cop."

"As much as I'd like to stand here and banter with you all night, there's somewhere I have to be. So how about this? I'll find you a place to stay tonight, and we'll figure something out tomorrow. Can you do that? Stay where I put you tonight and not get antsy?"

"No foster care."

"Not tonight. But I can't promise anything for the future. I'm sorry."

"Then I won't go."

"It's like this. Either you do it my way or you do it my way. If you don't like the very unethical idea I just offered, the one that could get my ass kicked out of a job, I'll haul you to social services right here and now. What's it going to be?"

Justin scowled at him. "I thought you were different."

"I am different. Let's go."

CHAPTER **FORTY**

From where she stood by his pickup, Alex watched Logan and Justin walk out of the alley. Neither looked happy. She could relate. She had the buzz of dread running through her head, and all she wanted was to talk to Charlie. Somehow, some way, she needed more information about this turbo empathy.

Logan neared the truck, Justin on his heels. "Justin's coming with us," Logan said. "Do you mind?"

"Of course not." She tried her best to give the battered boy a warm smile even as her insides clenched at the sight of his bruises. The poor kid. "Hello again."

Justin offered a tight grimace in response but said nothing. The thought nudged her, as it had when she'd met him a few minutes ago, that he looked familiar.

Logan pulled open the passenger door of the truck and signaled for Alex to get in.

As she scooted across the seat to make room for the teenager, she took note of his short-sleeved T-shirt and safari shorts. Considering her own tank top and shorts and the pickup's bench seat, avoiding accidental contact with the bruised-up boy wasn't going to be easy.

"Get in," Logan said to the teenager, sounding like a drill sergeant. "And try not to get my girlfriend dirty."

Mutiny flashed in Justin's blue eyes. "If you're so worried I'm going to stink up your ride, I can catch the next one."

"Shut up and get in," Logan snapped.

His uncharacteristic impatience surprised Alex, but then he gave her an apologetic I-don't-know-what-the-hell-I'm-doing look.

With a miserable glance at Alex that again tweaked her memory—she was *sure* she knew him—Justin hopped into the truck, and Logan slammed the door shut. The boy seemed just as leery of touching her, or perhaps of being touched, because he all but hugged the passenger door, putting as much distance between her and himself as possible. She forgot her own fear and worried instead about what would make a child so fearful of close contact.

Logan got behind the steering wheel and started the truck. He'd already pulled into traffic when Alex realized why Justin looked familiar. "Aren't you Toni Wells's son? The alderwoman?"

Logan's head swiveled toward her, his eyebrows arched. This apparently was new information to him.

"Nope," Justin said.

"You look a lot like her," Alex replied. "She has really pretty blue eyes, like you do."

Logan snorted, and Alex cast him a chastising glance. "What? His eyes are beautiful."

"Whatever," both Logan and Justin said at the same time.

Alex ignored their male disdain, even as she admired their bond. "It was a big deal when Toni and Senator Wells got married a couple of years ago. I took the photo of the wedding that ran in the newspaper."

"Good for you." Justin made a big show of looking out the passenger-side window.

"I'm pretty sure you were in that photo. One of the groomsmen."

"Nope. Wasn't me."

"Your hair was long. You looked very rock star. Why did you shave it all off? Not that it doesn't look great now, but you have such gorgeous hair."

"Maybe that's why. I'm a *guy*. Guys don't have gorgeous hair and pretty eyes."

Alex glanced at Logan, silently asking him if he caught the shift. Justin had just acknowledged that he was who she thought he was. Except Logan didn't look happy about it at all. In fact, a red flush crept up his neck.

"You're Senator Wells's stepson?" Logan asked, attention fixed on the road.

"Nope," Justin said.

"Why haven't they reported you missing?" Logan asked, as though the boy hadn't responded in the negative.

"Maybe they don't give a shit," Justin said.

"I'm sure that's not true," Alex said. "I've met your mother, and she's a very kind, caring woman."

"Yeah? Then why don't you know that I'm missing? You work for the snooze paper, don't you? That'd be pretty big freaking news, wouldn't it? Politicians' kid runs away from home? Sounds like page-one material to me."

"Justin," Logan said sharply. "She's trying to help you."

"Maybe I don't need help. Ever think of that?" He grabbed the door handle. "I'd like to get out now." He yanked up on the handle.

Alex seized a handful of his T-shirt. "Don't!"

The locked door didn't open, but Logan swerved onto the shoulder anyway and hit the brakes. As the truck jerked to a stop, he gripped the steering wheel in white-knuckled fists. "Son of a bitch," he said under his breath.

"Let me out." Justin's low voice trembled. "You can't keep me in here against my will. It's kidnapping."

"It's not kidnapping. I'm a cop, remember?" Logan said through his teeth. "Or did it never occur to you that your parents could take my badge if they found out I didn't turn you over to social services the first night I found you in that alley *three weeks ago*?"

He shouted the last three words, and Alex winced at the thunder in his voice. But she said nothing. He had a right to be ticked.

"I didn't *want* to go back. Why do you think I gave you a fake name?"

"This is such bullshit," Logan growled.

Justin heaved out a shaky breath and looked out the window again. "Fine. Take me back."

The tired resignation in his voice tugged at Alex. He was too young to be so beaten down. "Who hit you, Justin?" she asked.

"SpongeBob. I made fun of his pants."

"Damn it, Justin—"

Alex stopped Logan with a hand on his arm. "Why don't we give him a break for now?"

Logan looked at her as if she'd lost her mind. "We need to know—"

"I know. But he doesn't want to tell us. What are you going to do? Torture it out of him?"

Justin smirked. "Yeah. Are you going to torture it out of me?"

"Not a bad idea, actually," Logan said with a dark scowl.

"Just give him time," Alex said. "He'll talk."

"No, he won't," Justin said.

"Not a good sign, buddy," Logan said, "when you start referring to yourself in the third person."

"Ow, that really hurt." Justin grabbed his chest and pretended an arrow had struck him in the heart.

"Bite me," Logan muttered and pulled back onto the road.

The rest of the ride to Noah's office was silent, and Alex used the time to figure out how to get Justin alone. An empathic foray into his head could answer all of Logan's questions. It would hurt like hell, but if it helped this troubled teenager, she could suck it up.

Besides, whatever had happened to him couldn't be nearly as bad as what had happened to Butch McGee as a child.

CHAPTER **FORTY-ONE**

Alex hadn't visited Noah's office since he and Charlie had finished the remodel. The newly painted words on the frosted glass of the door said: LASSITER PRIVATE INVESTIGATIONS. When Logan pushed open the door to let Alex and Justin walk in ahead of him, the scents of new carpet, fresh paint and leather flowed over Alex.

The office's new décor screamed competent male. A cherrywood receptionist desk, dark brown leather chairs and a matching overstuffed sofa furnished a comfortable, reassuring waiting area. Freshly painted beige walls, plush light brown carpet and multiple plants kept the space from looking gloomy. Another door, sporting a glass window, led to an inner office that held Noah's desk and more furniture in the same vein. Charlie was perched on the desk, facing Noah, with a teasing smile on her lips as he idly caressed her knee.

Alex had to tap on the window to get their attention, and then Charlie hopped off the desk and strode out to meet them while Noah flipped closed the open files on his desk.

"What took you guys so long?" Charlie stopped when she saw the teenager. "Oh, hi."

"This is Justin." Alex set her camera bag on the floor. "I wouldn't shake his hand, though. We found him in the alley behind the Green Iguana."

Justin shoved his hands in his pockets. "It's not like I've got Ebola."

Logan nudged him forward a step. "How do we know? You wouldn't tell us if you did."

Alex grabbed Logan's hand and squeezed, trying to tell him without using words to lay off the kid. "Perhaps you could go in and talk to Noah while Charlie and I get Justin set up with a shower and some clean clothes?"

"And lunch," Justin added. "I'm starving."

"Make sure it's something healthy," Logan said over his shoulder. "Salad from somewhere. A big one. He really hates anything from McDonald's."

"Screw you," Justin called after him. "I'm getting my cooties all over the nice new furniture in here."

Justin plopped down into a waiting room chair, slumped back and rested his chin on his chest like a sullen kid half his age.

Anxiety, Alex thought. And fear. Both bled off him in waves.

Charlie inched closer to Alex so she could keep her voice at a level that stayed between them. "Okay, so, um, this is an interesting turn of events. What happened to the cranky teenager?"

"I'll explain later," Alex said softly. To Justin, she said, "There's a men's room that has a shower in it out the door and down the hall on the right."

She knelt on one knee to dig through the bottom of her camera bag, then came up with a plastic Publix bag filled with trial sizes of Dove soap, shampoo and conditioner as well as a change of clothes. You never knew when chasing a news story would make a mess of a girl's look. She'd covered too many hurricanes, dripping wet, and wild fires, reeking of smoke, to travel without backups.

"You're always prepared," Charlie said with an admiring smile.

Alex walked over to the chair and dropped the toiletries into Justin's hand. When he scowled at the labels, she said, "Yeah, they're girlie, but even you must be sick of the way you smell. While you shower, my sister and I will go to the clothing store next door and pick up some clean clothes."

"Isn't that a place for old farts?" Justin asked.

"I could lend you the clothes in my bag, but if you think the shampoo is girlie . . ."

"Just don't get me black socks to wear with shorts. I hate that stupid look."

"Agreed. Now, I'm trusting you not to hightail it out the door the minute our backs are turned," Alex said. "If you think Logan is ticked at you now, go ahead and do that and see how fast you regret it."

Justin's chin inched up. "He doesn't scare me."

"That's good, because he's not trying to. He's trying to help you. But the main thing to keep in mind is that he knows who you are now. If you take off, he'll have every cop in Lake Avalon looking for you. And there are no other cops around here who have the patience that Logan has. Got it?"

Justin didn't nod, but he didn't sneer, either, which Alex considered acceptance. "Take a long, hot shower. With lots of soap."

Once he'd left the office, grumbling under his breath, Charlie asked, "You trust him not to take off?"

"No. I'm hoping you'll do me a favor and pick up the clothes while I guard the bathroom door."

"Noah's got his gym bag with him," Charlie said. "His workout clothes would be too big, but they're clean."

"Perfect. We wouldn't want to force old-fart couture on the poor kid."

Charlie disappeared into Noah's office to retrieve the offerings while Alex opened the door that led into the office building's inside hallway and kept an eye out for an escaping teenager.

When Charlie returned with black gym shorts, a white T-shirt and clean socks, they both took up position outside the men's room door. Alex listened for a moment, then smiled as she heard the telltale whoosh of water from a showerhead.

"So what gives?" Charlie asked.

"He and Logan don't quite see eye to eye."

"Logan did that to his face?"

"What? No! God, no. Justin won't tell us who did it." Alex paused. "He's Toni Wells's son."

Charlie's brows shot up. "Really? He looks like a street kid."

"He has been for a few weeks now. Logan's been trying to help him."

"Doesn't he realize what Toni would do to him if she found out? She'd make sure he lost his badge."

"He didn't know who Justin is. Logan is fairly new here, remember? Justin gave him a fake name. And even if he'd given his real last name—Kale, Toni's maiden name—it wouldn't have rung a bell with Logan."

"Still. Toni's going to be majorly ticked."

"Don't you think it's weird, though, that she hasn't reported Justin missing?"

Charlie considered that a moment. "Yeah, it is."

"I think someone at home gave him those bruises. He's afraid to tell us who. And no one's reported him missing because they don't want anyone to find out."

"Toni wouldn't—"

"My money's on the senator."

"Oh, man, Alex, we can't go around making accusations. What if . . . wait." Charlie's brows shot up with realization. "Please tell me you're not thinking what I think you're thinking. Is your empathy back?"

Alex nodded. "This morning."

"Damn." Tears brimmed in her eyes. "I'm sorry. I know how much you—"

Alex cut her off with a dismissive wave of her hand. "I'll figure out a way to cope, but we can talk about that later. Right now, I want to focus on finding out the truth about what happened to Justin. If we know it, then Logan, or someone from social services, might be able to get Justin to talk. Or Logan can take some detailed info to the senator and get him to fess up."

"I don't think jumping into that kid's head is a good idea," Charlie said. "I *really* don't think it is."

"Don't tell me you haven't deliberately used your ability to get information quickly."

"I just don't think . . . considering what just happened to you—"

"Like I told Logan, I'm fine."

"Have I mentioned that you look like death warmed over? You're not fine, Alex."

"I'm a little tired. That's it."

"Well, I know from experience that you don't mess with what we've got. It's unpredictable."

"You seem to have yours under control."

"Do I? You apparently haven't noticed that I haven't touched you since Logan carried you out of that storage unit. I'm terrified of what happened to you."

Alex realized how closely they were standing and backed away from her sister. Careless contact, and Charlie would . . .

Charlie nodded as though Alex had just confirmed a suspicion. "Yeah, that's what I thought."

Alex frowned. "I never said it was a carnival ride."

"Look, let's make a deal," Charlie said. "I'll get up close and personal with Justin's memories, and—"

"No! I don't want you—"

"Well, I don't want you to, either. And I'm fresh. You've had a rough couple of days."

"But—"

"You're pushing it, Alex." Charlie's warning tone shut down her protest. "You need to let yourself acclimate. We don't know the extent of your ability's side effects. Besides, you might not even flash on what we need to know. You could end up way back in Justin's past when what we need to know happened a couple of hours ago."

"But I flash on the most recent traumatic event, too, and your flashes are so brief. What if you don't—"

"What part of 'I'm not letting you do this' do you not get? The kid is mine."

Alex felt her lips quirk into a humorless smile. "I can't believe we're arguing about who gets to head-trip the abused kid."

"I imagine this won't be the last time, either, considering your tendency to rescue every damn stray that crosses your path," Charlie said with a faint scowl.

"You say that like it's a bad thing. I mean, you saw Justin's bruises. Whoever did that to him *has* to go down. We have the power to make that happen."

"Power, Alex? You're calling it a *power* now?"

"Ability. Curse. Whatever the hell it is. Don't overanalyze my word choice."

"Fine, but just remember it's not as black-and-white as you think it is. Sometimes the consequences are too great." Charlie's intense gaze softened into concern. "Alex, seriously. Where do you draw the line? When does your need to take care of every wounded creature on this planet reach its limit? When it almost kills you? When it *does* kill you?"

"Now you're just being melodramatic."

"Maybe. Maybe not. I suppose that's something you'll have to figure out for yourself. In the meantime, Justin's mine."

Alex gave what she hoped looked like an acquiescent shrug. "Okay. Whatever."

CHAPTER **FORTY-TWO**

Logan holstered his cell phone and sat back in the chair across from Noah's desk with a heavy sigh.

"That good, huh?" Noah asked.

Logan massaged his temples, where a tension headache brewed like a tropical storm. He'd called Detective Don Walker to get the lowdown on where the Butch McGee investigation stood. "Don's faxing over photos from the security cameras at the rental car counter and storage facility. Meanwhile, FBI's on its way."

"No shit?" Noah asked. "How come you don't seem to mind the feds getting involved?"

"Because they know a shitload more about this guy than we do. Crime scene guys ran his DNA through the national database and got a bunch of hits. The fucker's a serial killer."

"Holy hell. How many has he killed?"

"Twenty-three that the feds know of. All across the U.S. Get this: The feds can't pin down his MO. He doesn't have a type. Young. Old. White. Black. Asian. Tall. Short. Fat. Skinny. You name it. They have only two things in common: They're all women, and they're all somewhat socially isolated."

"Christ," Noah breathed.

"He bounces all over the damn place, too, with no discernible pattern. They've been tracking him throughout the United States for years. The only link they have to all the murders is his DNA. He's apparently not worried about getting caught. He spreads it around like he's leaving presents for the feds. And that's all they have. No photos, no sketches, nothing. They didn't even have a name until now, let alone a decent picture from security cameras."

"Jesus," Noah said. "So with these other murders, did he contact any of the victims' significant others like he did you?"

Logan rubbed at his right temple. "No. His only pattern is to grab a woman, spend a few days raping and torturing her, then he kills her and moves on. When he took Alex, he broke that pattern for the first time, as far as the feds can tell anyway. He had a more specific goal with her." And that goal made Logan want to slam his fist through a wall.

"This could be the break the feds need to nail this guy," Noah said. "Alex is the only one to get away."

Logan reached for the MacBook open on Noah's desk. "Do you mind? I have a contact in Detroit who was going to e-mail me a copy of Butch McGee's Michigan driver's license."

"Go ahead."

Logan pulled up the Safari Web browser and accessed his e-mail account. Phil's message, with attachment, was at the top of his in-box. He clicked through to the attachment, and as the color copy of Butch McGee's driver's license opened on the screen, Logan studied it. Date of birth put the guy at thirty-seven. Dark brown hair. Gray eyes. In the photo, McGee's wide, genial smile exposed somewhat crooked teeth. What thirtysomething guy smiled that big for his driver's license photo?

"Well?" Noah prodded.

"Doesn't look familiar, but he matches Alex's description." He turned as Noah's fax machine came to life. "That might be the security camera photos."

Hopping up, Noah grabbed the sheets of paper as the machine fed them out and handed them to Logan.

Logan held the first one, a full-on shot of the guy standing at the Hertz counter, an amiable smile on his average-Joe face. Logan could tell without squinting that it was the same man from the driver's license. Whoever this guy was, he hadn't swiped Butch McGee's identity. He *was* Butch McGee.

Don Walker had told him that the alert they'd put out for him had yielded nothing so far. He might have fled Lake Avalon after his car was found at the storage facility. Logan suspected, though, that McGee wouldn't give up so easily. He'd killed twenty-three women without getting caught—and Logan suspected the actual tally went much higher. The man knew how to operate under the radar.

"So," Noah said. "From the look on your face, I'm guessing you still have no idea who he is."

"Not a clue."

"He said you took away his brother. Do you know what that means? Took away as in killed? Took away as in sent to prison?"

"I don't know," Logan said through his teeth. "I don't fucking know. After talking to Alex, I thought it meant 'killed,' because I had the one incident in Detroit. She mentioned the name Brian, the same name as the man I killed, but he apparently didn't have any siblings."

"What else do you know about the Brian you killed?" Noah asked. "He have any other relatives you can check in with?"

Logan shook his head. "Full name was Brian Lear. Picked up for hustling at twelve. He'd been living on the streets since he was nine or ten. No record of him before the arrest, and he spent the next six years, until he was eighteen, in and out of the system."

"Brian Lear probably wasn't his real name."

"He never gave up his real name, and social services couldn't track it down. No one ever showed up to claim their lost kid. Chances are, he started showing signs of deviant behavior early on and instead of getting help, the parents dropped him somewhere and drove away."

"That's just sick."

"Lear was a real piece of work, too. Liked little boys, if you know what I mean."

"Yikes."

"He was a regular at a brothel in downtown Detroit that catered to deviants. Run by a guy, Chad Ellis, who interestingly enough wasn't a deviant himself. More of a businessman."

"And his business was sex."

"Yep. Women, teenagers, little kids, you name it. The night I busted up his . . . business, I shot and killed Lear. Ellis was arrested and went to prison."

"Think Ellis would be worth a visit?"

"I don't know. The guy was tight-lipped as hell when he was arrested. I got the feeling he and Lear knew each other well—Ellis seemed broken up by Lear's death—but he'd never fess up to it. All of this is probably moot anyway. The name Butch McGee never once came up in that case. And his MO isn't to visit brothels. He likes ordinary women, not prostitutes."

"That you know of."

"True."

"McGee could still be connected in some way," Noah said. "I mean, if Lear's the only guy you've killed . . ."

Logan thought about it. Dead end, his gut told him. Even if Lear and McGee shared a connection, the chances that Chad Ellis would start sharing information after two years in maximum-security prison . . . Well, Logan didn't expect that to happen. Still, Noah had a point, and Logan had no intention of blowing off his only lead.

"I'll ask my former lieutenant to feel Ellis out," he said. "Maybe we could make a deal of some kind with him."

"Good idea." Noah picked up a pen and tapped it against the edge of his desk. "I don't suppose you've had an in-depth conversation with Alex about her time with McGee."

"I followed up with her on Don's questioning at the ER."

"I mean *in-depth*, Logan. The details. Alex is a damn perceptive woman. I'll bet you a hundred bucks she's got info in her head that she might not even realize is important. Info that could answer some of these questions."

Logan rose, his jaw tightening at the thought of asking her to relive her nightmare as McGee's captive.

"Listen," Noah said, "I know it's hard, but she's tough. She can handle it. You both can."

Logan flashed him a rueful smile before he opened the office door, just in time to see Alex collapsing, blood spilling from her mouth.

Charlie shouted her name and tried to brace her on the way down, succeeding only in keeping her head from bouncing against the carpet.

"Alex!" Charlie slapped at her sister's cheeks. "Alex, come on. Don't do this to me."

Logan dropped to his knees next to Alex's prone, unmoving body—Jesus, the blood, what's with the blood?—and pushed Charlie back so he could check for a pulse. The beat in Alex's throat drummed against his fingertips, strong but frantic. She was breathing, too.

He glanced up at Charlie's whitewashed face. "What the hell happened?"

"We agreed that I would be the one to do it, but then she pushed me out of the way."

"What did she do?"

"She touched Justin."

CHAPTER **FORTY-THREE**

*M*y *bedroom window is unlocked, just as I left it, and I tumble through the opening head first. As I get up off the floor, I listen for noise downstairs. Nothing. They're probably at the dinner table, cutting into thick steaks. I bet the topic of me living on the streets never even comes up.*

I sit on the edge of the bed. Man, I've missed this bed and its kick-ass feather pillow. The rest of the situation is shit, but what can I do? That cop is going to haul me off to social services and some fucked-up foster home that's way worse than this. At least here I have my iPod and Wii and a decent bed. Even if it is a farce.

I get up and start to strip out of my stinky clothes. The bedroom door flies open and Mom stares at me like I've got a Mount Vesuvius zit in the middle of my forehead.

Before she says anything—welcome home, you're grounded, where have you been, I'm divorcing your dip-shit of a stepdad—the scumbag comes up behind her.

"What is it, Toni?"

She shifts to let the bastard share the doorway. His snake eyes go to slits when he sees me. "Justin."

He says my name like it tastes like sewage. He's such a tool. Life was good before he came along and started screwing my mother. As if screwing the Florida taxpayers hadn't been enough.

"Apparently, you've decided to play by the rules," Senator Tool says.

"I'll do what I can, but I can't change the fact that I'm a dick-loving homo, and I plan to shout it to the world. I don't give a shit about your run for governor in an old-fashioned, conservative state."

Senator Tool's fat face flushes bright red, right to the top of his shiny bald head, and even though I know I've just screwed myself, I flash him a bite-me grin.

A glance at Mom says I've gone too far, and I regret it for about a second, because I hate disappointing her. Used to, anyway.

Senator Tool takes a step toward me, but I refuse to back up. He's going to hit me. That's his deal. If you don't jive with what he believes, he destroys you.

His fist slams into my jaw. Rockets explode in my brain. My head hits the bedroom carpet, and then I'm blinking away the stars. I have a full-on view of under my bed. Hey, there's the extra Wii remote I couldn't find.

He jerks me up by the back of my shirt. My head spins and spins. Mom turns and walks away. That hurts worse than the punches. I've stood up for her more than once.

The tool smacks me again. Hard. Fuck, that hurts. Blood floods around my tongue, metallic and salty.

He smashes his fist into my face again. When he lets go, I hit the floor, fading fast . . .

Logan cradled Alex in his arms on the sofa in Noah's office, his brain screaming at him to get her to the emergency room. Her head lolled against his shoulder, her breathing shallow and hitching as though she were still caught in the throes of a seizure.

But Charlie had steered him, his arms full of Alex, to the sofa. "Just give her a minute."

"She's not responding," Logan said. What the fuck was *wrong* with these people?

Charlie dabbed at the trickle of blood at the corner of Alex's mouth, her hand shaking.

"What's going on?" Justin asked. He had backed into the corner, looking small and defenseless in Noah's too-big shorts and T-shirt, his don't-screw-with-me attitude nowhere in sight.

Logan didn't even look at him. All he could focus on at the moment was Alex, limp and too fucking pale in his arms. He heard Noah say to Justin, "Let's wait in the other room, okay? I'm sure she'll be fine."

"She was fine just a minute ago," Justin said. "Is she epileptic or something?"

"Something like that." Noah steered the boy out of the office.

Alex shifted in Logan's arms then and opened her eyes, blinking as if against too-bright lights. Relief pounded through him a second before she went rigid, her head pressing hard against his shoulder. As quickly as she'd stiffened, she relaxed.

He looked at Charlie. "What the hell was that?"

She winced. "We should have tried to protect her from the flash of you finding her on the floor. Too late now. I'm just glad she's back." She pushed to her feet, a hand on his arm for balance. "I'm going to get her some water. I'll be right back."

Logan didn't watch her go. He was more concerned with Alex as she shifted in his arms with a soft moan, her tongue tentatively exploring some leftover blood at the corner of her mouth.

He loosened his death grip on her and helped her into more of a sitting position, keeping her legs draped over his thighs. Leaning toward the table next to the sofa, he plucked several Kleenex from a box there and gently wiped away the rest of the blood.

She looked dazed, not quite fully in the moment. Her jaw obviously hurt her, because she worked it with a pained wince. "Ow."

He lightly stroked a finger over the left side, where a large bruise had formed. Holy shit, how was that even possible? "You must have hit it when you fell."

She closed her eyes without agreeing or disagreeing and seemed to concentrate on slowly breathing in and out.

Charlie returned with a small bottle of Advil and a glass of water. She knelt next to Alex and tapped four orange caplets into her palm. "You should take these right now," Charlie told her. "It'll help with the pain. I asked Noah to run across to the Java Bean for some ice."

Alex's fingers trembled as she accepted the pills and swallowed them with the water that Charlie handed over. "Thanks."

"What happened?" Logan asked Alex. "Did you faint?"

Alex jerked her head up, as though just now becoming fully conscious. "Where's Justin?"

"He went with Noah," Charlie said. "Don't worry. He's okay. Kind of wigged, of course."

"Oh, God, that poor kid." Alex's voice thickened with emotion, and she gripped the front of Logan's shirt. "The senator did that to him. Senator Wells."

"He told you that?" Logan asked, stunned.

The kid hadn't told him squat in three weeks, yet he'd spilled his guts to Alex within an hour of meeting her? And what did that have to do with her ending up on the floor, unconscious and bleeding?

He had a feeling he knew what Charlie and Alex, even Noah, would say, and that just twisted his insides up even more. Fuck empathy. *Fuck* it.

"His mother," Alex said. "God, his mother . . . she walked away."

"Don't worry," Charlie assured her. "We'll take care of him. Now that we know what we're dealing with, it'll be easier."

"Wait a damn minute. Just . . . time out," Logan said. "How do you know what he's saying is true? I mean, I've known the kid for weeks, and he's never met a lie he couldn't tell."

Charlie glowered at him. "Are you deliberately playing dumb? Look at her. She's got the same bruises on her face that Justin has. You think I did that to her just to play some elaborate joke on you? For the love of God, are you—"

"Charlie," Alex said, the "back off" clear in her tone.

She shifted her legs off his lap and put her feet on the floor. He reluctantly let her go, concerned by her pallor and the gingerly way she held her head, as though she feared it would separate from her neck and roll away.

"Are you okay?" He kept his hand light on her arm. He knew she wasn't. She couldn't be. But, Jesus, he *needed* her to be. He couldn't think, couldn't function, when she wasn't okay.

"I'm great. Fantastic. Thanks," she said dryly. "Let's focus on what we're going to do to help Justin."

The knot in his stomach tightened further when she deliberately eased away from his touch.

CHAPTER **FORTY-FOUR**

Butch jimmied the window open and quickly stepped through, grumbling under his breath the whole time. This was so beneath him. Entering a woman's house like this—not cool. He preferred charming his way in, using compliments and warm smiles as keys. That was part of the game, part of the fun, proving that he'd chosen the right woman each time, unlocking each of her defenses with a skillful turn of words and appreciative looks.

A mad barking came from somewhere inside the house, and he froze in the office, his heart suddenly pounding. Dogs. He should have remembered, and he admonished himself for being sloppy. He hadn't done his homework with this one, had embarked on this quest without proper preparation. Proof that he normally wasn't a vengeful man.

When no mangy mutts charged into the office and tried to chomp into his private parts, he relaxed. They must be confined. Hopefully not in her bedroom. He really wanted to spend some quality time in there.

His frustration, and impatience, had built anew overnight as he'd staked out the house, waiting for the cop to bring his precious Alex home. When they hadn't arrived, he'd shifted his focus to John Logan's apartment this morning, but they hadn't been there, either. The cop must have taken his Alex somewhere else, to a hotel perhaps, where he'd spent the night making love to her over and over again, which is exactly what Butch would have done in John Logan's shoes.

The thought of being the one between her legs had his dick stirring behind the fly of his brand-new navy Dockers shorts. He resisted the urge to give himself a comforting pat. Time for that later.

Turning his focus to where he stood, he took in the standard spare bedroom used as an office. A laptop on the desk occupied a docking station that linked it to a monitor, keyboard, mouse and printer. Nothing too fancy, though the printer looked high-end. The photos—some framed, some not—that covered the walls reminded him that Alex Trudeau was a photojournalist. And a damn good one, he mused, as he stepped closer to inspect her work.

The eclectic collection included beach shots in which vivid blue skies, white-sand beaches and blue green water set off gleaming tanned bodies; house fires in which wicked yellow orange flames licked out of windows, sending thick white smoke into the night; stormy skies in which jagged streaks of lightning stabbed out of dark, rolling clouds; and the aftermath of hurricanes or tornadoes, where homes and businesses looked like nothing more than piles of debris waiting for the garbage truck.

One, of chocolate fondue, had a sensual quality as smooth, rich chocolate dripped from a ripe red strawberry.

Butch smiled. His Alex knew how to snap a picture. He wondered if he could talk her into taking his portrait. Or maybe she could teach him how to use a camera so he could shoot her photo after he was done with her. That would be a keepsake he'd treasure for the rest of his life. He imagined such a shot in a simple but unique frame, something that wouldn't detract from the masterpiece it displayed.

Sighing happily, he started to whistle "You Are So Beautiful" as he ventured out into the hall. He passed a closed door, the room that held what sounded like a dozen raucous beasts snuffling at the door, some whimpering, others woofing softly and still others barking their heads off. Butch wished he'd brought a gun, especially when he realized that that closed door most definitely did belong to his Alex's bedroom.

Frustration buzzed through his veins, and he stood in front of the door and glared at it, wondering how long it would take him to get to the hotel, get his handgun, which was stashed with its bullets in the room's safe, and come back. He hated guns. Hadn't used the Heckler & Koch pistol once since his brother had given it to him when Butch was seventeen. But sometimes you do what you have to do. Alex would understand once he explained it to her.

Resolved, he about-faced and went back into the office. With one last look at the fondue and strawberry picture, his cock expressing appreciation with an anticipatory little twitch, Butch climbed out the window and meticulously put everything back in place.

As he cut through neighboring backyards to the street parallel to Alex's but in the block behind her house, he started whistling again. Life was good when you had time with an interesting woman to look forward to. He imagined she'd be just as beautiful inside as out, pictured the red velvet of her blood as it slicked her pale skin, sexier than a strawberry dipped in chocolate.

As he got into the Ford Fusion, he happened to glance back toward the back of Alex's home in time to catch a glimpse between the houses of a police car easing down her street.

Someone must have seen him break in.

As much as he hated stinky, annoying dogs, this time they'd saved his butt.

CHAPTER **FORTY-FIVE**

Alex sat with a dishcloth-wrapped Ziploc bag of ice against her jaw and tried to focus on the teenager and not how much her face hurt. A check of her watch told her she had at least another thirty minutes before the bruises faded away as if they'd never existed. Justin, however, was not so lucky.

He sat in the visitor's chair next to her, his features drawn and pale. She'd scared him when she'd collapsed. Or perhaps she'd scared him when she'd regained consciousness with marks on her face identical to the ones on his.

She glanced at Logan, who leaned against the wall several feet away. He shifted his gaze away from hers and then rubbed his eyes with a thumb and forefinger. Just tired, she thought. She hoped.

She was tired, too. The effects of fifteen hours of sleep had vanished after only a few minutes inside Justin's nightmare, leaving behind a dull headache and a leaden feeling that seemed to permeate every cell.

She couldn't regret the excursion, though. Now they knew exactly what had happened. There would be no he said/

he said with his case. Alex was certain she could provide enough details to force the senator into a confession, especially once two *Lake Avalon Gazette* journalists—herself and Charlie—confronted him.

"Are you feeling up to sharing yet?" Charlie softly asked Justin.

Alex looked at her sister on the sofa next to Noah, who had his arm around her as if he had no intention of letting her get anywhere near Alex. Under normal circumstances, Charlie would have been all over her, soothing her and stroking her back and holding her hand. Not now. Maybe never again. The loss of such comforting contact settled in an aching lump in her stomach. The fact that Logan stood clear on the other side of the room, as though he didn't savor the idea of touching her, either, turned the ache to stone.

Alex shifted focus to Justin. He was the one who needed help now. She forced a reassuring smile. "Let's talk about Senator Tool."

Justin's eyes rounded with shock. "I wouldn't . . . I never . . . call him that . . . out loud."

"He was angry with you."

Justin squirmed, casting a panicked look at Logan. "I'm not sure I—"

"It's okay, Justin," Alex said. "You're among friends. Everyone here accepts you, no matter who you are. Do you understand that?"

He continued to stare at Logan, tense and unsure, until Logan nodded at him. "She's right, Justin. It doesn't matter what you've done."

Justin stiffened. "I haven't done anything—"

"What he means," Alex cut in, "is the only thing that matters to him is you're safe. Your stepfather is not a good man, and he was wrong to punish you for being the young man you are."

Justin's shoulders relaxed by slow degrees, especially after Logan gave him another encouraging nod. "It's not like I did it on purpose, you know? I mean, it's not like I *want* to be . . . this way. But he hates me. Hates what I am. He thinks it'll hurt him when he runs for governor. He said if he'd known, he never would have married my mom. I wish *I'd* known before he married her. I would have scared him off. He thought he was getting the perfect family, and then I screwed it all up for him."

Logan straightened away from the wall and moved to kneel in front of the boy's chair. He put his hand on top of Justin's sneaker, a show of gentle but not-too-forward support. "How many times has he hit you, Justin?"

Justin shrugged. "A couple."

"It's okay to tell the truth," Alex said. "We'll believe you."

The boy took a breath and held it. "It started last month. When he found out. He . . . he found a magazine in my room that I ordered on the Internet. And he just lost it."

"Was that when you ran away the first time?" Logan asked.

Justin nodded. "I knew he'd be pissed and Mom would be worried, but . . . he must have told her something, a lie, because no one came looking for me and it wasn't in the newspaper or on TV. She must not have known I ran away." His chin quivered. "At least, that's what I thought then."

Alex remembered how his mother, a woman she admired and a fixture in the Lake Avalon community, had turned and walked away while her husband used brutal fists on her only child. Alex would have assumed exactly what Justin had. Toni Wells had known her son had run away, and she'd let him go. To protect him, perhaps? A twisted form of protection, though, when she could have tried to rescue her son and had her husband arrested. Alex wondered if the antimaternal reaction meant Senator Tool was using his fists on his wife, too.

"I didn't know what to do," Justin went on. "I didn't want to go home. And I knew if I went to the police or something, my stepdad would get even madder. I figured, you know, maybe Mom didn't want me anymore."

"Oh, Justin," Charlie said, coming off the sofa where she'd stayed silent in Noah's arms. She swiveled the boy's chair toward her and pulled him into her arms to hug him close, her hands flat against his back. When she stiffened and let out a soft, whooshing gasp, Alex realized her sister had just landed in Justin's head. Charlie opened her eyes and met Alex's, and a tear rolled down her cheek.

Charlie's head trip, while painful, had been brief, and she came out of it on her own and unmarked. Alex envied that.

"I went back last night," Justin said when Charlie sat back from him, keeping her hands wrapped around both of his as they rested on his knees. "I thought maybe I could take it, you know? I didn't want to cause trouble for Mom. I thought maybe I could pretend I'm . . . normal."

"You *are* normal," Alex said. "You are."

Justin lifted one shoulder and let it drop. "But he got all over me right away, and he pissed me off. I wanted to piss him off right back." He paused with a shaky breath. "He started whaling on me all over again. And Mom . . ." He trailed off and lowered his head.

"She walked away," Alex said softly, remembering the harsh bite of betrayal.

Nodding, Justin sniffled and swiped at his eyes.

"Jesus," Logan pushed to his feet and paced away, enraged tension infusing his body.

Alex noticed the same tension in Noah as the men exchanged furious glances.

Charlie hugged Justin again, patting his back as he sniffled some more, all teen-boy attitude gone. He was just a scared child now, broken and adrift.

Logan cleared his throat. "I'm going to have to get the authorities involved, Justin. I'm sorry, but I have no choice. I want you to remember that you're safe, though, okay? He won't hit you ever again."

Noah stood. "If you want, Charlie and I can take care of Justin from here. I imagine you have an arrest in your immediate future?"

Logan nodded, one fist clenching at his side. This was one arrest he was clearly going to enjoy. "Yeah, thanks. I'll call it in on the way over to the Wells residence."

Alex felt a swell of pride, loving him more than she'd loved him before, assuming that was possible. He believed Justin without hesitation and jumped right to his defense.

A flutter of bitterness followed, though, because while he trusted Justin, he couldn't seem to bring himself to believe her. Perhaps with time . . . but she couldn't deny that his apparent doubt in her, when he professed to love her, caused some damage. She couldn't imagine spending her life with a man who didn't wholly believe in who she was and what she could do.

"I don't want to leave you unprotected," he said near her ear, and she flinched at how close he'd gotten without her realizing it. "Would you mind coming with me to make the arrest?"

She recovered quickly and nodded. "I wouldn't miss it."

She sat in the passenger seat of Logan's truck, her hands clasped between her knees. The headache still throbbed in her temples, but a gingerly exploration of her jaw with the tips of her fingers had let her know the bruises had gone. It had taken a little more than forty minutes.

In that time, Logan had said nothing, though he kept throwing her concerned glances, as though he worried about her but didn't want to acknowledge why. She'd noticed when he realized the bruises had vanished, because his eyes narrowed and he peered more closely at her face before closing his eyes and shaking his head.

Must be some powerful denial flowing with his blood,

she thought. Not that she could entirely blame him. If it weren't happening to her, she'd have trouble believing it, too.

"We need to talk," Logan said into the tense silence. "I know this isn't the best time, but . . ."

The weight on her shoulders lifted some. He wanted to talk about the empathy. Finally. Maybe they'd be okay after all. God, she hoped so. She didn't want to face the future without him. He was the only thing that kept her head from exploding.

Logan began to drum his thumbs on the steering wheel. "I need to know more about your time with Butch McGee. There might be something he said or did that can help us track him down."

Her heart sank. "Okay." She swallowed against the tightness of her throat. "What do you want to know?"

"I just need more details beyond the surface information you've already shared. I won't know what I'm looking for until I hear it. Can you start at the beginning?"

Alex closed her eyes and breathed through her nose. She didn't want to relive any of that, especially not with this throbbing headache. But she understood why he needed to know. "He rang the doorbell," she started. "I checked the peep hole, but he looked so . . . harmless that I opened the door. I know that was stupid, but my neighborhood is—"

"It's okay, Alex. I don't blame you for opening the door to him."

She laughed under her breath. She wished he could be so understanding about her high-powered empathy. "He zapped me with a stun gun."

Angry air whistled through Logan's teeth, but he said nothing.

"When I came to, I was tied up in the storage unit." She paused, remembering that she hadn't even gotten a glimpse of Butch McGee's face before the stroke of his hand on her cheek had catapulted her into the dark, dirty-sock-stinking closet where he'd tried to hide from his own kidnapper.

"And?" Logan prodded.

She skipped the part she knew he would have trouble believing. "I got sick, and he left to get supplies to clean up."

"He didn't say anything to you?"

"Not that I remember."

Logan thought about this for a long, silent moment. "And when he returned?"

"He told me that he picked me because he wanted to punish you for something you did to his brother."

"That's when he told you his brother's name is Brian."

She hesitated for an instant. Butch hadn't told her anything about Brian, not directly. But she saw no other choice but to lie. "Yes."

"What happened after that?"

She chewed her lower lip. "He left me alone, and the next thing I knew, you were carrying me out."

"You were unconscious when Noah and I found you. How did that happen?"

"I don't remember."

"Alex—"

"I don't remember," she repeated.

"When did he tell you about Tyler Ambrose?"

She struggled with how to respond. She was not good at manipulating the truth, never had been. "He told me that was his real name."

"He *told* you? Alex, come on. I can tell you're lying. You're terrible at it."

Her face heated in a heartbeat. "I'm giving you the information in a way that I know you'll accept it."

"I'll accept the truth."

"You don't trust the truth. Not when it's not what you want to hear. And apparently you don't trust *me*."

He started to respond but shut his mouth when he steered around the corner into a cul-de-sac jammed with police cars and an ambulance. "Shit," he said under his breath. "I guess the backup I requested got here before we did."

"You called for all of this?"

"Not quite," he said in resignation.

CHAPTER **FORTY-SIX**

Logan flashed his badge at the officer keeping curious bystanders at bay in front of the sprawling, Spanish-style, yellow stucco mansion on prime beach property. The Gulf's waves splashed in the background, and the fronds of palm trees rattled in the breeze. Amid the tranquility of the beach, what should have been paradise for a snow-beaten tourist, something ominous hung in the air.

"What's the situation?" Logan asked.

"Looks like a homicide, sir," the officer said.

Logan kept his expression impassive. Damn, shit, fuck.

"Detective Culver's inside, sir," the young officer said. "He told me to tell you to go in when you got here."

In other words: Let's not discuss what happened in front of the onlookers. Logan nodded and grasped Alex's elbow. He turned toward her, his mouth close to her ear so as not to be overheard. "Maybe you should wait in the car."

"Forget it," she said, lips moving as little as his had.

"I don't know what's inside. It might be . . . ugly."

"I'm a news photographer. I've seen ugly."

"Alex—"

"Stop trying to protect me, Logan. I've seen some horrific stuff just in the past few days. I can handle it."

The soft words, spoken with no hint of melodrama, hit him square in the chest. After the conversation they'd had on the way over, the way she'd hedged even simple questions, he . . . just didn't know what to think. She'd said, *You don't trust the truth. And apparently you don't trust* me. But he *did* trust her. He just couldn't trust the unbelievable. The supernatural wasn't reality, not in his world. He couldn't fathom how Alex and the people who cared about her could believe it all so easily.

He studied her, and the knot in his stomach tightened. Only an hour ago, her jaw had been swollen and smeared with purple. Exactly like Justin's. Empathic stigmata, AnnaCoreen the psychic had called it.

Jesus, it just wasn't possible.

Yet, he'd seen it with his own eyes. It *was* possible.

"Well?" she asked, nudging him out of his thoughts. "Are we going in or are you going to haul me over your shoulder and put me back in the car to wait?"

He let a small smile curve his lips as he imagined having her firm behind so readily available to his hands. "That certainly sounds tempting."

She must have recognized the naughty direction of his thoughts, because she returned his smile with a slight one of her own, though it appeared strained. But then she looked away instead of batting back a teasing response.

It struck him, like a fist to the temple, that he was losing her, and that thought turned his stomach inside out. "Alex—"

"Shouldn't you do your job?" she asked.

He sighed, frustrated and not even sure who he was frustrated with. Not her, not really. Himself, definitely. He needed to find a way to accept the unacceptable. No, he corrected himself. He needed to find a way to accept *Alex*. That shouldn't be nearly as difficult as he was making it. It was *Alex*, after all.

He focused on her face, so pale and punctuated by dark circles under her eyes that hadn't been there even a month after she'd died in the ER. He'd thanked his lucky stars every day since then that she'd survived, that he still had her in his life. And now what was he doing? Being a stubborn asshole, obsessed with finding logic where logic didn't exist. And petrified, if he did accept it, of what she would learn about him.

"Logan."

He blinked, realizing he'd stared at her for too long. Amazingly, concern for him created lines on her forehead. She was concerned about *him*, when she'd been the one bleeding and unconscious little more than an hour ago. Because she'd touched Justin.

Jesus.

He had to fight to focus. "I have to do my job. Right. Stay close to me, okay?"

She nodded, and she looked more tired than before, as though the impact of what happened to Justin, and her, hadn't quite worked its way through her system yet. Or perhaps his lack of faith in her was taking a toll. That thought twisted the already knotted muscles in his gut.

Shoving away his doubts, and concern, he led the way into the foyer of Florida state senator Preston Wells and Lake Avalon alderwoman Toni Kale Wells. The newly built home had all the upgrades of an expensive beachside house. Ceramic tile, palm-frond ceiling fans, arching ceilings and sliding-glass doors all across the back wall that displayed the beauty of Florida: a white-sand beach and infinite water that shot off diamonds of light.

The smell of blood reached Logan while he and Alex pulled on paper booties that would prevent their shoes from disturbing evidence. They didn't have to go far to find the source of that coppery scent. The senator lay face up in the middle of the living room floor, eyes open and staring. Blood soaked the front of his formerly white dress shirt and pooled on the tile beneath him. He'd been shot in the chest.

"Fuck," Logan breathed.

Beside him, Alex sucked in a shaky breath.

Detective Gale Culver spotted them from across the room and walked over, careful to skirt the crime scene with its small yellow placards bearing large numbers to mark evidence around the body. The gun lay near the dead man's feet.

"Logan," Gale said in greeting. He was a tall, rail-thin man with a goatee, bald head and crease-laden face. Logan knew him to be fifty-five, based on the big party their co-workers had thrown in the fall, but he looked sixty-five, thanks to a fishing hobby and resistance to sunscreen.

When he smiled at Alex, Logan quickly introduced them. "Gale, this is Alex Trudeau. She helped me talk with the alderwoman's son."

"Hell, Logan, Alex and I go way back." Gale reached out to shake her hand, and Logan tensed. Then he noticed the latex gloves the detective wore, standard operating procedure at a crime scene like this.

Alex must have noted the gloves, too, because she accepted his hand after only a slight hesitation. "Hi, Gale. Good to see you."

"You doing okay? I heard you had some drama the other day."

She nodded and smiled. "I'm fine. Thanks."

Logan watched the genuine affection between the two, reminded that Alex had a lifetime of history in Lake Avalon that he couldn't relate to.

"How's your dad doing these days?" Gale asked. "Enjoying retirement?"

"He seems to love it. You should stop by and say hi," Alex said.

Gale glanced at Logan. "Her old man used to drive me nutty back in the day, always trying to pry information out of me about even the most mundane cases. A regular old newshound, that one." He grinned at Alex. "He was tickled to death when his kids followed in his journalistic footsteps." He looked at Logan. "He thought this one"—he indicated Alex—"would be long gone by now, though. Working for *The New York Times* or doing some Annie Leibovitz–type work."

Alex smiled but said nothing as her cheeks pinkened. Logan found the blush as cute as always, and a warmth spread through him that happened only around her. How could he be so all-fired stupid as to toss that away because he couldn't buy something as simple as psychic ability? Jesus, he was an idiot.

"So you have the son in custody?" Gale asked Logan.

Logan forced his brain back on topic. "I wouldn't call it custody. But I know where he is, yes. He says the senator's been beating on him for the past month. I was on my way over here to haul the bastard downtown in cuffs."

"Christ," Gale said, shaking his head. "We'll need to talk to the kid soon."

"Can you tell me what happened here?" Logan asked.

"Looks like the alderwoman and the senator struggled over a gun, and the senator took a bullet." Gale jerked a thumb over his shoulder toward the back of the house. "The alderwoman is in the kitchen with the EMTs. She's pretty traumatized."

"When did this happen?" Logan asked. "We've been with Justin for hours, and you guys didn't get here until after I called in a request for backup."

"Late last night or early this morning. The first officer on the scene found the alderwoman sitting on the floor in the living room with the gun still in her hand. She was in shock."

"Is it okay if I go talk to her?" Alex asked. "We know each other."

"Sure, but she's completely zoned out," Gale said.

"Seeing a friend might snap her out of it so we can get a statement."

Logan watched Alex go, his muscles twitching to follow her. As much as he knew logically that Butch McGee wouldn't come near a house swarming with cops to get at her, he still didn't like letting her out of his sight.

"So, you and Alex, huh?" Gale said. "I've watched her grow from a spunky little thing. You break her heart, and you're going to have to leave town."

Logan laughed under his breath, not all that amused. "What makes you think I'd break her heart?"

"I'm just saying. I wouldn't be the only one wanting to kick your ass. You don't realize it, but you work with a long line of guys hoping you mess up so they can get their chance with her."

Logan bristled, whether with jealousy that other men coveted her or annoyance that they expected him to be an asshole to her, he didn't know, maybe both. Either way, he decided it best to steer the conversation back to the case. "What's your take here? Self-defense or premeditated?"

"Self-defense all the way. She's got the bruises to prove it."

"Bruises? The senator beat her up?"

"My guess is he almost killed her knocking her around and trying to strangle her before she got the gun and shot him. She's lucky to be—hey, where are you going?"

Logan's vision narrowed down to one thing. He found the kitchen. It had a bright and airy breakfast nook surrounded by more glass doors that opened onto a terra-cotta patio and a private beach. A salty Gulf breeze stirred through bamboo curtains.

Alex sat in a chair, facing the hunch-shouldered Toni Wells, who sobbed quietly into a wad of Kleenex. Alex had a hand clamped on the woman's sweater-covered shoulder.

Logan winced at the sight of the bruises on the other woman, especially the dark, finger-sized ring around her throat. A white bandage was taped to her temple, and her nose bore the signs of a recent blood fountain. She held a cold pack to the back of her head.

"I don't really remember what happened," Toni was saying, breath hitching and tears streaming. "I just remember Preston hitting Justin and yelling at him, and the next thing I knew, Preston was dead on the living room floor. They keep asking me questions I can't answer. I . . . It's just all a blur." She looked up and stared into Alex's eyes. "I need to find Justin. He's been gone for weeks. Preston said he was wanted by the cops for dealing drugs. I . . . I didn't want to report him missing and get him into more trouble until . . . Oh, Lord, I should have known that wasn't true, should have suspected. But I didn't . . . I couldn't . . ." She bowed her head and started to weep in earnest. "I'm a horrible mother, and they're going to arrest me now and send me to prison, and my baby won't have a mother."

A tear traced a path down Alex's pale cheek, and Logan swallowed. She felt other people's pain like her own, would do anything to try to ease a friend's despair, and his heart ached with love for this woman. How did he get so damn lucky? And when had he gotten so damn stupid that he'd risk losing her because he was too stubborn to open his mind to supernatural possibilities?

"I wish I could remember," Toni said between hiccups. "It had to be self-defense, right? I wouldn't kill even a cruel animal of a man, not in cold blood. I mean, I wanted to kill him. When he hurt poor Justin, that bastard. But I wouldn't actually do it." She turned pleading, drenched eyes on Alex. "Would I?"

A determined expression took over Alex's features, and her jaw clenched. She straightened in her chair, the hand on Toni's shoulder tightening.

Logan got what she intended to do just as she removed the hand from Toni's shoulder and shifted. He reached her in two long strides and caught her wrist before she could place it on the back of the alderwoman's hand.

Alex flinched and glanced up at him in shock.

"You don't need to solve this mystery," he said softly. "That's someone else's job."

Her eyes, so tired they appeared bruised underneath, widened. Unable to stand the exhaustion shadowing her face, he took her elbow and urged her to her feet.

"I'm so sorry to interrupt," he said to the alderwoman, "but I need to steal Alex away. I promise you that your son is safe, and you'll see him very soon. Now, if you'll please excuse us, Alex is late for an important appointment."

He tugged Alex toward the door that led back to the living room, but she resisted. "What are you doing?"

"I'm getting you out of here before you do something stupid," he all but snarled under his breath.

She jerked her arm out of his grasp and stopped. "Stupid? *Stupid?*"

He faced her, determined not to waver despite the fury in her eyes, just as determined to keep his voice low and between them. "You were going to touch her, weren't you? To see what happened to her. To *experience* it firsthand. Well, isn't it pretty damn fucking obvious what happened to her? That son of a bitch almost killed her. And you were going to relive it. Why? It's not necessary. My fellow detective—Gale Culver, remember him?—he knows how to do his job, and he does it well. He doesn't need you to figure things out for him."

"I can help her, Logan. She doesn't—"

"It doesn't matter if she doesn't remember. There's no mistaking what happened here. No one's going to try to send her away for something that was clearly self-defense. Justin's story supports hers, so—"

His ringing cell phone cut him off, and he swore at the intrusion. "Damn it." He whipped it out and checked the caller ID. "It's Don. I need to take this." He gave her an apologetic look. "I'm sorry."

Alex turned and walked out of the house without another word. He followed a few steps behind, not taking his gaze off her while he answered the detective's call. She didn't quite walk a straight line, and worry hammered at him. He hated that his buttheadedness had added to her stress.

"Don, hi. What have you got?"

"Listen, I think Butch McGee broke into Alex's house."

"Shit, did he—"

"Everything's cool, don't worry. The dogs must have chased him away."

"And they're okay?" Logan couldn't imagine Alex's devastation if anything happened to any of her mutts.

"They're all fine, but they barked up a storm. Neighbor called the police. We've got a squad car sitting out front for now."

"Good, that's good."

"We can't keep one there indefinitely, though. If we had the staff, we would have staked out her place and your place."

"Yeah, I know the deal. There's only so much the department can handle. So did anyone see McGee at Alex's?"

"Nope. But we found footprints outside a bedroom window that match the plaster we took of the prints at the storage facility. He got in and looked around but didn't disturb anything other than busting the frame on the window to get in."

"So he's not lying low."

"Nope. I've got officers checking the lodging in the area, but as you know, there are a lot of hotel rooms."

"He's probably using an alias now that he knows we're onto him," Logan said. "He's no moron, considering how long he's avoided getting caught."

Alex opening the passenger door of his pickup and climbing into the truck commanded his attention. Without glancing his way, she leaned her head back against the seat and closed her eyes. Exhaustion radiated off her like waves of heat.

"Logan, you listening?" Don said.

"Yeah. What was that last thing?"

"Two FBI agents are flying in tonight. Flight from Washington lands around eight. They're going to want to talk to Alex first thing."

"I figured as much. Let me know when and where."

"Sure thing."

Logan disconnected the call as Gale joined him on the sidewalk.

"Bitch of a day," the other detective said.

Logan nodded. He couldn't agree more. "Are you transporting the alderwoman downtown?"

"She's going to the ER first," Gale said. "I'll get her full statement there."

"I'll have a friend bring Justin to the ER then, if that's cool."

"Maybe it'll clear her mind if she sees with her own eyes that her son is okay."

Before Logan got into the truck, he quickly called Noah and arranged for him to reunite Justin with his mother at the hospital. Then he slid behind the wheel. Alex said nothing as he fired up the engine, her hands clasped between her knees.

He wanted to reach out and touch her, soothe her. But he hesitated. What if she saw inside his head? What if she flashed on the part of him he found it almost impossible to live with? And that just made him angry with himself. He couldn't just hurt her with his pigheadedness. He also had to be an absolute fucking coward when she needed comfort.

Alex would touch a hurting friend, as she'd tried to touch Toni Wells, knowing the action could thrust her into a life-threatening situation. And he couldn't bring himself to risk letting her see his darkest side. He told himself it was because he didn't want to stress her more, but he also wanted to never have to tell, or show, anyone what he'd done, the innocence he'd taken.

"Logan?"

He glanced sideways at her, concerned all over again by the tremor of fatigue in her voice. She looked back at him with equal concern, and he had to glance away. He'd never felt so ashamed. He'd doubted the one person he trusted more than he trusted even himself. He'd feared *he* would be exposed, and he'd made her pay for it.

"I'm sorry," he said, the apology rushing out. "I'm so, so sorry."

CHAPTER **FORTY-SEVEN**

Alex rubbed at her temples. Her brain felt thick and slow, as though she'd swallowed double the dosage of Benadryl. She didn't know why Logan was apologizing, but she was smart enough by now not to assume it meant what she hoped it meant. He'd certainly *seemed* to accept her empathy when he'd intervened before she could touch Toni, but who knew? He had a much stronger sense of denial than anyone she'd ever known.

"I'm sorry, Alex," he repeated. "For everything. I've been an ass."

She arched an eyebrow when he swallowed and looked away.

"I *do* trust you," he went on. "I always have. And this empathy thing . . . I believe you. Of course, I believe you. None of this has been about you or my lack of faith in you. It's me. It's all me, and I just—"

She released a frustrated huff of breath. Damn him anyway. "It's not me, it's you? Is that what you're saying? You're going to write us off that easily? After everything we've—"

She broke off as a choked sob caught her off guard, and she buried her face in her hands. Oh, God, she couldn't take it. She was frazzled beyond belief, couldn't think, couldn't feel, and now he was going to leave her. She'd have to deal with everything, *everything*, alone.

"Alex, God, no. I'm—" He twisted in his seat and grasped her wrists to pull her hands away from her face. "Look at me, honey. Look at me."

She did so reluctantly, emotion hitching in her chest. This was what it felt like to lose hope. She didn't think she could cope with her empathic life without her anchor, the one thing that kept her centered.

"I'm not leaving you," he said, his fingers gripped hard around her wrists. "I swear. I love you."

She narrowed her eyes, not sure she could believe him.

He must have seen her uncertainty, because he leaned forward and kissed her, gently at first, his lips warm against hers, and then more urgently, one hand releasing her wrist to curl around her nape and draw her closer.

Pleasure and the absolute rightness of his embrace swirled together through her, chasing some of the leaden cold from her bones.

When he ended the kiss, too soon in her opinion, he rested his forehead against hers and mingled their exhalations. "We're going to get through this, Alex. I promise. Whatever it takes."

She wanted to believe him. God, she wanted to believe him. But she wondered how much of what he said was Logan being honest and how much was Logan saying what he thought she needed to hear.

Silence again reigned as he drove to Charlie's and parked in the driveway. No one else was home, and Alex was glad. She needed a nap, stat.

But when the front door closed behind them, Logan drew her into his arms and kissed her again, deep and desperate, his hands sliding up under her tank top and over her ribs. His thumbs found the tips of her breasts, and she moaned against his mouth as they played and teased her nipples into aching peaks.

It took her a pleasure-dazed moment to realize that he was talking to her as he caressed her, as he kissed her senseless and backed her down the hallway toward the guest bedroom.

"I know you're doubting what I feel," he murmured, trailing kisses over her throat and back to her ear. "I know you think I can't accept who you are."

His tongue traced the shell of her ear, then teased the lobe. "I know I hurt you when I doubted you."

He pulled her into the bedroom and used one foot to gently kick the door closed, his lips sucking lightly at the throb of her pulse in her throat. "I know you didn't believe me when I said I love you and that I won't leave you, no matter what, so I'm showing you."

He grasped the hem of her shirt and pulled it off, tossing it aside. "I'm showing you how much I love you, Alex."

His fingers hooked into the waistband of her jeans, and he tugged her close, his nose in her hair as he worked the button free and eased down the zipper. "I love you so much," he repeated as he pushed the denim over her hips. He braced her as she kicked free of her shoes and jeans, then he backed her against the wall, swallowing her gasp of anticipation on a kiss that stole her breath, made her head spin. "I'm going to love you, Alex. For the rest of my life."

Still kissing, exploring her mouth with the light touch of his tongue, he slid his fingers into her panties and started stroking her. She couldn't stop the moan that tickled her throat, and she felt him smile against her mouth.

They stayed like that for a long time, Logan kissing and caressing, caressing and kissing, until her breath grew choppy and she could do nothing but hold on to his shoulders. He'd stopped talking, but she didn't care, no longer able to focus on words, consumed by the growing wave of pleasure that bore down on her.

Her body tensed, preparing to take the hit, and she gasped, "Wait, wait."

She wanted him inside her, wanted the connection. Wanted him to fill all her empty spaces.

"We have time," he murmured, holding her close against him with one arm around her lower back while his free hand stroked and stroked and stroked.

She stiffened, and the world turned white and blank as the pleasure rolled, tumbled, cascaded over her. He held her through it, still stroking but gently, easing her down but bracing her as smaller, undulating waves continued to wash through her.

He lifted her and turned toward the bed, where he laid her on it and quickly stripped out of his own clothes. She realized dazedly that she still wore her bra and underwear, so she started to shed them. Logan grinned at her when her fingers fumbled with the clasp on her bra, and she smiled back, probably looking goofy considering how incredibly smitten she felt. He brushed her hands away and took care of it for her, taking time to massage and knead until her nipples were tight and aching.

God, she loved him.

And as he crawled onto the bed with her, she saw how much he wanted her. She opened her arms to him, throbbing with need when he settled between her legs. She lifted her hips on a gasp of pleasure as he eased into her an inch at a time. He braced on his hands, and she heard his harsh swallow as he swiveled his hips against her, working his way in, filling her with more than she ever thought possible.

Her head arched back into the pillow. He was so big, so hard, and the pressure . . . it pulsed inside her, surrounding him, drawing him deeper.

His breath hissed between his teeth. "If you move, it's over," he said, gently kissing the corner of her mouth.

She wouldn't move. No way would she move. She wanted this to last. Forever.

"I love you," he whispered, his lips pressed to her temple. "I've never loved anyone like this. Never."

She tightened her arms around him and closed her eyes against the tears burning her lids. "I love you, too."

He started to thrust finally, gently at first and slowly, as though too much friction too fast would send him over the edge. The slow, easy glide, creating friction in places she could no longer identify as his or hers, renewed the pulse of pleasure, and when he did little more than continue the lazy rhythm, thrusting against her with no apparent plans to hurtle through the final countdown, she found herself rising to meet him with a growing need that blossomed and fluttered and built until she dug her nails into his back.

How could he stand it? How could he control his movements when it felt so damn good *everywhere*? It was like they'd become one, cliché as that seemed, but she really couldn't tell where he ended and she began, and she didn't care. All she cared about was how it felt. So. Phenomenally. Supernaturally. *Good.*

She heard herself release a strangled whimper.

He chuckled against her throat, his nose drawing feathery circles against her damp skin as he kept up the steady, devastating pace. "Think you could articulate that?" he asked, his own voice hoarse.

"No," she replied on a gasp as pleasure spiked sharply, and she strained against him. Oh, God, finally. Her body gathered its resources, and . . . and . . .

He put the thrusting on pause and kissed away her protests, using his lips and tongue to settle her, his fingers gentle and stroking on her breasts, over her ribs and hip, drawing her closer, branding her with his touch.

The sensation between her legs was unlike anything she'd ever felt. Pleasure and exquisite, highly sensitized pain. Soft, wet silk gripping and rippling. Iron-hard heat pulsing and twitching. She was herself; she was him. She was restraint; she was greed.

She was going to kill him if he didn't—

A gasp caught in her throat as he resumed, and this time he didn't tease or try to ease her down. He drove her up and over.

She clung to him, and mindless, soaring ecstasy flowed through her in molten waves, hitching her hips against him repeatedly and as frenzied as his thrusts. She had no time to float down as he started to come, jerking against her and groaning against the side of her neck.

The instant he collapsed on top of her, she felt herself turn inside out. Her world narrowed down to the fever and steel between her legs, nestled in silky softness and scorching heat, the pleasure spreading out in incredible, mind-blowing spasms that culminated in a geyser of heat spurting and spurting.

She couldn't stop the serrated moan as her head arched back and her body continued to tense and release, caught in the throes of his pleasure.

CHAPTER **FORTY-EIGHT**

Logan gathered a limp, damp Alex against him, his breath still coming fast and hard. His brain was working a mile a minute, though, as he put two and two together and realized why she had an extra orgasm every time they made love.

Holy shit, he thought. Holy freaking shit. And he had to laugh, and marvel. "I'm so jealous."

She laughed, also breathless, her muscles lightly trembling against him. "You should be. It's pretty incredible."

"I can't believe I didn't get what was happening to you before. I just thought you were so in tune with me that no matter what I did, I could make you come."

"Well, there's that, too."

He hugged her close. "I really am sorry it took me so long to . . . accept."

"Why?"

"Because I hurt you, and I hate that I did that."

"No. I meant why did it take you so long?"

"I'm a cop. I try to see the logic . . ." He trailed off and sighed. "I'm afraid, Alex. Of what you'll see in me. Have already seen."

"Your nightmare."

He nodded. "Yes."

"But that wasn't reality. You didn't really shoot a child."

He closed his eyes and pulled her tighter. "How do you know that?"

"Because I know you. If you did shoot that little boy, it was an accident. I think it's much more likely that your dream is a distorted version of the truth."

He held her for a long time, idly stroking her bare arm. This moment, with her relaxed and loving in his arms, might be their last such moment. Once he told her—

"Tell me," she whispered, trailing her fingertips through the hair on his chest. "Please?"

He swallowed, his entire body tight with tension. "He was six years old. Kidnapped three months before that night." He stopped, not sure he could get through the story in one piece. The last time he had spoken of that night, it had been to a jury in a cold, impersonal setting.

Alex gave his chest hair a slight tug. "Go on."

"I was on patrol in downtown Detroit, in an area some people would call the red-light district. I saw a little boy burst through this door in the next block, and a big guy, huge, run out after him. The man caught the boy and cuffed him a good one upside the head, then carried him back through the door. I didn't like the look of that, so I approached and flashed my badge. Things didn't go well, and . . . there was a shootout. Aaron Hastings was caught in the crossfire. Six and missing for three months, and the night I could have saved him, I killed him."

"You shot him?" Her voice was dull with horror.

"If I hadn't interfered—"

"You tried to help him, Logan," she said, the horror gone, conviction in its place. "You didn't mean for—"

"I know that. I know all of that. I've said the same things to myself over and over for the past two years. And none of it matters. That kid is dead because of me."

Alex sat up and stared at him for a long, intense minute, until Logan shifted and got nervous. "What?" he asked.

"Is that why you left Detroit?"

"I didn't run away—" He stopped. He was being honest now, right? "Okay, yeah, I ran away. Turns out two of my fellow police officers were on the take, paid to look the other way and even provide protection when the . . . sex providers organized their 'party nights.'"

"Party nights?"

"Two-for-one deals. Buy a blow job, get a rim job for free. Buy an hour with a woman, get fifteen minutes with a little girl. Sick shit like that."

Alex closed her eyes. "Oh my God."

"The guy who ran the shop was a creative son of a bitch. He probably could have founded the next Microsoft or Google if he'd used his brain for good. Instead, I showed up on a party night. Killed one of the best customers and sent the leader of the band and two fellow officers to prison. Then I left town. Arrived in Lake Avalon three days later and liked it. Sunshine almost every day of the year. Fresh air. Green trees and flowers year round. And water as far as the eye can see. Humbling yet comforting. Things were simpler here."

"Were?" she asked with a quirk of her lips.

He smiled, gathered her closer. "Until I fell in love."

"Sorry about that," she said.

"Yeah, you ruined my life." He pressed a kiss to her temple, lingering for a moment to breathe in her light, sweet scent. Stalling, really. "Can I ask you a question, about the empathy?"

She grew still in his arms but nodded. "Okay."

"When you were with Butch . . . you flashed on his past, didn't you?"

"Yes."

"What's his worst nightmare?"

The breath she took in shook. "He has several, it turns out."

"What do you mean?"

"He hit me with a stun gun, and it must have scrambled my system even more, because every time he touched me after that, I flashed on something different. Or maybe his entire past is a nightmare."

He forced himself not to stiffen as he imagined what she'd gone through. No wonder she'd been unresponsive when he and Noah had found her. The fact that she'd been able to function afterward for as long as she had . . . well, fuck.

"You need to talk about this," he said gently. "Keeping what happened bottled up will only tear you apart."

She shifted, as though she wanted to move away from him, but he tightened his arms, ever so slightly, to ask her nonverbally to stay put. She settled back into him, though she didn't relax. Anxiety vibrated off her body, and he did his best to absorb it.

"Take your time," he said.

After several long minutes, she inhaled a trembling breath. "He was kidnapped as a child and subjected to years of abuse and torture."

"Specifically?"

"I can't . . ."

"Try."

Her throat made a clicking sound as she swallowed. "Fists. Cigarette burns. Knives. He was locked up, not allowed to go outside. His captor told him his parents didn't want him anymore."

"Jesus."

"The kidnapper—Butch called him the dickhead—he taught Butch how to torture women, how to enjoy it. I mean, part of me thinks he couldn't have become a monster if he really didn't want to, but part of me has no idea how much a human being can take before . . . breaking."

Logan heard the double meaning, and the gravity of it pulled at his heart. "Are you worried about breaking?"

She didn't breathe for a long moment. "Maybe."

"You won't. You're the strongest person I know."

"But it's in me, Logan. Butch's memories . . . they're inside me. They feel like *my* memories. It's like there's this evil . . . seed planted inside me now. What if it grows?"

"Well, to continue the analogy, it would have to be nurtured to grow."

"It grew in Butch."

"But he chose to let it grow, Alex. He became a serial killer."

She shifted away from him, taking the sheet with her this time, and turned so she could see his face. "Are you serious? He's a serial killer?"

He nodded, wishing he hadn't dropped it on her like a bomb, but it was too late now, and he hadn't had a chance earlier to ease her into what he'd learned. "The FBI has DNA evidence that Butch McGee has tortured and killed twenty-three women."

The pink in her cheeks washed away, the hand clutching the sheet to her chest tightening until her knuckles turned white. "Oh my God."

"You're the only one that the FBI knows of who's survived an encounter with him."

Realization creased her forehead like pain. "I'm the one who got away."

"And the one who can help the feds put him away forever."

She raised her chin, her lips pressing into a resolute line. "Then I need to talk to them."

The muscles in his chest squeezed. Another woman might have been terrified that McGee might try to come after her again. Another woman might have wanted to hide or even demanded protection. Not Alex. She was so gung ho to help that it scared him, and he thought of the look of determination on her face when she'd reached for Toni Wells's hand.

She had no concept of the consequences to herself. And yet, she possibly held the key to catching a serial killer who'd eluded the FBI for years.

"I need to talk to them, Logan. You know I do."

A wave of protectiveness flowed over him even as he resigned himself to doing his job. "I know. A couple of FBI agents are due in tonight. They'll want to talk to you as soon as possible."

"Oh. Okay."

"I'll be with you the whole time, okay? Just . . . can you promise me something?"

"What?"

He caught her hand and threaded their fingers. "Promise you'll start thinking twice before you fling yourself into someone else's hell with the idea of helping them."

"I did help Justin, though."

"Yes," he conceded. "But there might have been an easier way."

"What could be easier than witnessing the truth first-hand?"

"But it *wasn't* easy," he said. "You came out of it bloody and bruised."

"The bruises faded in less than an hour, and there isn't any lasting damage."

"But what about on the inside? You're worried about how much you can take, Alex. That's damage, in my opinion."

Her brows drew together, and she settled back against the pillow. "I'm fine. For now, I'm fine."

Yeah, that sounded confident. Still, he didn't challenge her. Not this time. "I just want you to think before you do stuff that puts you at risk." He pulled her against him, rubbing her arms and resting his chin on the top of her head. "You can't save everyone, you know."

"I don't want to *save* Butch McGee. I want to stop him."

"I meant the Justins and Tonis of the world."

"You have to admit my method saved a lot of time. There are no shades of gray, no worries about who's lying and who's telling the truth. We kept a teenager from a potentially destructive path. Justin didn't think anyone would believe him, and we proved him wrong."

"And you got off on that power, didn't you?"

He felt her hold her breath in his arms, sensed her think carefully before she answered. So it surprised him when she said simply, "Yeah, I did. I'm the only one who could have done that. Besides Charlie, and her flashes are so short, she might not have gotten the full story."

He relaxed some, relieved that she admitted it, even if the substance of the admission worried him. "We're going to have to keep an eye on you."

"That's what I have you for, right?"

Smiling, he hugged her close and kissed her hair. "Damn right. You can't chase me away with your empathic . . ." He trailed off, hunting for the right word.

"Freakishness," she said.

He laughed, surprised that he could. "Well, it is kind of freaky."

"Tell me about it."

He put his fingers on her chin and gently angled her head back so he could kiss her, slow and sweet. His ringing cell phone interrupted right when things turned urgent.

Swearing, he swiped it up from where it sat on the bedside table and flipped it open. "Logan."

"Yeah, it's Don. I'm on the scene of a murder. Woman found by neighbors when they noticed she hadn't picked up her newspapers in the driveway like usual. They thought she might be sick so checked on her. Looks like Butch McGee has claimed a twenty-fourth victim."

CHAPTER **FORTY-NINE**

Butch gulped down an iced mocha and stared with narrowed eyes at the sunlight glinting off the fender of the recently washed royal blue Ford Escape in Alex Trudeau's driveway. When his retinas started throwing off black dots, he blinked and looked away.

He needed . . . a fix. Like a crack addict, withdrawal had set in. He'd slashed his pleasure into Sally Blake not that long ago, and already the need had built to a new high.

And Alex Trudeau, goddammit, was nowhere to be found.

He'd returned to her house with his gun, intending to kill the dozen or so dogs that guarded her bedroom so he could at least feel close to her, smell her, perhaps collect some souvenirs, but a cop car parked out front ruined his plan.

So instead, he sat in the Fusion, casual in sunglasses as he pretended to consult a map, and surreptitiously watched a woman who had to be Alex's sister, considering the resemblance, lead six dogs out to the SUV in her driveway.

Each dog was physically challenged in some way, he

noted. Missing a leg, an ear or an eye. One, a big German shepherd, appeared to be completely blind, considering the way the Alex-like woman kept making kissing noises at it to steer it toward the SUV.

Alex Trudeau liked damaged things. How interesting.

Spotting the cop leaning against the front fender of the cruiser looking toward him, Butch folded the map and tossed it into the passenger seat. He steered the rental around the next corner and did a U-turn in the middle of the road.

Hopefully, where Alex's dogs went, so went Alex.

CHAPTER **FIFTY**

Alex wandered into Charlie's living room, hungover from a three-hour deep-sleep nap, and found all her pooches in various positions of sleep and watchfulness scattered around the floor. Six heads lifted to watch her, but each mutt seemed to get that she wasn't up for a ground assault delivered with puppy love.

Instead, she stopped and visited each dog, murmuring reassurances accompanied by an abundance of ear and belly rubs. "Aunt Charlie brought you to her house so you wouldn't be home alone, huh? That was awfully nice of her. She's a good aunt."

In the kitchen, Charlie was emptying the dishwasher in slow motion. When she spotted Alex, she stopped, a guilty look on her face. "Did I wake you? I was trying to be quiet."

Alex shook her head as she ran a hand through her disheveled hair and sat down at the kitchen table with a graceless plop. "I didn't hear a thing."

"Logan and Noah are at the home of the murdered woman," Charlie said. "The feds went straight there after their plane landed, too."

Alex nodded wearily as Phoebe hobbled into the kitchen and nudged her long nose under Alex's palm. Alex obliged the not-so-subtle request with an answering chin stroke.

Charlie watched for a moment, as though gauging Alex's well-being, then went back to stacking clean plates in the cupboard. "There's a cop staking out the backyard and another one parked in front of the house," she said. "Logan wasn't keen on leaving you here, but Noah and I convinced him that you needed your beauty sleep."

Alex gave a soft laugh. Beauty sleep. A nice way of describing lapsing into yet another empathy-induced coma.

Charlie nudged the dishwasher door closed with her hip. "Want some coffee?"

"Make it espresso. A quadruple shot."

As Charlie retrieved a cup from a cupboard, Alex said, "How's Mac doing? I've dropped the ball the past few days on checking in with him."

Charlie filled the cup with coffee and brought it to Alex at the table. "I'm going to suggest that he spend some time at the cabin, like we talked about before."

"That good, huh?"

"He has good days and bad days. I just really think he needs some time away to get it together."

"We can gang up on him, if you want."

"Sounds good to me. When you're feeling better."

Alex couldn't suppress a timely, jaw-popping yawn.

"Maybe you should sleep some more." Charlie returned to the dishwasher to finish putting away clean glasses. "There's no point in fighting it."

Alex didn't respond at first, smiling softly when Raquel trotted into the kitchen, Dieter right behind her with his nose vying for a shot at her butt. Both dogs crowded around Alex, bumping Phoebe out of the way so they could get some attention.

Alex used both hands to fluff and scratch and pat, gradually relaxing when Dieter's pink doggy tongue gave the back of her hand an affectionate lick. If things got so bad that she couldn't touch other people, at least she could look forward to warm, loving contact from her mutts.

"Is it going to be like this forever?" she asked Charlie. "I have no control over my own body anymore. I mean, I haven't felt this exhausted . . . ever."

"I wish I could say you get used to the flashes and their aftereffects, but they take a lot out of you. And yours are a hell of a lot more intense than mine." Charlie wiped down the counter before draping the dish towel over the faucet and facing Alex. A moment passed in which Alex sensed her sister's intense scrutiny.

"You should go back to bed," Charlie said, her concern evident. "You're going to make yourself sick if you resist."

Alex sat back, dialing it down on the pooch lovefest to look at her sister. "So, what, I'm going to spend the rest of my life sleeping it off? Like a drunk after a bender? How am I supposed to do my job? How am I supposed to have a life?"

"You'll find a way, Alex. You're resilient as hell. And you're not alone. You've got me and Logan and Noah and Dad."

A bitter smile twisted Alex's lips. "I noticed you left Mom off that list."

"She's special," Charlie said with a rueful laugh.

Instead of laughing, Alex blurted, "I head-tripped her."

Charlie sat down across from her, eyes wide. "I'm almost afraid to ask."

"It was . . . awful. She found a man after he committed suicide."

"Oh, God."

"She felt responsible, like she'd driven him to it."

"How?"

"Some kind of con."

"Con? As in con *artist*? *Mom?*"

Alex nodded. "She wanted to return the man's money, but he'd killed himself. She planned to run away from home with another man . . . Ben, and—"

"*Mom? Our* mom?"

Alex nodded. "Yes, I know, it's unbelievable. Her name was different. Eliza. Oh, and she had sisters. Agnes and Rena. Older. I think they were all con artists. Like grifters or gypsies."

Gus wandered into the kitchen and bumped the top of his head against Alex's leg until she ruffled his floppy ears.

When Charlie remained silent, Alex focused on her sister to see that shock had arched her brows. "What?" Alex asked.

"Did you say Rena?"

"Yes. Agnes and Rena."

"Alex, the cousin who came to see me back in March? Laurette? Her mother's name is Rena. She wanted to reunite Mom and Rena before Rena died of cancer. They're sisters. Mom admitted it during a weak moment after you were shot, but she's refused to talk about it since."

Alex's mind began to race. Suddenly, she saw a way to get some answers. "You know where Aunt Rena is because of Laurette, right? Have you tried to go see her?"

"I've called a few times, but Laurette's sister, Jewel, has been resistant to a visit. I don't want to barge in on them during a bad time. She said Rena is very ill."

"Did Jewel say how long . . ."

"I don't know. It sounded as though it wouldn't be long. I think Laurette might have been shooting for a deathbed kind of reunion." Charlie sighed. "So I'm afraid that leaves us with Mom. The queen of denial."

"Right. That leaves Mom." Knowing suddenly what she needed to do, Alex got up from the table and headed for the door.

Charlie jogged after her and caught her shirttail to stop her. "Excuse me, but where do you think you're going?"

"Mom *knows*, Charlie. I made the connection before but was too out of it to do anything about it. I went completely catatonic on her, and it didn't faze her. She *knew* what was happening. That means she might know how to control it. And if she doesn't, then she might be able to get Aunt Rena to talk to us. I'm going to see her to—"

"You do remember that this is our mother you're talking about."

"Surely she'll talk to me once she knows what this empathy . . . *crap* is doing to me."

"You flashed right in front of her, for an extended period of time, and she didn't do anything to try to help you. That's not a woman who gives a crap about what's happening to her kid."

"As usual, you're being way too hard on her."

"As usual, you're being way too easy on her. Has she contacted you at all to see how you're doing since that happened?"

"I've been out of touch—"

"You have a cell phone."

"Look, you and Mom have always had your issues. But this is different. I need to talk to *someone* who knows what I'm dealing with. If I can't find a way to control this empathy . . . well, I don't know how I can live around other people. Any innocent contact could be a nightmare. And what happens when I . . . when I touch someone who's lost a limb or suffered an aneurysm or stroke? Or, God, what if I make contact with a woman who's lost her husband or a child? I can't even imagine what that kind of grief would feel like, and I really, really don't want to ever experience it if I don't have to."

"We can go see AnnaCoreen—"

"AnnaCoreen is just guessing. I get why you love her. She's been a huge help, but we—*I* need answers from experts."

"Alex, I'm just trying to protect you. Mom doesn't want to talk about this. Ever. Cornering her because it's what *you* want won't change her mind."

"Fine. Then you can stun gun me and hold Mom down

so I can head-trip my way through her past until I find what I need to know."

"What? Wait. What?"

Alex sighed, frustrated that Charlie wasn't keeping up. But, then, she couldn't really blame her sister for being behind when Alex hadn't told her anything about her time with Butch McGee.

To buy herself some time to get her thoughts together, Alex turned her attention to her menagerie of strays. "Who wants to go out?" she asked the four dogs now forming islands of laziness on the kitchen floor.

The two who hadn't wandered in from the living room yet, Artemis and Oscar, came running at the magic word—"out"—and the whole pack filed out the back door when she pushed it open for them.

Turning back to the kitchen, she saw Charlie striking her expectant pose: arms crossed under her breasts, head cocked. "I'm waiting," she said without saying it out loud.

As usual when confronted with that look, Alex caved. "Butch McGee zapped me with a stun gun. It did wild and wacky things to my empathy, and I bounced all over the place in his head. I got to see all the nasty things, or at least some of the nasty things, that happened to make him the serial killer he is."

"Jesus, Alex." Charlie slowly sat down, looking ill. A long moment passed in which she swallowed several times, as though fighting the urge to be sick. "I really think we should consult with AnnaCoreen before we—"

"Damn it, no. I don't want to sit around *talking* about it. I need to *do* something. And I need to do it before it kills me."

Charlie raised her hands in a supplicating gesture. "Okay, okay. But you know what? You're not operating on all cylinders at the moment. This doesn't have to be solved right here and now."

"The sooner, the better."

"I agree. But let me put it to you this way: We're not going anywhere, not even to Mom and Dad's, until Noah and Logan get back. Logan would kill me if I let you go anywhere without him. Okay?"

"Charlie—"

"There is no discussion. You're a smart woman, Alex, and there's a serial killer out there who might be gunning for you."

"He wants revenge on Logan, not me."

"I'm sure that even you, in all your irrational gung-ho tude, can see that that logic is flawed. He's already proved that he wants to use you to get at Logan. We're going to play it safe, end of discussion."

Alex opened her mouth to argue then stopped. Charlie was right. She needed to take a breath. And a nap. She was so tired she couldn't think in a straight, coherent line anymore.

"Do me a favor?" Charlie said. "Go back to bed. Please? Your reserves are seriously depleted."

Alex thought about arguing but gave in instead. At the door leading to the hallway, she paused and looked back at her sister. "Thanks, Charlie. You're my best friend, you know."

Charlie smiled at her. "Yeah. Sister Sam screwed herself out of some good times when she ran away from home, huh?"

CHAPTER **FIFTY-ONE**

Logan let himself into the dark bedroom as quietly as possible, stopping just inside the door to listen for Alex's even breathing. Smiling at the soft, rhythmic snoring that floated from the bed, he toed off his shoes and then emptied his pockets on the dresser.

It was two in the morning, and Charlie had informed him that Alex had crashed late in the afternoon and hadn't stirred since. He was glad. She'd looked absolutely beat when he'd left her, and he hadn't been able to stop worrying about her. He wasn't used to seeing her so exhausted. Or anxiety-ridden.

Shaking his head—she was peaceful now, and he'd focus on that—he shrugged out of his shirt and went into the adjoining bathroom. He couldn't get the scene of Sally Blake's bedroom out of his head.

The mingling scents of blood, sweat and sex.

The gory aftermath of a psychopath's idea of fun with a blade.

The quiet, almost respectful murmurings of the crime scene techs.

All of it coalesced in his brain in a horror-show haze.

"It's the work of Butch McGee," the newly arrived FBI agent in charge, Tom Boyd, had said as he'd smoothed a hand over his stubby crew cut.

Logan's brain had too quickly made the connection that what that monster did to Sally Blake, he easily could have done to Alex. Probably *planned* to do to Alex. And he was relieved, so fucking relieved, that Alex was safe.

Shit like this shouldn't happen in Lake Avalon, Florida. This was supposed to be paradise. This was supposed to be his escape from the darkness and evil.

And Butch McGee followed him here.

Sally Blake died because a killer followed him here.

Alex was terrorized because a killer followed him here.

He just managed to get the toilet seat up before his body expelled the churning contents of his stomach.

Afterward, he flushed, breathing heavily and repeatedly spitting the bitterness out of his mouth. He brushed his teeth, then took a shower and stood under the hot spray until he felt marginally human again, or at least clean enough to crawl into bed with Alex.

Then he slipped between the sheets, snuggled up to her warm back and lightly kissed the side of her neck.

She woke on a violent gasp, and Logan swore as he gathered her close against him to soothe her. "It's okay, Alex. It's me. I'm sorry, I'm sorry." Damn it, he should have realized she would flash on what he'd seen at Sally Blake's the minute he touched her.

"Oh, God, that poor woman," she murmured against his chest, her voice raspy from sleep.

He pressed his lips to her forehead. "Try to go back to sleep."

"Are you okay?"

Her fingers played over his cheekbones, coming to rest, light and delicate, on his mouth. He kissed their tips, unable to stop the curve of a smile. He was so damn lucky to have her. "I'm okay now," he said. "You?"

"I need you."

His heart hitched under the hand she spread over his chest, the way she draped a leg over his thigh and pressed closer. "Later," he said, even as he hardened in hungry response. He wouldn't mind losing himself in her, letting her love chase away the lingering, haunting images in his head.

But those images were in her head now, too, thanks to his carelessness, so he didn't protest when she nudged his shoulder. He rolled onto his back, and she made quick work of his briefs, then straddled him, trapping his ready cock between them. His heart thunked against his ribs as his hands settled at her waist. Oh, Jesus, she wasn't wearing underwear.

She pulled her T-shirt—*his* T-shirt, he realized—over her head, and her springy curls tumbled around her face. Those curls, scented like almonds and cherries, tickled his cheeks when she leaned forward to bury her mouth on his, her tongue lazily slipping between his lips, her hands soft and soothing and perfect everywhere they touched.

As the need built, he raised his head off the pillow, taking their kisses deeper, more insistent, his mind blank to anything but loving this woman, loving Alex.

She shifted, lifted off him briefly, before sinking down, sinking onto his cock, taking him inside the tight, wet heat that stole his breath, stalled his brain. His fingers dug into her hips, and he couldn't stop himself from bucking his hips up off the bed, driving himself deeper. Her intake of breath told him that worked for her, too, and as they linked hands, fingers threaded for balance, he did it again and again, meeting each downward thrust of her hips until, oh, Jesus, he was already . . . right . . . there.

He tightened his fingers on hers and gasped, "Wait, slow down, wait."

But she shook her head and rode him faster. He caught a glimpse of her features in the moonlight, saw the concentration on her beautiful, pale face as she tipped her head back and gave herself over to the pleasure, gave herself over to him. The image set him off like a rocket.

He released a long, jaw-clenched groan as he came, stars bursting in his head, every nerve focused on the woman wrapped around him, around his heart.

The instant he regained control of his brain, he opened his eyes and watched, waited, breathless with anticipation as his orgasm took her. She stiffened on him, head back and neck corded, as his secondhand waves tossed her high, higher.

He quickly sat up, and bracing her with a hand flattened against her back, he began to suck her right nipple, using teeth and tongue to work it, tugging and biting ever so gently, using his fingers on her other breast to match the effect, intent on overwhelming her with pleasure.

She made a helpless sound in her throat, something that sounded like, "Un*guh*," and then he caught her mouth with his and swallowed her scream while her body convulsed, out of control, in his arms, the tension-release of her own orgasm hitting her again and again.

When she was finally limp against him, her head resting on his shoulder, her breathing still ragged, he pressed a kiss to her throat, touched his tongue to the perspiration there. She tasted good, like she was his.

"Wow," she murmured. "That was supposed to be all for you."

"Glad it worked out for both of us."

"I love you, Logan."

He smiled at the sleepy words, relieved that she was already drifting off again. "I love you, too."

CHAPTER **FIFTY-TWO**

"A lex? Logan? Hey, guys?"

Alex blinked her eyes open to the dim light of early morning as Logan, bare chest pressed to her back, stirred with an unintelligible grumble. The hallway light behind Charlie silhouetted her figure in the bedroom doorway.

Alex propped up on one elbow, running a hand through her tangled hair. Too late, she realized she was naked and fumbled for the sheet. "Um, yeah, I'm awake. What is it?"

"I'm sorry to wake you, but I didn't know what else to do." Charlie paused and took a breath. "Dieter is missing. He must have jumped the fence when I let the dogs out before I hopped in the shower. Noah's out looking for him now, but I'm afraid he might not come for anyone but you."

Alex sat up, her senses jerked into lucidity by worry for the German shepherd. He'd jumped the fence? She'd never known him to do such a thing. Yet, Charlie's backyard wasn't his, so he might have gone looking for home. Or sniffing for it, rather, since he couldn't very well find it by sight.

She turned to tell Logan to go back to sleep, but he was already out of bed and pulling on his jeans.

Alex found the T-shirt she'd shed the night before and dragged it over her head before getting out of bed and groping through her suitcase for a pair of shorts.

While they dressed, Charlie stepped into the hallway and paced. "I'm so sorry, Alex," she said. "I didn't think I had to watch them with the fence and all."

With tennis shoes in hand, Alex left the bedroom and paused in front of her sister in the hall. "I let them out into your yard a million times yesterday and didn't watch them. This was a fluke. I'm sure Dieter's just looking for home and has gotten a little lost."

Charlie nodded and swallowed, miserable despite Alex's reassurances. "Okay. I . . . I'll help you look, though. He'll be fine. Everything will be fine."

Alex led the way out of Charlie's house and into the damp chill of early morning. A haze of humidity clung to the ground, and everything looked muted in the predawn light. The sun would be up in less than half an hour, burning off the chill and the damp.

"Noah went that way," Charlie said at the end of the driveway, pointing to the right. "I'm going to try to catch up with him."

"We'll go left then," Alex said as Charlie took off at a sprint. She glanced at Logan, who didn't look quite awake yet. "Actually, why don't you go left, Logan, and I'll go straight. There's a shortcut to the dog park between those houses across the street."

Logan blinked his eyes open wide a couple of times, then shook his head. "We stick together. No exceptions."

"It's a missing dog," Alex said. "A missing *blind* dog."

"No exceptions," he repeated firmly. "We don't know where Butch McGee is. He could be watching."

She didn't argue. To be honest, she was relieved, not relishing the idea of traipsing off by herself, even if it meant finding Dieter faster. She was confident the German shepherd could defend himself if he had to. Assuming that treats weren't involved. The big dog would follow someone off the side of a cliff if it meant he'd get a doggy biscuit afterward.

She and Logan walked side by side, all attention focused on scanning and calling for Dieter. After about an hour, Alex's voice began to tremble with growing concern. They'd traveled the same wooded path for the third time—one of Dieter's favorite places to walk near Charlie's house because of the myriad smells and wildlife—and hadn't spotted the lovable, protective dog.

Logan slipped his hand over hers and squeezed. "We'll find him."

She nodded, not trusting herself to speak and fighting the eye-burn of emotion. The sight of an elderly man shuffling toward them kept her from bursting into tears. He wore a hat and jacket, one hand plunged deep into a pocket and his shoulders hunched as if it were forty degrees instead of seventy. A cane helped maintain his tottery balance. Alex thought it odd that he would walk this secluded path. If he fell, he'd have a tough time getting help.

"Maybe he's seen Dieter," Logan said.

Alex sniffed and nodded. "I hope so."

The old man waved at them with his cane, an eager grin flashing his white teeth. Something about that smile set off a spark of familiarity in Alex, but she figured she must have seen him around Charlie's neighborhood before. Or maybe it just struck her as odd that such an old man would have such white teeth. Maybe they were dentures.

"Do you know him?" Logan asked.

"I don't think so. Maybe he's just happy to see friendly faces."

He faked a shudder. "Remind me not to get old."

The old man was about six steps away when he paused, dropped his cane and pulled his hand from his pocket.

Out of the corner of her eye, Alex saw Logan flinch before it clicked what the old guy pointed at them. A gun.

"Shit," Logan growled, and pivoted toward her, putting himself between her and the old man just as a strange snicking sound snapped through the air.

Logan's body jerked, and he fell to his knees in front of her and pitched forward, where he jerked and seized.

"Logan? Logan!" Alex grabbed at his shoulders, trying to roll him over, trying to steady him but not knowing what to do to help him.

She saw the tiny darts embedded in the back of his T-shirt, saw two thin wires connected to them and trailing away. A stun gun. The old man had Tasered Logan.

Then she registered the thud of footsteps and twisted around to see the old man striding toward them without his cane. Not an old man at all.

That's why his smile had looked familiar.

Butch McGee.

She pushed to her feet. She'd kick the bastard's teeth in for hurting Logan.

On the ground, Logan shuddered, valiantly fighting the effects of the shock. He grunted out unintelligible syllables that might have been "Run! Run! Run!"

Alex ignored him, focused on defending herself, and him, from the psychopath. She heard Logan grunt louder, more frantic, trying to get her attention, and glanced down just as he reached out a desperately twitching hand to try to stop her.

His fingers closed around her bare ankle, and the contact sent her spiraling into his latest, literal, shock.

CHAPTER **FIFTY-THREE**

Butch could barely contain his glee as he dragged a drugged, bound and gagged John Logan feetfirst through the brush to the car. He'd stashed his Alex a few hundred feet off the wooded path, well out of sight of any unlikely passersby. Despite the way she'd surprisingly dropped into a dead faint after he'd Tasered the cop, he'd tied and gagged her and administered a light sedative to keep her calm and quiet until he could return.

He'd left the Fusion parked on the side of the road that paralleled the wooded path. After popping the trunk lid, he built up a healthy sweat maneuvering Logan inside. The cop weighed a fucking ton.

The whole time he grunted and pushed and shoved the big man into place, the damn dog barked its damn head off in the large crate in the backseat. He should have killed the thing, but he hadn't in case he needed to use it to draw Alex and Logan to this relatively secluded area.

And now he had some ideas for later, too. Alex loved the dog. And Butch thought he might love using the dog against her.

As he slammed the trunk shut, he began the sprint back to Alex. He smiled the whole way, pleased at how smoothly his plan was working. Once he had them secured at the empty house he'd found online in a listing of foreclosed homes . . . well, then the fun could begin.

And, finally, his brother would be avenged.

CHAPTER **FIFTY-FOUR**

A lex opened her eyes to bright, piercing sunlight and the lightheaded realization that she was tied to a chair.

Oh, God, not again.

Butch McGee sat cross-legged right in front of her, on plush, off-white carpet. He looked for all the world like a normal guy participating in a little yoga before bedtime. His smile, more relaxed than any psychopath's should be, sent a chill through her.

"Hello, Alex," he said, voice soft, almost reverent.

She drew in a calming breath and tried to focus past the trepidation and dizziness. First things first: Logan.

When she saw him, her breath choked off in her chest. He was similarly secured several feet away, facing her. His head drooped forward so his chin rested on his chest. Was he dead? No, he couldn't be dead. He wouldn't be tied up. Please, please, don't let him be dead.

"Don't worry," Butch told her from where he sat between them, as though manning the middle in a game of keep-away. "He's just sleeping."

"What did you do to him?"

"Nothing he won't sleep off in a New York minute." He smiled. "How long do you think a New York minute is? Shorter than a Florida minute, right? I imagine a Florida minute is one of the longest minutes out there. Time moves more slowly here, don't you think? Considering all the retired folks and the vacation vibe."

While he entertained himself, she looked around, trying to get oriented. Big, fancy house. No furniture. The dueling scents of new paint and new carpet. Huge glass windows that looked out on lush acreage that went on forever.

"Hey, Alex, I'm over here."

She focused on him, trying not to shudder as she gave her wrists a subtle tug. Secure, just like last time. Logan's restraints were probably doubly secure.

"Don't you want to know what happened to the dog?" he asked, light and airy, as though he'd asked if she'd seen last night's episode of *American Idol*.

Dieter. Oh, God, not Dieter.

He smiled, no doubt thrilled by her tightly clenched jaw. Cocking his head, he said, "That German shepherd was the only one out of the brood that would follow me for a couple of Milk-Bones. How did it end up blind?"

"What did you do to him?"

"You haven't answered my question."

"If you hurt him, I'll . . . I'll . . ."

"Kill me?" he asked, gleeful. "Over a dead dog."

A *dead* dog. That *bastard*. She jerked at her bound wrists. "He never hurt anyone, especially you."

"True. But you know what? I'm enjoying how frantic you are about the animal's fate. It's really turning me on." He leaned back on one hand and fondled himself through his Dockers.

A new kind of fear whitewashed her vision, and she shut her eyes.

"Aw, don't be a party pooper, Alex. This party's just getting started."

"What do you want?" she asked through gritted teeth. Stupid question, really. But stalling was all she had for now. At least until Logan woke up.

"We've already had this conversation. Revenge."

She opened her eyes to meet Butch's gaze head-on, determined not to cringe. "I assure you that Logan doesn't know who you are or why you want revenge. You've made a mistake."

"Nope. I don't make mistakes. I learned very young not to make mistakes. The consequences can be very painful." He rose to his feet in a graceful motion and walked toward her, slow and casual. "But let's talk about you."

When he reached out to touch her face, she jerked her head back, away from him, but the restraints made sure she had nowhere to go.

His fingers, cool and damp, caressed her cheek.

Reality whirled away.

He's standing across from me, waiting. I can hear him breathing, heavy and deep.

I don't want to do this.

"I'm waiting, Butchie."

I want to close my eyes to the naked, white flesh restrained on the table before me. Her rosy nipples are puckered from the damp chill of the basement, and her breasts quiver as she sniffles and whimpers, the gag in her mouth shutting off any screams.

I can't look at her eyes. I did already, by mistake, and her tear-drenched terror almost made me piss my Levi's.

I should be curious. I am *curious. I want to look. Touch. I've never seen a naked woman before. She smells . . . nice. Like some kind of flower. I should know what it is. If the dickhead didn't keep me here, a prisoner, I would know.*

I decide she smells like lilies, or how I expect lilies to smell. Soft and girly. Sweet.

Like Mommy.

My sweaty hand tightens on the knife. Did she even try

to find me? She and Dad probably just fucked until they created another kid to replace me.

I watch the news every night on the tiny little TV he brought me, flipping through the channels one after the other and back again, looking for some mention that Tyler Ambrose has been lost for, shit, must be at least ten years by now, and never found.

I'm here. I'm right here!

But there's no amazing grace for Tyler.

"Butchie."

There's an edge to his voice. He's getting impatient.

He's less than three feet across from me. One flick with the blade, and I could open his jugular. I know where that is. He's insisted on anatomy lessons. I know how to cut and where, to prevent his idea of fun from ending too soon.

"Remember how I promised you a present? This is it. You've been a very good young man, and I want to reward you. I know it's difficult being confined to the basement all the time, but it's necessary. No one would understand, but what we're doing here is very important work, and you're my apprentice. You've earned it, Butchie."

A present. This . . . woman, trussed and gagged and naked and terrified, is my present. What am I supposed to do with her? I'd rather have one of those video game things I've seen advertised on TV. Nintendo. Or a Game Boy. Yeah, that'd be cool.

"Do you want to touch her, Butchie?"

I shake my head. He'd better not zap me with that fucking stun gun.

"Do you want to make love to her? Because you can."

My stomach cramps, and I squeeze my eyes shut. This situation doesn't resemble anything I've ever seen on TV that relates to making love. This woman and I haven't walked hand-in-hand on the beach or giggled while cooking dinner or thrown snowballs at each other or sprayed each other with the hose while soaping up a fancy car.

"You don't have to be afraid, Butchie. I'm here. I'm going to help you, so you do it right."

He moves around the table until he's behind me. He smells like sweat and cigarettes, and I almost gag. But I hold still anyway—stun gun fear—and try not to tense as he reaches around me and grasps my hand that holds the knife. Both of his hands are pudgy and damp. Disgusting.

"You don't have to rush," he says in his low, teaching voice. "You have all the time you need. In order to do things right, you have to go slow. Okay?"

I nod and swallow, careful to avoid the woman's eyes. She's jerking against her restraints, and the skin of her wrists and ankles is raw. Any second now blood will be flowing where the bonds hold her.

"Where would you like to start?" he asks.

Like she's a steak, cooked medium rare and topped with sautéed mushrooms, pink juices ready to flow at the first stab of the knife.

"How about here?" He angles the tip of the knife over the inside of her right breast, not breaking the skin, just skating the blade over that pale slope.

She sucks in a breath, and the hairs on my arms stand up.

"Yes," he breathes behind me. "That was nice, wasn't it? That soft sigh. Because she knows you have the power. You are in charge of her body. You can play it like an instrument. With your fingers. With your tongue. With your . . ."

He takes my hand and draws it down and back between us, presses it against the front of his pants, and holy God—

I jerk away from him. My hand burns, my face just as hot. I twist away from him and around, the knife thrust before me. "No!"

He walks around to the other side of the table, a grin on his face that I want to cut off, a grin that shouldn't be there considering the last time he handed me a knife. My arm still aches from where he broke it. A small price for the big satisfaction of making him bleed for a change.

"Relax, Butchie. I'm not into boys. This is what I'm into." He trails a hand over the woman's breast, his fingers leisurely toying with her nipple. "If you don't do something with your present, open her, for instance, I might be tempted to claim her for myself."

She whimpers, and I feel sick. And too warm. My hand, the one that touched him . . . there . . . tingles.

I hold my breath and watch. He lingers over the woman's body, his hands touching her . . . in places I've seen only in the pages of my anatomy book. I can't see those places now . . . but I am curious. Especially when her whimpers grow more desperate, and blood starts to slick her wrists.

"You want to touch?" he asks. "She's soft and warm." He grins. "She wants you, Butchie."

I close my eyes tight and concentrate, but that doesn't stop what happens to my crotch. Blood is engorging my penis, making it hard and erect, preparing it for the penetration of sexual intercourse. That's what I've learned from my anatomy books.

It's not the first time my body has done this, and I know what happens if I touch it and manipulate it and work it. It's feels pretty fucking good. But this is the first time I've gotten an erection in the presence of him.

And her.

His grin widens. "Ahh, there's my good little Butchie. I was beginning to worry about you."

I swallow hard, adjusting my grip on the knife. I could so easily plunge it right into his throat. I would, too, if I knew I could escape this time, if I knew where he put the booby traps. His fucking traps have stopped me every time. Stair steps that give way under my weight. A whole fuckload of ten-pound weights that drop from the ceiling when I open the door at the top of the stairs. It's like the bastard knows what I'm thinking, knows when I'm going to try to get the fuck out.

Jesus H. Christ, I hate that pasty son of a bitch.

"You want to fuck her now, don't you, Butchie? You want to fuck her until she screams."

I kind of do. My dick is starting to throb, starting to insist. It's like the more pissed off I get, the harder I get.

"I'll make a deal with you, Butchie. If you cut her, I'll let you fuck her."

My heart thuds, and I can feel it down there.

"As many times as you want. All day if you want. All you have to do is cut her."

I swallow hard, wet my lips. All I have to do is . . .

I raise the knife.

"Pick a good place," he says, soft and reverent. "The first cut, first blood, is always the best, so you have to make it good."

I set the tip of the blade just an inch above her belly button. Oh, man, I can't wait to get inside her. Can't wait for that first thrust. I've had nothing until now. Nothing but pain and captivity. No pleasure. No fucking sunlight. All I have are scars. And the memories of my own screams.

"Breathe, Butchie. Nice and easy."

The blade is against her skin. Her clean, white skin. So pretty and soft. The scent of lilies and . . . Mommy. Who let me get taken. Who never rescued me.

The blade slides in easier than I expected, and blood wells as her body convulses so hard it reminds me of what happens to me, and how good I feel, when I come in my hand.

And then I'm coming for real, spurting inside my pants . . .

Alex slammed back into herself with a choked cry. Her stomach heaved, and she bent forward, coughing and gagging, her head heavy and dizzy. She had nothing in her stomach to come up, but she stayed bent over her knees and tried to breathe while she waited for the spins to abate.

Hot tears stung her eyes, and she closed them tight. Oh, God, oh, God, oh, God.

That was the moment that threw the switch inside a teen boy's head. He'd resisted as long as he could, too afraid to try to escape, too terrorized to defend himself. And that was the defining moment, when pain and blood and a blade became the main ingredients necessary for the only pleasure he'd ever known.

"Your happy place?"

She raised her head, weary to the bone as a dull throb began its staccato beat in her temples.

Butch McGee leaned against the far wall, arms crossed, posture expectant.

"It wasn't your fault," she said, her voice hoarse and weak. Dizzy. She was so damn dizzy. And her head hurt, like someone had taken a power drill to the inside of her skull. She had to make this—him—stop. "He made you who you are. It wasn't your fault."

"Who?"

"The man who taught you how to cut a woman."

He straightened away from the wall, one fist clenching at his side. "What are you talking about?"

"You want to know about my happy place, don't you? Fine, I'll tell you." Stalling was all she had. Come on, Logan, come on. "When you touch me, I flash on the horrible things that happened to you in the past."

Butch stared at her in almost comical disbelief. "Come again?"

"It's a psychic ability called empathy."

Butch tilted his head. "And people think *I'm* crazy."

"I can prove it." Anything to keep him facing her and talking, leaving Logan uncovered. When he regained consciousness, maybe he could do something. "He . . . he burned you with cigarettes. He kept you prisoner in the basement of his house."

Butch's eyes narrowed to suspicious slits. "The FBI must have done a psych profile on me."

"No, no. I haven't talked to the FBI about you at all. I was going to, but . . . but you killed Sally Blake, and they had to deal with that crime scene before they got to me." She searched for something more to say, to keep his attention focused on her. "You have them stumped, you know. They don't think they'll ever catch you. You're too smart for them."

His tight lips curved slightly. "I am."

"But if you take revenge on Logan and kill him, a police officer, that will make them even more determined to find you and make you pay."

"But they won't find me. They haven't in twenty years."

"Because you've been so smart. And now you're risking getting caught for some twisted idea of revenge for something Logan doesn't even remember doing."

"He remembers. Believe me."

"But he doesn't know who you are."

"He will."

"You're going to lose yourself because of this. You know you are."

"Lose myself? I *found* myself a long time ago."

"But you're not Butch McGee. You're Tyler Ambrose."

His jaw hardened, muscles contracting at both temples. "Shut up."

"That horrible man kidnapped you, Tyler Ambrose, at the mall. He offered you candy, and you . . . you thought it was okay to accept it because he helped your mom shovel snow once. Remember that? Remember? And you felt so stupid about it, because he kidnapped you and tortured you. He . . . he made you his apprentice. And . . . and Brian—"

"How can you possibly know about Brian?" he cut in, his tone soft, deadly.

"I told you. Every time you touch me, I take a trip into your head, your worst memories, your defining moments. I become . . . you." She remembered the slide of the knife through soft flesh, the resulting surge of pleasure, and shuddered. How would she ever be able to separate his memories from her own?

Butch approached her, arms still crossed, brow creased with curiosity. He stopped a few feet away, close enough for her to smell his sweat. "Just now, in my head, what did you see?"

She couldn't believe he already bought it. Yes, it was the truth, but she'd expected him to assume she was bluffing. "The first time he made you . . . you didn't want to, but he made you do it. He made you cut . . ." She had to fight off the gag reflex.

"You're wrong." His voice was rough as gravel. "I wanted to. I always wanted to. That's why it's so good."

"But you kept thinking about how you didn't want to do it. You wanted to stab him with the knife instead, but you were afraid."

"I was never afraid!" He backhanded her.

We're going to do it when he brings dinner. Any minute.

"Are you sure, Butchie? Are you sure we can do it?" Brian looks unsure and more than a little scared.

"Get over it, Brian," Chad says, punching him too hard in the arm. "We'll be fine. Butch and I will take good care of you."

"Will we find my mom?" Brian doesn't complain about the punch. He's used to it by now. "I really want to go home to my mom."

The eternal optimist. As if any of us can go home after what the dickhead's made us do. Well, maybe Brian. Maybe it's not too late for him. He's not old enough to . . . play with the big boys, to kill and enjoy it, though he's definitely got issues, that's for damn sure. He arrived as a sick little fuck. Probably why the dickhead nabbed him to begin with.

Me and Chad, though, we're officially screwed. We've opened a few too many presents.

I'm glad I'm not alone there. Chad makes things easier. He liked it here, at first. He said it's better than living on the streets, hustling for cash. Offering a blow job for twenty bucks to the dickhead was the best thing he ever did. He got a warm bed and three squares a day.

Then he got bored. Didn't take long. A couple of weeks maybe. He doesn't enjoy the presents as much as I do.

I tense as I hear the dickhead's footsteps on the stairs. "He's coming."

Chad gives me a nod and steps into position so that when the door opens, he'll be behind it. Brian and I sit on the bed, the way we're supposed to, our hands where the dickhead can see them.

The key clicks in the lock. The hair on the back of my neck shoots straight up. This is it, this is it, this is it.

The door swings open, Chad hidden behind it.

The dickhead takes one step into our prison cell before he locks eyes with me and stops. "Where's Chad?"

Chad shoves the door closed so hard that it knocks the dickhead back on his ass, the tray of hamburgers and French fries splatting him in the chest. As the food falls to the floor, the smell of ketchup bursts into the air while Chad and I pounce on him as one. We punch and pummel and screech like little girls. I hit him, right in the face, and blood sprays upward, warm and wet and awesome.

And then I remember, and I yell, "Stop! Wait! Wait!"

It takes forever for Chad to hear me. He finally stops, and then he and Brian are staring at me like I'm the nutjob. The dickhead moans on the floor and makes a gurgling sound. I kneel beside him, my heart pounding with excitement, and work the stun gun out of the holster on his hip.

The first zap makes me hard. I ignore the ache of the boner and focus on the twitching dickhead while I reload the gun. I don't want to fuck him. Not like that, anyway. I just want to make him pay. I can't wait to make him pay.

The crackle of the stun gun as I depress the trigger, the business end pressed to the dickhead's throat, joins the buzz in my head until I can't distinguish between the two. This feels good. This feels so good. Finally. Finally.

I start to laugh. I sound hysterical. I am hysterical. And I love it.

The power.

The satisfaction.

Take that, you fucking son of a bitch, motherfucking cocksucker.

"Butch, Jesus, you've made your point."

Chad's in the doorway behind me, disgust in his voice.

The smell of ketchup and burned meat assaults me. The dickhead was going to feed us burned burgers. But then I glance down at his face, his throat. It's not the food that's burned.

Gagging, I scramble back off the dead fucker, the stun gun falling from my hand.

"Let's go," Chad says.

I look up. Blood has spattered his face like paint flicked onto a canvas. He looks crazier than I feel. But he also looks as determined as I feel. We're out of here.

My knees shake as I rise. I'm finally leaving this fucking hellhole. And all I want to do is throw up. The dickhead is dead. The fucking dickhead is dead. Ding-dong and all that.

I start to laugh, my breath hiccupping in my chest. Chad has to slap the shit out of me to snap me out of it.

"Hold it together, bro," he growls. "We're not done yet." He looks me over and then down at himself. "We should change first."

Good idea. Too much blood and people are going to stare.

As we change, adrenaline jacks up my excitement. I haven't been outside in . . . something like ten, maybe eleven, years. I can't wait to feel fresh air on my face. I hope it rains soon, because I really want to smell the rain.

I try to picture Mom's face when she opens the front door and I'm there on the porch, her little lost boy. Of course, I have no idea where my mother lives.

And I realize I really don't care anymore. Fuck her.

It occurs to me that if I don't go home, back to my stupid, careless parents who never tried to find me, what do I do?

"Hey, Chad."

He's tucking in his shirt when he glances up. "Yeah?"

"Where do we go from here?"

He shrugs. "I don't know. Get a job. Get a life."

"Where are we going to live?"

His next shrug is irritated. "I don't know. Jesus, Butch, you wanted out. I helped get you out. What the fuck you want from me?"

"We're brothers, though, right? That means we stick together?"

"Sure, it does. We'll always be brothers."

"Good." I've always wanted a couple of brothers.

I get up the stairs first, remembering too late to be careful of booby traps. But the dickhead must have disabled them when he came downstairs, or maybe he stopped setting them when I stopped trying to escape, because I make it out of the basement without a hitch. And then I'm running, sprinting, tearing through the house, not looking, not caring. It takes me a few tries to find the front door, ending up in a closet instead, then a bathroom. Right behind me, Chad laughs his ass off. What a dick. But I'm laughing, too, and so is Brian. Freedom . . . rocks.

Finally, I find the door and fling it open.

The light blinds me. The cold is a shock. Oh, yeah, it's winter.

Then I'm on my knees in the snow, and it's freezing and wet and fucking bizarre, and I love it. I love it. Laughing, surprised at the clouds of steam coming out of my mouth, I scoop up some snow and pack it into a loose ball, just like I've seen on TV. I throw it at Brian, catching him smack in the face. He looks like he's going to cry, but then Chad nails me in the back of the neck with a huge snowball, so hard I pitch face-first into a foot of the coldest, wettest, most awesome stuff I could ever imagine.

CHAPTER **FIFTY-FIVE**

Alex didn't open her eyes this time when she resurfaced, afraid Butch waited. She kept her head down and tried to think around the pain in her temples. She was still tied to the chair, immobilized and helpless, ready for the next head trip into the whackjob's tormented past.

Oh, God, she couldn't take anymore. Couldn't . . . just couldn't. His memories . . . they were her memories now. In less than a week, she'd experienced the highlights—lowlights?—of what he'd endured over many years. How much more before she broke? How much more before her mind snapped and she became as warped as Butch?

Maybe she was already broken and just didn't know it.

Her father used to tell her, "Sugar and spice and everything nice, that's what my little girls are made of." Not anymore. His littlest girl was made of anger and violence and a horrifying need to beat something bloody with her bare hands.

"Alex."

That sounded like Logan, but she didn't dare move.

Where was Butch? Waiting, no doubt, waiting to touch her, to drive her back into the depths of hell.

"Alex, baby, he's not here. We're alone."

She blinked her eyes open, raised her head. Battery-powered lanterns lit the living room now, and even that dim light stabbed into her head until she squinted.

Logan, still secured to a chair, sat about eight feet away, peering intently at her. "Alex, Jesus, thank God. Are you okay?"

She swallowed against her dry throat, moistened her lips and started to nod only to stop and clamp her eyes closed at the sick whirl. The side of her face ached where Butch had struck her, bestowing a hot, throbbing bruise that wouldn't fade in less than an hour. In some ways, she preferred the more lasting kind of physical pain. At least that was real. And, oh, God, was that twisted?

"Talk to me, baby. Are you okay?"

She nodded, eyes still closed, swallowing against a surge of nausea.

"I'm going to rip that fucker's lungs out," Logan muttered.

Forcing her eyes open, she focused on his face, his beautiful face, his blue, blue eyes, and felt the nausea ebb. "What about you? Okay?"

He smiled at her, really smiled. "Happy as hell to see your chocolate browns. You've been out for a while."

She shifted on the chair, retested the strength of her bonds. Still secure, though not so tight that her hands had gone numb. Butch had many years of experience using ropes and other restraints on women.

"Alex."

She blinked at Logan, realized he'd been talking to her. Worry put deep creases in his forehead, but she had no idea how to reassure him, or even if she could.

"We're in one of those ritzy neighborhoods near the Gulf," he said, probably repeating himself, considering the way his eyes locked on hers, intently searching. "A vacant

house. Big one. Lots of sprawling land on the side I could
see before it got dark. I imagine the house is surrounded on
all sides like that."

"Secluded." She had to force herself to talk, to focus,
her brain constantly sidetracked by the memory—Butch's
memory—of the first slide of a blade into flesh. And the
thump of fists against blood-streaked skin and hard bone.
The twitches and jolts of a stun gun pressed repeatedly
against skin and muscle. The titillating scents of blood and
sweat and fear and the intense sexual thrill that went with
them.

"No one to hear if we yell for help." Logan jutted his
chin toward a collection of knives laid out on the carpet
along the glass wall, large to small. "He wasn't here when
I woke, but he'll be back."

She rotated her wrists against the ropes, wincing as the
rough texture abraded her skin. Maybe blood would act as
a lubricant, and she could slip free.

"Noah will have called the police," Logan said. "Everyone is looking for us."

She didn't respond, eyes closed against the burn as she
turned both wrists, back and forth, back and forth, her
brain stalled on Logan's previous statement: He'll be back.

Alex vowed to kill the bastard then. For all those
women. For Dieter. For what he planned to do to Logan.

She knew how it felt to kill. Knew what happened when
fury blinded you to right and wrong, when you handed
control over to rage. It felt good to pummel your hatred
into the soft tissue of a helpless human being. The warm,
wet, salty spray of blood on your face could feel just as
refreshing, just as enjoyable, as water droplets thrown from
Gulf waves.

She imagined Butch's blood flying as she took one of
his knives and slashed at him with it. The image in her
head . . . it should have repulsed her. It didn't. She didn't
care anymore that he'd been abused as a child. He'd made a

choice when his tormentor had handed him a weapon. He'd chosen to plunge that knife into a helpless woman rather than end his own captivity. He'd made a choice to kill. A choice to torture.

"Alex?"

She blinked at Logan, found him watching her carefully, scrutinizing.

"What happened while I was out?" he asked slowly.

She shook her head against the emotion overtaking her. "He killed Dieter."

"What? Jesus!" He yanked anew at his bonds. "Son of a bitch. I'm sorry. I'm so sorry."

"Dieter never did anything to him. He was a good dog. The best."

"Yes, he was. He was damn lucky you took him in."

"Not so lucky now." Her voice fractured on the words, and a tear dripped down her cheek.

Logan peered at her, helplessness clear in his eyes. "Alex, honey, I need you to hang on. Don't give up."

"I'm not giving up," she said, cold now, determined. "I'm imagining what it will be like to kill the bastard."

Logan's brows arched sharply. "Are you . . . okay?"

She didn't know how to respond. No, she wasn't okay. She'd used a knife. Her fists. She'd stunned and reloaded, stunned again. And it felt good. It felt . . . incredible.

Logan's jaw clenched hard. "I scrambled your system when I touched you, didn't I? I was trying to get you to run, and all I did was fuck you up. God, I'm such an idiot."

Always with the guilt. He had no idea how easy it was to let it go and embrace the dark side. So, so easy.

"What did you see?" he asked.

She closed her eyes, swallowed hard. The rope biting into her flesh stung, made her head swim and her stomach churn, but her bonds slipped more easily now. A warm, wet trickle down one palm gave her hope. And that almost made her laugh. Of all the things to offer hope.

"Alex. Please, talk to me. Tell me what you saw."

She met Logan's eyes. He had such blue eyes, and she remembered how it felt to sink into them, to drown. She remembered the warm clutch of emotion deep in her chest, reached for it now to ground her, searched for her anchor. But there was nothing. Just cold . . . blank . . . nothing.

"Alex?"

"His first . . . kill."

"Fuck." Logan jerked at his bonds, nearly snarling with frustration. "Son of a *bitch*."

"I feel . . . it's like I did it. *I* did it."

"You didn't. You know you didn't."

"But I experienced it. I *felt* it. I felt what he felt, and it . . . it was *me* holding the knife."

"Alex, honey, it wasn't you. It could never be you."

Arguing wouldn't change anything. And he would never understand. Never grasp how powerfully she experienced the things that happened to Butch, happened to *her*. *Changed* her.

"I love you."

How forcefully he said it startled her almost as much as the words. She met his eyes, captured by their intensity, and couldn't look away.

"Don't think about him, Alex. Don't let what's in that asshole's fucked-up head take you down. Think about us. Think about what we've got, who we are together. We're good together. We're *great*. We have years ahead of us, Alex. Years and years. We're going to walk away from this. Together."

But one of us won't be the same, she thought. One of us will be changed forever. And not for the—

"Tell me what else you saw."

She shook her head. "I can't."

"Yes, you can. Tell me, Alex. Tell me and let me carry it. I'll carry it and you can forget it."

"It doesn't work that way."

"Just try. Please. For me."

She rolled her bottom lip between her teeth. "They escaped."

"They? Butch wasn't the only one?"

"There were two others. We . . . they killed their captor. Beat him first, then Butch killed him with a stun gun."

"Holy shit."

"Brian sat on the bed like we were all supposed to, and Chad hid behind the door, and I . . . *Butch*—"

"Wait. Chad? Chad *Ellis*?"

"I didn't catch a last name."

"Son of a bitch. This *is* about Brian Lear. I ruled him out because he didn't have a brother. But he and Butch must have *considered* themselves brothers."

Right, that's right, she thought. *We're brothers, though, right? That means we stick together?*

"I shot and killed Brian Lear," Logan went on. "The night I stumbled into the prostitution ring in Detroit. Chad Ellis, the ring leader, was arrested and went to prison. Butch was probably involved, too, but Chad never once mentioned him. Or maybe Butch was out doing his own thing and had nothing to do with the operation. Either way, that's the connection." He yanked on his hands so hard he winced. "Not that any of that helps in getting us the hell out of here."

The thought of Butch coming back sent her heart rate into the red zone all over again, compelled her to twist her wrists more urgently, no longer feeling the pain. She couldn't do it again, couldn't handle another nightmare trek.

"Alex, I can see blood dripping behind your chair. Did he do something to you? Did he cut you?"

She wrenched harder, desperation bearing down. "When he comes back, if he . . . if I get stuck in his past again . . . you have to find a way to get loose and hit me."

Logan gaped at her. "Jesus, Alex."

"*Hard.* Hit me as hard as it takes to get me out. Promise."

His face went sheet pale. "I can't—"

"It's not about you striking me, Logan. It's about protecting me from a nightmare. I want you . . . I *need* you to—" Her voice broke. "I can't keep doing this. I can't keep taking trips into his mind. It's . . . it's . . . changing me."

"Alex, please. Don't—"

"You have to promise. Do it for me."

"Fine," Logan said, the word barely audible.

"Thank you."

He snorted his displeasure at what he no doubt considered displaced gratitude but said nothing.

She sighed and wet her lips. Exhaustion weighed down her shoulders, pressed on her chest. She'd never felt so hopeless, so . . . dark.

"Listen," Logan said. "I've managed to loosen the rope around my wrists."

It took her a moment to process that. How could he have loosened his rope when hers stayed frustratingly secure in spite of the blood trickling down her hands? And then she knew why. She knew Butch, after all. "It's a trap."

"Really? But—"

"He's not sloppy. It has to be a trap."

"But he can't know for sure that he can control me."

"He's a psychopath, Logan. It wouldn't occur to him that he *can't* control you."

"Just—" He broke off and his gaze locked on hers as his whole body went rigid.

She'd heard it, too. The opening and closing of a door somewhere in the house.

Butch was back.

CHAPTER **FIFTY-SIX**

Logan held Alex's gaze for a long moment, trying to tell her without words that everything would be okay, they'd get out of this, before Butch intruded. The despondency in her expression worried him, though. The bruise on her face, its darkness reflected in her eyes . . . well, that just infuriated him. Butch McGee would pay for that. All of it.

As soon as he worked his hands free.

His heart raced with the need to hurry.

"Ah, so the happy couple is awake," Butch said in a sing-songy voice as he ambled into the massive living room.

Logan immediately noticed the bandage on his lower forearm, blood spots soaking through in two somewhat parallel lines. Like rows of teeth. "What happened to your arm, Butch? You have a run-in with a pissed-off German shepherd?" he said, hoping to steer the man's attention away from Alex.

Butch's jaw tightened, but he ignored Logan to bestow an adoring smile on her. He made sure to angle his body so Logan had a full view of every move he made, though.

"I'm sorry for my abrupt departure earlier," Butch told her.

"You didn't have that bandage before." Her eyes blazed with anger . . . and renewed hope. "You lied about killing Dieter."

"I *implied*," Butch said. "In fact, I planned to kill him, but then I saw how much the devil dog means to you and changed my mind. Instead, I've expanded the beast's role in tonight's festivities."

He tilted his head and studied her so speculatively that Logan's legs began to twitch. If only he could—yank, yank—get—yank, yank—loose.

Butch sighed. "I'm sorry for this." He tried to stroke his fingertips over the bruise on her cheek, but she pulled back before he could make contact. Which just multiplied the size of his smile. "I'm afraid I lost control. It won't happen again. At least, not in a way that's unproductive."

"Leave her alone," Logan ground out. If his hands had been free, they would have been clamped around the bastard's throat. Just the thought of Butch touching Alex, even without the empathic spike through her heart, set his brain on fire. "Your beef is with me."

Butch cut his gaze to Logan, his smile turning bitter. "Surely you've figured out by now that I prefer to hurt you the same way you hurt me. Through someone you care about."

"It's not the same. Alex hasn't done anything to you. And Brian tried to kill me. Right after he murdered a defenseless child."

Butch turned more fully toward Logan. "Ah, so you *do* remember my brother."

"Alex helped me to remember. That's what you wanted, isn't it? You shouldn't punish her for helping you."

"You're acting as if life is fair, and we all know it's not."

"You've already hurt her enough to punish me for a lifetime. Start on me now."

"Logan, no."

He ignored Alex's soft plea. He knew she feared Butch

would flat-out kill rather than toy with him. Her concern for him hardened the lump in his throat. He'd failed to protect her from so much, and look how it had worn her down. He wouldn't fail her anymore, damn it.

"It's *my* turn," Logan insisted, his attention locked on Butch. "Make me pay for killing Brian and sending Chad to prison. I took both your brothers from you. They were all you had of family."

Butch's lips twitched. "You think you can manipulate me that easily?"

"I think you're a sick son of a twisted bitch, and if my hands were free, I'd kill you and enjoy it. Just like I enjoyed putting a bullet in your brother's head."

"Logan, God," Alex said. "Don't."

"You should listen to her." Butch's voice was low now, and rough, as though Logan had squarely hit the nerve he'd aimed for. "She knows me pretty well."

"Yeah? She knows what I know. You tie up helpless women and use them for your own sick pleasure and then you kill them. You can't even kill like a man, can you, Butch? A man would cut them loose, give them a fighting chance. But you're a coward. A weak, pathetic coward. You're the pussiest of the pussies."

Butch, his face flaming red, lunged at Logan and struck him with the back of his hand.

Logan's head whipped back under the force of the blow, and the taste of blood only enhanced his satisfaction. He had the psycho's attention. Just like he wanted.

He spat a wad of blood onto the carpet at Butch's feet. "You hit like a girl, Butch. Don't you even know how to make a fist? That must be why you have to tie up your victims. Because you know you can't control them. If they got in one little slap, you'd have to run crying to your mommy."

Butch strode to the lineup of knives on the floor and snatched one up, a long one with a wide, serrated blade, then stalked toward Logan, murder gleaming in his eyes.

"His name isn't Butch." Alex's even, calm voice didn't sound at all like she addressed a crazy man about to take a slash at her lover. "His name is Tyler. Tyler Ambrose."

Butch stopped in midstride, and Logan's insides twitched. Shut up, Alex. Jesus.

Butch's shoulders relaxed some as he turned toward her.

Logan's heart clattered with fear, but he took advantage of the opportunity to tear at the bindings at his wrists. Almost there. Come on, come on.

"I'm not Tyler anymore." Butch's tone was just as calm as Alex's had been. "I haven't been for a long time."

"That's what he *made* you think," she said. "That's why he changed your name. Because he wanted to make you into someone you're not. Someone you never wanted to be."

"Not at first. But that changed."

"He didn't give you a choice. You were only a kid. What were you supposed to do? He kept hurting you. It was only natural that you'd take the opportunity to let someone else hurt for a while. You're only human, Tyler."

"Tyler," Butch repeated softly, almost reverently.

Logan, stunned that she seemed to be getting through, felt the rope give a little more and stifled a triumphant grunt.

"You don't want to hurt anyone anymore," Alex said, soothing. "I can help you. No one understands, not like I do. I've been there, Tyler. In your head. I can help you explain everything. We can find your mother. She'd be so happy to see you again. Her sweet little blond-haired boy."

Logan managed to pull his hands a few inches apart.

"You want to see her again, don't you?" Alex asked Butch. "You want to see your mother?"

"She let me go. She should have kept looking."

"She did," Alex said. "She's been looking all these years. Your name is in a database of missing children. Why would your name be in there if she didn't want to find you?"

Butch moved toward her, the knife clenched tight in his hand.

Logan's fingers blindly fumbled with the knot as sweat began to run down his temple. At the same time, he noticed that the blood spatter on the floor at the back of Alex's chair had widened. Had she gotten her hands apart? Jesus, was she free?

"You don't want to hurt anyone anymore, Tyler," she said. "It's not who you are."

"You think you know me. You think that a few glimpses of my past are all it takes to understand who I am. You're wrong, you know. You're so very wrong."

Logan pulled the knot apart and shook his hands loose. Yes! He kept them behind his back, though, and put the scowl back on his face. If he'd thought he could get to Butch before the psycho had time to plunge the knife into Alex's throat, this would have been over by now.

"All of this? Here and now? It isn't about me," Butch said, circling behind her chair, narrowed eyes fixed on Logan over the top of her dark head. "It's about *him*. About what he took from me."

Butch reached around Alex with the knife, his smug gaze never straying from Logan, and traced the blade, featherlight, over her collar bone and toward the hollow of her throat.

She didn't flinch, didn't breathe, as her gaze, deep and dark, met Logan's. Her lips moved, formed three silent words that shook his world as much as the sight of that blade hovering over her jugular. *I love you.*

"This is what I'm taking from you," Butch said to Logan. "Watch carefully."

Alex closed her eyes. "Tyler—"

"I'm not Tyler!" He jerked the knife up under her chin, nicking her skin.

Logan launched himself out of his chair, her pained

gasp and the sight of the slow dribble of blood down her throat more than he could stand.

Butch, a feral, satisfied grin curving his mouth, whipped the stun gun out of the holster on his belt and fired.

CHAPTER **FIFTY-SEVEN**

Alex couldn't stop the scream as Logan fell, his body going violently haywire.

Butch laughed while Logan jolted on the carpet. "What took you so damn long, hero? I figured you'd be free of those pitiful knots by the time I got back. Who's the pussy now?"

Butch swaggered over and kicked Logan viciously in the ribs. "I'm not done yet, you stupid bastard. I'm going to kill her slowly. She's going to scream like you've never heard a woman—"

He broke off and half turned toward Alex, as though he'd sensed rather than heard her move. But he was too late, and his eyes widened in stunned disbelief, his breath catching on a shocked gasp as she drove the knife between his ribs and into his heart.

He fell slowly, first to his knees, his body sliding off the blade with a wet slither, and then to his side and over onto his back. His arm flopped against Logan's still-seizing legs, and his disbelieving gaze locked onto hers.

She stood over him, the knife in her hand dripping his

blood onto the carpet, and watched the life drain from his eyes.

She didn't remember slipping her bloody wrists out of her bonds. Didn't remember pushing up from the chair. Didn't remember picking up one of his knives—one at the long end of his collection on the floor. Didn't remember deciding to take this man's life.

"Alex?"

She heard Logan say her name, heard the question in it. But she couldn't tear her attention away from Butch and the blood that had stopped spreading beneath him.

He was dead.

She'd killed him.

Her head felt light and dizzy, not at all like it belonged to her. She thought she might have enjoyed sliding that death-sharp blade into the man who'd tormented her with his memories. Who'd kicked Logan hard enough to break bones. Who'd tortured and raped and murdered and . . .

"Alex, please. Look at me."

The break in Logan's voice shifted her gaze to his. His muscles still weren't responding to his efforts to move, yet he tried desperately to push himself up. His pale face shone with sweat and pain and . . . worry.

She dropped the knife and moved to help him. "Are you okay?" The voice didn't sound like hers. Too calm, too even.

He grunted and tried to nod, the seizures of his muscles finally slowing to a fine trembling. Grimacing, he held a shaking hand to his ribs and looked her over. "Jesus, Alex, your wrists."

She hadn't noticed her own raw and bloody skin, didn't feel the pain that should have been agony. She was numb.

"Alex, baby, are you okay?"

No, she wasn't. She'd somehow lost contact with . . . reality. With herself. Butch had severed her connections.

She wanted them back. Now.

She reached for Logan, intending to kiss him, intending

to orient herself, but as soon as she touched him, she felt
her body snap taut and muscles start to jitter.

Fuck! Shit!

Alex was right. The son of a bitch set a trap!

Too late, too fucking late, and now he's going to . . .

Oh, Jesus, Alex. She's free! She's—

The aftermath of the impact of Logan's open hand on
her face stung. Then he dragged her to him, muttering into
her hair, "I'm sorry, I'm sorry, I'm sorry."

She closed her eyes and let out a relieved sigh. He'd
done it. He'd fulfilled his promise.

Then she registered that along with the roar of blood in
her ears, she was hearing something new, something distant but familiar. Something precious. "Is that—"

"Dieter," Logan cut in with a laugh. "Barking his ass
off. He must be locked in a room. Upstairs, I think. He
certainly sounds healthy."

"Oh, thank God."

Logan's warm, blessed lips settled on hers . . . and reality fell away all over again.

*It's just as fucking cold in this dingy hallway as it is
outside, and the soft cries of children permeate the dark
as I ease my way along the wall, Glock heavy in my hand.*

*I should be outside, waiting for backup. But they're
going to be too late. I know it, and I can't let this shit go
on for one second longer. They're little kids, for the love of
God. I just can't.*

*I see him in the dim light of the dank hall. I see the
boy I'd spotted on the street. He looks so small. Lost and
desperate and scared. A huge monster of a man, tall like a
basketball player, broad like a football player—the same
man I saw grab him outside—has hold of his hand and
drags him along behind him.*

*The boy whimpers—very pale face and very red lips.
Maybe six, maybe seven. Terrified. "Where's Daddy? I
want Daddy."*

The big man turns to roughly cuff him upside the head. "Shut the fuck up."

The child stumbles and cries out, and the man yanks him off his feet by the arm, flinging his small body up against the wall and pinning him there with one meaty forearm across his small, vulnerable throat. "What part of 'shut the fuck up' do you not get, you little pissant?"

Rage burns in my chest. I should wait for backup.

I don't.

"Freeze! Police!"

And I thrust my badge out in front of me with one hand, like this scumbag is actually going to take a second to study it. My finger flexes on the Glock's trigger, ready to squeeze at the slightest provocation—give me a reason, asshole—as he turns his head to look at me, eyes glittering in the dim light.

"Let the child go and step away." Despite my rage, my voice sounds steady, firm. I'm a cop first, a pissed-off man second.

He releases the boy, lets him fall maybe four feet to the grubby floor, and doesn't even have the decency to flinch at the nauseating sound of snapping bone. The boy's screams are piercing.

My finger twitches. No one would blame me for putting a bullet hole in the middle of this fucker's forehead. Not. One. Person.

He knows what I'm thinking. He must. He gives me a smug smile, thinks I won't do it. I'm one of the good guys. I uphold the law.

As the boy continues to howl in pain, the scumbag shows me his hands. And shit! He's got a gun! He points it at the shrieking kid.

And fires before I can do anything more than flinch.

The gunshot deafens me. Or maybe it's the abrupt cessation of the screams. Or the absolute black horror that blanks out my brain for an instant.

And then I'm yelling and running. "NO!"

Throwing myself down the hallway. To do what? To do . . . what?

I stop several feet away, head spinning, mind trying to grasp what has just happened. And it finally registers: I'm too late. I'm . . . too . . . fucking . . . late.

For a moment, I'm frozen. Stunned. He shot the kid point-blank. Right in front of a cop. In front of me. Because of me. I should have waited for backup.

My gun hand levels, and it's shaking with the rage roaring through me. Rage that tells me it's okay to take a life. I can kill this man. I'm his judge and jury. He deserves to die for what he's done. Fucking bastard child killer.

I hear sirens right outside. Shouts inside. Scrambling feet and childlike cries for help. The cavalry is here.

I'm going to fucking kill this guy. Right fucking now.

As luck would have it, he gives me yet another reason to shoot him, one that qualifies as self-defense. He has the balls to point his weapon at me. What an idiot. He's got to be high, got to be whacked out of his head on heroine or crystal meth.

Either way, I have no choice but to pull the trigger.

CHAPTER **FIFTY-EIGHT**

Logan poked a finger at the doorbell and listened to the answering clamor of dogs on the other side of the door. It twisted him up inside all over again that she hadn't taken her best friends with her. She'd fled Lake Avalon, left everything she cared about behind. Her sister, her parents, her menagerie.

Him.

For the first two weeks, he couldn't blame her. She'd been through hell. It still rattled the shit out of him when he remembered carrying her into the ER, limp and unresponsive and ashen. When he hadn't been able to slap or shake her out of her latest flash, he'd found Butch's keys in the kitchen and car in the garage, and driven like a madman to get her some help.

A panicked Charlie had arrived at the ER shortly after Logan called her. She'd started firing off suggestions about beta blockers, alpha blockers, tranquilizers and God knew what else at the perplexed doctors. Soon, Alex had been stabilized. Crisis over. At least until the next day, when contact with Logan, Charlie and her dad had sent her into empathic overload all over again as she flashed on their intense, emotional reactions to her ordeal with a serial killer.

The next day, Alex left Lake Avalon. Hell, left *Florida*. She hadn't said good-bye, see you later or fuck you. She'd just taken off.

Charlie knew where she went but, ever the loyal sister, wouldn't tell him.

"She needs time."

"Give her space."

"She'll come around."

Well, fuck that. He was tired of waiting. If what he had with Alex was over . . . Well, shit, he didn't even want to think about it, about what would happen to him without her. Just imagining losing her made him want to sit down, drop his head into his hands and weep like a goddamn little kid. That or smash his fist through the nearest wall.

He rang Charlie's doorbell again and checked his watch. Maybe she wasn't here. He supposed he could call her cell and beg over the phone, but he wanted to do it in person. Again.

When he heard footsteps on the other side of the door, he straightened his shoulders.

Charlie pulled open the door and gave him a tired smile. Alex's absence had been tough on her, too. "Hi, Logan. Come in."

He stepped into the cool house, grinning in spite of his dark mood when six mutts, led by Dieter, tried to take him down. "Well, hey, guys. I've missed you, too."

Once all the puppy love had been taken care of, he looked at Charlie and took a breath. "I know you're protecting her, but—"

He broke off as Charlie held out a single key attached to an old leather key chain.

"What's this?" he asked. The key looked ancient, the gold worn to copper and the edges smooth from years of use.

"Key to the family cabin."

His heart jumped with hope.

"It's in the Shenandoahs outside DC."

Logan's eyes started to sting. "Thank you." He cleared the gruffness from his throat. "Thank you, Charlie."

"It's a long drive," she said, handing him a map with an address scrawled on it.

He took the map, handled it with the respect one would give a thousand-year-old treasure map and looked it over. When he spotted the circle in Sharpie black, his pulse started to thud hard and fast. That was where he would find his treasure. Alex.

He raised his head. "I'm thinking I'll fly and rent a car. It'll be faster."

Charlie nodded. "I'm not going to tell her you're coming."

"Thanks. I think that's a good idea. I don't want her to run again."

Charlie gave him a quick, warm hug. "Bring her back, Logan. I miss my sister."

CHAPTER **FIFTY-NINE**

Alex liked chopping wood. She sucked at it, though, having to work hard to heave the damn ax blade out of the wood every time she buried it. And it took her *way* longer to make any significant progress than it would a big, strong man. But the physical labor felt good, felt real. The ache in her muscles afterward . . . also real. As was the fresh scent of the wood as she stacked it against the side of the cabin.

She had no use for firewood now, other than the chopping and stacking as distracting activities. The end of May in the Shenandoah Mountains was pleasantly warm during the day and warm enough at night that an extra quilt on the bed kept out the chill.

When she heard the snap of twigs and crackle of dead leaves underfoot, she knew Logan had arrived. Frankly, she was surprised he hadn't shown up sooner. Charlie had apparently kept her location secret longer than Alex had expected.

Her heart kicked into a higher gear, anticipation and trepidation taking turns churning her stomach. She'd prayed he would come, even as she'd hoped he wouldn't. Such was her state of mind these days.

Taking a breath, she turned, the ax resting on her shoulder like she was Paula Bunyan without a blue ox.

He stopped in midstride and flashed her the broad smile that she'd desperately missed. "Hey," he said.

She smiled back, heart tripping and flipping. He looked good . . . great, in faded jeans and a long-sleeved navy T-shirt only half tucked in. The strong breeze swept his hair back from his face, plastering the cotton of his shirt against his muscled chest. Her entire body heated at the absolute masculine beauty of John Logan. God, she'd missed him. She ached to run to him and jump into his arms and kiss the daylights out of him.

But she stayed where she was, practicing a new form of restraint. She called it self-preservation. Someone else might call it cowardice. Either way, the practice would keep her firmly in her own head and out of anyone else's crazy.

"Hey," she replied.

"Nice place," he said, gesturing at the small log cabin surrounded by woods alive with the songs of birds, the croaks of insects and tree frogs and the soft whisper of new leaves. "I almost missed the tiny driveway."

"Charlie must have given you good directions."

He nodded, hands sliding into his back pockets. "She says hi."

Alex released a soft laugh. "I know. I just talked to her on my cell an hour ago. She didn't mention you were coming."

"So you get cell service here, huh? Interesting."

"Only if you stand in a certain spot." Guilt brought the heat of a blush. "I'm sorry I haven't returned your calls."

"First week, I figured, okay, you'd been through a lot. I'd give you the time and space you need. Second week . . . my patience started to wear thin. Third week, here we are."

"I'm sorry." She held his gaze for a long moment to make sure he knew she meant it.

He shrugged one shoulder but didn't glance away. "Don't be sorry. Just tell me why."

She dropped the weight of the ax to the ground, blade first, then kicked at the broad side of the blade with the toe of her hiking boot. "I couldn't . . . I can't handle it, Logan. I can't."

"You're not alone, Alex."

"It doesn't matter. There's nothing you can do, nothing anyone can do. And how am I supposed to deal with it? Spend the rest of my life wearing long sleeves and long pants . . . and asking cashiers to put my change on the counter so I can pick it up without fear of making accidental contact?"

"We'll figure out a way to control it. Both of us together."

"I know it sounds that easy, but it's not. You haven't lived in a killer's head. You haven't felt what he felt, did what he did. It's all over me, Logan. I feel . . . tainted. Maybe I'm a little crazy. I certainly *feel* a little crazy."

"You're not crazy, Alex. You're human. We're all human. And the odds of you encountering another serial killer with a stun gun are practically nonexistent. You know that, right?"

She did know that. Didn't help. Even the tiniest possibility scared the crap out of her. And that was on top of the fear of tumbling into any random stranger's nightmare. But instead of agreeing or disagreeing, she turned the conversation back on him. Pot, meet Kettle, and all. "So if we're all so human, why do you feel like you killed that little boy when you didn't?"

She watched the slow drain of blood from his face. Before turbo empathy, she would have reached out and rubbed his arm to reassure him. Now, she stayed where she was, a safe, empathic-free three feet between them.

He tunneled both hands through his hair. "I figured that's where you went in my head the last time. I . . .

was afraid maybe that's why you ran away, because you couldn't live with what I did."

"Oh." Surprise arced through her. "I'm sorry I gave you that impression, because that had nothing to do with it. In fact, I'm not even sure what I'm supposed to be so repulsed about."

"I took it upon myself to be judge and jury for Brian Lear. And then I killed him in cold blood."

"He was pointing a gun at you."

"I was glad for the excuse to take him out. If I'd waited for backup in the first place, maybe he wouldn't have killed the little boy and I wouldn't have killed Lear."

"And maybe other people, other kids being kept prisoner there, would have died, too."

"I know that's logical. I just . . . I made a mistake. A *rookie* mistake. And it got an innocent kid killed."

"I was in your head, Logan. You made a choice based on the information you had available. You feared more children would be harmed if you didn't act quickly. In my opinion, that makes you a hero."

"Then you have low standards," he said, lips quirking.

"I have perspective." She didn't smile at his joke. "Remember: I spent some time in Butch McGee's head, too. What happened to that little boy, and even what happened to Brian Lear, is *very* different from what Butch did to all those women over the years. The difference is *intent*. Butch was a cold-blooded killer. You're not. And there's no argument you can make to convince me otherwise. I've been both of you. And there's a *huge* difference."

Shaking his head, he sat down on the stump of tree she'd been using as her wood-chopping work area. "Not too many people can say that."

"Like I said, I'm a little crazy now."

"Thing is, what you said makes perfect sense. I never thought of it that way."

"So you're cured? All guilt is gone?"

He chuckled, rubbed his hands over the thighs of his jeans. "Sure. Why not?"

"Yeah, right," she said with a smirk. "Now you're just trying to get into my pants."

His eyes went dark and promising. "Believe me, when I try that, you'll know. And don't think for a minute that I didn't notice how you steered the conversation away from you and onto me."

She smiled faintly. At least it worked for a while. She propped the ax against the tree stump. "Want some apple pie? I made it from scratch."

He massaged the back of his neck with one hand. "Alex—"

"Come in and have some pie. Please?"

When he nodded, she led him inside and through the hardwood interior that had been dark when she arrived but wasn't now, thanks to the wide-open windows that let in the sunlight and fresh air. The stone fireplace along the outer wall of the small living room still smelled of the fire she'd burned the first chilly night. It smelled like vacation and carefree times spent with her father and sisters.

In the tiny kitchen, which had a closet-sized dining area with a small wooden table and four chairs crammed around it, she cut into the pie while Logan murmured his appreciation for the homey cabin. Without asking if he wanted any, she poured coffee from a thermal carafe into two cups and put them on the table along with the plates of pie.

They sat down and dug in.

"Excellent pie," Logan said around a mouthful.

"Thanks. It's my Nana's recipe."

All so normal. Real. She liked normal and real. Needed both, especially now.

He set down his fork halfway through. "Look, Alex . . ." He trailed off, took a breath. "When all that happened in

Detroit . . . afterward, my life went to hell. My mistake cost a little boy's family more than I can ever imagine. And instead of dealing with the fallout, I bolted. I should have stayed and dealt with it. Maybe I'd be in a better place about it now."

"I'm not running from fallout, Logan."

"Then what are you doing?"

"Look around. There's nobody else here. Just me . . . before you got here, anyway."

"So . . . what? You're a recluse now?"

"Yeah, I guess I am."

"You're going to spend the rest of your life alone, never having to risk landing in another person's head."

"Another person's *nightmare*. There's a difference. This isn't Charlie's brand of empathy. A quick trip, and it's over. Mine . . . Well, in comparison, hers is easy. I mean, not easy, because none of this is easy, but it's just not as . . . traumatic." She blew out a frustrated sigh at her inability to make sense anymore. "You know what I mean."

"I've done research, Alex. A ton of it. I probably know more about empathy now than you do. There are ways to control it. Maybe not as easy as smudging your aura or having a mantra, but there are things we can experiment with until we find what works for you. I mean, come on, can't we at least *try*?"

She couldn't stop the curve of her lips. "Smudging my aura?"

He shrugged with a sheepish, adorable smile. "You do it with sage."

"Really." She gave a serious nod. "Did you happen to bring any with you? We could make some cornbread stuffing, too."

"You're enjoying yourself way too much, considering."

She sobered. He was right. Instead of appreciating his efforts to help her, she was being flip. And, God, she loved him. Her own mother hadn't tried to help her, despite Alex's attempts in the past couple weeks to reach out to her for answers. "Sorry," she murmured.

He didn't let her linger on the guilt. "Charlie and the mutts miss you, you know. Especially Dieter."

"I miss them, too. She and Noah are going to bring the dogs up in a couple of weeks. After that, we'll adjust. It's not like we'll never see each other again. I'm not going to guard the perimeter of the property with a shotgun. People can come visit."

"What about us? You and me."

Tears filled her eyes, and she looked away, trying hard to blink them gone before they could overflow. She missed him so much it ached in her bones. "We had a good time, Logan. Things were really good . . . and fun. And now they're not. Now they've gotten all serious and dire."

Irritation, and a touch of hurt, flashed across his face. "You think I love you just for the good times? Because that's the biggest load of shit I've ever heard."

"You didn't know what you were getting yourself into. It's not fair to you—"

"I don't care about any of that," he cut in, his voice rough. "I care about you."

"Still, I'm not the same woman. I've changed."

"Maybe we both have. I'll accept that what I did in Detroit wasn't my fault if you'll give us a chance."

"It's not that easy—"

"Of course it's not that easy," he shot back. "It's not supposed to be."

"You're not listening, Logan. I'm not the same person anymore."

"And *you're* not listening *to me*, Alex. I love you no matter who you are. Isn't it unrealistic to expect to fall in love with someone who's never going to change? How boring would that be, anyway?"

"Logan—"

She broke off and straightened in her chair when he stood suddenly and shoved aside the table. Before she could do or say anything, he had her by the arms and hauled her to her feet. His mouth closed over hers, and she let loose a tiny squeak before every protest, every argument, every thought, flew right out of her head.

Her knees went liquid, her breath gone as his tongue sought hers, and she grasped at his muscled arms to keep from sinking to the worn hardwood floor.

He didn't give her time to catch her breath, didn't let her move, his arms enfolding her, one hand tangling in her hair and tugging her head back so he could take the kiss deeper.

Her back bumped into the wall, and she realized he'd walked her the few steps backward. Now, as the air backed up in her lungs, he slid his hands under her shirt and up, rough skin on smooth, and she started to shiver even before his thumb massaged a nipple through her bra. The back of her head knocked against the wall as she dropped it back and closed her eyes.

Oh, God, she hadn't been touched in weeks. Not even a hug or a pat on the arm, a kiss on the cheek. No one had even ruffled her hair.

She missed it. The human contact, the tactile sensations of . . . life.

She missed *Logan*.

And then he let her go. Just stopped the staggering caresses and backed off, hands falling to his sides.

Alex stared at him, panting and aching. "What are you doing?" She couldn't care less about the telltale catches in her breathing.

"I'm leaving." He turned on his heel and started for the door.

"Now?" Her voice rose an octave.

"That's what you want, isn't it? To be left alone?" He

stopped and faced her, folding his arms and cocking his head, eyes narrowed with purpose. "No one around to touch you? Ever."

"Okay, you've made your point. Now come back here and finish what you started."

"First, you have to come home."

"Wait, what? You're not going to make love to me unless I go home with you?"

"That's right."

She angled a pointed look down at the bulged-out front of his jeans. "That's going to be an uncomfortable ride back."

"I've got a hand."

"Wow, that's cold."

"What's cold is making me go home without you."

"You think you can lure me back to Lake Avalon with sex?"

"It's not sex with us, Alex." He strode back toward her but stopped close enough to touch, far enough away to frustrate her. "It's love. It's the booming finale of the fireworks on the Fourth of July. It's rockets' red glare and bombs bursting in air. Don't you think for one nanosecond that I'm here just because of sex. I'm head over heels for you, and there's no way in hell I'm going back without you, so you might as well just suck it up and agree and save us both some energy that we can spend on this."

He tugged her forward with a hand in the waistband of her jeans, and when his mouth closed over hers, she melted against him, totally, willingly his. Wherever he wanted to go.

Breath fast and shallow, his hands roaming up and down her back, under her shirt, over her skin, hips nudging insistently against hers, he murmured against her lips, "Is this a yes?"

"Yes." Her heart soared as she said it, and the weight bearing down on her shoulders lifted. It wouldn't be easy, but with Logan at her side, she felt she could handle anything.

He grinned against her mouth. "I love you."

"I love you, too."

"Now where's the bedroom?"

Keep reading for a special preview of

TRUE CALLING

The third romantic suspense in
Joyce Lamb's **True** trilogy

Coming soon from Berkley Sensation!

CHAPTER ONE

Zoe was dead.

Dead.

Sam closed her eyes and gritted her teeth against the throb of pain in her shoulder.

Focus, damn it. It's what you're good at. What you're trained to do.

Soldier on. Accomplish the mission. Get to the cabin. Hunker down. Hide. Get warm. God, she couldn't wait to get warm.

Blinking cold rain from her eyes, she squinted into the growing dusk, trying to get oriented. The cabin was around here somewhere. She was sure of it.

Unless she'd gotten herself lost.

No. She wasn't lost. She knew where she was going.

Just like you knew where you were going when you ran away from home fourteen years ago?

Don't think. Focus.

She peered through the rain running in rivulets over her forehead and into her eyes. She couldn't see a damn thing. Just towering trees decorated in gold and orange and red. The same coppery red that spattered her Nikes and the leaves squished underfoot. Her feet were cold and wet, just like the rest of her. At least she still shivered, the body's way of creating its own warmth. But, crap, she'd been shivering for so long and so hard that she should have generated enough heat to warm a small house. If she didn't find the cabin soon, she was toast. And not the warm, golden brown kind.

She was probably toast anyway. No way was he going to let her go. He'd hunt her down like an animal. Have her shot down like they'd shot down Zoe—

She battled back the wave of grief that tried to steal her breath and forced herself forward, one foot after the other. Don't think, don't think.

But she couldn't help but think.

Zoe was dead. Her closest friend.

Don't go there. Don't *go there.*

Then she saw it. The Trudeau family cabin. Materializing out of a copse of amber gold and dark orange trees. An honest-to-God log cabin.

A rush of much-needed warmth spread through her blood. Almost home. As close to home as she'd gotten in a decade. Wouldn't it be cool if her sisters and parents waited for her there? Alex and Charlie and Mom and Dad.

She pictured the cozy living room with its stone fireplace and polished wooden floor, the big, overstuffed couch with the red-and-black-plaid blanket draped over the back. She imagined that blanket draped around her shoulders, imagined sinking into the poofy cushions and drifting off, wrapped in the familiarity of home away from home.

She found the key in its place, tucked into a cleverly carved notch three feet up from the planks of the porch. Her half-frozen fingers fumbled with it, missed getting it into the lock on the first three tries. Hot tears streamed through the cold rain on her face.

Stupid, so stupid. Crying *now*, after everything that had

happened, after so many years of not crying. N3 operatives didn't cry. N3 operatives carried on.

But Zoe, poor Zoe.

Her hands trembled as she finally nailed the lock and heard the tumblers squeak open. The door swung inward, and she all but tripped over the raised threshold and into dust-choked air and a musty odor that didn't smell at all like the cabin she remembered. Where was the scent of fresh-chopped wood? The hint of fabric softener that spoke of clean sheets on big, soft beds?

She dropped her dripping bag on the floor and pushed the door closed, her arms and legs leaden now, weighed down by her sodden denim shirt and jeans. All she had to do was make it to the couch and get the blanket, and she'd be warm in no time.

But her knees buckled, and as they hit the floor, a fist of pain slammed through her shoulder. A burst of light flashed the world bright, and she flinched. A deep, quaking rumble vibrated the worn wooden floor under her knees. Thunder.

On the next burst of lightning, she noticed the pink water pooling near her left knee.

Oh, yeah. She'd been shot in the shoulder. Funny how she couldn't feel it anymore.

In fact, she couldn't feel much of anything. Maybe that should alarm her, but somehow it didn't.

It figures, she thought. Make it almost home, and it wasn't going to matter.

She was still going to die alone.

CHAPTER **TWO**

Mac Hunter squinted against the rain slashing the windshield and hoped he was going the right way. He had no way of knowing at this point. No street signs for miles, just this crappy, pothole-ridden road that kept going. Thank God for four-wheel drive, or his back end would have sunk into three feet of mud by now.

A flash of lightning made the towering trees pressing in on all sides look menacing against the night sky. Christ, why had he let Alex and Charlie talk him into a week by himself in the middle of the Shenandoahs with nothing to do but brood? He didn't need to get away to get his act together. He was fine.

Okay, yeah, he was a little burned out, and, yes, he'd started drinking more than he should. But it wasn't like he was downing shots at the local bar every night and then stumbling home at two in the morning with no memory the next day of how he got there. He wasn't sneaking drinks at work from a bottle stashed in a bottom desk drawer. He wasn't slipping out at midday for a three-martini lunch. The Trudeau sisters acted as though a few drinks after a stressful day had him veering onto the off-ramp to alcoholism.

If he were perfectly honest with himself, he could see their point. His father had drunk himself to death, after all. Because of that, Mac had always been careful about his alcohol intake in the past. So, yeah, maybe he did need someone to slap him upside the head. Maybe he was lucky that Alex and Charlie had staged their version of an intervention before more serious measures became necessary. They wanted to stop the self-medicating drunk before he became an alcoholic. And he had to appreciate the depth of their friendship, whether he agreed with them or not.

Finally, he saw it.

The dark clouds of the storm lightened, and there sat the Trudeau family cabin, nestled among tall trees dressed up in the golden colors of fall. For a brief moment, he wished he knew what kind of trees those were, but he had no idea. Some people knew plants. Mac Hunter knew inverted pyramids and how many picas were in an inch. He knew how to write a story hook that'd pique your interest, even if it was about nothing more exciting than a city council meeting. He knew nut graphs and hammer heads and how to get a shooter to the scene of a fire in less than ten minutes. But trees? The closest he came to knowing anything about trees was that the newsprint he spent his days filling with stories and photos started out as trees.

With a relieved sigh—because now he wouldn't have to drive the hour back down the mountain to find a crappy motel for the night—he parked the Jeep Commander and stepped out onto the soft, squishy ground. As rain pelted his leather jacket, muddy water oozed up around his loafers. He should have put on his new Gore-Tex hiking boots when he'd stopped for supplies, but he'd been eager to get here. The flight had been long, picking up the rental SUV a hassle, and it had thunderstormed the entire way. So far, not a fun trip.

On the porch, he found the notch where Charlie said the key resided. Three feet up, a handy little nook. But there was no key.

His heart thumped. Shit. Maybe he was destined to spend the night in a ratty motel after all. But with his luck, the road he'd just traversed would have washed out by now, trapping him.

He stuffed his hand into his front pocket and retrieved the new Swiss Army knife Alex had given him for the trip. Maybe he could pick the lock.

After a few seconds of fumbling with the knife, trying to figure out which tool to use, he gave up. Before beginning the slog back to the truck, he tried the door, just in case it wasn't locked, and the knob turned.

He pushed the door open and blinked several times as his eyes tried to adjust to the gloom inside. Alex told him a lantern sat on a table right by the door. Pop in some batteries, and you're good to go until you can get the generator going. Batteries, of course, that he didn't have on him.

He sprinted back to the Jeep, figuring his shoes were ruined anyway, and it was kind of liberating, really, splashing through mud puddles like a kid.

Batteries in hand, he stepped into the cabin while ripping into the packaging. Within a minute, he cranked the light on and, eager to see where he'd be spending the week, held up the lantern.

And just about dropped it.

CHAPTER **THREE**

Earlier the same afternoon

Zoe, you have to calm down and tell me what's wrong."

"They did it to me, they might have done it to you."

"Done what? You're not making any sense." Sam tried to guide her friend out of the entryway and toward the sofa. She'd arrived home in DC less than an hour ago, relieved to drop her bag by the door and start shedding the persona she'd worn for the latest assignment. She'd gotten as far as shrugging out of the denim shirt she'd worn as a jacket when Zoe started pounding on the door.

"Come sit down and talk to me," Sam said. "I'll pour us some drinks."

"No!" It burst out of her, and Zoe covered her tear-streaked face with shaking hands. A wild sob quickly followed. "I can't . . . I can't . . ."

Seriously concerned now, Sam pulled her weeping friend into her arms and held her tight, smoothing her hand over Zoe's quaking back. "It's okay. Everything's going to be okay."

She didn't even know what was wrong, but it seemed like the right thing to say. At the same time, her alarm grew. This was *Zoe*. Stoic, ramrod-straight-posture, I-didn't-cry-at-*Bambi*-as-a-kid Zoe Harris. She never cried, rarely even showed much emotion. What the hell had happened while Sam was undercover in San Francisco?

"No, it's not all right," Zoe said and pushed her back with surprising strength. "Everything will *never* be okay. He betrayed us, Sam. We trusted him, and he betrayed us."

"Who? Who betrayed us?"

"Flinn."

Sam's stomach did a flip. "What?"

"I'm pregnant," Zoe blurted.

More shock had Sam shaking her head, denying herself the leap to conclusions. "You and Flinn?"

Zoe's blond spiral curls bounced as she violently shook her head and stalked into the living room as though she couldn't stand still. "No! Never."

Zoe sank onto the sofa and dropped her face into her hands as stronger sobs tore out of her. "I don't know when it happened. I . . . he must have . . . must have drugged me or something. I don't . . . remember . . ."

Drugged her? Sam's heart took off at a sprint as she thought of a night a month and a half ago when she'd suspected Flinn had drugged *her*. But she'd decided then that she was wrong. The days of N3 experiments on her to help the team were over. Weren't they?

Zoe raised her face to Sam, her brown eyes red and puffy. "He's using me as an . . . as an . . ." Her breath started hitching, and fresh tears poured down her reddened cheeks. "As an . . . *incubator*."

Sam's stomach rolled with dread. She knew when she needed backup and never hesitated to request it. As soon as she picked up the phone to call Sloan, though, Zoe clamped iron-strong fingers around her wrist and twisted until Sam yelped at the burning pain.

Before she could think to block it, a memory that wasn't hers crashed into her.

"Why would you do this? What kind of sick bastard does this to someone he cares about?"

Flinn pats my shoulder. "It's going to be okay, Zoe. Just hear me out."

"Why should I listen to you? You're the one who did this to me!"

"You're part of something critically important, Zoe. Something that's going to change the world. You were chosen—"

"Fuck you!" I shove him back, wanting to do worse. If I had a gun in my hand, I would kill him. "I'm not some breed mare to use to grow super soldiers!"

Sam fell out of the empathic memory as Zoe jerked her up close so that they were nose to nose. For the first time since she'd come weeping through Sam's front door, Zoe looked coherent and deadly. "Do you get it now?" she hissed. "Did you *see*?"

Sam resisted the instinct to try to break Zoe's grip on her wrist. They were both battle trained, both knew the moves and countermoves for incapacitating an attacker. But this was her friend. She knew Zoe had no intention of hurting her.

Sam relaxed her muscles and waited until the taller woman's shoulders sagged. Regret added to the emotional chaos of her expression as Zoe dropped Sam's wrist and took a step back. "God, I'm so sor—"

Her brows arched sharply, and shock wiped the despair from her eyes.

The splat of something against the front of Sam's shirt had her flinching back and glancing down to see a spray pattern of red against the white backdrop of cotton. It took a second to register.

Blood.

Sam lunged toward her friend. Pain burned through her

left shoulder as she tackled Zoe to the floor. Too late. Her training had failed her. She'd let the enemy take her by surprise.

She scrambled to her knees and pressed shaking fingers to Zoe's neck. That was when she realized trying to find her friend's pulse was pointless: Her eyes were open and empty.

Sam fought down the nausea and grief that crowded into her thickening throat and forced herself to remember her training. The sniper who just killed Zoe no doubt waited for Sam to come into view so he could kill her, too.

She had to *do* something. Move.

A ticklish feather-stroke down her arm drew her gaze, and she watched the thin stream of blood tracking over her forearm. Numbness spread from her shoulder into the hand resting palm up on her thigh.

The sound of breaking glass snapped her out of her paralysis, and she slithered across the slippery hardwood floor toward her bag, toward her gun. With cold, hard—comforting—metal pressed to her palm, she flipped over onto her back and fired one shot into the chest of the intruder tearing toward her.

He dropped about a yard from her feet, crumpling into a heap, and she kept her SIG trained on him, waiting for a twitch to tell her he wasn't dead. She didn't so much as breathe until she saw his fingers go lax on the trigger of his weapon.

Heart slamming against her ribs, she crawled to him and shoved him over onto his back with both hands. She studied him as she aimed her gun at his head. In head-to-toe black, he looked like any other assassin, but something about the shape of his body seemed familiar.

She yanked off the black balaclava obscuring his features and sat back on her heels with a startled gasp.

She knew him.

He wasn't a fellow N3 operative, but he was part of the

team, one of three men Flinn called "the muscle." This man was a sniper.

And Flinn had sent him to kill Zoe, to kill Sam.

Disbelief lightened her head. Betrayal tightened her lungs.

She had to run.

Discover Romance

berkleyjoveauthors.com

See what's coming up next from your favorite romance authors and explore all the latest Berkley, Jove, and Sensation selections.

See what's new

~

Find author appearances

~

Win fantastic prizes

~

Get reading recommendations

~

Chat with authors and other fans

~

Read interviews with authors you love